THE CRITICS HAIL
REINDEER MOON

(more . . .)

Elizabeth Marshall Thomas

REINDEER MOON

POCKET BOOKS

New York   London   Toronto   Sydney   Tokyo   Singapore

The poem on page ix is reprinted with permission of Macmillan
Publishing Company from *In These Mountains* by Peter Sacks.
Copyright © 1986 by Peter Sacks. Originally appeared in *Seneca
Review*.

Map and kinship chart by Leslie Evans

POCKET BOOKS, a division of Simon & Schuster Inc.
1230 Avenue of the Americas, New York, NY 10020

ISBN: 0-671-72778-8

First Pocket Books printing March 1988

10 9 8 7 6 5 4

POCKET and colophon are registered trademarks of
Simon & Schuster Inc.

Printed in the U.S.A.

TO STEVE
LORNA AND MARION
ROBERT AND STEPHANIE
JOSS AND RAMSAY
INGRID, DAVID, ZOE, AND THE TWINS

Even if all the hawks in the world were to vanish,
their image would still sleep in the soul of the chick.

—JOSEPH CAMPBELL,
The Way of the Animal Powers

"Master, you know that I sit waiting for the moon
to turn back for me, that I may return
to my place. That I may listen again
to my people's stories, which come from
a long way off. . . ."

—PETER SACKS,
In These Mountains

CONTENTS

List of Characters   xiii

Prologue   1

I   The Trail   3

II   The Wolf   93

III   The Lodge   145

IV   The Moon of Walking   239

V   The Cave   285

VI   The Reindeer Moon   347

Sources and Acknowledgments   389

CHARACTERS

Graylag's Family

GRAYLAG, headman of the lodge on the Char
INA, Graylag's elder wife
TEAL, a shaman, Graylag's younger wife
TIMU, a young man, son of Graylag and a deceased wife
ELHO, a young man, son of Graylag and Teal
OWL, Timu's sister
CRANE, Owl's husband
RAVEN, son of Graylag's deceased brother
BISTI, Raven's wife
WHITE FOX, a young boy, son of Raven and Bisti
JUNCO, White Fox's sister

Ahi's Family

AHI, brother of Graylag's wife Ina
LAPWING, Ahi's wife
YOI, Lapwing's sister and co-wife
YANAN, daughter of Ahi and Lapwing
MERI, Yanan's sister
KAMAS, The Frog, son of Ina and her first husband, Marmot
HENNO, The Stick, The Frog's brother

Mammoth Hunters

SWIFT, headman of the mammoth hunters
RIN, Swift's half-sister
ANKHI, Swift's young kinswoman
ETHIS, Ankhi's sister

CHARACTERS

People at the Fire River

BLACK WOLF, elderly woman, sister of Sali Shaman
EIDER, Black Wolf's daughter
OTTER, Yoi's second husband
KAKIM, The Frog's stepson

Spirits

MARMOT, a spirit-helper, elder brother of Graylag
GOLDENEYE, a spirit-helper, younger brother of Graylag
SALI SHAMAN, Teal's mother

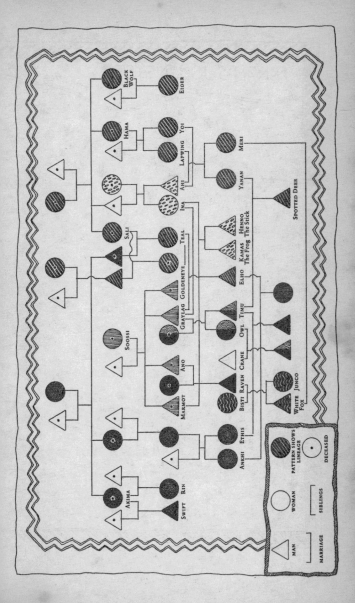

YANAN'S JOURNEYS

HAIR RIVER

9

GRAYLAG AND SWIFT TO CHAR RIVER

YANAN AND OTHERS TO HAIR RIVER

GRAYLAG'S PEOPLE TO FIRE RIVER

SPRING RIVER

AHI'S PEOPLE TO PINE RIVER

4

FIRE RIVER

8

WOMAN
LAKE

8

N

W   E

S

GRASS RIVER

BLACK RIVER

2

3

3

10

GLACIER RIVER

GLACIER

7

6

ANTLER RIVER   MARTEN RIVER   PINE RIVER

1   YANAN AND MERI TO CHAR RIVER

5   CHAR RIVER

10

3

3

1   GRAYLAG'S LODGE ON CHAR RIVER
2   SUMMERGROUND OF GRAYLAG'S KIN
3   WINTER LODGES OF GRAYLAG'S KIN
4   SUMMERGROUND OF FIRE RIVER PEOPLE
5   CHAR LAKE
6   AHI'S LODGE ON PINE RIVER
7   AHI'S LODGE ON MARTEN RIVER
8   WINTER LODGES OF FIRE RIVER PEOPLE
9   SWIFT'S CAVE ON HAIR RIVER
10   FORDING PLACES

～ TUNDRA   ✹ LONG GRASS
✹ SHORT GRASS   ⚜ TUSSOCK GRASS
• LODGE   ■ CAMP
▲ CAVE, OCCUPIED OR OTHERWISE
🌲 MIXED EVERGREEN FOREST

0   50   100

SCALE OF MILES

REINDEER MOON

PROLOGUE

MY STORY ISN'T BIG like the stories some of the mammoth hunter men could tell. Mine doesn't end with a huge pile of meat. My story has no captured women, only the gifts of a marriage exchange, and no battles, only arguments about the gifts. My story isn't very long, and perhaps lacks wisdom, since the beginning was told me by other people and the end came sooner than I wanted. I was still a young woman when I left the world of the living and became a spirit of the dead.

So there was much about life I never learned. Still, I knew where all the berries grew, and how to find the seeds hamsters store in their burrows. Better than most of the men, I knew the animals who eat grass and the animals who go hunting. I remember the children who lived and the children who didn't, the women who bore those children bravely or in fear, and men I liked and men who scared me. I was scared by some of the mammoth hunters the first time I saw them—by those with pale eyes and grass-colored hair. To me, they looked in every way like lions. I was shocked the first time I met such people. My aunt agreed to marry one of them before she saw him, and then was very rude because his looks gave her such a surprise.

Thinking of his pale eyes watching me, I remember a big pile of meat in my story after all. And a big swarm of flies. But when we got the meat we already had plenty of other food, so I don't think about the pile as often, say, as I think about a scrap of marrow from a tiger's kill we found when we were starving.

I

THE TRAIL

◄ 1 ►

My name was Yanan and my story began where it ended, in Graylag's lodge on the highest terrace above the north bank of the Char River. The lodge was big, with two smokeholes instead of one, and very well made, the best I've ever seen. Graylag built it with his three brothers before his brothers died, while they were still young. The pit of the floor was dug deep. The walls were braced with the legbones of mammoths, which in turn were braced with boulders and wound with spruce branches tied on with strips of reindeer hide, which shrinks when wet, so wind didn't move the lodge and rain didn't make it leak. Water drew it tight.

The arch of the roof was made of cast antlers forced together as if the deer were fighting, and was so high that only a few of the men had to stoop when they stood up. Over the spruce branches and antlers were hides, and over the hides were strips of sod. The lodge was so strong that people, or any amount of snow, could stand on it without breaking it, and so thick that weather came in only through the smokeholes. Thieving animals never came in, since we kept a dead spruce to pull, butt end first, into the door of the coldtrap.

On top of the lodge Graylag and his brothers put a wonderful thing, a group of very long antlers from huge spotted deer almost never seen around the Char. Each antler was almost as long as the lodge, and standing on it, they looked like a grove of birch on a low hill, or like a herd

5

of spotted deer lying down. The antlers stood out against the sky and could be seen far up and down the river—a sight that always told us we were reaching home.

Behind the lodge, a low cliff rose to the plain, so storms from the north blew over us and the south-facing rock cast sunlight on the lodge all day. Below the lodge, other terraces fell away to the floodplain of the river, where roe deer and sometimes horses browsed the willow scrub. The river was fast and shallow, and rushed around boulders so, except in the coldest part of winter, holes of open water showed in the ice. From our lookout in front of the lodge, we could watch for red deer or horses or reindeer following their trails down the terraces to drink.

On the south side of the river grew a wide spruce forest where bearded lichen hung from the little trees. In winter we hunted the reindeer who sheltered among the trees eating the lichen until The Woman Ohun sent them on their long spring walk back to the open plains. The forest was crossed through and through with trails, those made by reindeer and also by us, since in winter Graylag made the young people of the lodge gather firewood every day.

In the east, where the river rose, stood a range of hills with larches and pines on their south slopes. The hills were far, almost half a day's walk from the lodge, yet when Graylag and the other men could not kill reindeer, we went to these hills to gather pine nuts and to look for the dens of sleeping bears. When we dug out a bear and killed it, its meat fed us for a long time, perhaps the length of a moon.

In the west, the Char River joined the Black River and ran north. Every spring, when the reindeer were gone and pine-singers filled the woods across the river, when deerflies and mosquitoes filled the lodge, when the terrace stank from our feces and other foul things that lay thawing in the melting snow, we followed the rivers to the steppe to find the reindeer again. There, on the banks of the Grass River, we camped together with many other people from lodges far from ours, lodges belonging to Graylag's kin on the upper and lower Black River.

Graylag owned the winter hunting for many days' walk in any direction along the Char. He and his kinsmen owned the summer hunting everywhere on the huge steppe drained by the Grass River. Wherever Graylag went, we followed, because he owned the meat.

The handsign for headman is the raised right thumb. All my life this sign made me think of Graylag, because like a thumb he was short and strong. I've been told that his first wife was also short, but I never saw her, since she died before I was born. His next two wives were his brothers' widows, both as tall as he. The other men were taller. But as the right thumb is the strongest, most important finger, Graylag was the most important of us. He was also the eldest, with white hairs in his beard and at his temples. And he seemed tall, standing straight with his chin raised as if he faced the wind.

Clasped hands are the sign for a lodge, for marriage, and for strength, since the fingers are the joined antlers of a roof and also the joined people who live under it. So I will show with my hands about the other people of our lodge and how we lived together.

The hand palm down with fingers spread is the sign for men. If I count the grown men of the lodge on the backs of my fingers, I find eight. On my right hand I find a man on every finger—Graylag himself, his two sons, Timu and Elho, his brother's son, Raven, and his daughter's husband, Crane. On my left hand I find Father and his nephews, The Stick and his brother, The Frog.

The hand palm up with thumb and fingers tight together is the sign for women, water, and berries. So I count the grown women on the pads of my fingers and find six. On the first and second fingers of my right hand I find Graylag's two wives—Ina, who was Father's sister, and Teal, who was a shaman. On the third finger is Graylag's daughter, Owl, and on the fourth finger is his nephew's wife, Bisti. On my left hand are Father's two wives—my mother, Lapwing, and her sister, my Aunt Yoi.

Fingernails are the sign for children, because nails look like children's faces in the hoods of their parkas. On my fingernails I find five children, two on the left hand for me and my spoiled sister, Meri, and one each on the right hand for Junco, for her brother, White Fox, who was almost grown, and for Graylag's little grandson, a baby born to Owl.

Those were the people of our lodge, the people I've shown on my fingers. Now I clench my fists, because a fist is the sign for fire. As I have two fists, in our lodge were two fires. One was at the back, in the warm end, and the other was in the front, in the cold end by the door. The people named on my right hand slept at Graylag's fire in the back, because they were Graylag's family and Graylag owned the lodge, while the people named on my left hand slept at Father's fire by the door, because they were Father's family and Father was just the brother of one of Graylag's wives.

Men own the meat, so men own the places where we find meat—the hunting grounds, the lodges, and the hearths inside. Women own the families, the lineages. The people of a lineage are not joined to a place, but like milkweed seeds are scattered over the world of the living or clustered in the Camps of the Dead.

So the opening fist is the handsign for lineage and also for milkweed. As my fists open I see my own lineage, the largest in the lodge. Some of us are on my left hand—Mother, her sister, my sister, and I. Others are on my right hand —Graylag's younger wife, Teal, and their son, Elho. Mother and Teal belong together because their mothers were sisters. Before them, their mothers' mother had sisters who had children, and these people too were in our lineage, but they didn't live on the Char. I didn't even know them.

Again I open my fists. Now I see Father's lineage—Father and his sister, Ina, elder wife of Graylag, with her two grown sons, Henno The Stick and Kamas The Frog. Again I open my fists, and again and again. My fists are like milkweed pods with a few seeds clinging. Seven times I find lineages in Graylag's lodge. In the sixth lineage I find Owl and Timu, two of Graylag's children, and Owl's little baby, Graylag's only grandchild. But in the last lineage I find, like a single seed caught by its tuft of hair, just one person—Graylag himself, alone since the death of his brothers.

Again I clasp both hands, making the sign for a lodge. Again in my hands are strength and marriage, our group with our lineages joined. So we are solid. So the locked antlers in our roof make the lodge solid over our heads. And so Graylag's people of my right hand and Father's people of my left hand once lived together.

8

When I was a girl, I liked our lodge the way it was and was satisfied with the people in it. But the grown people were not satisfied, since some of our men had only one wife, some had no wife, and some were widowed. My cousins, The Stick and The Frog, once had wives and even children who were drowned crossing Char Lake, snatched under the spring ice by The Woman Ohun.

By listening to the grown people one night in winter, a night I remember very well, I learned that our men could not find wives among the women we met in summer when we followed the reindeer to the steppe. The women we met there were married or else were in the same lineages as our men, with mothers who were sisters, or mothers' mothers, or even grandmothers' mothers. So said the adults who crowded together, sitting on their heels around Father's fire.

This surprised me. On summer nights Graylag's sons, Timu and Elho, often visited two women secretly to have coitus with them. Thinking that everyone knew, I reminded the adults of those women. "What about Tunne and Lilan?" I asked.

The words were not out of my mouth before the adults fell silent. Round-eyed like owls, they stiffly turned their firelit faces toward me, making me feel I had said far too much. Father stared. Mother showed me the palm of her hand, threatening to slap if I said more. And Aunt Yoi very stealthily reached down in the dark where no one could see to give me a terrible pinch that brought tears to my eyes and left a blue mark on my thigh for days after.

Graylag, however, looked sideways at his sons. "I hope my kinsmen know less about their wives than Yanan knows," he said.

"Some things are better unknown," said Father.

Speechless at first, Elho and Timu soon began shouting. "Yanan shouldn't speak until she gets sense!" cried Timu. "Are we animals, that a child talks about us freely?"

I tossed my head to show him I thought nothing of his words. "You must be an animal! You look like an animal!" I said.

For this Mother clapped her hands loudly like a slap, so I dropped my eyes to show I would be quiet. But as the adults began talking again, I stole a glance around the fire, thinking that the other children might have liked my joke. Just as I hoped, Junco and White Fox were snickering at Timu. Only my little sister wasn't laughing. Ready to nurse at any moment, she sat between Mother's knees, face to face with the two bare breasts in Mother's open shirt. Too young to like my wit and daring, Meri looked triumphant, as if Mother had really slapped me.

In their usual way, the adults must have decided to overlook what I said, to pretend nothing had happened. Very soon they took up the talk of summergrounds again, and then I heard something I didn't like at all. We might not follow the reindeer to the Grass River this summer, but might visit some campsites at the place where the Fire River drains Woman Lake. There, people were saying, we might find unmarried women.

Anxiously, I listened to the adults. I knew very little about that place except that some people from our lineage lived there and it was very far. I hoped we wouldn't go. No one likes strangers, and to me all the people would be strangers, kin or not. But the adults were now counting the quarter moons we might see along the way. A decision had been made. We were going!

What about the distance? I wanted to ask. It took us almost the length of a moon to reach our summer campsite on the Grass River. To reach the Fire River would take much longer. I hated to think of walking so far, crushed by the weight of a heavy pack while my sister sneered down at me from her place on Father's shoulders. I hated to think of the number of days we would spend hungry, cold, and wet, bitten by mosquitoes and scratched by heather. All this only so that men could find wives? Why couldn't the unmarried men go by themselves?

Sad, I wanted to ask Mother if we really had to walk so far. But Mother was cross with me now, and I knew better than to speak. Instead I listened, and heard more. Not only would men find wives, but we would tie ourselves to their fathers' lodges. This would be good, said Graylag. Who could say why or when we might need to use new hunting grounds?

We would also collect presents owed us from a marriage

exchange. Many of us had been promised presents for the marriage of Graylag's daughter, Owl. Graylag was owed an obsidian knife. Owl's brother, Timu, was owed ivory beads already carved and drilled for stringing. Owl herself was owed amber beads and special rainbow feathers from the necks of Woman teals, the birds who nest in the reeds by Woman Lake. Years had passed, and no one had seen those presents. This year we would get them at last.

Mother sighed. "It's been so long since we visited our kin at the Fire River that we don't know who's dead or who's living," she said. "Perhaps our people don't use their old summerground. If not, how will we find them?"

Father answered. "Won't they make trails? Won't their fires smoke? We'll find them the same way Graylag and his brothers found women when they went to the Fire River. The same way we found you. We just went. There we found you. You didn't hide from us."

"Do you expect to find three unmarried women at the Fire River?" asked Teal. "Three women are too many to expect."

Three? That also surprised me. I thought at least four men—Timu, Elho, The Stick, and The Frog—had no wives. Not to mention White Fox. But I knew I shouldn't ask questions, so I listened, hoping that Teal would name the men.

She didn't. "Perhaps my son won't find a wife there," she went on, speaking of Elho. "Too many people at the Fire River are in our lineage."

Then everyone began to talk, naming the women they remembered at the Fire River and tracing their lineages. I was bored by the talk, since most of the people named seemed to be dead. The only lineage I knew was my own, and at that, just the people of our lodge. Also, the only one of us being mentioned was Elho. If he couldn't find a wife, I didn't care. I waited for the talk to turn to Timu, hoping to hear that no wife could be found for him either. But the talk of lineages passed over Timu to Father's nephews, The Stick and The Frog.

Graylag interrupted the long lists of names. "You must expect trouble finding unmarried women," he said to Teal.

11

"You talk as if trouble surprised you. If finding husbands and wives was easy, we wouldn't have to give so many presents to our in-laws."

"We give too many presents," said Timu. "And for what?" He gave me an angry look I didn't understand. "I've heard of men who don't give presents. Those men capture their wives!"

"Horses do that, not people!" cried Teal.

"Capture!" said Graylag. "Listen to him! Take care, Son! One of those big hungry women at the Grass River will pick you up and run away with you."

Now everyone laughed at Timu, me most of all. Even my sister, Meri, showed all her little teeth, although she didn't understand why. But Timu looked ashamed. He hadn't meant to joke, but to remind us of other people's customs. So Graylag put an arm around Timu's shoulders and said in his kindly way, "We must all wait for wives. Yours is growing every day. Soon you will sleep in her deerskin, and my kinsmen at the Grass River will be glad."

People laughed again, but I was startled. Timu had a wife? Was that why his name wasn't in the talk of lineage? Curious, I pulled at Mother's sleeve. When she looked down I whispered, "Timu's wife—who is she?"

Mother blinked in mild surprise. "Why, Yanan," she said, "she's you!"

I must have shown how much this shocked me. Mother looked at me strangely. Suddenly my face grew hot, and I leaned back from the fire so the light wouldn't shine on me. I wanted to hide until my thoughts stopped spinning.

I didn't want to be married at all, and here I was and hadn't known. Couldn't someone have bothered to tell me? I looked at Timu across the fire. *You?* The skin began to crawl on the backs of my thighs. He would make me have coitus with him! His arms would pin my elbows and his breath would smother me! A baby would grow inside me until I suffered as I had seen other women suffer! I would bleed! I could die!

I looked up at the bleached antlers in the arch of the roof, their sharp tines white in the firelight. Usually I saw life and strength when I looked at the antlers, but that night I saw rutting and fighting. I looked at all the many things wedged among the tines—Father's hafted greenstone ax, Mother's flint knife, Aunt Yoi's ivory necklace that she never let me wear or even touch, a necklace given her by Timu's sister, Owl, in a marriage exchange. Perhaps my marriage exchange! Suddenly tears filled my eyes. Surely I was the person exchanged for that necklace! Who else but me? And Aunt wouldn't let me touch it! Nobody cared what I wanted or thought! I would die in childbirth while people praised Aunt Yoi for the necklace.

I looked from the necklace to the hole in the roof, where gray smoke curled like a cloud against the dark sky. Suddenly a herd of red sparks rushed up to the hole, each on its own path, all knowing the way. How did they do it? Did something scare them? Did the wind lift them? Or did they just go of their own free will to find places in the sky? They must die there, I realized, since we never see them later. They don't become stars, because stars are white. I thought of all the things I didn't understand that no one would explain to me. Aunt Yoi had worn the necklace ever since I could remember, but not one person had ever said why.

I looked across the fire at Timu, who had forgotten his embarrassment while everyone made more jokes about the hungry women. In fact, he too was laughing. "She'll sit on you," said Elho. "You won't get away."

Suddenly, still smiling, Timu looked straight at me. My face burned! I dropped my eyes as if Mother had slapped her hand over them, and then, staring at my feet in great confusion, I wrapped my shirt around my legs and pulled it tight.

Before I knew I was married, I thought of Timu and his half-brother, Elho, almost as if they were children. Gathering firewood was their work as well as Junco's and mine. If they didn't help us, we didn't wonder where they were or what else they might be doing—we only wondered how to get the adults to scold them for leaving the work to us.

But after I learned that Timu was my husband, although I pretended never to notice anything about him, in fact I noticed more than ever. When we were gathering wood I listened for his voice or for the sound of breaking branches to show where he was; I looked for his tracks in the snow. I seemed always to know where he was, as if I could feel him. I didn't like it, and became uncomfortable.

Timu felt a difference in me. After all, he had known we were married all along, so his thoughts didn't change, as mine did. "What's wrong with you?" he would ask. "Am I a stranger? Stop staring."

Before I knew I was married, I never gave a thought to other people's marriages. I knew married people had coitus in the dark, under their deerskins at night when other people were supposed to be sleeping, but I never saw anyone have coitus, and tried not to think about how people did it or why. Down at Graylag's end of the lodge, Timu's sister, Owl, and her husband, Crane, sometimes showed that they were having coitus by an accidental change in their breathing or by a grunt or a sigh which would escape one of them. The rest of us were supposed to take no notice of the noises.

I never thought about the older adults. Since I never imagined my parents having coitus, I never wondered why Father preferred Mother to my Aunt Yoi, so that he almost always chose to sleep with Mother, forcing Meri and me to sleep with Yoi. That Father preferred Mother seemed natural—Meri and I preferred her too. Mother was nicer than Yoi, who always spoke to us sharply, sometimes pinched if we displeased her, and when asleep selfishly turned her back and pulled the deerskin over herself, leaving us in the cold. If we instead of Father had first choice, we would sleep comfortably in the warm curl of Mother's body while Father struggled for the deerskin with Yoi.

But after I learned I was married, I became more curious about my parents. Surely they had coitus. I was stupid to think they might not. Perhaps Father would rather have coitus with Mother than with Yoi. This unpleasant idea would explain why he always chose Mother. And also, I thought, it would explain why Yoi was childless.

Graylag, on the other hand, slept with both wives at the same time. Teal and Ina once pierced sewing holes in three reindeer skins, so the skins could be laced together, as if with a seam. Like the three parts of an enormous parka, this sleeping-skin opened out in three pieces, and under it

Graylag slept with a wife on each side. Yet Teal was the only one of Graylag's living wives to have a child with Graylag, and their son, Elho, was a child no more. Might this mean that Graylag and his wives did not have coitus?

I seemed to need knowledge that I didn't want and had no way to get. People said that coitus before initiation harmed girls, so I knew I wouldn't have to lie with Timu for a while. Initiation followed menstruation, and mine hadn't come. But I saw how my menstruation must have been in Graylag's mind when he told Timu of men waiting for their wives to grow up, and I saw how Timu must be waiting for me to menstruate, thinking about me in a way I hadn't realized, and didn't like. His waiting made me uneasy and confused, and began to fill my mind whenever I had nothing to do. I found I didn't always hear when people spoke to me. Mother took to rapping her knuckles on my head and accusing me of daydreaming.

But of course, if Timu was thinking of me, I was also thinking of him. One windy day in the woods, Elho and White Fox, Junco and I were standing around a spruce that Timu was cutting. His little ax marks ringed the trunk, and every now and then his chopping would loosen a flake, yellow and stringy with the cold. With each loose flake the trunk got weaker. We were waiting to push the tree over, but my mind wasn't on the work. Instead I was watching Timu. I saw how wide his shoulders were under his parka, and how his eyes were dark but had lights in them, and how his big hands were grasping the ax powerfully. Perhaps I was standing too near him, for he turned suddenly to look into my face. "Get back," he said rather proudly. "I don't want my ax to hit you by mistake."

In earlier times I would have jeered at him, saying that he was boasting, or that he chopped like a woman, or that since the tree seemed safe from his ax, so would I be. But now no jeers came. I simply took a few steps back, just as he had asked. This he noticed. Dropping his ax, he grasped the trunk, and with his parka straining handsomely over his shoulders, he forced the tree, popping and cracking, to the ground. The moment he started, the rest of us threw our weight onto the tree, but Timu was ahead of us. Before we could rightly get hold of it, he had it down. As all of us could see, he was strong.

That winter, when the full Moon of Roaring rose into the long blue dusk, a new hunter came to the Char valley. One night in the lodge, when the adults were all talking loudly about finding women at the Fire River, Graylag suddenly reached across some of us and grasped Father's arm. Seeing that Graylag was listening carefully, the rest of the adults stopped talking and listened too. Far away we heard a voice: *"A-a-a-oo-ong."* We strained our ears but heard nothing more. Were we mistaken?

Not bothering to put on outer clothes, we crawled one by one through the coldtrap and stood up to listen, chilled by the night wind. Above us the stars were coming out. We heard the wind in the spruce trees and the river under the ice. And then, far away among the eastern hills where the Char rose, where a pale yellow light now showed that the moon was coming, we heard the voice again: *"Oh. Oh. Aagh. A-aa-oong."* A tigress! A tigress calling a tiger!

We listened for his answer, but none came. We waited, standing close to the lodge for shelter from the gusting wind, straining our ears for the answer. A long time passed, but we heard no more that night, not even from the tigress.

The following dusk we heard her voice again, clear but faint in the cold hills, very far away. She called *"Aagh! Aagh!"* as if she was angry. In the still night we heard her perfectly, an unhappy, echoing, booming sound: *"Oo-o-o-oo-ooong!"* May she always be lonely, we thought. But the next night her calls were answered by a tiger, and then we began to see huge round tiger tracks on both sides of the river.

This made us very careful whenever we went into the woods to gather fuel. But by now we had gathered all the dead wood within easy distance of the lodge. We tried to remember the trees we had ringed to kill, but we couldn't find all of them. So because our search for wood took us far, we tried to walk slowly, watching the thickets carefully and looking closely for tracks, since tracks aren't easy to find on bare, frozen earth or crusty snow.

One day in the woods, when the sky was hazy and the air

seemed to be getting warm and full of snow, I climbed the
south side of the Char valley and went into the low, rolling
hills beyond. There, to my surprise, in a long patch of snow
I found fresh tracks, not of a tiger but of my Aunt Yoi. She
had walked there quickly, all alone. The sight amazed me,
since I thought all the grown women had gone to gather pine
nuts in the hills half a day's walk upriver.

Aunt Yoi seldom gathered firewood, since this was the
work of children, and Aunt was not one of the adults who
liked to help the children. Was she lost? Curious, and even a
little worried, I followed her trail. Not far beyond, her
tracks vanished on hard, bare, windswept ground. Then,
among some little trees, I found them in the frost. But now
someone else was following her. I looked at the new tracks,
each footstep neatly printed over my Aunt Yoi's, and saw
that they were Timu's.

I felt relieved. Yoi was gathering firewood after all,
helping Timu. Thinking no more about it, but watchful for
the tiger, I followed the two sets of tracks over the crest of
the low hill. Here, on a bare, southfacing slope, I saw both
people had knelt and rolled together! And not so long ago!
The red grass stalks were freshly bent, their coats of frost
broken. The sight shocked me, and set my thoughts spinning. Coitus! Timu and Yoi had had coitus. Right here on
the red grass, Timu had done with Yoi what he did with the
women on our summergrounds. Had he been married to me
last summer? I didn't know! Since he now was, should he be
with my aunt? Again I didn't know! But Aunt Yoi! She
shouldn't be with Timu! She was married to father!

Unhappy and confused, without much dry wood, I hurried back to the lodge. There I found Yoi alone in the dim
light from the smokehole, calmly working her awl in the
leather of a moccasin she was making for Father, boring a
row of holes for the needle. My face hot, I threw down my
firewood and started out again, feeling great confusion. As I
left I caught her watching me, her eyebrows lifted, her eyes
curious and cool.

That night I watched Yoi and Timu for a sign of what had
happened between them—an exchange of glances, perhaps,
or a touch—but neither took any notice of the other. I
watched Father for suspicion or anger, but he was talking

with Graylag about the tigers. I watched Mother, feeling
that if anyone knew the truth about her sister, she knew it,
but Mother simply drowsed, having walked since midday
carrying Meri and a large bag of pine nuts. So I tried to put
the memory of the crushed red grassblades out of my mind.

For a few days the two tigers stayed mostly in the pine
woods and open meadows of the hills, hunting the red deer
by day, roaring together by night. After a while we heard no
more calling. But soon we began to find the tigress's
footprints in the spruce woods of the river valley. We then
knew that the tigers must have made the red deer wary, hard
to hunt, so that the tigress, at least, was now hunting our
reindeer.

During a spell of fine weather Father and his nephews
killed a reindeer doe, but by the time the meat was gone, not
even Graylag could get near the little herd to kill another.
The tigress, said Graylag, was teaching lessons to the deer,
giving them frights and making them shy.

Without reindeer, we feared hunger. By now the Moon of
Cast Antlers was in the evening sky, and a few cast antlers
lay on the snow in the forest—a sign that the reindeer
would soon start their spring journey to open ground.
Before dawn one morning when I took Meri to the spruce
grove we used as a latrine, I found a one-antlered doe
scraping her tongue on someone's frozen urine—another
thing the deer do, for reasons of their own, before they leave
in the spring.

Whether the reindeer went or stayed, they were now too
wary to hunt. Graylag wondered whether we should leave
soon, traveling early to the Fire River, hunting for game and
searching for winter-killed carcasses to eat along the way. If
not, he said, we should go into the hills and dig out a
sleeping bear whom we had been saving since autumn. He
was the only bear whose tracks we found leading to his den
after the first snowfall, which proved that he lacked experience, or he would have gone inside his den when the snow
began. Then snow would have covered his tracks instead of
showing them plainly. The adults decided to kill and eat
him, and to begin our long trip later.

The next day was clear, so we started our hunt early,
leaving Timu's sister, Owl, with her nursing baby; also

Junco's mother, soon to give birth, and my sister, Meri, too bothersome to carry and too young to keep the pace. Since there was a tigress somewhere nearby, Graylag told his son Elho to stay behind with the women but not to use his spear on the tigress unless she tried to come into the lodge. And when Elho was told to stay, Aunt Yoi decided to stay too. "I'm sick," I heard her say to Mother.

Our way led east into the hills, to a pine wood on a slope that we reached in the afternoon. After looking about for a while, Father found the den under the roots of a pine, by a little hole melted by the bear's breath in the snow. Sending Junco and me to gather firewood so we would keep out of the way, the adults took their antler picks to the frozen earth that hid the bear. We hadn't gone beyond the first row of trees before we heard a roar, and hurrying back, we saw the young bear on the snow, blood bubbling and squirting from his nose and mouth, with everyone's spear sticking out of him. From the side he looked like a hedgehog. In the sky the ravens screamed, calling other ravens.

During the long twilight we ate our fill. Then some of us slept, but most of the adults sat awake by the fire. Not long after dark, four hyenas came by. We heard them whooping as if they were trying to scare us, then saw their blunt dark snouts and wide green eyes in the firelight. "You are few! We are many! Be gone," shouted Father. To see us better the hyenas bobbed their heads, but they didn't leave. "Go!" shouted Father, grabbing up his spear and taking a step toward them. They moved off slowly, looking at us over their shoulders. During the night they came back three times, trying to catch all of us sleeping. On their third visit Graylag threw burning sticks at them.

In the morning we tied the meat in bundles and started the long walk back to the lodge. Under the heavy loads, the women traveled much more slowly than the men. Soon all the men were out of our sight and at last even out of our hearing. So we didn't hurry, since we knew we would arrive long after them. As we got near the lodge, we heard everyone shouting at once. Knowing that something was wrong, we began to trot, and arrived breathless to find everyone crowded around Father and Aunt Yoi.

Father seemed to have forced Yoi to one knee, and now

19

was standing over her, holding her braid to twist her head painfully. I had never seen him so angry. "What of the gifts?" he was shouting. "Who will return the gifts I gave for this woman? I'm talking to my wives' lineage—to your wife Teal and your son Elho! Where is Elho? Where is he hiding?"

"There's time enough for Elho," said Graylag reasonably. "Be calm, Ahi. You can have your gifts back, if you want them."

"I want them!" shouted Father. "I have no more use for this woman." He yanked upward on Aunt Yoi's braid.

"Let go," said Mother firmly, struggling out of her pack and hurrying forward to catch Father's arm. Meri ran to Mother, screaming. Father flung his arm so that Mother stumbled backwards. I ran to Mother's side, ready to fight Father. Now both parents turned on me. "What?" cried Mother. "What has this to do with you? Get away before I get angry." So I crept away, to sit unseen with Junco at the edge of the group, where we looked at Yoi past other people's firmly planted legs.

Aunt Yoi was strangely calm. Father's grip on her braid kept her chin down and her head still, but except for her eyes, which were wide open and fixed on Mother, her face showed no emotion. She sat quietly on her foot, one knee on the snow, the other raised, with her hands in her lap. For a woman as quick to pinch and slap as Yoi, she wasn't giving Father much of a fight.

In the group around Father and Yoi, Teal and Mother joined arms. The two women had their heads together, watching thoughtfully. Perhaps they were wondering how to deal with the trouble. Presently they moved next to Father, and speaking softly and soothingly, they pried his fingers from Aunt Yoi's braid. Yoi crouched low until Mother led Father aside, then she jumped up and, pushed forward by Teal, ducked into the lodge. The rest of the people began to look around for Elho.

When Aunt Yoi was safely out of sight, Mother asked Father what was wrong. Father said that as he and the other men had come along the trail, they had overheard Yoi joking and laughing with Elho in the woods. When Father stopped to listen, he heard Elho call Yoi "wife," as men sometimes call women with whom they might have coitus. Very angry, Father shouted at them through the trees. They didn't answer, and instead ran away in different directions. Father dropped his pack and followed Yoi, caught her, and dragged her home. She denied doing anything wrong with Elho. She denied that Elho had called her "wife." She even denied that she had run away from Father. This was so ridiculous, claimed Father, that he had to laugh. "Where is Elho, if I'm lying?" he asked.

I heard a pebble or a bit of ice roll down from the trail above the terrace, and looked up to see movement in an evergreen thicket. Deer were passing, circling up the sloping cliff to stay far away from the lodge. Suddenly many pebbles scattered downward. We heard scrambling feet. The deer were startled, hurrying. In a moment Elho appeared on the trail down the cliff, as if he were on his way back from hunting. He hadn't been hunting, of course. He didn't even know about the deer until he crossed their trail. "Waugh!" he cried when he saw their fresh tracks.

My father and his were waiting for him. Taking him by the sleeves, they drew him aside, talking to him angrily but too quietly for the rest of us to overhear. Whatever they said, Elho pretended to be surprised. Timu, I noticed, also widened his eyes, looking innocently from one person to another as if he had no idea what the trouble was about.

After a while Yoi came through the coldtrap, pushed out by Teal, who still wore her parka and her knee-high moccasins but now dragged a spear. Calling to Mother, me, and Elho, Teal set off for the woods with Yoi behind her. By the spear Teal carried and by the pair of firesticks thrust in her belt, I could see we were going to be gone for a while but not for the night.

Teal walked proudly, without ever looking back or slowing her pace, sure that the rest of us were following. Behind her, Elho walked defiantly. Behind Elho, Yoi walked more slowly than the others, so that a gap widened in the line. Mother carried Meri, and I closely followed Mother, noticing how dark the woods were growing and how I was the last person in the line.

We came to a clearing. Once a hemlock twice as tall as a man had grown here. Now it lay on its side under a dusting of snow. While the rest of us broke branches off it, Teal took out her firesticks and rolled a fire.

Even the last red glow of the sun was gone from the sky. We smelled snow. It was a night to think of animals who hunt, and sure enough, in the hills beyond us we heard wolves. We listened, noticing how far the wolves were from us, wanting to hear whether the woods around us were empty or something was waiting there. I hoped we would hear the tigress far away, so we could be sure she wasn't near us. But after the wolves stopped calling, we heard only the wind.

At last Teal spoke. "We at this fire are one thing," she said, "the kindred of Sali at Graylag's lodge."

Sali? Uneasy, I crowded with Meri against Mother. Sali was Teal's mother, and in life had been a shaman like her daughter. But after her death Sali became a dangerous spirit whom I hated to hear mentioned in full daylight, let alone on a night like this, out in the dark, windy woods.

Teal was still speaking. "In the name of Sali Shaman," she said, "I want my son and my kinswoman to tell me why they called each other 'husband' and 'wife.'"

No one spoke. Our little fire snapped a spark, and far away in the woods one of the wolves called again. The rising wind moaned in the branches of the hemlocks, and Teal said, "I'm waiting."

At last Yoi leaned forward. "Aunt," she said to Teal in an appealing voice, "every night Ahi chooses my sister. He doesn't come to me. My sister has two children. I have none. Isn't this Ahi's fault?"

"So you would get a child with your kinsman?"

"No, Aunt. We didn't try to get a child. We played. Your son is young. I'm young, and I'm lonely."

"Doesn't your husband have two widowed nephews? Who else are The Stick and The Frog? If you must 'play,' as you say, can't you play with your husband's kinsmen instead of your own?"

"Aunt! Those men are ugly! I don't want them! And since they're my husband's kinsmen, wouldn't they tell him what they had done with me?"

"Who else do you play with?"

"No one, Aunt," said Yoi.

"Why do you lie, Sister?" asked my mother, very angry. "Are we your in-laws, that you must lie? Timu was your lover too. We know it. Admit it!"

"Timu was my lover too," said Yoi.

Teal stood up, so that her face was lit from below by the fire. Leaning on her spear, she looked down at her son and said, "Elho? What about you?" But Elho just lifted his shoulders and shook his head. He wouldn't speak.

For a moment Teal said nothing, but looked down at Elho scornfully. "Now listen to me," she said at last. "You, Elho, and you, Yoi. Yanan, look at me. Lapwing, make Meri face me. Even Meri should hear this. Look at me when I speak to you."

So all of us, even Meri, looked at Teal's face. She said, "We here are the lineage of Sali. Sali was my mother. Her sister was the mother of Lapwing and Yoi. I want to know why you, Elho, and you, Yoi, who are the children of sisters, should act like a husband and wife! If a child came of your games, it could be put to death."

Angrily Teal stared down at Elho, then at Yoi. Ashamed, they looked at the ground. After a moment Teal went on. "When I lived on the Fire River," she said, "a girl was born without arms. People knew she was surely gotten by a kinsman, so they put her out in the snow for hyenas." Teal waited, giving us time to imagine the scene in the snow, then asked, "Why do you think coitus is forbidden within a lineage?" By now even Meri looked worried. Teal stared down into Elho's eyes. In a low voice she whispered, "Where is your sense? Do you think that because Ahi hasn't yet gotten a child from Yoi, you couldn't?"

Elho couldn't meet Teal's eyes. Yoi stole a glance at Mother. But Mother leaped to her feet to stand by Teal. "You don't answer!" said Mother. "Yet people of your lineage have already suffered from doing what you did. I will tell you of Sali and her kinsman. This story of our lineage is also the story of Sali's death!

"Sali loved her kinsman but hated her husband. Her kinsman got her with child. One winter night in her husband's lodge, Sali went into labor. So that her child would be clean of the taint, she asked help from her sister, our mother. She asked her sister to shed blood for her, to beg help for the baby from The Woman Ohun.

"When her husband heard what Sali was asking, he guessed what she had done. He wouldn't let her sister help her. 'If the child is spoiled, it is spoiled,' he said. 'We won't change it.'

"Although she was in great pain, Sali wanted to spite her husband. She called out the name of the child's father for everyone to hear. Then her husband knew he had guessed the truth. He pressed his foot against Sali's vulva so the child couldn't come.

"People tried to pull him away. 'The baby will die,' they said. 'I want it to die,' said Sali's husband. 'And it will die. If it's born, I'll make Sali kill it. If she dies and it lives, I'll kill it. I'll dash its brains on a rock, just like a hare.' That night, Sali and the baby died together.

"After Sali died, her husband divorced her. He told our old people to give back his marriage gifts. But the old people refused, saying that what had happened wasn't their fault. He tried to get presents from Sali's kinsman-lover, but this man ran away to a place none of us knew, to his wife's relatives. No one has seen him since."

Mother sighed deeply, making a cloud of breath. "Now I'll tell you why people fear Sali," she said. "After her death, we began to see her in the woods. Then we knew she wasn't going to the Camps of the Dead, as other spirits do. Instead, we saw, she meant to stay among us. Surely she was very angry at us for letting her lose her life.

"Next fall her husband found the carcass of a deer in a thicket. While he was gathering up the scraps of meat, a tigress attacked him. The old people told him the tigress was Sali, who had left the carcass as bait. So for the rest of his life, her husband knew he was in danger. He later died of sickness and his spirit went to the Camps of the Dead, but we don't think that Sali knows he's dead, because she still hunts for him on the trails and riverbanks.

"We know because we see her in the woods or following a river, anywhere between Woman Lake and the glacier. Sometimes she comes in human form, naked and carrying a stillborn baby. Sometimes she comes as a tigress with a cub in her mouth." Mother sat down on the far side of the fire from her sister. "That's all," she said. "I've finished speaking."

"Who is the tigress in this valley?" asked Teal, looking first at Yoi, then at Elho. "Is she Sali? Has she come to punish you for spoiling our lineage? Has she come to protect you from Ahi?"

"If the tigress kills any one of us, she will punish our lineage," said Mother. "If she kills Ahi, she will protect you from his anger. Are we to lose our lives or our husband because of your doings? Did you think you could hide your play from a spirit?"

Yoi and Elho had no answers for these questions. They looked at the woods, as if the tigress were watching us. The wind blew stronger, moving the branches of the trees and filling the air with the first flakes of snow. "Now," said Teal, taking off her parka, "we will do what must be done."

Dropping her parka in the snow, she took off her shirt, untied the sinew thread that held her braid, and shook out her hair. Then, half naked in the falling snow, her bare skin red in the firelight and striped with shadows from her swinging hair, Teal threw back her head and pulled a flint knife from the top of her knee-high moccasin. Slowly she drew the blade up the inside of each of her arms and across the pads of all her fingers. Beads of blood sprang from the tracks of the knife.

Sweeping her hair from her face, Teal set her blood-stained fingers at the midline of her forehead and drew her hands apart, marking herself with streaks of blood in the same pattern as the black stripes on a tiger's forehead. Then, taking a deep breath, she gave a full-throated tigress's call: *"Aa-oo-oong!"* While the echoes of the call died in the woods, none of us moved or breathed. I found that I was trembling. Again Teal called as loud as she could, *"Aa-oo-oong!"*

This time, from far away, the tigress answered, short and startled: *"Aa-ng!"*

Teal held her arms over the fire, letting her blood splatter on the coals, making puffs of steam. Looking up at the sky, she called, "Blood is in the smoke! Come for it! Take it for those who will be born. Do not harm them!"

Now we listened very carefully, hearing the gusts of wind in the hemlocks and the hissing of the blood; a smell seemed to fill the clearing as the blood boiled away to nothing on the burning sticks. Suddenly the tigress called again: *"Aaa-ooong!"*

"Good," said Teal. "Stand up, Kindred of Sali. Open your shirts." So we stood and opened our shirts. Carefully Teal pressed the tip of her knife against Mother's breast-bone, then Yoi's, then Elho's, then mine, then Meri's, catching on her thumb the drops of blood and flinging them into the fire. In the distance the tigress must have been listening for an answer, and getting none, she must have decided to learn for herself who else was in the forest, because now we heard her again, nearer. *"Aaoong!"*

"There," said Teal. She picked up a little of the new-fallen snow to wash her arms and face. "Since the tigress is coming, we should go."

"Aaoong!" roared the tigress from our side of the river, her call echoing from the high bank. She was coming!

But Mother wasn't ready to leave. "The people in the lodge may hear the noise tonight and guess what we're doing," she said. "Even so, it would be better to admit nothing."

"Yes, Sister," said Yoi hastily. "Let's go."

"You brought us here," said Mother. "Now finish what you began."

"The tiger, Sister," said Yoi, biting her lips.

Mother ignored this. "You should tell our husband that Timu was your lover," she said. "Timu can't deny it. Ahi doesn't want to think you had any lover. He might rather believe part of the truth than all of it."

"Ahi knows about Timu," said Yoi, looking anxiously toward the edge of the woods. "He pulled my hair until I told him. And he knows about Elho because he heard us together."

"He told me he heard you talking."

"He did. He guessed the rest."

"Talking isn't coitus. What if you have a child and he kills it? Tell him he guessed wrong."

"If you like," whispered Yoi.

26

"Please, Mother! Let's go," I begged, pulling Mother's sleeve.

Mother paid no attention. "I'll tell him the same, Sister," she said, calmly settling Meri in the sling on her back. Elho, Yoi, and I, expecting to see shining green eyes at any moment, would have run for the lodge by ourselves if we weren't afraid of the trail. "But," Mother added slowly, "when I lie, I'll also say something true. You risk all of us by acting as you did—all of us and perhaps an unborn child too. If Ahi decides to beat you, I won't interfere. The truth is, you make me very angry!"

"I'm sorry!" cried Yoi.

"Being sorry doesn't do any good," said Mother.

A third time we heard the tigress, now very clearly. We thought we even heard a rattle of breath in her throat. "You can scold them later, Lapwing," said Teal. "Let's go." And we did, hurrying quietly through the snowy woods, leaving the fire for the wind to scatter and leaving the clearing to the tigress, if her curiosity brought her so far.

When we reached the lodge and went inside through the coldtrap, we saw that most of the others were still awake, sitting quietly around the two fires, waiting for us. The adults met each other's eyes, but no one spoke. Timu— wide-shouldered, strong, tall person though he was—sat beside his sister in the back of the lodge with his head bent as if he was ashamed, while Junco and White Fox stole triumphant glances at him. As Yoi came through the coldtrap, Father and Graylag slowly raised their chins and gazed at Timu coldly and thoughtfully. They seemed to have given him quite a scolding. He alone, I saw, was going to take the blame for lying with Yoi. The adults didn't even like to think of Yoi and Elho together.

Beside Timu, his sister looked up angrily when Elho came near. But Elho went innocently to his sleeping place and soon rolled himself in his deerskin. As Yoi stood up from crawling through the coldtrap, Father stretched out his hand to her and drew her down beside him. Later they too rolled themselves into a deerskin. Very late at night we heard them whispering, and after most people were asleep, Meri and I, allowed for once to sleep with Mother, heard Aunt Yoi and Father making the struggling, breathless noises we weren't supposed to hear.

Although the trouble caused by Yoi and Graylag's sons seemed to pass, in fact people still thought about it. After being nice to Yoi for a while, Father began to watch her suspiciously, and once even stalked her to learn whether she went where she said she was going—to the latrine. His finding her there shamed both of them.

My cousins, The Stick and The Frog, seemed to see Aunt Yoi with new eyes. Once they had treated her with great respect because she was married to their uncle, but now they ran their eyes up and down her as if they were trying to imagine having coitus with her themselves. Father noticed this and began to make angry jokes. "You ugly pair, how do you think a woman could want either of you?" he once asked.

"He who has eaten can't believe others are hungry," Cousin The Frog answered. "Why do you with two wives make fun of me?"

Many people, Graylag among them, seemed not to want to understand that Elho had done anything more than joke with his kinswoman, so no blame fell on Elho. But people blamed Timu all the more. Graylag seemed to want to make Timu do hard jobs, like pegging out and scraping the bearskin, although the skin froze solid and to scrape it Timu had to spend the day on his knees, holding the icy scraper with bare hands. Both my parents and even my cousins gave him angry looks, as if he had wronged all of us. Even Meri stared at him! And my Aunt Yoi treated him almost as if he had forced her, so coldly did she speak to him. Only his married sister, Owl, seemed to stand by him. If he looked sad and sat alone in the dark part of the lodge, she sat with him, her head by his as they spoke in low voices.

Every day, when I went with the other young people for firewood, I tried to talk to Timu, to tell him that I, at least, knew the truth—that although he and my aunt might have done something wrong, his half-brother and my aunt did something terrible. One day I found myself alone near him, and I looked up at his face. "I know about my aunt," I whispered. "She told us everything."

But Timu turned angrily away from me. "Am I a woman, to talk of your aunt?"

In earlier times Timu's sulky words would have delighted me. "You must be a woman! You look like a woman!" I could have shouted. But though the wasted chance hurt me, I was more hurt by the sight of Timu suffering unfairly. So I let him be.

One night we heard above the lodge a hurried, exciting sound like a lot of people talking at once. Geese! Graylag was already asleep under his deerskin, but the sound woke him, and he got up to sit naked by his fire. Eyes half shut, he listened with his face raised as if to let the sun warm it. When the sound faded, he smiled at all of us and said, "Listen to them! Hear how their headman keeps his people together in the sky. Even in a wind they travel, even in the dark! They are many! They are brave! And they're going to their summergrounds, the same as we will do."

Just as hearing someone laugh can make others feel like laughing, so we suddenly felt happy because of the geese and Graylag. Suddenly the moaning east wind made me think of asparagus and sedge root, and the sight of Father already sorting through his tool kit, getting it ready to pack, made me think of wading thigh deep in a rushing river, catching salmon with my hands.

That very night we made our packs to leave for the Fire River in the morning. Mother began to sing a Fire River song: "Save my life, hunters! Kill ten horses, one for each of my fingers! Save my life, hunters! Kill ten ground squirrels, one for each of my fingers!" The song went on with "kill ten mammoths, kill ten reindeer," so easy to learn that soon many of us were singing. The trouble started by Yoi and the bad feelings that followed seemed to vanish like frost in the sun, and as soon as the sky was light we left, walking in single file down the terraces to the river, crossing the river mostly on boulders, taking just a few steps on the rotting ice, just this one last time.

At a bend of the river I turned to look at the lodge, not

knowing what would happen to us before I saw it again. Like a low mound of earth with a grove of trees on it, the rounded roof held the high, upreaching antlers, very tall against the gray sky. A raven, I saw, was perched on the uppermost tine. And from one of the smokeholes came a billow of heavy yellow smoke, all that was left of the gift of burning bearfat we threw in the fire for a spirit who watched over our lodge.

◄ 2 ►

THE NAME OF THE SPIRIT who ate our burned bearfat was Marmot. He was Graylag's brother and Ina's first husband in life. At the time of his death Teal captured his spirit in a shaman's net made with powdered feathers, burned ocher, and the burned red vine of a gray pea that grows in clearings. In this way she made him her spirit-slave, for use not just in our lodge in winter but at our summer campsites as well. So now I think the raven I saw on the roof when I turned for a last look at the lodge was probably not a real raven but Marmot in the form of a raven, Marmot ready to travel.

I met Marmot on a bright, cold, moonlit night one year in early fall. On that night, although I was still a young woman, I realized I was dying. The other people in Graylag's lodge must have realized it too, since by the time my body was dead and my spirit had wiggled free of it, some people around me were crying, and Teal had prepared a spirit-net, which she threw over me. The next thing I knew I was fighting hard but was caught like a hare, and soon I found myself on the roof of the lodge among the shafts of the huge old antlers, tall and black against the moonlit sky. At the far end of the roof a boyish man-spirit squatted on his heels, wearing a shabby deerskin shirt, ragged trousers, and worn moccasins. I, on the other hand, was naked, because earlier, perhaps unwisely, I had let the people help me out of my clothes.

At first I hardly saw this man-spirit. Made desperate by my struggles, I was looking frantically for an owl. Ever since my childhood I had been told that birds guide spirits to the Camps of the Dead. But just as the grub-eater bird won't wait to lead a person to a beehive, no bird will wait long to guide a spirit. The grub-eater flits away if the honey hunter isn't ready, and the guiding bird leaves to do something else if the spirit isn't there.

As I stood naked on the roof, I was dismayed to hear a gray owl booming deep in the woods across the river. Surely that was the bird who would have led me. I heard the owl's voice again, farther away this time, and saw that Teal's net had held me back too long. My guide was gone. I was a spirit-slave, just like the young man-spirit. Never again would I be Meri's sister or Graylag's daughter-in-law or Timu's wife. I might never even find the Camps of the Dead, where the elders of my lineage could give my spirit to a bird to bring to a newborn child. Down in the lodge beside the good fire, where my bed used to be, I heard people talking about my burial. Not for a long time had I felt so much like crying.

At the other end of the roof, the young man-spirit watched me with round eyes, making me uneasy with his stares and curiosity. I knew who he was, of course. All my life I had heard about the spirits of Graylag's brothers who helped the people of our lodge, and who else but Graylag's brother could this man-spirit be? At last I looked straight at him. "What should I call you?" I asked rather sharply, then wondered if I should have spoken more respectfully. He was, after all, the most senior member of the lodge, and I was one of the youngest. Perhaps I should have called him by his mother-name, Child of Soossi, as I would have called Graylag if I needed to be very respectful.

But the young man-spirit didn't seem to notice disrespect. "Marmot," he answered simply.

"Well, I am Yanan, Child of Lapwing," I said.

"I know," he said. "I know all the people of this lodge. I was one of the people who started this lodge. I was killed by winter, giving my life to hunt food for the others. Did they tell you?"

In fact they did not. Or if someone did, I hadn't paid attention. The lodge had spirit-helpers, and once in a while we burned fat for them—that was all I knew. But now I saw

32

how my ignorance could hurt Marmot's feelings, especially since he seemed to be waiting hopefully for my answer. "Oh yes, they told me," I answered. Then I wished I hadn't lied, because Marmot looked disappointed. Perhaps he would have liked to tell the story.

Time passed, and neither of us spoke. I looked around at the woods and sky, full of wind and bright moonlight. Free from my braid, my hair whipped my face, but I didn't feel cold. Even so, I would have been happier in my clothing, and I asked Marmot where his clothing came from. "They'll bring yours outside tomorrow," said Marmot.

"Could I go inside to get it now?"

Looking down through the smokehole, Marmot pointed with his lips at a bundle of jointed pine and bears' teeth tied menacingly to the lodgepole, a charm against spirits. "By now you know you're not feeling hunger or cold," he said, "but if you go inside the lodge, the charm will cause pain all through you. They want us out here, not in there with them."

At dawn the people came through the coldtrap, dragging behind them the corpse of a thin young woman. They also carried picks to dig a grave, since the earth was not yet frozen hard. The body was mine, of course. The people behind it carried all my things.

Later, by the cold smell of freshly turned earth I found the grave, and took out of it the spirit of each piece of my clothing. When I put on the spirit-clothes, I felt better. But that night when I heard the people talking about me, I was hurt at what they thought to say. "What of the necklace we buried with her?" asked Timu's sister, Owl. "That should have been my necklace, since it was promised me in Yanan's marriage exchange. I once told Yanan to make the gift first and finish the work later. If she had, when she died she would have been working on my necklace, not her necklace, and the beads wouldn't have been wasted in her grave."

"Wasted?" cried my sister, Meri. "You call them wasted?"

"Yanan was away a long time," said Owl. "Do you remember how tough and dirty she was when she came back? She was almost like an animal. No wonder she didn't understand giving."

Meri lost her temper. "You're the one who's like an animal," she said, and a fight began. Angry to hear his sister insulted, Timu leaped to his feet and said that Meri was the animal. Meri cried. Other people joined the quarrel, some taking Meri's side, some Timu's.

"Leave my sister alone!" I shouted down the smokehole. "If you make her cry, you'll be sorry!"

But no one paid any attention except Marmot, who said, "Never mind their quarrels. You don't belong with the people anymore."

Of course he was right. Things were no longer the same. I leaned my head back and looked up at the sky where the Reindeer Moon, very high and far away, floated in thin clouds. When I trusted my voice, I said to Marmot, "Tell me then, Marmot, where do I belong?"

"In the air," he said.

In the air? The puzzling, matter-of-fact answer made me turn for a close look at him. "Why in the air?" I asked.

"Where else?" he asked. "There are only four places you could be. You could be in the Camps of the Dead, which are owned by the lineages. Or you could be in the lodges or campsites, which are owned by the people. Or you could be out on the steppes and tundra or in the forests or lakes, which are owned by the animals. The only other place is the air, which is owned by the shamans. Your sister is in a lodge. You're in the air, since you were caught by a shaman."

"And what do I do?"

"You'll see soon," said Marmot. "Look at the sky."

"I am looking at the sky," I said. Around the moon was a faint white ring—the track of The Bear tramping a bed in His den.

"The Bear is going to His winter's sleep," said Marmot. "The people are thinking of hunger. My wife," he added, speaking of Ina, "will soon have Teal up here to ask for our help. My wife doesn't like hunger."

"She's Graylag's wife now," I said, feeling much more at ease with Marmot. He must have been feeling more at ease with me. Raising his eyebrows, he gave me a long look that said, *I am the senior of us, so don't correct me.*

Later that night, when Marmot lay wrapped in his deerskin by Graylag's smokehole, as if asleep, I looked through the other smokehole and saw the people building a big fire. When they took off their shirts—all but some of the women, who kept their shirts to hide their little babies from the strong things that would soon be going on—I knew the people were about to help Teal trance, and I threw a bit of snow to waken Marmot. "Marmot!" I whispered. "They're starting!" Marmot got up and with his deerskin draped over his shoulders came to sit on his heels beside me. Now both of us looked down into the lodge.

In the darkest place at the back we saw Teal, dressed in her shaman's shirt with fringe on the sleeves like birds' feathers. While she loosened her braid and painted her face with ocher, the people began to clap and sing:

> Calling The Bear's head! Hona!
> Calling The Bear's neck!
> Calling The Bear's hump! Hona!
> Calling The Bear's back!
> Calling The Bear's legs! Hona!
> Calling The Bear's feet!
> Feet turn toward us,
> Bring animals toward us.
> Hona! Wiri! Hona! Wiri!
> You of the double trail,
> We are burning fat!
> Fat is in the smoke!
> Hunter of bees,
> Come for what we give you!
> You whose trail crosses the sky,
> Come for it! Come!

Suddenly we heard the high scream of a falcon. It was Teal, dancing from the back of the lodge, singing in a bird's voice over the voices of the people. "Hariak! Hariak!" she sang in the voice of a goose, flinging her arms wide like a bird's wings and beginning to turn, slowly at first, then faster and faster as she sang in the voices of a lapwing, a woodcock, a kestrel, and a mosquito. As the thin voice of the mosquito died in her throat, she tore off her shirt and

35

threw it down, threw herself onto her hands and knees, washed her chest and arms with burning coals, and set her hair on fire.

On her feet, she began to turn again. Soon she was spinning, her burning hair standing out from her head, sparks flying to all corners of the lodge and up the smokehole to the sky. Suddenly Teal fell forward into the open arms of the singing people. Carefully they laid her on the floor, squeezing out the last smoldering sparks in her hair and gently rubbing her back.

We spirits then saw something the people couldn't see. Teal's back split lengthwise and her spirit began to wiggle through the split, as a springfly wiggles out of its casing. When her spirit broke free, it flew up the path of the smoke, chasing the sparks through the smokehole. Then in the cold air over the lodge Teal stood in front of us, transparent but faintly shimmering, like heat.

"Greetings to Teal Shaman," said Marmot as he sat on his heels.

"Greetings, Honored Spirits," said Teal, looking proud although she was about to ask a favor. "In the name of The Bear, I ask your help, since we are getting hungry. The reindeer don't come. We find nothing to hunt. As in life you hunted animals, help us hunt animals."

"We hear you, Teal Shaman," said Marmot.

In the lodge below us, around Teal's prone body, people were calling her name. "We will be grateful," said Teal, her voice growing faint. "We promise you a gift." Then she vanished. Down in the lodge we heard her murmur as she came out of trance.

We then heard something sizzle and smelled something good. Marmot became alert. "Here's our gift!" he said, putting his tongue into the smoke. I did the same and got a little taste of fat!

What happened next surprised me. Marmot stood up and stretched his muscles. "Well?" he said, looking down at me. So I stood up too. Marmot turned his back as if to step off the roof, and then, before my eyes, he vanished. Where he had been standing I saw the haunches of a large gray wolf sliding down the sloping roof. On the snowy ground below, the wolf nosed at some scraps of bone thrown away by the people, then ambled toward the woods.

Suddenly my head filled with strong odors. I smelled the bodies of many different people, their hair, their sweat—I smelled the urine of a baby, deer meat dead for many days, burning feathers and woodsmoke. I smelled snow in the air, cold spruce needles, river ice, and open, moving water, and I caught a whiff—a warm, sweet, tickling whiff—of a nearby birch mouse! Where was it?

Then my skin prickled between my shoulders and my eyes stretched wide—I smelled the strong male smell, the heavy fur, the breath, the feet, and the anal glands of a male wolf! Although the power of the strange smell frightened me a little, it also drew me. I felt myself sliding from the roof. Spreading my fingers and toes to slow myself, I looked down at my feet and saw that I too had turned into a wolf.

Slowly, holding my head and tail low and folding my ears as politely as I knew how, I stepped carefully toward the large male. With his ears stiff and his tail raised slightly, he watched me come. Wanting no trouble, I let myself sink to the snow. Marmot took my nose in his teeth, and giving my head a downward push just strong enough for me to feel it, he looked right into my eyes with his frank, rather friendly yellow eyes. Then he let me go. I sneezed, he turned and trotted off, and I picked myself up from the snow and followed him.

Running as a wolf was very easy. I found myself leaping over rough places on the trail almost as if I were flying. I saw how this was the right way to travel fast and far at night, to find out everything about the Char valley so we could tell the people. And when we started off, we seemed about to do just that.

But as time went by and we got farther from the lodge, I found myself thinking less about the people—except that they were telling the truth when they said there was nothing much to hunt—and more about the few trails of scent we crossed, all of them too stale to follow. Perhaps the people were hungry, but I was now hungry too. The scent of a hare ahead of us filled my mouth with saliva. Excited, I ran faster, passing Marmot without knowing that I did. But suddenly I was caught by a blow on the shoulder. Marmot didn't want me ahead of him, so he had given me a shove. Obediently I fell behind.

On a high bank overlooking the river we stopped. We were only a short way from the lodge, and could still smell, on the spruce trees by the trail, the stale odor of some people who had passed this way recently. But by now the smell seemed sour and dangerous, and made my skin prickle. Much more interesting was Marmot's marking the place with a scat. I soon squeezed out a scat of my own and with much satisfaction looked at the two together, quiet in the grass. *We are here,* the scats said, *showing the land of our makers, our place, our pack, our hunting. Let those who find us know this and take care.*

And then, softly at first, Marmot began to sing. Starting high, his perfect note grew loud, lasting long, and at last fell, a great, stirring cry that sent a shock of excitement through me. With all my heart, and all the breath in my lungs, I joyously threw my voice after his voice, singing low as he sang high, so that my song rose as his song fell. Shivering with delight, I sang louder than ever as we sent our voices through the width of the sky, up to the moon, out to the far corners of the valley where our echoes rang!

The joy of singing cleared our minds completely of the slightest thoughts of any of the people. In fact, when the song was over, we felt so pleased with ourselves that we had to touch noses, to wave our tails, to smile and thank each other. Ah! Now I felt hopeful! Now my heart was ready for anything! Now I would help Marmot do whatever he wanted and follow wherever he led!

But as we began to lope in single file along the rim of the valley, we stopped as quickly as we started—stopped in our tracks, because far away we heard the voices of other wolves, also singing. Their calls could only mean that they had heard us and now wanted us to hear them!

We held our breath, so carefully we listened. A deep voice, a loud, low, female voice, we heard singing above the others—but so many others! Oh, there were several loud, strong males! And other females! And a youngster—last spring's pup! With my hair lifting on my shoulders, I looked uneasily at Marmot. Those singers were many and strong!

That, of course, was what they wanted to tell us, we with only two voices!

Marmot's hair was standing, but he didn't seem worried. Instead he looked long in the direction of the large pack, then lifted his nose to test the air. I too tested the air with a quiet sniff, to learn what I could from Marmot. No real fear there, although a trace of annoyance seemed to rise from his skin.

Well, the large pack was in the southeast, in the hills where the river rose, and we were heading west, along the north rim of the valley. We would have to turn back if we wanted to meet the other wolves. But of course we had forgotten all about turning back. We meant to keep going, and didn't want to meet them.

Our hackles up, we touched noses again, just to be sure we could count on each other. Then, on a frozen grass tussock chosen by Marmot, we carefully placed marks of urine, scratched backwards to draw the attention of any newcomers, nosed our marks, and marked again, first me, then Marmot. It almost seemed as if four had marked here, something those other wolves might think about if they ever came this far!

With that we turned our minds to serious hunting, and ran loping through the draft of air that rose from the valley. Marmot ran first, carrying his tail rather high. I followed, my eyes on the pale fur of his rump, which showed me the way in the moonlight. Low to the earth among the little, sparse trees that grew on the valley's rim, the yellow moon shone, sinking. Ah? Did I smell roe deer? Yes, but not strongly; two roe deer had passed this way just after dark. Their pellets of dung were already frozen. We ran on.

It soon became clear that Marmot knew the country. In the form of a wolf he must have ranged around the Char valley many times before. In life I had thought I knew the country as well as anyone could, but now I saw that what I had known was mostly the people's many trails and the places they led to. It was also soon clear that Marmot knew what to look for. All the other animals who used the trails seemed to leave signs on them, urine or scats or marks of musk or rubbings of chin glands or tail glands or scratches on the earth or on the bark of trees—boastful warnings to others of their kind. But Marmot too nosed these signs with interest.

The larger the sign, the more care he took with it. When I saw him tasting the scat of an old he-bear, I did the same, and found a carrion flavor, as if the bear had found and eaten meat. That had meaning, since we were not finding much to eat anywhere, alive or dead. The meaning wasn't clear to me but seemed clear to Marmot, since he surely knew the old bear's range. I saw that I had much to learn about the Char valley before I would know as much as Marmot. The carrion flavor was a start.

By dawn we found ourselves on the eastern shore of the frozen Char Lake. Far out on the wide stretch of snowy ice, between the pink moon setting in the west and the red light gathering in the east, we saw something moving. Three things! Three reindeer! Bulls, they were, all trotting, their breath steaming, their chins high to balance their sweeping antlers, the masses of white hair on their chests and shoulders swaying. Oh!

For a moment Marmot and I stood gazing at them. Then, unable to check myself, I rushed them. With a grunt of surprise Marmot bounded after me and we ran side by side across the open lake. Up went the tails of the three bulls as they raced for the lakeshore, leaving behind them a great cloud of snow. The next thing I knew, the bulls were almost on the shore, going faster than I would ever have imagined. The sight took away some of my speed—my headlong dash became a discouraged trot.

Then suddenly, beside me, Marmot stopped still. His head and ears rose but his tail drooped. I looked where he looked, and my tail sank too. Dashing at the reindeer from the shore came a gang of hyenas.

And what now? One of the hyenas leaped at the foremost reindeer. The bull kicked and spun around, showing his antlers to the hyenas, but the hyenas were all around him, grabbing at his nose and hindquarters. Although he kicked fiercely and slashed with his antlers, a hyena took a bite out of his haunch. The bull's two friends didn't slow their pace for a moment. While the wounded bull bellowed and kicked at the many hyenas who now grabbed at him, the pacing legs of the other two bulls quickly carried them out of sight.

We couldn't stop ourselves from moving closer. Some of the hyenas were busy snatching bites from the bull's hind legs and belly, gulping pieces down in case the rest of him managed to escape. A few of the largest hyenas didn't loosen their jaws to eat but kept their teeth sunk in the bull's nose and legs. The gobbling hyenas got in the way of the determined hyenas, who at last jerked the bull to his knees. Above the whoops and snarls I heard the bull's last bellow choke to a gurgling, hopeless grunt.

It made me sad, that sound did. It should have been ringing in our ears, not the hyenas'. We saw the bull first, and we ran at him first. Now we had to watch others eat him.

We couldn't leave though. The smell of blood, of opened muscle, of bared, fresh bones, even the smell of crushed evergreen from the torn intestine, was too much for us. Inside my mouth, my saliva stung. I ate some snow. It was tempting to try to steal from the hyenas, but they were so big and so many, and they were so noisy and so often turned in our direction just to show us their teeth, that though we ran back and forth for a while hoping to find a way to the carcass, every scrap of it, even the antlers and the bones, went down their throats. We would have to give up and hunt somewhere else if we wanted to eat.

We went back to the river to hunt horses. We found a herd near the trees at the edge of the floodplain, but with a great stretch of hard, flat ground before and behind them, so however we came toward them, they could easily bolt away. Their smell was everywhere, but their dark, furry bodies were hard to see beside the dark trees. These horses must have known that there weren't many reindeer to keep hunters busy, since they acted as if they thought themselves in terrible danger, always snorting and throwing up their heads.

And all of a sudden, with bloodthirsty screams, the stallion attacked me! My whole attention had been taken up with a mare in the distance, and I didn't even know the terrible horse was near me until, like avalanching rocks, his heavy hooves whizzed by my head! I tucked my tail and dodged for my life with the stallion pounding after me, his teeth bared. How I hated horses!

41

We slunk away, hiding ourselves in the willow scrub along the river. Here we found the faint smell of horse in a thicket drenched in tiger musk. While I looked behind us, Marmot nosed the place very carefully, his neck stretched, his eyes wide. At last he crept into the thicket, where I heard him chewing. I followed. He was chewing a hoof. I ate a lone, frozen scrap of meat, then chewed on the hoof after Marmot dropped it, but my hunger wasn't satisfied.

One night later, after I had forgotten that we were anything more than a pair of wolves who badly needed food, we suddenly smelled woodsmoke with another smell inside it—something wonderful, delicious, like marrow in a bone. Our mouths watering, we quietly, cautiously, followed the smell and found ourselves in the shadows of the moonlit trees that circled Graylag's lodge. Inside the lodge the liver of a roe deer was cooking!

We were so hungry and the smell was so good that in spite of the bloody, bitter fumes of human beings, we crept to the lodge from the rear, then scrambled up onto the roof, where the liver smell was rising, so delicious that I felt a little faint. But on top of the roof we found something even better than the smell—we found strips of deer meat hanging from the antlers! In no time we were jumping, pulling down and gobbling the strips!

Inside, someone must have heard our feet scrabbling. We heard muffled shouts, then saw people popping quickly from the coldtrap like pellets from a startled deer. "Get gone!" a deep, loud voice rang out. "Go on!" and "Get out!" cried other voices, while spears and bits of wood and snow began to fly by us. We leaped off the roof and dashed halfway up the trail behind the lodge.

But suddenly Marmot stopped and turned around as if he remembered something. Then he vanished and I stood alone beside his footprints on the moonlit snow. I waited, but nothing happened. So I put my nose in the air and howled a long, loud call that rose quickly at the beginning to show my surprise and fell slowly at the end to show my loneliness. Nervously, hopefully, I listened for an answer, but heard only bits of snow dropping from the trees and the sudden *hrou-ou* of an owl. At last I remembered who I was—nothing but Teal's spirit-slave—and slowly, sadly, I scrambled downhill to the lodge.

I must have changed to human form without noticing, because when I looked down at my feet while I climbed to the roof, I saw on my legs my spirit-clothing, my knee-high moccasins and trousers. And huddled by Graylag's smoke-hole, with his spirit-deerskin wrapped around him, was the human form of Marmot. Annoyed, I sat down by the other smokehole.

"Why did you leave me alone?" I asked him.

"I was hungry. Do you see this meat hanging here?" Of course I saw the meat. In the form of wolves, Marmot and I had just been trying to steal pieces of it. I didn't bother to answer what seemed a pointless question, but simply stared at Marmot as if he hadn't asked. "Well," he went on, seeing that he wasn't going to get any help from me, "the meat belongs to the people. They won't let wolves or any other animal have any of it. But they'll burn some for spirits. That's how we'll get a share."

As usual Marmot was right. Before long we smelled fat burning. "Here it comes," said Marmot, dropping on his hands and knees to hold his open mouth above the smoke-hole. I did the same, and got a little taste.

"They didn't give much," I said, after cleaning my lips with my tongue.

"They don't have much," said Marmot. "When they get more, they'll give more."

Again Marmot was right. A few days later, large herds of migrating reindeer began to ford the partly frozen river far downstream. All the men and women except the nursing mothers crawled out of the lodge armed with spears and axes, and without any help from us went to slaughter the deer as they struggled between the open water and the ice. After two days the people came home carrying forequarters, hindquarters, necks, and ribs, then went back again for more. Then strips of meat hung so thickly on the antlers and cast such a heavy, bloody smell that all day the ravens called in the sky to other ravens, bringing flocks of them from far away. And all night the woods around the lodge seemed alive with animals moving in the cover of the trees—first the large pack of wolves from the hills to the east, later the hyenas from Char Lake.

Dangerously outnumbered, what could the two of us do but withdraw to the woods, out of the way of the greedy robbers who swarmed over the roof to snatch meat? I couldn't help but start when I suddenly noticed the tigress crouched low under a spruce branch, looking with round eyes at the hyenas as if she disliked them. I was relieved to see her thin haunches and long tail vanishing among the trees as she went away to hunt her own deer.

However, although the two of us were as helpless as the tigress against the many thieves, the people were not. Like hornets from a nest, they kept rushing from the coldtrap whenever they heard toenails scratching on the roof.

Between trips to clear the roof, the people sang to praise us. If we had handed them the meat ourselves, they could not have been more grateful. "We will live," they sang. "We will eat fat. Our mouths will shine. Our lodge will grow and our children will be many. Find fat in the smoke as our thanks."

Were they sending a large gift? Hurrying to the smoke-hole, we smelled a vapor of reindeer fat rising. Ah! The smoke was thick with it! As in life we might have sat ourselves down at a fireside for a heavy meal, we eagerly sat beside the smokehole to catch the greasy vapor on our fingers. Under our heels the roof trembled with the strength of the singing. "How simple these people are," I said.

"We're simple too," said Marmot, exploring his palms for the last greasy traces. "Look how easily we're satisfied."

≪ 3 ≫

ALTHOUGH I WAS STILL young when we went to the Fire River
to find wives for the unmarried men, I remember parts of
our trip very well. I remember looking back to see a raven
on top of Graylag's lodge, and then looking up to see flock
after flock of geese in the gray sky, below the high clouds.
Where the geese came from, none of us could say. But
Father knew that after flying all night, the flocks were on
their way to rest and eat in the marshes of the Black River.
Should we go there and try to kill some? he wondered.
Graylag found the thought tempting, but said that the
marshes were very far. Too far, said the other adults. The
geese could leave before we got there. We decided not to go,
knowing that before we reached the Fire River we would
often think of those geese hungrily.

This became so. Although we brought our bear meat, we
also looked for food along the way. Sometimes we found
pine nuts or evergreen cones with kernels, but more often
we found carcasses—sometimes the kills of wolves or
hyenas, which we drove off; sometimes winterkills we found
by watching the sky for ravens. Some evenings we went
hunting, and every night we set out lines of snares, but each
day's travel didn't always bring us to a good place to find
food. Many days we didn't eat enough, and after the bear
meat was gone, some days we ate nothing, or just snow. So I
remember hunger.

I also remember walking. Soon after we crossed the Char,
the adults settled into their regular, distance-eating stride,

which carries them on and on as if the journey can never end. They didn't mind that there was no trail to follow, but took turns breaking trail. They didn't talk or sing, or complain about their packs. The bitter wind didn't make them cold, and hunger didn't make them tired. If their feet were wet, they ignored their feet. If the sun grew hot, they just opened the fronts of their parkas. The bad thing was that they expected the children to do as they did, and wouldn't let Junco and me walk together lest we start talking, forget to walk fast, fall behind, and cause a gap in the line. If an adult caused a gap in the line, the other adults were very polite about it. But if I caused the gap, I was shamed and scolded and made to walk in front of Mother so she could force me to keep up. And not a word of complaint could I speak, either. If Mother even thought from the tone of my voice that I wanted to complain, she would draw in her breath sharply: a warning.

I remember some of our camps. At the start of our journey, while we walked by the Char's southern floodplain, we sometimes found groves of hemlocks which made perfect shelters. I loved to sleep under the hemlocks, protected from weather by their thick branches, comfortable on their beds of dry needles, dizzy with their sweet, cold smell. And bits of their gum were tasty to chew, or made wonderful sparks in the night's fires.

When we reached the plains, we had to take shelter wherever we found it—beside rock ledges or in thickets—whatever protected us from the wind. If we couldn't find thick, sheltering bushes, we made little shelters like bushes out of branches thatched with grass or heather. And whenever we camped, Meri and I always wanted Father to choose Yoi so we could have Mother, and we were happy that he often did.

I remember many things about Mother. I remember how at the start of our trip, when we passed the place where the Little Char River leaves Char Lake, she noticed open water and decided to bathe. At least it was the warmest time of a sunny day. Mother made everyone stop walking while she and Yoi took Meri and me to a rapids. There they made us take off our clothes and scrubbed us in water so cold we couldn't catch our breath to scream. After that, Mother and

Yoi stripped and waded in. Without any of their heavy clothes, their naked bodies looked very thin, like the bodies of animals after being skinned—like bears, perhaps, but smaller. Mother and Yoi crouched and scrubbed themselves, then stood straight to undo their braids. Suddenly I noticed that their bodies looked different. Yoi's belly was flat, sunk between her hipbones. Mother's belly bulged and her navel stuck out. She was pregnant!

That was in the early spring, when the Icebreaking Moon was a waning crescent and the first mosquitoes of the year began to trouble us, just before our way led through the mixed birch and evergreen wood over the hills beyond the Char. We crossed those hills to a very wide plain where many herds of animals grazed and where, at night, we heard hyenas and lions. When the Icebreaking Moon left the sky and the new rim of the Moon of Foals showed in the afternoon over the plain like a woman pregnant in the springtime—thin, with a huge moon in her belly—our way crossed a steep range of rocky hills. On the south slope of this high land we tried to find a stream called the Spring River. Sooner or later it led to the Fire River. But in the hills the stream was very small. We couldn't find it. So Mother and Teal went to look for it, since the country was familiar to them from their childhood. Teal took Elho with her. I would have liked Mother to take me, but she wouldn't. Instead she made me stay to mind Meri. After Mother and Teal were gone, I thought about that. At first I felt hurt, as if Elho were being rewarded for the bad things he and Yoi had done. But soon I saw that Teal had taken Elho because she didn't want to leave him behind with Yoi. Mother didn't need to keep her eye on me. I felt proud of that.

After they were gone, Junco and I went to gather bristle-cones for the tasteless wooden kernels we thought would be our only food that night. We heard the sound of water, followed the sound, and found a pool with tiger tracks around it. Perhaps I was not worthy of the trust Mother seemed to have placed in me, but I reminded Junco that since the people in camp had no water but snow, we could be sent all the way back to fill a waterskin at a scary time of evening, if we told about the pool. Junco agreed, so we said nothing.

Late that night, when we were all sitting at a small fire burning the feathers off a ptarmigan, I heard footsteps crunching softly on the pine needles. Something large was moving slowly, pressing one foot, then waiting, then another foot. In the cold air I noticed a strong, musky scent, and in the darkness of a clump of evergreens I saw a cloud of breath. Scared as I was, I couldn't resist scaring Timu. "Behind you," I whispered to him. "Is something there?"

Timu turned, then leaped to his feet. Then everyone leaped up, snatched spears and axes and branches from the fire as the tiger showed himself between two trees, looking at us. He was enormous—as tall as a bison, I thought, with a face as broad as a man's body. His white chest and striped shoulders were wide and heavy, and his fur was very thick. His eyes were partly shut and his mouth was partly open so the tips of his lower teeth showed. "Uncle! Old One!" said the men. "Go back. The ptarmigan is ours."

But the tiger wasn't looking at the smoldering bird. He was looking at us, and seemed to be listening to us too. His ears were partly turned in our direction. "Go now," said the men. "Our spears will hurt you." But the tiger seemed to be filling his nostrils with our scent and his eyes with the sight of us. In time he twitched his ears so we glimpsed the white spots on the backs, turned his head slightly, and then, with a few slow paces, moved his great body between the trees, his shoulders high, his long, strong tail curved low. Only his terrifying musky smell remained behind him.

Our camp was no good, we could see that. We wouldn't sleep with him nearby, and we wouldn't be able to hunt. A tiger his size would have the game as shy as warblers. Now Junco and I had no choice but to tell the whole story of finding the pool and his tracks. The other people were quite angry at us for keeping such a secret, but what could they do? The pool was the source of the Spring River, which Mother and Teal had gone to find.

The adults decided to leave camp as soon as it was light. If we didn't meet Mother and the others, they could find us later from our tracks. Or so said Father and Graylag, spreading out their sleepingskins and rolling their firesticks and axes inside them.

I didn't like to leave without Mother. Plucking Father's sleeve, I said so. But he said kindly, "Your mother is all right. We'll find her."

"No, Father," I said. "I'll wait here for her."

"You?" said Father. "Alone here?"

I made up my mind not to show the way to the pool. But the others never bothered to ask me. By dawn they had figured out where it must be and left in single file, straight for it. Stubbornly, I stayed sitting by the embers of the fire while the sky in the east turned pink. As Father was about to move out of sight behind a clump of trees, he turned to look back at me with a little smile. I saw that I couldn't wait alone, so I got up and followed, down the southern slope of the hills while the sun rose.

As we kept just east of the tumbling stream which was the Spring River, we saw a figure among the birch trees ahead of us, a man carrying on his shoulder the foreleg of a horse. The man was Elho and the meat was part of a stallion, he said, the gift of people who were camped about two days' travel down the Fire River, where it flowed onto the steppe. Mother and Teal were now with those people and had sent Elho back for us. Since we had eaten nothing but pine kernels and ptarmigan for many days, we gathered fuel, rolled a fire, and sat down to cook the meat while we heard what Elho had to tell us.

About twenty people were camped along the river, said Elho. All of them were strangers. Not even Teal knew the men, and no one knew the women either, except that a few were related to people in our lineage. We looked at the present they had sent us. One foreleg for so many of us from so many of them seemed almost stingy. And although their women had welcomed our women, the men had made Elho uncomfortable. Their speech, he said, was strange.

"Your news is disappointing," said Graylag, looking rather uneasily at the foreleg. "What did these people tell you?"

Elho hesitated a moment. The rest of us glanced around at each other, distressed that he was having trouble choosing words. "They weren't really unfriendly," said Elho at last. "But they told us that our kinsmen don't come here

49

anymore. Instead they go from their lodges to camps on the steppe, to the calving grounds of the mammoths by the Hair River, very far."

"How do these men know that?" asked Graylag, scowling.

"One was the widower of a woman of my lineage."

"A widower?" asked Father. "Who has died?"

"Tchene?" said Elho. "I didn't know her." The adults looked at each other and shook their heads. They didn't know Tchene either. "Mother and Aunt knew Tchene," Elho added. "They cried very much to hear that she was dead."

"What else?" said Graylag.

"When I asked how long it would take us to find our kinsmen if we traveled there slowly with women and children, they told me it would take more than the length of a moon."

Thoughtfully, Graylag rubbed his lip. "Did you learn where the strange men came from?" he asked.

"From winter lodges in the west," said Elho. "If we left from here now, taking our direction from the Reindeer Stars, we would reach there when the Reindeer Stars start down to their winter shelter."

"Very far," said Graylag, still thinking. "Why are they here?"

"To fish."

"Have you news of other people?"

"Yes," said Elho. "Out on the steppe, hunting mammoths, are two big groups of people from lodges in the northeast. The strangers don't know them but think they're from the lower Black River."

"Ah!" cried Graylag. "Two big groups from the Black River? Aren't all the people along the Black River related to me?"

"I don't know all your kinsmen," said Elho reasonably. "There was no way for me to learn more."

"No," said Graylag happily. "I will ask them myself. Now we must go, to thank them for this good meat."

And so we did. Two days later we came over a rise of ground and saw the smoke of the strangers' fires. We walked slowly until we could see the tops of their grass shelters, then we put down our packs, and the men of our group went off to meet the men of their group, taking with them a winter reindeer skin to show our thanks very generously for the rather stingy present the strangers had sent to us. Our men left their spears, their axes, and even their knives behind, to show their peaceful way of thinking. I would have liked to run ahead of the men to see Mother, but Father wouldn't let me. "When we meet strange men, we must greet them quietly, without confusion. How else can they be sure we come in peace?"

In the afternoon sunlight, the rest of us sat by our packs and dozed. In time the men came back with Mother and Teal, followed by one of the strangers. He was a tall man, Father's age, with braided hair, a beard, and brown eyes. His shirt, his trousers, and his moccasins looked very much like ours but he wore a necklace of pierced seeds and deer's teeth of a design I didn't know. He too had put away his weapons, and his empty hands hung at his sides. He nodded to us politely, then opened his mouth and began to say such thick words that I gaped. I could hardly understand him, and had never heard such ugly speech. "Greetings to the women" is what I think he was saying. "You are welcome. The hardhead trout are running. We ask you to make your camp near us on the river so you can share the fish."

Catching myself gaping, I tried to think why he sounded so terrible. Where we said *fff*, he said *vvv*. Where we said *ssh*, he said *zzh*. Where we said *th,* he said *dth,* and where we said *p,* he said *buh.* Our speech was clear and right. His was all wrong and muddy. How did his people know what he meant? Glancing around, I saw Junco and White Fox, Timu and Owl, all with puzzled looks on their faces, all getting ready to laugh. Elho stood by, enjoying the surprise we were getting. But the adults held themselves very straight and stiff, their eyes flashing dangerously from one to another of the young people, so we knew to pull long faces and pretend nothing unusual was happening. The moment the stranger left, though, leading some of our people away with him to find a campsite, we laughed and imitated him. Timu and I, in fact, jumped to our feet and pretended to be the stranger and his wife having an argument. I thought we sputtered and grunted just like he did, and we must have been quite funny, since Junco, Owl, and White Fox laughed until their tears came.

We made a nice camp at a distance from the strangers' camp, hiding our half-dome shelters in the long grass of the plain by the river, under a hazy sky where swallows flew, catching things too small for us to see. We burned bleached, dry wood and even bleached bones washed up on the riverbanks, and bison dung we found on the plain. For the first few days our men sat at the strangers' camp talking with their men while their women went out along the river and over the plain with us. Teal and Mother already knew their women, most of whom (unlike their men) came from lodges on the shores of Woman Lake and so of course spoke naturally.

Spring had come to the lowland by the Fire River. Like a bear, Mother led us along the bank, nosing out asparagus and fern fronds and many other kinds of good spring foods to eat.

And fish! By now the Moon of Foals was rising at the end of night, carrying in her belly the Moon of Flies. When the spring moon's back turned north, the whitefish started running! With the strangers' women, we took off our moccasins and trousers, rolled up our sleeves, and waded in the rapids to catch whitefish with our hands. Otters, kingfishers, an eagle, an osprey, and some bears came to fish too. If we saw a bear, we laughed and pushed each other toward it and splashed and screamed. Before the Moon of Flies was a crescent, the women knew all about each other and were kissing and calling each other "Sister."

It was different with the men. They spent the first few days sitting and talking, not only in the day but far into the night. We brought them fish, sedge, goosefoot sprouts, and bulrush shoots. They ate without looking at their food, but kept their eyes fixed on each other. Their words, whether the good speech of our men or the ugly speech of their men, sounded stiff and guarded, as they carefully measured how much they told each other.

Then one night Graylag came back to our fires very excited. He had learned, he said, that he knew the mammoth hunters on the steppe, as he had hoped. One of them was Chelka, none other than his father's little brother. If Chelka was there, Graylag might know some of the other men, and because no group is too big for mammoth hunting, the mammoth hunters would welcome him. Graylag spoke quickly and his eyes shone. It seemed clear that when the strangers went to join the mammoth hunters, he would go with them.

After a time the whitefish grew fewer, then stopped running. We still saw hardhead trout but these were not as plentiful as whitefish. We worked hard but caught only a few. The time of plenty at the Fire River was ending. Now we would go.

On the last day the strange men decided to take our men hunting for meat to eat on the trail. One group invited Father to hunt with them in the willow brakes along the river for a musk deer, a small animal that is hard to find, since it lives alone, walks out at night, and by day hides in a form like a hare. The strangers wanted to keep the meat but offered the rest to Father.

Father accepted gladly. A musk deer's hide, taken off the carcass like a shirt turned inside out and knotted at the elbows, knees, and neck, makes a good waterskin. On a trip across the plains we would need a good waterskin. Also, a musk deer's tusks look pretty on a necklace, and its musk can be rubbed on snares. So Father was in a very good mood when he left in the morning with the strangers.

But that night he didn't come home. After dark the rest of us began to worry. The strangers were back—we heard them talking at their fires. At last Graylag called the men of our group together and they strode off to visit the strangers, to find out what had happened to Father or to fight. The rest of us listened, and soon heard Graylag and the strange men shouting with laughter. It sounded as if there was a joke on Father.

Then Graylag and the rest of our men came back, relaxed, laughing, and carrying the musk deer skin, which they handed to Yoi as a gift from the strangers, since her husband couldn't give it himself. He was still on the far bank of the river.

According to the strangers, Father had been so eager to get a musk deer that he had waded across to hunt on the far bank. While he was there the river rose suddenly, and he was caught. Meanwhile, the strangers found and killed a musk deer on the near bank. Stranded, Father watched them do it.

In the middle of the night, Father came home. His clothes were wet, his braid was loose, and his face was drawn and strained with anger. The strangers had persuaded him to cross the river, he said, knowing that the water would rise. During the night four lions had come to find him. He had seen their eyes in the moonlight, and had stood up to tell them to go. Just then he had heard a burst of laughter from the strangers' camp, laughter that showed how much the strangers were liking this.

The noise had startled him and spoiled his speech to the lions. Distracted, he had turned his head. Noticing this, the lions had moved toward him, giving him no choice but to jump in the water. He was swept downstream and dashed against rocks, and although he finally managed to pull himself out on the near bank and make his way back to us, his ax and firesticks were gone.

Balancing his spear, which he had managed to keep while he was in the water, Father stared toward the camp of the strangers. Perhaps because it was so dark, since our fires were low, or perhaps because Father looked funny, like a wet animal that drags itself, ashamed, from a river, the men of our camp didn't see how angry he was. Or perhaps they wanted to joke away his anger. Anyway, they laughed at him. "You should see yourself, Ahi," said Graylag. "Where are you going with that spear?"

Father turned and stared at Graylag. "Where am I going? I'm going home. Get up and make your packs," he said to Mother and Aunt Yoi. "We're leaving as soon as it's light."

At first we didn't believe he meant it. Mother and Yoi just looked at him in amazement. "What's wrong, Ahi?" Mother cried. "Did someone hurt you?"

"The strangers robbed us of the skin, and now Graylag makes fun of me."

"No one robbed us!" said Mother. "They gave us the skin. Look! My sister has it. They gave it to her."

"And what was she doing while I was gone, that strangers should give her a skin?"

Many people began to shout at Father. Yoi tearfully said she had done nothing. Mother begged him to sit down until his anger left him. Meri cried, and I shouted at Meri. The noise brought several of the strangers, all men, who began to laugh when they saw Father in his wet clothes. Meanwhile, Graylag spoke in a low voice to Father's two nephews, The Stick and The Frog, who then took Father's spear away from him.

"Let everyone go away now," said Graylag. "We will leave Ahi to dry his clothes. There's no need for anger. We will talk in the morning, to put an end to this."

But in the morning Father threw the musk deer skin on the fire and made us roll up our packs. His sister, Graylag's wife Ina, came over to reason with him, begging him to stay. But he pushed her aside. To her sons, his nephews, he said, "You may come with us or stay with Graylag and your mother. But if you stay, remember that you don't know the people you'll meet on the steppe. As these strangers treated me, perhaps those strangers will treat you."

Father's nephews were shy of strangers. Why not? Those two young men were afraid of their own hurtful nicknames. Cousin The Stick had a withered, useless right arm and a left-handed throw with a strange twist to it, and Cousin The Frog had a broad face with popping, yellow-brown eyes so like a frog's that Timu could always make people laugh by offering him flies. When Father began to make his pack, his nephews began to make their packs too.

At last Graylag himself came to sit by Father, cheerfully at first. But slowly he grew more annoyed, as Father stubbornly refused to listen to him. "Whoever wants to go with those strangers may go," said Father. "But no one must go."

In the end Father and Graylag agreed that Graylag with his wives, his sons, his daughter and nephew and their families would follow the strangers to the mammoth hunters. In the fall they would probably start back to the lodge on the Char, bringing as much ivory as they could carry. Father and the rest of us would visit the lodge where Father was born, a lodge that was abandoned long ago but had good winter hunting, which might be useful to us all someday. We would go there to learn how the hunting seemed, and meet Graylag on the Char next winter. "So be it," said Graylag. "Then we'll meet again before the snow."

"Come, all of you," said Father. "The day is growing old and we're still here talking."

What could we do? As Mother said later, "The raven waits for the tiger," meaning that no matter how clever the rest of us may be, the hunter makes the decisions. The decision had been made, so we stood up, and with many tears for all the people we were leaving behind, we followed him.

We walked a long way. The sun grew hot, and deerflies found us. My pack seemed to want to bury me, and my feet hurt. Since the earth was very rough and stony, Father must have thought to try higher ground, because we climbed to the edge of the valley. At the top I turned and looked back at our old camp and saw, very small and very far away, Junco, Timu, Elho, and White Fox still looking after me. When they saw me turn, they waved!

And so began our summer. Father's old lodge, I learned, was on the Pine River, about half as far northeast of the Char as the camp on the Fire River was southwest. And we couldn't travel fast because of Mother, who had to eat and rest often because her pregnancy was well along. We spent a good part of each day finding food, looking for blueberries and raspberries and bearberries. And each night we stopped early to set snares. I soon realized that we couldn't reach the Pine River before early fall.

Aunt Yoi and my cousins must have realized the same thing. One night after we made camp we told our thoughts to Father. He agreed. But he had never really thought that Graylag could be back on the Char by next winter. As Father saw it, Graylag might spend the winter with the mammoth hunters and we might spend it in Father's old lodge. Then I suspected that he and Graylag were only pretending when they said they would meet in the winter. Without telling the rest of us, they may have thought of separating their groups for a while. This made me as sad as I could be, since I knew I would find no one of my age for a year or more, and would have no one to talk to but Meri!

* * *

THE TRAIL

One day we came to a birch grove where Mother made us stop to gather birch fiber. We stripped every birch in the grove and scraped the brown inner fiber. Mother put it in her pack. After that, it seemed, we covered less distance every day. One night at our fire, The Stick and The Frog remembered that they had traveled between the Fire River and the Black River in ten days' time. They were sorry, I'm sure, that our group was so slow. But Mother was slow because she was soon to give birth.

On the morning of the day we started down the northern slope of the hills between the rivers, Mother's labor began. All morning she lagged behind the rest. I lagged with her. From time to time she would lean on her digging stick and blow the loose hair from her braid out of her eyes. Even with her huge belly she seemed small to me, under the gray sky, against the dark of the hills behind her. Her face, always smooth and pleasant, was full of pain. I remember her telling me that when I was born, her water broke into her trousers, and her trousers hardened up afterwards so she had to throw them away. Sure enough, in the middle of the morning she stopped to take off her trousers and roll them into her pack, then went on barelegged. Presently her water broke with a gush down her legs. She stood in a pool of it, and in a cloud of its faint smell. Mother and I began to dig up the wet earth with our digging sticks, then carried the mud to a place far from the trail. "We'll stop here," said Mother.

She began to look for a place to hide, and finally chose a spruce with low branches that made a shelter so thick that only heavy rain would get through. We gathered moss for her to sit on when she leaned against the tree, and got out the birch fiber to soak up the blood. She brought her firesticks out of her pack and asked me to roll a fire. I found wood and tinder and began to roll, but I was still learning how to do this difficult thing, and my fire wouldn't start. Finally Mother left her place and came, crawling painfully, to do it for me.

Then she crawled back and braced herself against the tree, with her parka over her shoulders and a pad of her birch fiber between her legs. "Sit down. Keep still," she said, and I did.

57

After a while she told me to get up again and bury with fresh soil the spruce needles and earth soaked by more of her birth-water. I did, then sat down to wait again. I didn't dare watch Mother, who sat with her head on her arms, but I listened to her panting; her breath seemed to whistle in and out of her mouth. When I smelled blood, I stole a glance, and saw that her fiber pad was soaked with it. She used a stick to push the pad away from herself. "Bury that too," she told me. While I did, she made herself another.

The woods were very quiet. No birds sang; not even wind rustled the trees. The sky was overcast—we couldn't see the sun, but we knew it was by now late in the day. I began to feel afraid. Were we making a great smell? Would we attract a bear? A tiger? I tried not to think about this, but when the sky grew dark I began to hear soft footprints all around us, and I tried to take Mother's hand. "Leave me alone," she said in a weak, cross voice, and she brushed my hand away.

Soon we were sure we heard footsteps, and Yoi appeared on the trail. She had come back to look for us at last. "Oh," she said. "No one thought it would be today. How is it, Sister?"

"It's starting," said Mother between her teeth.

"The men have camped already, far ahead. Can you walk to them?"

Mother shook her head. "No," she said. "Just let me be."

But Yoi looked worried. "Yanan," she ordered, "run ahead and tell your father to move the camp here."

So then I had to start after Father all alone, when the valleys were already filled with dark, at the time of day when the animals start their hunting. I knew if I thought about it I would be too frightened to go, so I tried not to think about it, but just took my digging stick and set off at a trot.

The trail wasn't a good trail made by mammoths but by simple reindeer, who hate to follow each other exactly so go slightly different ways. Yoi hadn't bothered to tell me about a fork she had taken in the trail. Hares had used it since, so I had trouble finding Yoi's tracks. By the time I did, it was almost too dark to see at all. I groped along, feeling with my feet for the bare hardness of the trail or the spruceneedle softness of the edge of the trail, trying to remember when the moon might rise, even in the clouds. Then my fear found me. Like a spark in tinder, it began to grow until it was like a flame. I was afraid for myself, alone in the dark woods, and afraid for Mother, alone with only Yoi and a little fire, in pain and in danger.

Yoi, I then saw, was also afraid of the trail and had sent me instead of going herself. *I am only Yanan,* I thought, *alone in the woods, but if a tiger comes for me I will hit him as hard as I can.* I cracked my digging stick against the trees so that a tiger would know he would be hit very hard if he came near, and I kept walking, and in this way I arrived at Father's camp.

I found Father and his nephews on their feet, looking for us. "Where are the others?" they demanded angrily, as if it were my fault that I came alone. When I told them, they slowly began to pack up their things. Cousin The Frog had just put a strip of dry fish on the fire and wanted to cook it. Cousin The Stick's waterskin was empty. He handed it to me to fill for him at a stream which he said was nearby. Meri was tired and cried when I told her to get ready to travel again. When I tried to fix her clothes and her braid she cried more, and Father's nephews told me to let her be. Then I sat by the fire and fixed my eyes on the horizon while my anger at the men burned. When the fish was cooked, I refused to eat any.

Father and his nephews then put most of their bundles up in the trees, and when the moon rose and we started, they carried only small packs, spears, and axes. Meri and I followed, Meri with a pine-cone doll and I with the waterskins, now heavy and cold. For a very long time they slid back and forth against my legs as we walked in silence. Meri cried for me to carry her. "Crying?" I whispered. "Do you want to bring a tiger?"

Father turned around, picked her up, and put her on his shoulder, where she looked down at me with a nasty, babyish pout. In the past I might have told Father she was teasing, or said something mean to her, but tonight I didn't have the heart. I was too hungry and too tired on that dark trail where even Father had to walk slowly, almost feeling his way. For a moment I tempted a smile from Meri by playing hide-the-eyes.

The moon rose very high, the wind blew in the trees, and

the branches made a scratching sound. We sometimes heard our own footsteps and our own breathing, and we heard animals several times—reindeer thumping their front feet. I smelled the spruce needles in the night air, and a whiff of carrion—Cousin The Frog's dried fish. Then I smelled smoke—Mother's fire—and in a moment we came to her camp.

Both Father's nephews went to sit by the little fire, which was burning very low, but Father and Meri and I crept under the overhanging spruce branches where Mother sat with Yoi. Mother was now supported between Yoi's legs, leaning against Yoi's body. We saw that Mother's eyes were shut and her face was twisted with pain. She made no sign that she knew we were there. Yoi looked at Father with tear-swollen eyes, and reaching across Mother's large belly, lifted the edge of her shirt to show that a tiny foot stuck out of Mother's body.

Mother's belly suddenly seemed to grow tall. She held her breath, her back arched and her head rolled, and the tiny leg came out to the knee. Yoi rubbed the belly until Mother seemed to relax, the leg drew back in a trickle of blood, and again only the foot was showing.

"The head should come first," whispered Father.

"Yes," said Yoi.

"Why don't you fix it?"

"I can't. I don't know how."

"Have you ever seen this before?"

Yoi shook her head and Father went quickly to sit with his nephews. They spoke in whispers. We sat in silence. The only sounds were branches cracking as The Stick built a shelter. Even Meri was quiet, looking from Mother's face to Yoi's face and sucking her thumb. When Mother stiffened with another pain, Yoi stroked her face and hugged her.

"Is it coming feet first?" Mother whispered.

"Yes," said Yoi.

"We must turn it," said Mother. "Let me lie down. Then let Yanan do it. Her hands are small. Yoi, you help her." And so, very gently, Yoi lay Mother down flat on her back.

I brought a new torch and lit a fire right under the spruce branches. The flames leaped up and singed the spruce, but the needles were green and didn't burn. By the light I saw big clots of blood clinging to Mother's thighs and darkening the pile of moss and fiber under her. More blood was draining from her body, but the little foot was gone.

Mother said, "Slide in your hands and try to turn it. Push its feet toward my head. Look, like this." She showed me her cupped hand. So I knelt in front of her, shut my eyes, and did as she said.

The baby was so soft that at first my fingers were too coarse to feel it. Then I found something small between my fingers and realized it was the tiny foot, with toes. Suddenly my hand was squeezed terribly, crushing against the baby until my fingers became numb. The force moved the baby slowly down my wrist until the underarm was caught by my thumb. I held the little body and opened my eyes. Now, beside my arm, were two small feet.

"Did it turn?" asked Mother.

"No," said Yoi.

"Try again quickly," said Mother, "before the pain."

So I pushed until my hand disappeared almost to the wrist, while Yoi pushed the side of Mother's belly. "Turn, Little One," she cried softly to the baby, as if, inside, it could hear, and do as she said.

"Can you feel the face?" asked Mother. "Can you feel the head?"

Something lumpy slid by my fingers. The face? "Yes, I can feel the face," I said.

"Slowly take out your hand," said Mother. "Now," she whispered, and her muscles tightened very tight. This time we saw the top of the baby's head and with the next few pains the head came out. Even in the dark I could see its face, all wrinkled. Most babies come out looking down at the ground, but this one was facing up, facing me.

"The head is out, Sister," whispered Teal.

"With your hand," said Mother, "turn the shoulders." She was talking to me, but Yoi took over again. Yoi understood this kind of birth, and she sent me out for more fiber.

When I left the shadow of the spruce, I found that the sky was turning gray and the dawn sounds of the woods were starting. Father and The Frog were dozing by the fire. The Stick was awake. "Yes?" he asked me.

"The baby is coming," I said. Father woke up, rubbing his eyes. "We need birch fiber."

Father pointed to a pile of freshly peeled fiber, which I took back to Yoi. Under the tree I saw a tiny pale form between Mother and Yoi, and when I knelt to look at it, I saw that it was a little girl, lying perfectly still with a huge, twisted cord attached to the middle of her belly. Painfully, Mother asked Yoi to help her sit up. She reached out her hands. Yoi and I pulled her to a sitting position. She picked up the baby and moved the tiny arms, then put her face to its face and breathed in its mouth. Suddenly the baby trembled and gasped, a very faint sound. Yoi took out her knife. "Not yet," whispered Mother. "Wait for the heart to leave the cord and go into the body." Yoi waited, watching, then cut. Blood oozed from the stumps. Then Mother braced herself on one arm and held the baby with the other, while Yoi pushed hard on Mother's belly. The afterbirth gushed out.

"Bury this," said Yoi to me. So I buried all the birth matter. Father and his nephews then came cautiously to look at the baby. We brought Mother a drink of water, but she was fast asleep.

All day we rested, making one long trip with the water-skins to a stream. More fog settled on the hills. A few animals walked past us late in the day—reindeer moving down the slopes. Father and his nephews took spears and went after them, but the forest floor was so deep in sticks and cones that they couldn't go quietly. The reindeer heard them.

Mother lay with the baby under her deerskin. My mind was with the baby inside the cape, where I could see her tiny fists and her face with its closed eyes. Sometimes we could hear her make a little sound, sucking or starting to cry, but mostly she slept. And I had helped her! She must have been glad to be born at last, with the terrible squeezing stopped.

Shortly before dark, rain started. We crowded into the two sprucebranch shelters that The Stick had built and watched the rain put out our fires. Late at night Mother asked me to bury a new pile of blood-soaked fiber.

A spruce forest is a bad place to find food, although we all

THE TRAIL

went looking for it. We found mushrooms and some gray peas in a clearing, but nothing more. The men set snares and caught a squirrel with tufted ears. All of this we ate in one meal. After it, Mother herself buried many pads of fiber.

On the third day after the birth, Father asked Mother how soon she would be willing to travel. She wanted to go soon. She didn't like the forest because there was no food in it. "Hunger is making me sick," she said. So we divided her pack into our packs, leaving her with nothing to carry except the baby in a sling inside her shirt, and we took up the trail.

All day we walked down out of the hills, toward the swamps on the upper reaches of the Black River. The reindeer trails were no use to us now—we took a direction for the east side of the swamps, about a day's walk. Travel was difficult because the hills were rocky and steep and the footing was unsure. By midafternoon Mother was walking behind Yoi, and then behind Meri. When she was next to me, I walked more slowly to keep pace with her.

When I offered to carry the baby, I thought Mother would refuse, but she gave me the soft little body to put inside my shirt. I felt very proud and important. No one looking at us would know we were two; the person would see only me. Yet I could feel the baby inside, tickling me softly as she moved.

Near the end of the slope, Mother undid her belt and removed her trousers. We were both frightened to see that they were wet with blood and that her fiber pad was soaked with it. She buried the pad by the trail. Then, making a fresh one from more of the fiber, she dressed again and we walked on slowly.

But soon I saw that blood was running down her legs and showing in her footprints. "Mother," I said, "look at the ground." She looked down and saw it, and started to cry. I couldn't remember ever seeing her cry before.

"What is happening to me?" she whispered.

"Let's hurry," I begged, catching her hand and trying to pull her along the trail. "The others will help you." She tried to follow, but soon she had to lean on my shoulder. I put my arm around her waist, and we struggled along the narrow trail side by side.

Inside my shirt, the baby began to cry. "We must stop now. Give her to me," said Mother. Sitting on her heels, she opened her shirt and gave her breast to the baby who, feeling the nipple touch her cheek, groped for it with her mouth. She found it, sucked hard, and then began to cry again. "We'll rest," said Mother. "After I sit still, my milk will come." She waited a moment as if gathering her strength, then added, "Meri is betrothed to White Fox. You should know that." She touched her necklace. "His parents gave this."

Then suddenly Mother collapsed. She was sitting one moment, lying crumpled like a deerskin the next moment, with the poor baby lying near her on the ground, screaming. I screamed too. "Mother! Mother!" But she lay still, mouth open, eyes shut. Some flies settled on her. On the ground where she lay was a large pool of blood.

Nothing made sense. I didn't know what to do, and no thoughts came to me. I stood still. Then I thought, *She must have a drink of water,* and taking the waterskin out of my pack I started to look for a stream. But the baby's screaming stopped me, and I went back. The baby lay naked on the ground, her tiny hands in fists, her feet waving, her face all wrinkled with crying. I picked her up and put her in my shirt. She held her breath, and suddenly the world was quiet—I heard the droning of the flies. Then she cried again, this time muffled by my shirt. I thought, *I must run to get Father.* Holding the baby against me, I ran down the slope as fast as I could, and when the branches whipped my face I didn't feel it. But suddenly I thought of Mother, all alone, with no one to protect her, waking to find no one there, not even the baby, and I turned around and ran back.

I found Mother trying to sit up, and I took her hands to help her, but she lay back without speaking. When she tried to moisten her lips with her tongue, I could see that her tongue was almost white. Finally she whispered, "Stay with me."

And I said, "I will."

When Father and Aunt Yoi finally returned to look for us, the shadows of the reeds were long. Mother lay still in a patch of faint sunlight while flies tasted her skin at the corners of her mouth and eyes. On the ground her blood was spoiling, making a heavy, foul smell. The baby, exhausted, no longer cried. I wondered why Father and Yoi had taken so long to come back, but I felt numb myself, almost dead; I couldn't find the words to ask. Father stood staring at us. Yoi seized Mother's hand and began to rub it, meanwhile calling Mother's name: "Lapwing! Lapwing! Sister! Sister!" But Mother's spirit was almost free of her body, off for the sun's place in the west, and only when the baby began to cry again did her spirit look back for a moment, to make her eyelids stir.

Suddenly a blow struck the side of my head, and then two more. I saw lights, and threw up my arms to protect myself. Yoi was hitting me. "You worthless girl!" she screamed. "Why didn't you run after us? You lazy, worthless, thoughtless animal, not worth the food you eat!"

Father caught her arm. "Stop!" he said. "She did right. This is no time to quarrel."

But I could say nothing. I couldn't even cry. I wished I had done as Yoi said.

Giving his pack to Yoi, Father lifted Mother onto his back, and we followed him down the trail. The baby began to cry faintly, without stopping, until Yoi turned around to face me and angrily held out her hands. I gave her the baby and she gave me Father's pack, which made me go so slowly that by the time I reached the little shelters that Father's nephews had made while waiting for us, Mother was dead. Already the others had straightened her clothes and tied her arms and legs tightly against her body. Like a bundle, she lay stiffly at the edge of camp with staring, half-open eyes.

Meri ran up to me. "Where's Mother?" she asked.

"She's there." I pointed. "She's dead."

"That's not her," said Meri. "That's Aunt Teal." And I could see that Mother now looked a little like Teal—her cheeks were stiff and her eyes hollow, which made her face look square, like Teal's, not smooth and round, as hers used to be. It seemed to me that her spirit was not near the camp any longer, although it is said that the spirit of a woman who dies from childbirth waits for the newborn child.

Aunt Yoi had soaked a piece of deerskin in water and was letting the baby suck it. When I came into camp, she sobbed and held out her arms. "Who will help me? I have no mother, no father, no sister, no one now," she cried. I stared at her. Meri also held up her arms to me so I could lift her. When I did, she clung to me.

I heard chopping, and looking through the bushes, I saw Father and his nephews crouching with digging sticks, making a grave. They worked long after the moon rose, stopping to eat the last of the fish and part of a large root that Aunt Yoi had gathered. Then they went on digging. When their sticks hit the deep earth that never thaws, the blows of their digging became clear and sharp, and we knew from the sound that their work was nearly finished. I filled a waterskin and brought it to Mother, and in the moonlight Yoi and I washed her face and combed and braided her hair. On her braid we tied her ivory pin. Then, weeping, Father carried her to her grave and put her inside.

As he did, Yoi and Father's nephews all shouted at once. "Stop! That's wrong!" they cried. Father turned his tear-stained face to look at them. They were pointing in different directions. "Face her there," they said.

Slowly Father looked at the moon and the slope of the hills, and said carefully, "I'm facing her right. She was born on Woman Lake."

"She was born on the Fire River!" said Yoi.

"Were you there?" asked Father angrily. Of course, being younger, Yoi had not been there. She stared at Father but didn't speak. Father turned to his nephews. "Were you there?" he repeated.

"No," admitted The Stick.

"You see?" said Father. "She had a winter name for an animal, to honor The Bear. So she was born in a lodge, not on the summergrounds on the Fire River. Her father lived in a lodge on Woman Lake. Yes?" He stared angrily at Yoi, who shrugged. Father then turned back to the grave and looked at Mother for a long time in silence before dropping her parka down on top of her.

Although we realized too late that we couldn't be sure where she was born or whether she was facing the right way, we threw the rest of her things into her grave: the strings of her pack, her belt, her scraper, her twine, her awl, her bone needle, her bison horn full of tinder, her flint knife with its

66

perfect edge, and her antler necklace with pendants, the betrothal gift for Meri.

Then Father, weeping, threw earth on his head, and drawing his own knife, cut a gash on his chest. "See how I grieve for you, Lapwing," he said. He held out his arms to Yoi and said, "Give me the baby." Yoi took the baby from her shirt and handed her to him.

The Stick and The Frog turned their faces away while Father carefully set the baby down beside Mother. Father took Mother's deerskin and was about to spread it over both of them when I suddenly snatched the baby and put her quickly inside my shirt. "I'll feed her, Father," I said. "Let me take her."

He looked at me for a long moment. Fresh tears ran down his face. Then he turned back to the grave to cover Mother with the deerskin and began slowly to push in the earth. The cousins didn't wait but went to gather stones to mound over the grave. They asked me to help them, but I couldn't.

I stood with the smell of the fresh earth in my nostrils, listening to the sound of it falling, handful by handful, on the deerskin. Inside my shirt the baby cried faintly, on and on. No one mentioned the baby, and when the grave was full and covered with stones, we returned to our fire.

The moon was sinking, huge and red as it lowered itself to the hills where we had been when all this began, when the baby was born. By the faint light I found the bit of root that was my share of our food. I took a bite and chewed it hard. When it was a paste I put some on my finger and smeared it on the baby's mouth. She sucked my finger eagerly the moment she felt my touch, but her face slowly wrinkled and she began to cry again. Yoi opened her shirt and put the baby to her breast. The baby sucked quickly for a while, then suddenly fell asleep. I went to lean on Father's shoulder where he sat by the fire, and fell asleep as if I too were dead.

Before dawn the baby's crying woke me. Yoi was holding her loosely, almost angrily, and when I reached out my hands, Yoi dropped the baby into them. I tried to put a paste of chewed root into her mouth, but she didn't swallow it. Instead she began a steady, weak crying like a wheeze.

"She should be with Lapwing," said Cousin The Stick. "Without milk, she can't live."

"Yoi fed her!" said Meri.

When we were ready to travel, Yoi asked to carry the baby again. "No use asking. I won't carry your pack for you," I said.

Yoi took out her breast. "You took her from her mother, but you can't quiet her," she said. We looked at each other full of anger, then both drew back quickly as if we saw something dangerous.

Yoi was right: the baby cried less if it could suckle. Yoi's breasts, although high like a girl's, were full-grown even if they had no milk. My breasts were just starting to show. Yoi tied the baby's sling under her shirt and we walked all day without stopping or speaking, getting farther and farther from Mother in her grave.

When the baby was quiet, I thought of Mother, unable to follow us, curled under the earth, all alone. She would be there in the fall, when the birch trees near her would drop their leaves on her grave. She would still be there in winter, in the spring, a year from now still there. However far we traveled, she would never join us or feel our warm fires or see the good sun. Her mother too was buried somewhere, I realized, never having thought of this before. Alone in a wood, not even by a trail? I didn't know.

When the baby was crying, I cried too. We stopped near the end of the day to gather food and eat, and we tried to feed her again. All of us tried, but Yoi's breasts were still empty and the baby wouldn't eat paste. At sunset she stopped crying. I thought Yoi's milk had come at last.

We walked all the next day and at night camped at the eastern edge of the marshes, on a small, wooded island that stood above the wet. Our campsite was thick with pine needles smelling of summer, very sweet. We didn't make shelters but simply rolled ourselves in our deerskins by the fire.

Toward morning Yoi said, "She's cold," and held the baby out for us to see. When we looked, we saw that she was dead.

Yoi simply laid her by the fire, naked, still, her spirit lost, as Mother's spirit had gone by now without her. We had nothing but the sling to cover her, and when in the dawn light we dug her grave, we had nothing to put with her except that little scrap of leather. Nothing else belonged to her.

Inside the hole, her small, naked body was so tender and pale that I didn't think we could put earth on her skin, but finally Father threw the first handful, then quickly the rest, then the stones, then threw earth on his head. "I mourn for you this way, my child," he said to the baby's tiny spirit as it hung, bewildered, in the air. "We're sorry you're alone—we didn't mean harm. Speak well for us if you find the Camps of the Dead." After the sun rose, we made up our packs and went on our way.

◄ 4 ►

WE WALKED EAST, crossing the Char River the day after we
passed south of Graylag's empty lodge. We followed the
Antler River up the west slopes of the hills, then followed
the Marten River down the east slopes until we heard the
roar of rapids where the Marten River and the Glacier River
join. On the far side of this wide place, where water tosses
into the air and rainbows hang, was the mouth of the Pine
River, Father's childhood home.

It took a long time—more days than I could count. When
Mother died, the Mammoth Moon was waning, and when
we reached the Marten River, the Yellowleaf Moon was
almost gone. Every night we set snares, and every day we
stopped to gather and eat food when we found it. Even so,
we traveled far every day. Father wanted to reach his old
lodge before the snow.

I didn't like the trail. The farther we got from Mother's
grave, the more I missed her. One day the air was filled with
big white flakes like feathers. Meri turned up her face and
put out her tongue for a snowflake, but I waited for someone
to say "Geese are flying" or "Goosedown." Then I remembered that Mother was the one who said this when she saw
big snowflakes in the fall. The more I missed Mother, the
less I wanted to be shut in a lodge all winter with Meri and
Yoi. Most of all I didn't like it that Father and Yoi had made
their bed together from the day Mother died. I even noticed
that once or twice in the middle of the night they forgot
their mourning and made those soft, struggling sounds and
changes in their breathing that the rest of us were supposed

70

to ignore. Every night when we camped I sat by myself, until Yoi began to call me Egg, for a silent person who is hiding something that grows large inside.

One day we came to a very old lodge on the bank of the Marten. The roof of the coldtrap was caved in, and the smokehole was filled with fallen pine needles and leaves. We crawled over the dung of the hares and wolverines who once had hidden there and found the room dirty and very dim. But the walls were still in place, and the locked antlers bracing the roof were hardly sagging. The lodge was made well, and I asked Father who owned it. His father had helped build it, he said. It was the second lodge of the Pine River people, where he himself had lived when he was a child. When I asked where the owners of the lodge were now, Father gestured to the air, to the west. They were spirits, he meant. There were no owners. When I asked why we didn't stay, he said that for as long as anyone could remember, a large herd of reindeer spent the winter in the valley of the Pine, where his people had built their main lodge. We were going to live near those reindeer.

We reached the Pine River lodge by noon the next day and found it badly broken. This lodge was wider than the lodge on the Marten, so the roofspan, being weaker, had fallen in. We camped and began to fix it.

The valley was sunny and sheltered. Down the middle, the Pine bubbled over rocks and watercress. Here, and through the hills beyond, the trees were taller than the trees I was used to—many were much taller than a man—and grew closer together than the trees by the Char. We would have firewood and shelter from some winter storms. But the most interesting thing at the Pine was something I had never seen before: the shining white tip of a glacier reaching from a cleft in the hills beyond.

I found myself always looking at the glacier. While we gathered wood and sedge root, it shone white like a lake in winter, and when we built our fires in the evening, it turned pink and then red in the sunset. Best of all, after dark but before the moon rose, the glacier made the night sky lighter, the same as fallen snow.

Soon after we arrived at the Pine River, Father told us that the glacier had moved. When he was a young man, he said, the glacier was back in the hills. Now the glacier was coming out of the hills, and at its tip trees were leaning forward as if the glacier was pushing them. Yoi and Father's nephews doubted this. How could it be, they asked, when the land was flat so the glacier wasn't going downhill? And of course the glacier wasn't alive, so it couldn't crawl. It was ice, they said, which can't move by itself, and it was also like a mountain, which can't move at all. No one could argue with this, of course. They were right. Even so, during the winter we spent by the Pine River, the leaning trees were pushed down. Perhaps the glacier did this at night, when we couldn't see it moving. Or perhaps the mountains also crawl and no one notices.

By the time of the next full moon, the Reindeer Moon, there were scattered herds of reindeer, red deer, horses, and bison in the Pine valley, and our lodge was mended well enough to keep out the wind. Then the wind blew the last of the yellow leaves from the birches, and the trees stood in the woods like naked people, thin and pale. I remembered a riddle Mother once taught me: "Who is the girl with twigs in her hair? In summer she's clothed, in winter she's bare!"

On the night of the second snowfall, The Stick and The Frog offered a prayer for our safekeeping, while gusts of tiny flakes came down the smokehole and the wind moaned. "Give us life," they prayed. "Give us food in winter, Ohun. Give us children."

"Hona," said the rest of us, and burned a piece of fat.

We then settled into our winter life, different in our small group from what it had been in Graylag's large group. Yoi said that life was very hard for us because we were so few—people only need one fire, she said, but when there are many people, the wood for that fire can be gathered quickly. She and I, with some help from Meri, spent a large part of every day just getting enough wood to keep ourselves from freezing. At first we snapped the dry, dead branches of the evergreens beside the lodge, but later we had to go farther and farther. Even so, no one had gathered firewood here for a long time, so it wasn't as scarce as it was around the Char River; we didn't need to chop so much; we usually found enough.

The Stick and The Frog also complained because there

were so few of us. Hunting was hard without many people, they reminded Father. "You should have gone with Graylag to the mammoth hunters," Father would tell them. "We are the same number now as when we left the Fire River. Nothing has changed." He meant, of course, the same number of hunters, of men.

"Let Yoi help us," said Cousin The Stick. So the four adults went hunting every few days. I thought that Yoi would be slow and not pay attention. This turned out to be true. After the first few hunting trips the men left her behind again. Then she and I looked for pine nuts, winterberries, deerberries, and even bristlecones, at least to notice where we could find them if all other food was gone. And we set snares for small game.

In fact, Yoi and I brought more food than the men. Our snares often held something, a hare or grouse or ptarmigan. And almost every day we gathered enough so that all of us could satisfy at least some of our hunger. But the three men didn't manage to kill anything until the Storm Moon was a crescent. Their kill was a reindeer doe. When The Frog came for Yoi and me to help carry the meat home, Yoi was so happy she sang. And when the meat was in the lodge, we cooked and ate far into the night, and again the next day and night, so a lot of the meat was eaten quickly and we didn't have much to freeze.

At the end of the Storm Moon, Father made his trip to the Char River, taking his spear, his ax, and his firesticks rolled in his deerskin. Not having to wait for people who travel slowly, he came back after only eight days, bringing with him from the lodge several greenstones to make spearpoints. No one was there, he told us. The lodge was still empty. Then we were glad we had come instead to the Pine River.

At the beginning of the Lodge Moon, the weather turned warm for a few days. Then the dry, cold wind came back, and the wet snow froze on the ground like ice on a lake. We could hardly walk without falling. After this, many of the hoofed animals left the valley. Because each blade of grass was held tight in solid ice, the animals had no hope of grazing, and because they had already browsed high on the trees, they couldn't reach higher. Only a few reindeer stayed, eating bark, as they do when all other food is gone. Our snares caught nothing. We were frightened, and one night we appealed humbly to The Bear.

> You in the northern lights,
> We are calling
> Hear us calling
> Hear us in the wind, Hona
> Calling The Bear
> Calling The Bear's head, Hona
> Calling The Bear's teeth
>
> Calling The Bear's legs
> Calling The Bear's feet, Hona
> Hona! Wiri! Hona! Wiri!
> Feet turn toward us,
> Bring us food,
> Give us meat,
> Send us game,
> Hona! Wiri! Hona! Wiri!
> Help us in winter.

So we prayed, and burned a bristlecone (the only food we had) for the smoke to carry to The Bear. Sometimes at night we heard the wolves howling. They called together, letting their voices rise and fall as if they too were praying. But in spite of our prayers, hunger came to us as it does almost every winter at this time, which is why the moon that rises next is called the Moon of Starving. We had very little hope of catching the reindeer with their wide, hairy hooves that cling to the ice, but we heard them outside our lodge, passing in small groups. Something in their feet makes a loud ticking. The sound mocked us. And wolves came at night to eat our frozen feces outside our lodge. We ate nothing.

Meri began to cry for Mother until I wanted to stifle her. One night when the sun set, Aunt Yoi looked at it, glowing red on the horizon, and she said, "In the Camps of the Dead they eat the sun. Every night of the year they have plenty. They don't have to walk in the cold all day searching but finding nothing—their food sits down in front of them.

Because of this winter, we will all go there. I wish I were there now."

"Don't envy them yet," said Father. "Every winter has a hard time in it. Soon this time will pass. Soon enough we will all go to eat the sun. Don't reach for death."

He made us exhaust ourselves walking all day in the cold without food. We followed the tiny trails of mice around the stalks of bushes, looking for the seeds that mice store in their burrows; we watched the sky for ravens, which might show us a kill we could rob. Far away one day Father found some broken bones and part of the tattered, frozen skin of a red deer, killed but not finished by a tiger. We ate this gratefully.

The Moon of Roaring came and went, and the dry, icy weather went on. The Moon of Cast Antlers followed. When it was full, Father and his nephews killed a second reindeer, a small one. We finished it when the moon waned. Just as we did, Father and his nephews found wolves eating the carcass of a winterkilled stallion, chased off the wolves, and brought the carcass home. On this we lived a little longer. Before the Icebreaking Moon, a blizzard filled the woods with snow that packed easily. Our lodge was buried; we dug our way out the door and saw that the bearded lichen and edible twigs were easily within reach of browsing deer now that they could stand on snowdrifts. We hurried to set snares.

The next day we visited the snares. Leaving Meri in the lodge, Yoi and my cousins went one way while Father and I went another. When we were near the first snare, we heard ravens, then saw them looking down at the branch that held the snare, which was moving with short, irregular jerks. Above the bushes we saw the ears and antler buds of a reindeer, then we saw its rolling head with eyes bulging and tongue out. It was a doe. She looked dead, but she was moving. Something was tugging at her, trying to pull her down. Motioning me to wait, Father went forward in a cautious crouch until the ravens screamed and flew up. When I heard Father say "Get along!" I ran up to him, knowing that the robber was too small to deserve respectful speech. I found Father working to untie the snare's frozen knots, ignoring a wolverine which was arching its back in the bushes, watching him. It was a large wolverine, black and silver, surely very hungry and unwilling to give up the deer. It circled us twice, then came nearer to circle us again.

Father loosened the knot and laid the deer down on the snow while the wolverine circled a fourth time, coming closer. Father reached for his spear. Suddenly the wolverine dashed up to snatch a bite of meat. Father threw his spear, pinning the wolverine through the hindquarters. Then, grasping the spear shaft to hold the wolverine down, Father swung his ax at its head. But the twisting wolverine dodged the blow, and before Father could lift the ax for a second blow, the wolverine was hanging by its teeth from his hand. Father grunted with pain, let go of the spear, and grabbing his knife from his belt, stabbed it into the wolverine's ribs. Nothing changed. I snatched up the ax from where Father had dropped it and began to chop at the wolverine's head, but still it hung on. Father tugged at the knife, which came out of the wolverine's chest with a spurt of blood, followed slowly by the pink tip of a lung, which I saw was still breathing. "The ax," said Father, and catching it from my hand, he chopped the wolverine's neck again while blood flew. "The knife," said Father. I groped for it in the snow. Seizing it, Father forced it between the wolverine's jaws, which, when the teeth broke, slowly pried open. The wolverine, still living, fell to the bloody snow, where Father stood over him, raised his spear, and pinned him.

Then Father sat down to look at the bite. I peered at it over his shoulder. The eyeteeth must have met between the bones of his hand, which was quite torn from the shaking and was beginning to swell. The incisor teeth had cut gashes, which were bleeding fast. Father packed his hand in snow. We looked for something to bind it up, and I was taking off my parka to offer my deerskin shirt when Father showed me that the snow was already helping and the bleeding was beginning to stop.

Father calmly started to skin the reindeer. After a moment he sent me to get Yoi and his nephews. They were very happy about the reindeer and glad that the snare-robber was destroyed. They were worried to hear of Father's bite, though, and sorry that the struggle had spoiled the wolverine's skin, which could have been a hood. Together we found Father beside a fire with many strips of liver cooking on the coals. We looked down at the wolverine, its breath shallow, its pink tongue stuck out, and its blood-matted hair frozen to the snow. The Stick jabbed the spear into its neck, and when it still refused to die began to skin it anyway.

We all stopped work when the liver was ready to eat. The food was so good and so welcome that we felt glad, we laughed, we liked each other, and when we had eaten we worked quickly and willingly to finish cutting the meat and carry it to the lodge. There was so much, we had to make two trips each. Father even took the chewed lichen and spruce twigs from the rumen—he called it "winter vegetable." On the second trip we made sure to gather up every last scrap, even the wolverine's torn skin. The Frog hesitated a moment over the wolverine's flayed carcass, in which a spark of life may still have clung, then took it too. The ravens sitting in the trees flew down to eat the bloody snow.

At the lodge, with more liver cooking and the meat freezing in the coldtrap, The Frog and Father looked at the bite again. Father's hand was sore, but at least the wounds had stopped bleeding. We ate, then rested, then ate again, until we were full of meat and almost asleep. During the night wolves walked over our roof, sniffing at the smokehole for the smell of our good food. Now and then one of them scratched at the smokehole, whining. In the morning we found where they had trampled the snow around and over the lodge, leaving their scats and urine and even round hollows, their beds, in the snow.

Starting early, the men visited the snares again, then went hunting and were gone all day. They came home at night to say that although we had killed the wolverine, the snares were now being robbed by wolves.

Father said that his hand hurt and he had pain up his arm. We built the fire to roast meat while The Frog looked at Father's hand carefully. The Stick looked too, and even Yoi took Father's hand in hers and turned it over and back. Then The Frog said that poison was in the hand and the wounds should be opened. Taking his flint knife, he tested its edge, then with his antler chisel and a stone from the fireplace, he chipped a very small sharp place near the tip, which he pierced into the toothmarks. Father watched this without flinching. Some blood came. Then The Frog heated a stone in the fire and told Father to hold it, to let the heat drive out the pain. Father did. During the night I saw him sitting by the fire heating the stone again.

The next afternoon when Father came home, he had trouble taking off his parka. When he tugged the sleeve over his hand, we saw that his hand was swollen hugely, with a wrinkle in his wrist as in the wrist of a baby. Even his arm looked fat. Father sat up again that night, and in the morning he was sweating with fever. He was quiet, but we knew he was angry and kept out of his way.

"The wolverine's spirit is making you sick," Cousin The Frog told Father in the morning, and taking the wolverine's carcass from the coldtrap where it lay frozen, he wrapped it in its skin again. Then he cut a bit of fat from behind the reindeer's eyeball—one of the few bits of fat to be found on the reindeer after a winter of hunger and much traveling—which he forced between the wolverine's broken teeth. Carrying the wolverine outside, he lifted it into the branches of a tree, saying, "This is how we mourn for you. Forgive us."

Also to help Father he made many small cuts on Father's swollen arm and packed them with snow to cool the heat inside. But this made Father both hot and cold—he was both sweating and shaking.

Our fire was gone. Meri and I were sent to get more firewood. Father seemed so angry that we hated to stay in the lodge with him, so we came home slowly. At the door we heard him talking, and thinking that The Frog was inside with him, we went in. But we found him alone, sitting at the back of the lodge, his legs straight out in front of him, his back against the wall. But for the deerskin wrapped around him, he was naked.

Not an ember remained of the fire, and in the cold lodge Father's breath made a great cloud. "I'm glad you've come," he was saying. "I greet you all. Sit here by the fire and take food." He didn't seem to see me in the doorway but kept his eyes fixed on the air in the middle of the lodge. I stared at him a moment, then suddenly the skin at the back of my neck and shoulders prickled so sharply it hurt me. Quickly I backed out.

"What's he doing?" asked Meri, looking at me. But I couldn't answer. I didn't know.

Meri sat on her heels to suck her thumb. I sat beside her and took her other hand as we tried to catch what Father was saying. His voice grew warm, then friendly; then he laughed at something. Hearing his laugh, Meri glanced at me and smiled. But I clutched her hand so tightly she withdrew it, and we sat without touching, our teeth chattering with cold.

The sun was near the horizon, but the dome of the sky was bright; with the return of the long, cold days of early spring, the light would last a long time, and we knew that Yoi and Father's nephews might still be far away. A thin stream of snow blew off the top of the glacier, showing the wind from the north. It blew in the trees, waving the branches, and made our faces numb. I saw that poor Meri was crying, her tears freezing on her cheeks and under her nose, and after putting my arms around her and telling her to wait for me, I crawled very quietly inside to the crack in the wall behind my bed where my firesticks stayed. It was so dark in the lodge that I couldn't see Father, but I felt his eyes on me. I crept out quietly and rolled a fire, feeding it with the firewood we had brought, and soon we were warm.

When the last rays of the sun shone on top of the glacier, turning the bright ice pink over the darkening trees, Yoi and Father's nephews came home with a ptarmigan. They were astonished to find no smoke in the smokehole and us by a fire outside. "You left your father alone without a fire?" asked Yoi angrily. "Is this why we sent you for wood?" Meri hung her head miserably, as if she had done something wrong, but my face didn't change. The Stick, often more thoughtful than Yoi, looked around carefully, then asked me why we were sitting outside. I glanced at the doorway but still didn't speak. I didn't know how to answer, and I thought that if we waited, Father would talk again. Soon he did. The Stick and The Frog looked surprised, then leaned their spears against a tree, as if they thought strangers were inside.

"Why didn't you tell us that people came?" asked The Frog.

I still didn't know how to answer, but when The Frog

started to crawl down the passageway I said, "We couldn't see the people." Quickly, The Frog backed out.

He and The Stick exchanged a worried look, then went bravely inside. Yoi sat on her heels beside our fire, her hood thrown back, her eyes wide. She hadn't brushed her snow-blown parka and didn't notice that the front of it was slowly getting wet.

After dark The Stick and The Frog came out. They showed Yoi by their faces that they didn't know what was happening, but they got firewood and soon sparks were rising from the smokehole. Inside the lodge Father stopped talking and we heard the snap of the fire. When The Stick and The Frog came quietly out for the meat but not their spears, we all went in.

Father was lying in his deerskin, asleep. The fire burned fresh and bright—his nephews had made a large one—and over it strips of the reindeer meat were roasting. The lodge looked warm and welcoming; my heart lifted. But after turning the roasting meat, The Stick and The Frog excused themselves rather stiffly and went outside. We heard them talking together in very soft voices. Yoi, Meri, and I sat quietly waiting for the food, and when it was ready Yoi began to eat. When Father sat up and asked for some, she brought him a portion. He ate a little, thanked her, and lay down again. Once he said, "The lodge is hot." Then he asked, "Did my nephews kill anything?"

"A ptarmigan, Ahi. We haven't cooked it yet," said Yoi.

"No, you gave me reindeer meat," said Father, dozing again.

When his nephews returned to sit on their heels at the fire, we tried to see from their faces what they might have talked about, but their faces wore no expressions. They were hiding their thoughts. Yoi whispered to ask who was talking to Father, and Cousin The Frog seemed to want to tell, but suddenly he stopped himself and glanced around the lodge. We waited. Finally The Frog leaned forward to whisper, "I don't see the people. But I think they are many. Ahi was planning with someone to hunt a bear. He calls someone else 'Uncle.' Maybe the Pine River people are here."

"Now?" whispered Yoi.

"Maybe. Whoever they are, I don't know them," whispered The Frog uneasily. "Uncle Ahi and Mother knew them, since they grew up here. My brother and I never came to this lodge." Then he added, speaking louder, making his voice congenial, "Move nearer to Yanan there. We must leave room for our hosts at this fire. And cut more meat." He bowed his head politely to the empty space beside the fire, a gesture that made Meri shrink closer to me. "We are your guests," he said to the empty space. "We were brought here by Ahi. We are **his** sister's sons. We thank you for giving us shelter. We are here in friendship, in peace. The spear there belongs to Ahi. Our spears are outside, in a tree." He smiled as if expecting an answer, his broad face wrinkling pleasantly, but no answer came. The fire crumbled, making a little sound, the smoke rose coiling to the smokehole, and the bleached antlers that arched under the roof showed dimly in the firelight. I wondered whether the people were still here.

"You are tired from a long trail," said Cousin The Stick. "This good meat, we cooked for you. Now eat your fill to please us. Hona." The cousins began to eat, while the many strips of meat that they left on the fire slowly grew small, turned black, and flamed. The adults seemed not to notice.

Later, Cousin The Frog spoke to the spirits again with carefully chosen words. "Hosts of the lodge, we are grateful that you have come to welcome us here. Hona."

"Hona," added The Stick respectfully.

That night all of us except Father spread our deerskins near the door, leaving the back of the lodge, the best and warmest part, for the use of those who owned it. When Meri asked why, I reminded her of the lodge at the Char River and how Graylag and his family slept in the back because they were the owners.

Meri looked hopeful. "Is Graylag coming?" she asked.

"Not Graylag. The owners of this lodge. Father is talking to them now, so be quiet."

I lay awake, listening to the whispering voices of The Stick, The Frog, and Yoi, so soft that I couldn't overhear them, and also to Father, who began to talk again. The hosts must have asked him about Mother, because he lied about her, saying she was with her relatives on the Fire River. They must also have reminded him of the past, because he began to speak of the past in a hearty voice, as if he were speaking to men of his own age with whom he must have hunted. They seemed to be reminding him of the plain that lay beyond the Marten River, sheltered from the wind by the glacier, where many animals came in early spring. Father seemed to remember this place well—he showed his agreement by repeating some of their words. "Yes, sheltered from the north, very good, I remember," he said seriously. "Yes, many animals, many. Wolfskins, we got them. Speared them. Even red deer. Yes, I remember now. We did that. Yes, bison. Yes, you and I."

In the morning Father got dressed to go hunting. When The Stick and The Frog asked him what the hosts had told him, he looked puzzled. "People talked to me?" he asked, frowning. "I was asleep." Then he added, "I'm going to hunt on the riverbank. Did you kill yesterday?"

"I told you last night," said Yoi. "The Stick killed a ptarmigan."

Father looked unhappy and confused. "I'll eat now," he said at last. Going to the coldtrap to cut some meat, he put a large strip on the fire. "I'll go far today," he said. "Yanan, get plenty of firewood."

"Yes, Father," I answered.

"If you go out through the woods," said Father to The Stick and The Frog, "visit the snares. Take Yoi as far as the last snare. Then she can get firewood and come back." But The Stick and The Frog were in the back of the lodge rolling up their packs. Then, with serious faces, they came to sit on their heels beside Father, who was eating.

"We're going to find Graylag," The Stick said at last. "This lodge belongs to your people. We must not stay."

Father stopped chewing. "Graylag?" he asked. "My people? What people do you mean?"

"The people you spoke with yesterday, Ahi," said Yoi. "They were here, many of them."

Father swallowed, looking troubled. "My people died or left here long ago," he said at last. "The lodge was my father's, and is nobody's now if not mine."

"You talked with them all last night," said Yoi. "How is it you don't remember?"

Father thought for a long time. "Their spirits came?" he asked softly. "So they're all spirits." He looked very sad.

"You hear us, hosts of the lodge," said Cousin The Frog. "The meat is your meat, the lodge is your lodge. We thank you for your hospitality and we're sorry we must go."

"Where will you go?" asked Father at last.

"To Graylag's lodge," said The Frog.

"No one is there," said Father.

"They may be there by now," said The Frog reasonably. "Or they may be on the Black River, or going to the Grass River, as they used to."

"You must come with us," said Yoi to Father. "I'll carry some of your pack for you."

"What?" asked Father angrily. "Are you leaving, Wife?"

Yoi looked fierce. "We can't stay here," she whispered. "I must leave. You must too."

Father sat as if thinking. Absently, he ate a bite of meat, but most of his cooked meat lay cooling by the fire. At last he said, "I feel weak for traveling today. Any pack would hurt me, and my legs still shake when I stand. I'll go hunting by the river now, and eat and grow stronger, and later I'll follow you. If you go down the Black River, leave me a sign. What about the snares?"

"We'll get ours on the way," said The Frog.

"Then Yanan can visit mine this morning," said Father, "because I'm not going that way." He turned to me. "If you find something large, carry home what you can and call for me."

"We must give something to the hosts of the lodge," said The Frog seriously, and he cut more meat to lay on the fire. "Accept this meat," he said. I watched it burn, noticing that today he gave less than the night before. When it was crisp The Stick said "Hona," lifted his pack and started for the door. The Frog followed. Yoi quickly tied her pack. As The Stick and The Frog ducked out the coldtrap, she dropped to her hands and knees, and without looking back, showing us the seat of her trousers and the soles of her moccasins, she followed them and was gone.

We sat by the fire until a patch of spring sunlight through the smokehole made a circle around it, showing us that it was almost in ashes with only a few sticks left to burn. I heaped the ashes over the coals to save a few embers. Father sat on his heels, not speaking. His breath was fast and shallow; his eyes were on the smokehole, where a tiny icicle dripped. The lodge was cold again, although outside the air was soft and the sun warm.

I thought to look at the meat in the coldtrap to see what Yoi and Father's nephews had taken and what they had left behind. Father's snare had killed the reindeer, so some of the meat was his; a hindquarter and a forequarter belonged to Yoi and the other hindquarter to The Stick and The Frog. These were gone, as was the ptarmigan. One forequarter should belong to Father, and sure enough, although a lot of it had been eaten, it was still there, and so was a piece of the belly, usually the spirits' portion, which Father's nephews had left for the hosts. The head and feet had been left behind too, and even the skin, with meat still on it. We had enough for a while.

Just outside the door I saw where The Stick and The Frog had stripped the meat off the bones to make small pieces, easily packed and carried. They must have done this when they had gone out to talk privately the night before. I picked up the scattered bones and brought them in for the marrow. I showed them to Father, but he took no notice.

I wanted to ask what we would do now. Would we wait until later in the spring before traveling? Would we go back to the Char River? The Black River? What sign would Father's nephews leave us? People sometimes tied a bundle of grass in a tree, pointing to where they had gone. Sometimes people broke a sapling, or left a small, a middlesized, and a large pile of stones in a row. Where might they leave their sign? But I saw that Father was sad. He was lonely already, with his old home empty except for the people of long ago, who by now perhaps had also gone. I couldn't find a way to mention traveling.

When I got up to get firewood, Meri came right behind me. She made no fuss about the way I helped her into her trousers and parka, but followed me obediently into the woods. When we were far from the lodge she whispered, "Where is Aunt Yoi?"

"Visiting the snares," I said. "She'll be home later."

"Why did they take their packs?"

"The snares are far."

She followed in my footsteps as we went, snapping dry branches as we found them. I thought to visit Father's snares and led us to the nearest, which was large enough for reindeer and was empty. Farther on we came to the second, also empty. But in the third, set on a tiny path that led to a juniper, hung a small grouse. I took its body and reset the snare, carefully spreading the noose over its pegs, hiding the string with snow, and placing three dry berries in the center. Then we crossed the river on the ice to look for wood in the trees on the far side, and found a line of tracks in the snow. They were the tracks left by Yoi and Father's nephews, going west in single file on their way to the Marten River. Each footprint was filled partly by a shadow and partly by a little drifted snow. The sight of them made me want to cry.

When our bundles of sticks were big enough to bring home, we came out of the forest by the river and turned north toward the lodge across the plain. In the middle of the plain we saw a small figure sitting on the snow: a man wearing a hooded parka, with his back to the wind. Surprised, we stopped. Then, thinking that he might be The Stick or The Frog come back for some reason, we hurried to him and found that it was Father.

When we came up behind him, he turned his head and nodded to us. I thought to sit beside him, but leaning heavily on the shaft of his spear, he got to his feet and led us off toward the lodge. I followed in his footsteps, noticing that the steps he took were even shorter than mine, when always before I had to stretch hard to put my feet where his had been. But I didn't want to pass him—I followed him as Meri followed me, and the walk home took a long time. I didn't ask if he had killed anything to eat.

When we reached the lodge, he went in first, going straight to his deerskin to lie down, without even taking off his outer clothes. I took mine off, then helped Meri and hung our clothes from the roof to dry. When I sat beside Father and took his hand, I found it very warm and very dry. Gently, it clasped mine. "The fire," said Father, and I got up to build it. When it was burning well, I sat beside him again.

"Let me help you take off your parka, Father," I said.

"I'm cold," he said. "I'll take it off later. Now let me rest a while."

"Please, Father."

"I'm all right. Just let me rest," he said. "Go and cook something. Cook the ptarmigan." But Yoi and Father's nephews had taken the ptarmigan. So I plucked the grouse and placed it over the fire. When it was ready I brought him a piece but he was asleep. We tried not to eat too much but we were very hungry, so when Father didn't wake up we ate his share. Soon we heard him ask for food. I cut some of the reindeer meat and was putting it on the fire when he called me angrily. "Why do you make me wait?" he asked.

"I'm sorry, Father. It's cooking," I told him.

"Bring it," he said. So I did. I gave it to him although it was barely warm. "This is raw!" he called angrily. "Must I do everything? Can't you help at all?" He struggled to stand in his heavy, wet clothes and came to the fire, where he threw the meat back on the flames. Then he tried to take off his outer moccasins but the laces were wet and the knots were hard and by now he could only use one hand. When I tried to help him, he struck me in the face so hard he knocked me over backwards. He had never struck me before, and it shocked me so much that I lost my breath. Meri started to cry. Father took out his knife and cut the laces. Then I almost cried, as I knew of no other laces he could use except the strings of his pack. What was he doing? He was sick, and didn't seem to know it.

When Father tried to take off his parka but couldn't get it over his swollen hand, he called me to pull the sleeve for him. I did, then hung up the parka while he lay down again. By the time the meat was cooked he was asleep. Then I put Father's piece of meat beside his head and lay down with Meri in our deerskins.

In the middle of the night Father woke and asked for water. We had no water—the waterbags belonged to The Stick, who had taken them. But Father begged. "Please get some water," he said. "I'm burning." So I went outside.

Under the trees lay shadows where an animal might be hiding. I made a snowball quickly. Father took a few bites, then put it down and fell asleep again. I sat by him while the snowball grew small and vanished in a puddle, and then I went back to bed.

When I woke, morning was near. Hoarfrost from our breath covered the walls. While Father and Meri slept, I built up the fire and made plans for the day. I hated remembering that Father had cut his laces; I could have used them for snares. I wanted to cut strips from one of our deerskins, but I was afraid to cut a skin without asking. I knew I should set snares, many snares, but I was afraid that if I left Father alone he would go out again, perhaps to wander away, perhaps taking Meri with him. I was afraid that I would come back to the lodge to find myself alone.

But I was also afraid that our food would run out and we would starve here, as the hosts of the lodge had starved before I was born. So I decided to visit the snares and gather wood and come back quickly. I woke Meri, who looked at me with an anxious frown. "Don't worry," I told her. "I'll be back soon. If Father wakes up, get him an icicle or a snowball. His meat is by his head. Tell him I'm right outside." I wondered if I should tell her not to follow him anywhere, but decided not to. After all, if they left, I could follow their tracks. She saw that I wanted to say more and waited, but I just smiled at her. "Comb your hair," I said. "I'll braid it when I get back."

The first snare, at a hare's run, was empty. When I got near the second, I prayed that The Bear would have put an animal in it, and sure enough, I heard something flapping, then saw that the snare held a grouse. I broke its neck, reset the snare very carefully, and went on to the third, which was also empty. Then I wondered if I should move the empty snares, but decided to wait for Father's advice. Maybe he would soon be well enough to help me find new places.

The fourth snare was for a reindeer and was empty, but had been sprung, so that the noose dangled uselessly from the branch of the now straight tree. I didn't know how to reset it, and when I climbed out on a branch to try to get the leather thong, the branch bent, dropping me to the ground. I thought for a while, wondering if I should go back to the lodge for Father's ax and try to cut the tree, but the cutting would take a very long time and Father kept his ax beside his bed—he might not let me use it, or be angry if I tried to take it secretly. Then I noticed wood that I could gather and went to break it, then saw more wood, and was soon quite far away. I decided to wait and ask Father, knowing that he would be angry if a marten took the thong in the meantime.

When the sun was high, I had a large bundle of wood, and I started back toward the lodge, looking at the snares again on the way. But there is almost no hope of filling a snare in broad daylight—the animals move at dusk and dawn—and as I feared, the snares were still empty. I decided to visit them in the late afternoon and went home through the empty, quiet woods.

The lodge was very dark after the bright day. When my eyes got used to it, I saw Father now undressed completely, still lying on his deerskin, and Meri crouched on the opposite side of the lodge, far away from the fire, with her hair all loose and tear stains on her face.

Father's eyes were partly open, but he didn't seem to see me. Suddenly terrified, I thought he was dead, but he was breathing softly, and when he turned on his side I showed him the grouse. "Look," I said. "From the second snare." But he didn't look. Quietly, I got the comb and braided Meri's hair; then I plucked the grouse, forgetting to take it outside, so the lodge filled with feathers; then I combed and braided my own hair and suddenly felt so tired that I thought I would fall asleep before this was done. I lay down between our deerskins and dreamed for the first time of Mother, who stood on the far side of a bearberry bush and talked to me while we picked.

Meri woke me later by crawling under the deerskins with me. Father was standing up, trying to get dressed. But he couldn't put his shirt on over his arm, which was black and terrible, and finally he stopped trying and crawled out the door. Soon he came back and lay down again, having gone out only to urinate or eat snow. I saw from the light in the smokehole that the daylight was almost gone, so I hurried to visit the snares. The first three were still empty. Deciding to forget the fourth, to lose the leather thong if need be, I went home. Meri and I cooked the grouse and divided it, bringing a share to Father. He wouldn't wake up, so I left his portion beside the uneaten strip of meat. Then I blocked the door with the fir tree and went back to bed.

In the middle of the night, I heard Father softly call my name. I got up and sat beside him, and found him awake and sensible, so I asked his advice about the snares. He had very good ideas for places to set the ones I had found empty, and he told me to forget the leather thong. An animal would have stolen it by now anyway, he said. He told me he was sorry he was so ill, but thought he was getting better slowly. I asked him to eat, and he did, a little. I got him another snowball and he ate it all. When I asked him if I might use his ax, he told me to use whatever I needed but to take good care of everything, and to cut a skin if I thought we needed more thongs. "You're almost grown now," he said gently. "You keep us warm with wood and you brought food today. That's good. Perhaps you should have gone with the others, but you're here and so am I." He paused. "I'm sick now, but when I'm well we'll have plenty. Or we'll find your father-in-law." I realized he meant Graylag. "Anyway, the ice on the rivers will soon be gone. It's rotten now, too dangerous to cross. The others shouldn't travel at this time of year. And soon there will be fawns to hunt. Winter is nearly over."

Tears came to my eyes. He was speaking as he always spoke, without anger or strangeness. I wanted to creep into his arms and cry, as if I were little. I wanted to tell him I was frightened, but of course I didn't. Instead I thanked him for his praise and asked if he needed more water. He shook his head. "I knew when I saw my moccasin laces that I wasn't thinking clearly. It's part of my fever," he said. "I thought you cut them. Now I know I cut them myself. I woke you because I wanted to talk with you while I'm thinking well. I may think strangely again before I'm better. If I do, don't pay attention. You're a good child, and so is Meri, and while I'm sick you're doing everything right. That's good. Now I'll rest again." And he lay back and pulled up his deerskin.

In the morning he was asleep. I brought Meri with me while I visited the snares, all empty, and moved two of them to the places Father wanted them to be. We gathered wood and went home, and found him still asleep, the uneaten food beside his head. "I don't think he likes it. We'll eat it," I told Meri, and we did.

That night I heard him say something but when I went to sit beside him I knew the hosts of the lodge were back. That frightened me, and I burned a piece of meat for them. Father didn't talk long—he seemed to be listening to someone. I sat alone by the fire, not daring to lie in the dark.

During the next three days the snares set where he had suggested held two hares, a grouse, and a ptarmigan. Each one I brought home hopefully, wanting to show Father, but he didn't wake. On the fourth day I cracked the reindeer bones for marrow, finding it all dark and shrunken, without fat. Everyone likes fat marrow; I had hoped to give Meri a treat. When she saw the bad marrow, she began to sob helplessly and clung to me until I cried too. Then we ate some marrow anyway and brought some to Father, who was still asleep. The marrow too we put beside him.

During the night, as I watched the firelight on the roof, I realized I had known for several days that Father was dying. Perhaps his spirit was already going, struggling free of his body, waiting for the breath to stop. Would I ever see him again? I wondered. Meri and I would go to Mother's people in the Camps of the Dead.

I lay awake a long time, listening to the sounds of the night—I heard the wind in the trees, a fox far away, Meri's childish breathing, the crumbling fire, the soft creaking of the lodge, but nothing else. I listened carefully. The space at the back of the lodge was perfectly quiet. Father was gone.

I woke Meri and we looked at him. His eyelids were open. His face was drawn. I took his hand and found it cold, his fingers tight. We couldn't bury him, I saw, or put him in a tree as people sometimes do for the dead in winter, and strangely, I felt glad about that. It seemed a terrible thing to put a person in the earth, where it was always close, always dark and cold, and more terrible still to put a person in a tree to freeze like meat, perhaps to be picked by martens or ravens.

We left him where he was. But before we tried to follow Yoi and Father's nephews, we put all our wood on the fire.

We made the lodge brighter than we had ever seen it, and very hot. While the wood burned I cut up the meat in the coldtrap and divided it into three piles ready for carrying. I gave the smallest to Meri and took the next myself for our trail, and put the large one on the fire for Father and the people with him, for their trail.

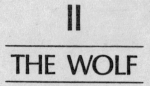

II

THE WOLF

≪ 5 ≫

THE YEAR I BECAME a spirit, I found myself thinking night and day about my father. One spring evening when I heard geese overhead, I decided to visit the lodge on the Pine River to learn whether some sign of Father, perhaps even his spirit, might still be there. The Pine River seemed so far that I wanted Marmot to come with me, and taking the form of a wolf, I frisked at the edge of the clearing to invite him. But Marmot seemed to be waiting for something. Instead of coming with me he sat on the roof watching the sky, so I gave up and went alone. Soon I forgot all about Marmot. Feeling free and hopeful in the spring twilight, I trotted beside the north bank of the Char, making for the plain beside the Antler River.

A fresh wind blew, rich with the smells of heather and hamsters. When I glimpsed a flash of white and orange by a tussock, I pounced on it and felt the tiny creature fighting hard between my teeth. But I knew I must go a great distance, so except for snatching a few voles, I didn't take time for hunting. Instead I ran until I was tired, but by then I was already in the peaks of the hills where the Marten River rises, and it was already the next morning.

On the eastern slope I stepped out of the juniper onto a rocky ledge with a smooth hollow on it, and after searching the hollow to be sure that no one else was using it, I turned and turned in the smallest possible circle until I fitted it. Then I lay down gratefully with my face but not my ears buried in my tail. I slept, ignoring the caws of ravens who flew overhead to see what I was doing, ignoring the moan of the wet south wind, which now seemed to be carrying snow.

When I was rested I stood up and stretched, first my spine and front legs and, with a yawn, my tongue and jaws, then—oh, the good feeling!—my hind legs, even clenching my hind feet so the stretch went all the way to my toes. After that I shook myself and looked around. To the east I thought I saw water flash in the sun—the Pine—and remembering a row of dry boulders in the river, I made for them, and hardly had to slow my pace to cross.

In a clear, high mood, I ran freely through the rushes on the bank of the Pine. My mind was on a reindeer I had spotted among the trees, who, with the help of a noisy jay, knew I was coming and was facing me, when suddenly I saw the lodge. Then I remembered why I was there. I noticed the wind and felt cold.

With care I nosed the opening of the coldtrap. It seemed unlikely that a wolverine or anyone else used the lodge, and less likely that someone was inside now. Even so, I tested the air carefully and listened a long time before creeping through the door.

The lodge was gloomy, even though daylight came through a break in the roof. Around the empty hearth lay dusty, broken feathers and old wolverine scats. By the wall lay a greenstone with flakes broken off it. And on the floor lay a man's bones—Father's, of course—scattered by the wolverine. I found two delicate bones from one of his fingers, then a thigh bone, then a rib. His skull lay in the corner, upside down.

As if he were in a grave with all his things, not much was left to help me remember him. His few tools that lay scattered on the floor looked like the broken, forgotten tools around a lodge that melting snow uncovers after winter. We seldom see the bones of the living, so Father's bones with their faint smell of carrion made me think of other bones, nothing more.

But suddenly the image of Father came into my mind as clearly as if he were in the lodge with me. I had caught the scent of his body. Unsure, I searched for it, then found it clinging faintly to his deerskin, among the smells of mice and wolverine and mold. On his parka, still hanging from the tine of an antler, I found his scent again. So in a way something of Father was there after all. The strange feeling this gave me lifted my hair very slightly, almost as if someone I couldn't hear or see were in the lodge.

Wanting to tell Marmot of my finding, I carefully rubbed each side of my head on Father's deerskin, then rolled on it to gather the scent into the hair of my mantle, so if Marmot met me in the form of a wolf and buried his nose there, as was his habit, he would know what I had found.

I didn't want to stay in the lodge, but I didn't want to leave it, so I lay in the doorway beside the broken tree that once was used to block the entrance. I was glad to feel the wind and see the sky. Although it seemed a time of day when spirits might be passing, no spirits were there—only the wind in the branches and a few ragged lines of geese high overhead. I slept, dreaming of running as one of a pack, and woke when the shadows in the woods were growing long and the air was turning cold. The moon rose. At last I stood up, shook, and ran back the way I had come, with the moon at first behind me, then above me, then in front of me, where it set after the dawn.

The wind blew from the west along the Char, carrying in it the smell of meat. The people must have killed something while I was gone. Sure enough, when I caught sight of the lodge, I saw strips of meat hanging from the antlers. We might get a taste of fat tonight.

I leaped onto the roof of the lodge, ready to tell Marmot what I had found and then to rest until the fat came. But to my surprise Marmot was sitting beside a strange man-spirit over Graylag's smokehole. From the fact that they sat so close together I saw they knew each other well, and from the strong, square body of the stranger, I thought he might be Marmot's kin.

Marmot pointed at me with his lips and said to the stranger, "Here comes Yanan, Lapwing's daughter."

"So!" said the stranger. I could tell I was no longer in the form of a wolf because of the way his eyes searched me. "Everyone remembers Yanan," he said, and laughed. "Does she remember me?"

He was young, but I felt he might be my senior, so I answered respectfully, "No, Uncle."

His name, I learned, was Goldeneye. He was the youngest of the four brothers who had built the lodge, and was Teal's first husband in life. She had caught his spirit when she caught Marmot's, but since then she hadn't spent much time helping the people of the lodge. Instead, I learned, he had traveled widely with a flock of geese whose summerground was our winterground. These were the geese Marmot had been watching. Soon after sunrise, as a string of geese passed high over the lodge, a gander had flown down out of the sky. The gander was none other than Marmot's younger brother, Goldeneye. Marmot seemed very glad to have him.

Goldeneye spent the day telling Marmot of his travels with his goose family. I listened too, sometimes asking questions to which Marmot already knew the answers. But since Goldeneye now seemed to belong to a flock, I couldn't help but wonder what geese were like, that they would welcome a stranger.

They hadn't welcomed a stranger, said Goldeneye. It had taken almost a year for him to join them. When he first met the geese in the marshes of the Black River, their many flocks were just leaving on their autumn journey, so in the form of a goose he followed. During winter, which they spent in sweet grass with heavy seeds on a warm, sunny shore far away, they grew more relaxed about his standing or grazing near them, and in spring one of their widows married him. After that he flew with her, followed by her grown children and their husbands and wives. That summer their big, strong flock took first choice of nesting places in the marsh.

By the end of summer the sinking water turned the marsh stagnant, and many geese got sick. The widow died of the sickness, and Goldeneye didn't have the heart to do all the flapping and shoving or even the hissing and staring he would have needed to do to try to keep his rank. He fell in importance, not as low as when he joined the flock but lower than he was with the widow. Anyway, since Goldeneye was a medium-sized man in life, he was only a medium-sized gander. Any large, important gander could get the better of him, and all the geese knew it. On the long flight south in the fall, other geese kept dropping behind him, making him do more than his share of trail-breaking. They did the same again on the long flight north. For now, Goldeneye was tired of them. Let them do their own work, he had said to himself. He was going to see his big brother.

Why had he joined the geese? I asked. Because of their strength, he answered. He made his first visit to the marsh simply to learn if geese were there, but when he saw them leaving and followed, he found himself at the southeast end of Woman Lake after just one day's flying. The speed and distance greatly pleased him. Then, since he didn't feel like going home and also was too far to go by himself, he kept following. After that, one thing led to another.

From listening to him and Marmot, I knew this wasn't his first visit since he had joined the geese. Surely Teal knew he visited, so why hadn't she made him stay to help the lodge?

"Ah, Teal!" said Goldeneye. "As soon as she caught my spirit and stopped me from finding the Camps of the Dead, she couldn't wait to marry my elder brother and have a new child with him. Elho. What could she say to me that I couldn't say to her?"

At sunset, when we noticed from the vapor in the smoke that people were cooking, we began to speak of hunger and bad winters. Marmot then remembered where I had gone that day, and asked what I had found. I told him that although years had passed, a deerskin in the old lodge still faintly held my father's smell.

Saddened by memories, the three of us sat in silence for a long time. My thoughts went back to Father, but Marmot and Goldeneye must have been thinking of the bad winter that had killed so many of our people, because in a while Goldeneye said, "Winter. Everything tries to find safety from winter. When geese fly south, they see below them long lines of animals and people also going to their winter-grounds. Animals with short legs make lodges under the snow. Red martens dig round holes among the roots of trees, and burrowing voles dig long, narrow holes underground. Even hamsters fear winter, and begin to gather food against it as soon as they can in spring. Only insects are too small to try to save their lives from winter."

Suddenly someone in the lodge below said "Hona," rather loudly. Our attention caught by the prayerful word, Goldeneye stopped talking and we waited. Sure enough, up with the smoke came a cloud of fat, which we caught on our tongues and fingers. It was reindeer fat from perhaps the last doe to leave the wintergrounds, a small doe who had found the river too full to cross.

After we licked our lips and fingers, Goldeneye told us more of his thoughts. "Now, bad winters make me unhappy," he said. "I don't like to see the sun come up only to go right down again. I don't like the frozen river or the cold woods where nothing moves but blowing snow. Trees must wait with their feet in the earth, but geese don't wait. It's spring now, but another winter is coming. I'll stay with you this summer, Brother, and next fall perhaps you'll come with me."

"Perhaps," said Marmot. "But haven't we always had winter?"

To me Goldeneye said, "Marmot won't come. He was the eldest of us. He got used to taking care of everybody. Even at the start he wouldn't leave his children. But I had no children to leave. So he stayed and I went."

Marmot might not want to travel far, but what about me? Couldn't I go, at least for the winter? "Uncle," I said to Goldeneye, "I'd like to go with you."

Marmot and Goldeneye looked at each other. "Teal wouldn't let you," said Marmot at last. "Goldeneye was her husband and her senior in the lodge. It comes hard for her to refuse him. She'd feel differently about you. I wouldn't go far or stay away long if I were you."

"What would happen?"

"The shamans own the air," said Marmot. "Who knows what would happen?"

‹ 6 ›

BEFORE MERI AND I had walked far from the lodge and the cloud of yellow smoke from the fire we burned for Father, I knew that our packs were too heavy. Mine, rolled in our deerskins, held my firesticks and most of the meat, but it also held some things that, with terrible misgivings, I had taken from Father's side—the ax from its place near his bed, his bison horn filled with tinder, and his heavy greenstone knife. Poor little Meri had rolled everything she could find into a piece of reindeer skin—some grass from her bed, her three pinecone dolls, a broken scraper that Father had once discarded but then gave her for a toy. I had made her pack her share of the meat and a second piece of reindeer hide to cut into thongs for snares.

Within sight of the lodge I made her sit down and unpack the grass, the dolls, and the scraper. She started to cry, but did as I said. Suddenly I hated to see her this way, weeping but obedient, and I let her keep one doll. But then the thought of two dolls left behind in the snow made us both so sad that we each took one, not to pack but to carry in our hands.

Numbly we trudged off to visit the snares. Two were empty—we took them with us—but the third held the frozen forepart of a rabbit. Around it were the tracks of a fox and blood was on the snow where the hindquarters had been. We took the snare and the piece of the rabbit and looked for the trail left by Father's nephews and Aunt Yoi. At first I couldn't find it, although I had seen it soon after they left. Then we walked in a circle, hoping to cross it.

Meanwhile, the sun climbed to the top of the sky, but we were almost no distance on our way. No smoke was rising from the lodge, I noticed. The fire we had made for Father had burned out.

Poor Meri was already tired and hungry. I saw, too late, that I should have cooked our meat before packing it, to make it lighter to carry and ready to eat at any time. "Eat some snow," I said, and Meri scooped up a handful. We circled twice near where I thought the tracks might be before we found them, just dents drifted over with snow. We followed them.

After a while Meri fell far behind me. I rested while she caught up. Twice this happened. Then I saw that she wasn't getting a chance to rest at all, so at the edge of the wood, just where the tracks led onto the plain, we sat down in a birch grove and ate twigs. These take away hunger, people say. Meri looked miserable, but she didn't complain. "You're being very good," I told her.

"Where are we going?" she asked.

"After Yoi and our cousins," I said.

"Where is that?"

I wasn't sure, of course, but didn't want to tell her, so I said, "Graylag's lodge."

"It's so far," said Meri. Then she asked, "Are you sure Father is dead?"

"Yes, I'm sure," I said.

"But what if he isn't? He might wake up and no one would be there. Let's go back."

"We can't go back," I said. "Father is dead there. I'm sure. And spirits are there too. They won't help us. How can we get food? Do you remember the lodge on the Marten River where we stopped on the way last fall?" Meri didn't seem to remember. "We went in. Father said he was born there."

"Does Junco live there?"

"No. Junco lives with her parents, with Graylag."

Meri said, "Oh."

"Today we're going to the lodge on the Marten. Yoi and our cousins went that way. Maybe they're still there. But we must get up now. It's far."

"Must I still carry this?" asked Meri.

"Your pack? Yes, of course."

"I don't want to."

"Well, you must, and all the way. We'll go now." I stood up.

"I can't," said Meri.

"I'll leave you behind. Good-by," I said. She came, of course, sulkily at first to show me that she was unwilling; but out on the vast, snowy plain, where the trail left by Yoi and our cousins lay straight as the track of a fox as far as the eye could see—though drifted over in places and crossed many times by animal tracks—she tried hard to keep up. The loneliness of the plain, the wind, and the many distant herds of animals must have frightened her. Walking where the snow had drifted was especially hard for her, as she sank in almost to her knees with every step. Every few steps she would ask me to wait for her, but I could only tell her to hurry because it was so late.

Small groups of horses, saiga, and bison, their rumps to the north wind, stood with their heads down, pawing through the snow. In the distance a herd of mammoths drifted, slowly moving in the direction we were moving. They stood close together, touching each other with their trunks from time to time, leaning on each other, gently shouldering each other, like people who know each other well trying to talk as they travel. There were ten of them, one for each of my fingers, and then several more. All were females, I saw from the breasts between their front legs, and some had calves. The biggest of them looked in our direction, then suddenly pointed at us with her ears and trunk and gave a little scream. She scared me—I didn't like being noticed. We looked at our feet and kept walking.

Later we came near a herd of five horses grazing: a stallion, a yearling, and three mares whose sides bulged with foals. I expected them to move away from us, but instead they raised their heads and watched us curiously. Then, necks stretched and ears forward, they ambled toward us as if they wondered what we were and meant to find out.

They made us quite uneasy. Meri stood close behind me and I stood as tall as I could. "Stop! We're people, Old Ones," I said respectfully. "Go away." I didn't add the words "we will hurt you," as adults usually do when speaking to animals, because the stallion, with his ears pricked and his neck long, was nosing my parka. One of the mares stretched her neck to nose Meri, who ducked behind me and clutched my hand. "Keep still," I whispered, and she did. The mare snorted, and the stallion fixed his bland eyes on something over my head. Right beside us, they weren't nervous! Was this how dangerous we seemed? Soon the other mares and even the yearling sniffed us, then some began to paw snow for grazing while others ambled on, and as carelessly as they had come, they drifted away. Suddenly the yearling frisked near Meri. Clearly the horses saw that we were harmless, but did they also see that we were young? Did the yearling want to play?

The sinking sun was turning the snow blue when we reached the edge of the plain, and long rays shone on the undersides of the clouds. I was frightened of the woods but didn't dare think about them—I was also afraid of the size of my own fear. The tracks of Aunt Yoi and our cousins were now hard to find, which made us go slowly. Meri's face was drawn and her lips were blue with cold, although long ago she had stopped complaining. Once she said that pine needles were in her moccasins, so I knew her feet were numb. I was cold too, and very hungry, and kept remembering the meat we had given to Father and the spirits of the lodge. I could still smell it and still hear it crackle as it burned. I wondered if we should stop, make a fire, and eat, but fear of the woods kept me walking. I didn't think we would live one night in the woods without adults.

Then, among some little trees ahead, I saw the hump and shoulders of a bear. Seizing Meri's arm, I forced her to crouch, shutting my eyes and putting my hand over her mouth so she wouldn't speak. The bear, his hairy shoulders high above the bushes, seemed to be snuffling for something. Large male bears, we were often told by our parents, leave their dens early because of hunger and are very dangerous to meet. Remembering how often we had been told that running from a dangerous animal can make it chase you, I knew that we must stay still. "Don't move, don't speak," I whispered. The bear came so near that we could smell the stench of his fur and hear his tongue clapping against his teeth as if he were cleaning them. His shoulders stood higher than my head, and when he moved between us and the lowering sun, he cast us in shadow. Now and then he muttered something, as a person will who thinks of something bothersome while he works. We stayed still for a very long time after the bear passed us, then hurried on.

As we reached the middle of the woods in the early evening, tiny, grainy snowflakes began to fall. Making Meri hurry again while the tracks lasted, I looked for landmarks and at the place of the sun, wondering how I had ever thought we might follow these footprints to somewhere far. Perhaps I had forgotten about falling snow. But the footprints gave me the direction—when the snow covered them, I kept going the same way, keeping over my left shoulder a distant range of hills and over my right the yellow glow made by the setting sun behind the clouds. We went slowly, though, because the sun and the range of hills weren't always in sight when we were among trees.

At the top of a rise, the country opened out before us into a wide valley where an icebound river ran. I was sure this could be no river but the Marten, and sure that by following its near bank, no matter how dark the night or how heavy the snow, and by feeling the slope of the valley as it fell to the river, I would find the lodge, unless of course I walked past it. I said to Meri, "Not far now."

But poor Meri didn't answer. I looked back and saw her dark figure stumbling behind me: she was too tired to lift her feet. When she caught up, I saw that her nose was running and her face was dusted with snow. I knelt and tied my pack around my hips. "Get on my back," I told her, and she climbed on slowly. I saw that she had lost her pine-cone doll. She seemed surprisingly heavy, but then, I was tired too.

At last I saw the snow-covered mound of the roof of the lodge, with a black hole below it which was the door, and I knew from the darkness and silence that Yoi and our cousins were not inside. Then I saw how our lives had been saved by the snow—if snow hadn't hidden the tracks, we would have followed them far from the lodge, where night would have found us. Of course Yoi and our cousins weren't camped here. If Meri and I had made the trip in less than half a day, the three adults, hurrying, would have reached this lodge in a morning and made their first camp far beyond. Probably they didn't even come into this valley. Their trail would have badly misled me.

I crawled into the entrance carefully, sniffing and listening for an animal inside—a wolverine, perhaps. When I heard nothing and smelled only the stale dampness of an empty lodge, I dragged my pack after me and called to Meri. She followed into that cold, hollow place, and didn't complain when I left her alone for a moment while I went out again to get kindling. Then I groped in the dark to open the knots on my pack and find my firesticks to roll a fire, which came hard because my hands were stiff with cold. By the light of the first flames I saw the lodge dimly. It too had mammoth legbones in the walls, which were braced with many large boulders and a mammoth skull. In the arch of the ceiling were interlocking antlers just like in Graylag's lodge. Little Meri stretched her hands to the fire. Tears were frozen on her cheeks, snow was frozen in her braid, and her teeth were chattering. I hated to leave her to gather firewood.

When I was far from the lodge, I heard her calling. Thinking she was frightened at being left alone, and feeling nearly exhausted, having to force myself on to tree after tree, I ignored her. At last I found two rather small trees blown down together, which would give us fuel for days to come if need be, even for longer than the meat we carried could last. Since there now seemed no way to catch up with Yoi and our cousins, no choice except to stay where we were, the fallen trees seemed a sign that all could be well. With a sense of relief and thankfulness, I broke their branches.

Again I heard Meri calling urgently, her voice so clear that I knew she was outside the lodge. Wrapping a thong around the broken branches, I went back to find her standing in the snow. "What now?" I asked. "Did you think I wasn't coming?"

"There's something inside! I'm afraid of it. Don't go away anymore."

My pack and firesticks were inside too, I remembered with alarm. "What's in there?" I asked angrily.

"I don't know," she said, "but it's moving."

"Is it big? Is it small? Is it a spirit?" I asked, but Meri just clung to my hand and looked unhappily at the doorway. She shook her head. She didn't know. Well, I had to go inside. I knew it, so I did, crawling very cautiously. With some relief I heard Meri following right behind me, so I thought that whatever it was couldn't be so bad that she would rather be outside alone.

At first I saw nothing. Then I threw wood on the fire, and in the blaze I saw something small move in the corner where the floor met the wall. A weasel! Very relieved, I was about to scold Meri for frightening me when the eyes gleamed pale green in the firelight. I knew that a weasel's eyes gleam almost yellow. Looking closely, I saw that the animal was brown with partly lopped ears—not a weasel but a cub.

A fox? I went to look carefully, and in a gap between a stone and the mammoth skull that braced the wall I found four cubs. Three were dead and frozen, their lips drawn back and their pale tongues showing, but the fourth cringed away from me. Although its short, thick fur was dirt-colored like the fur of a fox cub, its body was too large to be a fox. It was a wolf.

I felt a twinge of pity for the hopeless little creature and the three others who lay dead. Perhaps their parents, like ours, were dead. Perhaps their group, like ours, had gone away. Then I thought, *We can eat them.* But where to put them? As the meat of young animals spoils faster than the meat of old animals, I knew they shouldn't thaw while we still had part of the snared rabbit and part of the reindeer to eat. I wedged the dead pups in the thick frost behind the mammoth skull, where the heat from the fire wouldn't touch them and where I could keep watch for thieving mice or weasels. Again I felt hopeful. Now I had time to find a good place for our snares.

"Will you kill it?" asked Meri about the living pup.

"Don't be afraid," I said. "It's too small to hurt you. We'll eat it after we finish the rest of our food." I didn't want to talk about the death and rotting of young animals, because Meri was so young.

When the fire made coals I put strips of our meat to cook, and soon we were eating. I felt much better, warm and fed. Meri too was looking better with the blue gone from her skin. I blocked the door with my pile of firewood, hung our outer clothes from the prongs of the antlers in the roof, put the meat from my pack on the mammoth skull where the pup couldn't reach it—not that it seemed able to chew—and unrolled our deerskins, making our bed. In no time at all we slept.

When I woke in the middle of the night to feed the fire, I felt sick with loneliness to find no one at all, not even Aunt Yoi or Cousin The Stick or The Frog, sitting by the fire. Then I looked around for the cub. Even he seemed to be missing. Perhaps he had gone outside to escape us. Not wanting to look for him, I went back to the deerskins. There he lay asleep, pressed close against Meri. The sight made me so sad that I almost wept—two young, sleeping creatures without parents to care for them, perhaps both without long to live. I lay down, and putting my arms around Meri, I fell asleep again.

I dreamed that someone found us. The dream woke me. Then I thought I wasn't dreaming—I smelled a wet parka. I sat up, pulling the deerskin off Meri. The pup was gone, I saw, but nobody was sitting by the embers. A dream after all, I decided, and lay down, but the smell was so real, almost overpowering, that I sat up again. This time I saw what looked like a bundle of fur blocking the entrance to the coldtrap. A wolf was lying with its rear toward us and its head in the door.

The wolf was enormous. Although I was frightened, I groped in the dark for the ax in case the wolf got up. Then I thought, *If I hit it, I may only hurt it and then it will kill me.* Even so, holding the ax made me feel better while I did the best I knew to do: I lay still and tried to look around without waking Meri.

Light was growing in the smokehole, showing a snowy dawn. The wolf knew about us, I saw, when I noticed large, ashy footprints right beside our heads. I looked for our clothes. Mine were still hanging from the antlers, but Meri's parka was gone. With growing panic, I saw shreds of it by the wall! I looked for our meat. The top of the mammoth skull was bare! Then I saw that the frozen pups had been moved to the middle of the lodge, where they lay in a row, very still.

I remembered the meat in Meri's pack, rolled in the

reindeer hide with the snares. Wonderful to see, Meri's pack was untouched. I tried quietly to reach it, using the ax to drag it toward me. The wolf moved its ears at the scraping sound, but seemed to pay no more attention. I held the pack against my side, wondering whether to fight for it or to give it up if the wolf wanted it.

Seeing Meri's eyelids stir as if she might wake, I put my hand over her mouth. Her eyes flew open. I whispered in her ear, "A wolf is lying in the door. It knows we're here; stay still. I have the ax." She stared at me. I lifted my hand.

"A wolf!" she whispered.

I nodded. "It may go. Keep still."

"I have to go outside," she whispered urgently.

"You can't."

"I must!"

"Then go on the floor. We'll clean up later," I whispered, trying to help her with her clothes in a struggle that made the wolf lift its head. We froze. But the wolf merely looked at us, then raised its thigh to nose or lick something by its belly, something that then made a sucking sound. So I understood where the pup was, and that it wasn't abandoned after all. The large wolf was its mother, who had just been away for a while.

I gripped the ax as Meri crawled slowly away from the bed and relieved herself noisily, then hurried back and crept under the deerskin. At these sounds the wolf looked at us again. Then she sighed and slowly laid down her head while we waited nervously for something else to happen. But nothing did.

During the day the snow turned to sleet, then to rain, then to sleet again in the afternoon. Once the wolf rolled over, making the pup climb across her to find its place under her thigh. Otherwise she did nothing. Her side gently moved with her breath.

Neither was there anything for us to do. Not daring to move around, we didn't feed the fire but stayed in bed watching the rain fall through the smokehole and make the ashes wet. Once I crept near the wolf to see whether she might get up and go out, but she raised her head and with a forceful growl showed me her teeth, so I hurried back to bed. As the day dragged on, it became clear that the wolf had no plans to leave, but also might spare our lives if we didn't anger her. Slowly boredom took the place of fear. By late afternoon we were so bored we slept.

We were asleep when night came. I woke up in the dark when the wolf sighed and rolled over for a second time, making a noise with her mouth while she settled her tongue. Having slept so much, I couldn't sleep more, so I listened to sleet on the roof. Once I heard snuffling, and the footsteps of a large animal passing the lodge. A bear? The wolf stood up. When the footsteps and snuffling faded, she lay down again.

Toward morning the sleet stopped. The wolf got up, had a good shake, and started through the coldtrap. Her pup followed. She led it back, but it followed her again. She picked it up by the head, carried it to the middle of the lodge, and dropped it on the floor. When it still tried to follow, she showed her teeth and growled. But the pup crept toward her anyway, whining and almost crawling, its tail down, its ears folded, and its nose held up to hers. Suddenly she hit its head with the side of her bared eyetooth, making it cry terribly, but even as it cried, it tottered behind her when she started for the door. Finally, to my surprise, she slowly led the pup toward us, then dashed around behind us and out the door before we understood what she was doing. The pup was also puzzled—by the time it stumbled all the way around us, its mother was gone.

By now it seemed quite clear whose lodge this was. The wolf might be out for a while, but at any moment, I was sure, she could come back. I knew there must be something I should do while she was out, but I couldn't think what. I wanted to leave, but knew that we couldn't until the weather cleared, because without a parka Meri couldn't travel.

Since we had to stay, I wanted to keep perfectly still inside the lodge. But even this I couldn't do. If I didn't get food, we would starve. We should have stayed at the Pine lodge, I thought. Perhaps we could have put snow and stones over Father's body. Perhaps the spirits would have gone away. Perhaps people from Graylag's lodge would have come to rescue us. Or perhaps we should have tried to find the Char ourselves.

One day we would try to find the Char, I thought, but we

couldn't try now. Now, even if the weather grew warm, the ice on the rivers would be melting. We couldn't cross them. We couldn't cross the mountains in the cold and wet with nothing to eat. We couldn't camp in the open. *We may die here,* I thought. *Maybe the wolf will kill us. Maybe we'll starve. If I don't find food, we'll starve for sure.*

Suddenly I wondered if, instead of waiting for the wolf to kill us, I could use the ax to kill the wolf. I liked the idea until I tried to plan how to do it. No plan came. Several blows of the ax hadn't killed the wolverine that attacked Father; the wolf was much larger than the wolverine; unlike the wolverine, the wolf was not wounded, and unlike the wolverine, the wolf wasn't busy with her teeth. In my mind's eye, I saw myself standing by the wolf with my ax raised, and the wolf waking up and sinking her long teeth in my throat.

If I killed the pup, I wondered, would the wolf leave? She might, but she also might kill Meri so that I would feel pain as she felt pain. I dropped the idea.

Could I put the pup outside? I wondered. Could I block the door with a fallen tree or build a fire in the coldtrap? Not in the coldtrap! Flames where the ceiling was low would set fire to the lodge! If we were inside while the angry wolf was lurking outside, we would be trapped. In fact, I was afraid of angering her in any way. I didn't understand her, or know why she wanted the lodge or why she didn't live with other wolves or why she didn't kill us. Was she saving our flesh for later, as we wanted to save her pup?

Somehow I thought not. Bears kill us when we wake them; mammoths kill our hunters; lions kill people sleeping in the open, and tigers kill people who surprise them in the bushes. Hunger kills us, winter and the cold kill us, The Woman Ohun kills us, but wolves don't. Wolves steal our food and leather things, but they kill only reindeer, bison, saiga, and horses, the same as we do.

The only thing for it, I saw, was to live quietly in the back of the lodge, to put out snares for food, and to cook and eat only while the wolf was away. I would have to hang my own outer clothes and what was left of Meri's in a tree, and I would have to hide whatever I snared. With this as my only plan, I rolled a new fire. Then, leaving Meri beside it, I set out to search the wet snow for the trails and feeding places of small game. Soon I had set my snares.

When I got back, I found Meri and the pup under the deerskin together, keeping warm by the fire and with each other's heat. I cooked the reindeer meat from Meri's pack, and we ate while the pup looked on.

The next day the wolf came in for a little while, and when she left again, I visited my snares. But the weather stayed so cold and damp that most animals weren't moving. My snares stayed empty until the wind changed and cold, dry weather came from the north. Then I caught a grouse, which I plucked and carried home hidden in my parka.

Just after we ate the grouse and were burning the bones, the wolf came back. At first she seemed suspicious, then she stalked right up to sniff our mouths. With her big nose near my lips and her yellow eyes staring into mine, I sat very still, knowing how right I was not to try to block her out of the lodge or even to think very much about killing her pup. She then sniffed Meri, who also sat still, surprisingly unafraid even while the wolf tasted her mouth. Meanwhile the pup stumbled around the wolf's feet, crying. After sniffing quickly at the burning bones, the wolf lay down in the coldtrap to sleep, raising her thigh to make a place for the pup.

As the next days went by, I began to envy the pup, fed with milk, folded against its mother's warm body, because when our reindeer meat was gone, Meri and I began to starve. The few grouse in my snares were very lean, and we, lean to start with because of the hard winter and the long, tiring walk, became almost wasted. Meri grew so thin that her arms looked like two long fingers.

One day while the wolf was out we ate the dead pups. The wolf didn't seem to notice that they were gone. Later I found better places to set snares, and so, slowly, we began to eat a little more. And as long as we cooked and ate while the wolf was away, she didn't take our food from us.

Without a coat, Meri stayed in the lodge when I went out, although even if she had a coat I probably would have left her behind; she was so weak and thin that walking was hard for her. When I went out, I would tell her to play with her doll and keep warm by the fire. She did, but if the wolf was away, she and the pup would cuddle together. Presently I began to expect to find Meri and the pup cuddling. Then it came to me that the wolf also expected them to be together. Whenever she led the pup behind us before making her escape, she seemed to depend on Meri.

But the wolf paid no attention to me. When she was home, she never lay anywhere but in the doorway, and wouldn't move to let me by. If I was in when she came home, I couldn't get out. Meri and I would have to lie still or move quietly, trying not to excite her, sometimes for two days at a time. We relieved ourselves in the corner, then cleaned up when she left. Although we never had enough fuel to build a large fire and we used fuel sparingly, we sometimes ran out of it and couldn't get more. Then we had to lie in our deerskins to keep each other warm. I tried to pass time by sleeping, but I couldn't sleep forever. When I was awake, I would whisper stories to Meri of animals and people long ago, to keep my mind off two or three weasels, a marten, and two foxes who I knew were robbing my snares. We liked best the stories of how Wolverine got blinded and how Whitefish got his feet cut off, when real animals were causing us so much trouble.

Getting back inside the lodge was also hard sometimes. If the wolf was in the doorway when I came home, she wouldn't let me in but showed her teeth and growled at me. If I came too near her, she would stand up, bristle, and bark. Once I sat outside the door from noon until night, hoping the wolf would change her mind and let me in, but she was just back from a long trip and sleeping soundly. After dark I heard animals walking in the woods around me, and I got very frightened. Inside my parka I was hiding a snared ptarmigan until Meri and I could cook it, but I was so frightened of spending the night alone in the dark without a fire that I took the bird out and held it up for the wolf to see. She opened her eyes, then came out of the door as if a flame had touched her; I threw the bird at her and jumped aside just before she bit my arm. While she ate the ptarmigan, shaking her head to get rid of the feathers, I crawled inside.

Next day I made the smokehole bigger, so that even though I couldn't climb out of it, I could always climb in.

Yet after a bear scared us badly one night by snuffling again and again in the doorway, I was glad of the wolf. Each time she heard the bear she growled and barked, and each time the bear moved away. While she kept watch, I didn't need to. I found that if I could sleep, I didn't get as hungry.

Sometimes Meri seemed less hungry than I might have expected. She complained less every day, and after a while no longer cried if she heard that the snares were empty. One day when I had to tell her that I had caught nothing, she said, "Never mind. She fed me."

"Fed you?" I asked. "What do you mean? With milk?"

"No. With what the pup ate."

"What was that?"

"She vomited."

"What are you telling me?" I asked.

"She vomited, and the pup ate some, and then I ate some. I was too hungry." Meri looked sorry.

"How could you eat vomit?" I asked. "She might be sick."

"She isn't," Meri insisted. "When she comes home, the pup licks her mouth, and she looks at him, and she looks at me, and she heaves her stomach until she vomits. He asks her for it. Anyway, she isn't sick. The vomit wasn't sick vomit. It was meat."

"What have you done?" I asked. "No one can be that hungry." Meri now seemed downcast, but I couldn't bring myself to comfort her. What she had done bothered me so much that if my stomach hadn't been empty, I would have vomited myself.

Soon after that the wolf took to following my tracks through the woods and robbing my snares. She checked the snares before I could, because of course she always left the lodge first, and I would find her large tracks covering mine of the day before. I tried new places for snares, but she found them too. Finally I learned to wait until she had robbed me and gone on her hunt, then to reset the snares quickly in new places and to visit them soon. This helped, but very little. And so in time, in spite of myself, I too ate the vomit. I was surprised at how fresh it tasted, if bitter and foamy. But as Meri said, it was meat, and not just the lean meat of grouse and hare which sooner or later starves a person, and not just hairy winterkills, but sometimes the meat of newborn foals or calves, milkfed, with liver and fat.

She was a very large wolf with long thin legs, big feet, and pale yellow-gray eyes. Her gray fur was heavy and smelled when it was wet. Sometimes she seemed to love her pup as a woman loves her child. When she was home, she held the pup between her thigh and the eight pink breasts in the fur of her belly. Often she would lick her pup all over, even its urine and feces as they came out, which made me think she was too loving, but the licking kept the lodge clean.

Like a person, she relieved herself outside before going hunting. Also like a person, when she came home, she usually brought a meal. When the pup ran to greet her, she would lower her head, arch her back, and begin to heave while the pup and also Meri watched eagerly. Up would come the food as the wolf took one step back to lay out a long, shallow pile. That way three of us could eat together. She would watch for a time while we ate, almost never trying to stop Meri from sharing but sometimes staring hard at me. Still, she didn't try to stop me very often. When she did, she put her face near mine and barked sharply, with her eyes, ears, and nose all pointing at me. Then of course I'd move away. After giving up her food, she would rest in the coldtrap. And since we couldn't get out, we rested too.

When spring came finally and I found sedge root and mushrooms in the woods, I knew that we could live, if hungry, through the summer. With the spring weather, the wolf stopped holding the pup so close to herself, perhaps because the pup grew teeth and learned to bite. Then the wolf nursed it only for a short time when she came home, and kept it from sleeping with her by lying sideways to the coldtrap, so that not even the pup could get in. The pup would sleep or play with Meri, and when they played, the wolf would watch them with a mild expression.

I remembered how, the last summer I was on the plains by the Grass River, a stallion and his mares were grazing near a herd of reindeer, and when some of the colts began to

frisk and play, one of the fawns frisked with them. It made
me feel happy—if I had thought that the colts and the fawn
would wait for me, I would have tried to play too. Even so, I
never would have thought a person and a wolf could play
while almost starving, nor did I feel like playing when I
watched them. But like the wolf, I did feel mild.

◁ 7 ▷

ONE NIGHT I WOKE UP to hear geese calling, and when I went back to sleep, I dreamed of Graylag praising those strong birds for keeping their groups together. *You didn't keep your group together,* he seemed to say to me. Weeping, I tried to explain that I couldn't help what had happened, but with a clapping of wings much louder than my voice he rose into the air and vanished. I woke again and tried to look around, hardly able to remember where I was. The dark, the cold, the quiet, and the smell of stale ashes and wet fur reminded me. Then I thought of Aunt Yoi and my cousins, who by now must have returned to the Char River and told the people that Meri and I were here alone. Someone, I thought, must come for us.

But of course that couldn't be, and if I had been thinking clearly, I would have seen it. If the people thought Father was alive, they would wait for him to come to them. If they thought he was dead, they might think Meri and I were dead too, starved. Still, I wanted to believe that someone would come, because I didn't know how else we could join the other people. I didn't think I could find the way from the Marten River to the Char River without help.

Later in the night it came to me that someone wanting to look for us would look on the Pine River. Learning the truth from Father's corpse, the searchers would see that Meri and I were gone, but they wouldn't know where. Then I was very sorry that I hadn't left a twist of grass in a tree or three piles of stones pointing to the Marten River, and I made up my

117

mind that when daylight came I would go back to the Pine to leave a message.

But I didn't know what to do with Meri. Since the wolf had destroyed her outer clothes, I couldn't take her outside for long; I couldn't think of taking her on a trip when a storm might rise or the weather turn cold suddenly. And I didn't dare leave her behind. Our group was now only two, but like two geese we should keep together.

In the dark I heard a sigh of contentment—the wolf. She always seemed untroubled. Perhaps because of the cold, this was one of the few nights recently that the wolf had slept in the doorway. By now she usually slept in sunny places near the lodge or in her favorite bed on top of the lodge. From there she could see the door and the open space in front where Meri and the pup spent their days playing. If she thought the woods were safe, empty of roaming, dangerous animals, she would sleep curled, muffling her eyes, nose, and feet from mosquitoes but listening with open ears to hear what might come along. If she thought something dangerous was near, she might bark once sharply to make the pup raise his head, then jump to the ground to trot past the pup and into the lodge with the pup at her heels. Meri had learned to follow.

Then the wolf would block the door against the danger. If I was outside, I had no choice but to climb on the roof, since the wolf wouldn't let me pass her. Usually even from the height of the roof I couldn't see what had frightened the wolf, but once I saw the bear who bothered us at night come out of the woods in the daytime to snuffle at the wolf's beds, where she kept bones. When he came near the door, the wolf pushed herself half out of it, showing so much bristling hair and so many teeth that I thought she would throw herself on him. He must have thought so too, since he backed off. She rushed him, and he ran.

Then it struck me. If the wolf was using me as a helper, perhaps I could do the same with her. She couldn't help but protect Meri if Meri stayed with the pup. All Meri had to do was pay attention, and Meri paid more attention to the wolf than she did to me anyway. I went to sleep happily, planning to go to the Pine River as soon as it was light.

But when I woke again, the wolf was gone. She often did

this, going hunting at times I couldn't foretell. A person gets ready to go on a journey, taking things that show where he or she is going and for how long. A wolf just disappears. She was gone almost two days, never doubting—it seemed— that I would watch her pup for her, never thinking that I might want to take a trip too. How selfish, I thought.

How generous, I thought after she came back in the night and gave up her food to those who still ate it. For herself she kept only one squirrel, whose hind feet I saw dangling in her gape before she gulped it down. Knowing that the squirrel would keep the wolf from hunger until I got back, I told Meri I was going to the Pine. I explained that I would leave a signal for the people looking for us and would try to get home by night. The wolf, I said, still had food in her stomach and wouldn't be leaving for a while. "If she barks, go in the lodge," I told Meri. "Whatever she seems to want, do it."

"She just sleeps," said Meri.

"Well, let her sleep," I said. "But stay near the lodge and pay attention."

"She makes us stay near the lodge," said Meri.

I left, taking the ax. From her bed on top of the lodge, the wolf opened her eyes to glance at me. Perhaps she thought I was going for wood—something she knew about. Before the lodge was out of sight, I looked back. Her eyes were hidden in her tail. Only Meri and the pup were watching me.

It was early in the morning. The little pines were full of mist. Now that the long days were back, the sun moved north again. I noticed it to help me find my way.

When I reached the plain, I saw the glacier in its cleft in the hills: my landmark. All morning I walked toward it. Besides the ax I carried only my knife and my firesticks, and with so light a load I traveled quickly. I found food on the way—new shoots of ducksfoot by the river and tender, bitter leaves of deerflower among the heather on the plain. In a nest in a thicket I found six red eggs with brown spots—ptarmigan eggs—and ate two, meaning to come back to the nest on the way home to get the others for Meri.

The herds of mammoths, bison, and reindeer were off for their summer grazing on the steppe, leaving the plain to scattered herds of saiga and horses, all with young. Small herds of hinds grazed near the treeline. The plain, once white with snow, was now in bloom with follows-the-sun and sweet-root, all tumbling with bees. A cold, fresh wind blew from the north, and the sun shone.

Beyond the plain I saw the outline of Father's lodge among the trees. When I stood near its door, not daring to go in, I looked around for signs of people but found none. Then, gathering smooth stones from the river so that people would know my sign was a message about a river, I put them in three piles, large, middle-sized, and small, pointing toward the Marten. I also gathered long grass, which I knotted and put in a tree in case passing animals scattered the stones. That was what I had come to do, and I thought of starting back to the Marten. But as I sat for a moment beside the lodge, listening to the wind in the empty forest, remembering when all of us first came there and how different our lives had seemed, I knew that if I didn't look inside, I would always wonder what I might have seen, or always imagine something that would give me dreams; so although I was frightened, I made sure that no animal was lurking inside and then went carefully through the coldtrap.

The lodge was quiet and very dark, except for a dim light from the smokehole, showing the old ashes. An odor hung there, the odor of carrion and mildew. In the corner Father's body in its deerskin lay covered by a delicate white mold, as thin as mist. The greenstones he had brought from the Char River lay in the corner, partly worked, their cores exposed, hiding among their fragments a bit of antler carved in the shape of a lapwing.

As I looked at the carving, I remembered Father sometimes whittling in the evenings, and suddenly I thought I knew what the carving was—a memory of my mother. I didn't touch it. I knew I shouldn't touch anything else either, yet I couldn't help reaching out suddenly to take Father's firesticks and spear. As I did I felt terror, as if a spirit were watching, and I quickly put them back. Then I overcame the terror and took them anyway, because I needed them so badly—Father's sharp spear in case something happened to my knife, and his firesticks in case mine broke. I stole them. Holding them up so they wouldn't make a dragging noise, I crawled outside without looking back and walked quickly through the woods toward the Marten.

On the way I made plans for the spear. Animals whose flesh gives us strength are not to be caught in snares; I could use the spear to help get fat for Meri, still dangerously thin. Although I wasn't good at throwing the spear and found it very heavy, I thought I could try on a moonlit night to stab one of the swans nesting on an island in the river. I remembered that these birds have some fat all year, even in spring.

I reached the lodge in the evening. The wolf lay on the roof, her face and legs in her tail. She raised her head as I came near and watched me carefully. Meri and the pup came out the door, where Meri, and perhaps the pup too, had been hiding from mosquitoes in the smoke from the fire.

Meri looked at me hopefully, and the pup ran to my feet, licking the air as if he were begging. Going inside, I gave Meri the eggs, which she gulped. The pup must have been very hungry too—he ate the shells. I gave Meri a large bundle of greens, which she stuffed into her mouth while the pup pleaded, but two frogs I had caught while following the river I kept in my shirt to cook after the wolf went hunting.

Meanwhile the wolf came in to see what we were doing. She smelled the pup's lips while Meri tried to swallow the great mouthful of greens. She couldn't swallow quickly enough—the wolf sniffed her mouth too, but turned away, uninterested, to sniff me. As if she suspected that I sometimes carried food she couldn't see, her nose lingered long over the hidden frogs. Then she looked me in the eyes a moment, and because I was in fact hiding something, I found I couldn't meet her stare. At last she glanced between her front legs at the pup, who by now was sucking as quickly as he could. Relaxed for a moment, the wolf sat with her ears partly folded, her eyes squinting, and her tongue rolling out, letting him nurse for a time. Very soon she stood, swung her leg over his head, and as he tried desperately to cling, shook him off and left the lodge. From the scrabble on the roof we knew she was again in her favorite resting place, out of his reach.

The moon rose. I took the spear to the riverbank by a long, thin island where I thought I might find a swan's nest. At the water's edge I took off my clothes and put them with the two frogs in the top branches of a little tree. Then I waded up to my waist in water so cold I ached, so cold that for a moment my heart wouldn't beat. But I caught my breath at last and waded toward the island slowly, so that the river's noise would cover mine. In the moonlight I saw a swan's white form among the reeds. I raised the spear. As the swan bent its head, perhaps to touch the eggs under its breast, I stabbed it. It screamed and beat its wings, and something hit my head so hard I saw a bright light. Then blows fell over me and something enormous hit the arm I flung over my face.

I tried to lift the spear again and found it too heavy, so while blows and bites rained on me, I dragged it toward the shore. Somehow I fell, gulped some water, and managed to pull myself out on the bank. Behind me on the reedy island a huge swan beat its wings. I had been frozen and bitten for nothing, it seemed, but then I saw under the moonlit water the white body of another swan on the end of my spear. Wondering how I could have dragged something so heavy and not known it, I heaved it up beside me.

Suddenly I noticed a large pair of green eyes watching. I was about to dive into the water again when I saw it was only the wolf. She must have heard the noises. Quickly I lifted the dead swan on the end of the spear to lodge it with my clothes and the frogs in the cleft of the tree, out of the wolf's reach. But instead of trotting forward as she usually did if she thought I had food, she stopped in her tracks, bristled, barked once, and ran a few steps away. Had she seen something behind me?

In fear I looked over my shoulder, but saw only the moonlit river and the island beyond. Was the wolf afraid of the swan? The spear? Or—and I felt a fear colder even than the river—a spirit come after the spear? Slow with terror, I pulled my clothes out of the tree and put them on.

The moment I was dressed, the wolf came cautiously up to me to sniff uneasily. Her bristling mantle drooped, her eyes went from round to normal, and she glanced around casually, then up at the swan; she sniffed along the river-bank and in the reeds, then walked away as if nothing had happened.

What had she seen? Nothing dangerous was in the river and I didn't think a spirit would abandon a spear so quickly after following it so far. Then I knew—she had bristled at the sight of me! Me naked! She must have been as startled as I would be if she suddenly lost her fur. I was afraid to make more noise, or I would have laughed aloud at her. Instead I laughed inside.

Later that night she disappeared, probably to hunt. When she was gone, I went back to the tree to get the swan and saw from her footprints that she had leaped for it, but the spear had helped me put it high. Meri and I plucked and cooked the swan that very night to make it ours, eating the liver and the yellow fat while they were still so hot they burned us, as the pup begged for a share in vain. We got strength from that meal.

Then I knew that with the spear Meri and I could eat better. I might be able to kill more swans as long as they were sitting on their nests, or to use the spear to drive them off their nests and take the eggs, or to kill fawns hidden at the edges of the plain. I might be able to throw the spear at something, but even if I couldn't, it still greatly lengthened my reach.

Very soon the fawns would be running, the eggs would be hatched, and the swans and cygnets would be swimming where I could never catch them. I knew I couldn't wait. Planning to kill the other swan the next night, while the moonlight lasted, I used the morning to look through the grass and low bushes for a fawn.

The thought that one of us should watch the lodge was the wolf's, not mine. Her pup might wander off but Meri wouldn't, and although the wolf might wait for me to get home before going hunting, I saw no reason to wait for her. Feeling much safer, much more dangerous, with the spear than with the ax or the antler pick, I went to the plain, hunting for young animals in every patch of long grass, in every clump of bushes.

In time I heard faint hoofbeats and looked up. Two mares and a colt were running toward me, followed eagerly by a wolf—our own long-legged female. Now and then the horses would stop running to glare at the wolf, who held herself back at a distance so she wouldn't scatter them. Then the horses would dash off again with the wolf alert behind them, not on their heels but far off, swinging out to the left or out to the right in a way that made the horses run toward me. A stallion driving them would not have moved them better, except that he would have been on their haunches, driving them with shoves and bites. I couldn't at first imagine why she was chasing horses to me. Then I thought she might want help. Did she know what the spear was for? She couldn't know that! Perhaps she saw me standing on the plain and hoped I might snatch one of the horses with my hands, to hold it until she could set her teeth in it to start it bleeding or drag it down.

In the next moment the horses thundered by. Then everything happened at once—I threw the spear just before the hooves of the first mare lifted me off the ground and sent me flying. Drawing up my knees and hugging my arms over my head as I landed, I caught a second blow as if a tree had fallen on me, then I felt a stab of pain from a third, terrible blow on my shoulder, which I thought would crush my bones. I screamed.

The hoofbeats grew faint and I dared look up to see the wolf with her teeth sunk in the colt's hindquarters, dragging it to the ground. While its little feet battered her, the two mares spun, but instead of rushing back to the colt, they jounced against each other, confused. The colt screamed and the two mares answered, and when one of them charged back to us, I rolled myself up like a ground squirrel. In the silence that followed I opened an eye to see, very near me, the colt stretched in a pool of blood, still living, with the mare bowed over him, her head by his head. At a distance sat the wolf, eyes half shut and tongue rolling. Remembering a wolf that Timu and Elho and I once found, killed and battered into the earth by a horse—a story the tracks told clearly—I lay perfectly still, hardly daring to breathe. After a very long wait, during which the mare ran at the wolf several times and ravens set themselves down on the plain around us, the colt died and the mare gave up hope. Then both mares went away. Again I dared to peek, and saw the wolf taking big bites from the colt's haunches.

I stood up carefully, my head ringing and my body very sore. But the wolf snarled at me so fiercely I sat down again. After that she ate more quickly while keeping an eye on me, and any move of mine brought her almost to her feet, snarling. By now evening was coming with other hunters; the open plain next to a dead animal was no place for me. I would gladly have given up any share of the colt to find my spear and go home, if only to learn how badly I was hurt and to lie down. But whenever I tried to stand, the wolf seemed to think I might try to take her meat and showed me her teeth, reminding me of the adults of our group when they sometimes got wrong ideas fixed in their heads and wouldn't listen to any explanation. So I sat still, feeling sad and hungry, with no hope of a share.

At dusk the wolf walked heavily away to throw herself on her side and clean the blood from her fur. I stood up on numb legs and dragged myself home, bruised, sore, and ashamed to have been gone all day only to return with nothing. Late at night the wolf strolled through the coldtrap door, and lowering her head, heaved once, heaved twice, and vomited a pile of pale, shredded flesh, which Meri and the pup bolted.

From my point of view, what had happened with the horses wasn't promising, yet afterwards the wolf seemed to want to use my help in hunting as well as in keeping watch. Although she wouldn't leave the lodge if I was leaving, she would come to meet me if she saw me on the plain. Often she would trot ahead of me, chasing nesting partridges and nightjars up from their cover. Since whatever she caught she ate herself, I didn't want her with me and tried to make her see this, but she didn't pay attention. Twice more she tried to chase animals to me. Someone to surprise an animal, to make it falter, was, I think, how she saw me, but her plan didn't work. When she managed to chase a young bison mother and calf far from the herd, I was so terrified to see them charging at me that I dropped Father's spear and dove into the mouth of a badger's burrow, where I curled tighter than a birch mouse and prayed to The Bear to spare my life.

Another time the wolf chased a herd of little asses: the stallion, his three mares, and his colt. The wolf was almost as big as the mares, and she frightened them so much that she made them run from their cover of brush at the edge of the woods right across the short grass on the open plain, with the stallion after them, trying to make them turn back. When I saw them coming I knew why, and had the spear ready. From Timu's and Elho's talk of spears, I remembered that you must throw before the animal reaches the place you aim for, because the spear takes time to reach its mark. Steadily and carefully I waited, and when the asses got very near I threw, using all my strength. The spear flew past their chests and pierced the ground, the asses dashed by, and when the wolf saw what had happened, she dropped her pace from a run to a trot and, showing me her furry hindquarters, made off toward the glacier.

We saw her at the lodge late the next day; she stayed long enough to heave up some limp, wet food—a gray hamster, three or four voles, and two nest-building mice. As Meri and the pup began to eat eagerly, the wolf nosed the hamster for a moment. When attacked, these fierce animals sometimes throw themselves on their backs to bite and scratch. Sometimes they leap at you. Perhaps this hamster had shown more fight than a wolf might expect. Although it was dead, she stared at it, then suddenly flipped it in the air and, when it fell, barked at it. Finally she gulped it.

As the summer grew, we began to hear more voices at night. We heard the owls, or the bear snuffling and grumbling to itself, or the high, fine squeak of bats over the smokehole. One night we heard lions roaring from the plain, the first sign since we came to the Pine with Father that any lions were near. This frightened me; I listened to a far lion answering a near lion just as if their voices were telling me not to visit the plain anymore. How selfish they were, I thought, to take for themselves even a plain as small as this, when they make us expect to find them on wide plains, on the steppe and tundra, where the large herds graze. Finally I crawled out the coldtrap to learn, if I could, how the wolf felt about these distant bellowing voices.

She was resting on the roof, curled up as usual to protect herself from mosquitoes, and although she glanced at me when I came out, she seemed not even to hear the lions, although of course she could. This encouraged me, and I was just about to go back inside when I heard a faint, far howl of wolves, one voice at first, pure and rising, then joined by many others, some high, some low. This brought our wolf to her feet, her eyes wide, her fur bristling. Inside the lodge the pup howled an answer, and to my astonishment Meri joined him, lifting her voice to pass his voice as his was falling, just as a wolf would do. Did they do this together when I was away? They must, but why? Were they calling? I would have gone inside to ask Meri, but the wolf, looking very anxious, made many little cries and wagged her tail, then raised her chin and howled too. At the sound of her voice, Meri and the pup held still.

Then came a great silence. The wolf listened, Meri and the pup inside the lodge must have listened, and I listened. Out on the plain the near lion, having nothing to do with the howling or the wolves, thinking only of the far lion and of whatever they meant to each other that made them roar, began the drawn-out grunts that meant he was going to bellow again. But the wolves must have heard our wolf, because suddenly they answered her. She scrambled off the roof and vanished in the deep shadows among the trees. Then the near lion bellowed, the far lion bellowed too, and I went back inside the lodge to think where best to stay in case the lions should come into the forest. Would we be safer in the lodge or in a tree? Although matters would have been much better with the wolf keeping watch, I decided to stay in the lodge even without her. On the plain were bison and saiga, horses and asses, colts and calves. Surely the lions would kill something there and not bother us. Besides, the lodge was well made, with a small coldtrap.

So I told myself, and lay down with Meri and the pup under our deerskins, but I found I couldn't stop listening for the lions and couldn't sleep. During the night the far lion came much closer to the near lion, and in time, like the excited voices of two furious people, the two roars mixed, very loud and sharp. Then came silence. Where had the lions gone? Soon the silence became more frightening than the roaring, which was the way with lions, as I remembered from our summers on the plains by the Grass River. The pup and Meri slept peacefully, never doubting that they were protected from all harm, while I listened for the scratch of the wolf's feet on the roof, wishing she still slept in the coldtrap so I could sleep too.

During the night I heard a lion breathe outside the door, or thought I heard it, and by morning, when the time came to go for food, I was nervous and tired. Taking my digging stick and Father's spear, now badly chipped from being thrown into the ground, I went unwillingly to the edge of the plain for onions and lily bulbs. After digging a few I smelled fresh meat, and thinking that I might find carrion to bring home, I carefully followed the odor. It came from a low thicket in which I heard, as I went nearer, the buzzing of flies. Ravens and magpies stood on the grass nearby, there being no trees for roosting, and two foxes ran off in opposite directions at the sight of me. Asking myself why these animals were not in the thicket eating what the flies were eating, I knew to go no closer, and started a wide circle to go by. The smell of meat grew stronger, mixed now with the fragrance of sage and the musk of lion, and just as I felt relief that the lions who made such noise at night were now eating, I saw between the bushes that the odor didn't come from a carcass but from one of the lions, a male lying on his side with his head raised slightly, his eyes shut by wounds. He may have heard me or smelled me or seen me between his swollen lids—baring his teeth, he growled. A crowd of meat flies rose from his body as he moved. Very frightened but remembering not to run, I backed away until the thicket stood between me and the lion, then I turned and hurried for the edge of the woods, where, if necessary, I could climb a tree.

When I reached the lodge, I tried to be sure I understood everything I could about what I had seen. A lion lay in a nearby thicket, alive but alone and wounded, surely not able to hunt large game. Not only that, but it knew I was around—it had shown its teeth to me. Soon it would need food, and what food could be easier to catch than me or Meri? Now I knew we needed the wolf, who could hear more and smell more than I and who, being an animal—or so I reasoned—would be likely to know where another animal might be. But the wolf didn't come back.

I began to wait for her, and to sit on the roof in her old place, partly to keep watch over the woods as she had done and partly to look for her, so anxious was I to see her again. Two days passed. After we ate our last scraps of food, I made Meri stay in the lodge and even blocked the door with the fir tree. I tried to leave the pup outside, so that if the lion came he would eat the pup and not Meri, but this made them both cry so much that I shoved the pup inside to stop the dangerous sound.

I didn't dare look for food on the plain, so I tried the river, stalking among the reeds with my digging stick lifted, ready to strike one of the thin green frogs which early in the year poise on the riverbank, singing. But where once there had been many frogs, now there were none. Then from the reeds ahead of me a large crane lurched into the air and crossed the river. Perhaps he had eaten the frogs. I looked for strawberries at the top of the bank and found a patch with a few berries left, but the bear had been there before me. He had eaten many bulrushes too, and the sedge roots, but I found some he had bitten and dropped, and these I took with me. Then I saw he had been almost everywhere that food grew. He had overlooked some broken asparagus, some lily bulbs without stalks, and some slug-eaten mushrooms. All these I took gratefully. He had trampled some purslane. Even this I took, although one can't live on purslane. When the sun was starting down the sky, I still didn't have enough to feed both me and Meri, but the thought of what the wounded lion might be doing began to worry me, and I went back.

On the way, when I stopped to pick bits of the sweet gum the larches bleed in summer, I tried to listen carefully to the woods. All around me pine-singers were starting their evening songs, and the late-afternoon wind made a watery whisper in the branches. I strained to hear beyond these sounds, and at last I heard a high, clear call, a wolf's howl, which rose, trembled, fell a few notes, and stopped. After a long pause, as if for listening, the call rose again. I felt the skin between my shoulders prickle and my eyes grow dry and round. Forgetting the sweet gum, forgetting even to walk quietly, I hurried toward the lodge as if someone were calling me. Halfway home I heard the howl once more.

I'm not sure what I expected to find or why I hurried. I think I hurried because I was so relieved to hear the wolf. I must have been more frightened than I realized without her, and must have been excited to hear her again. But also the howl seemed to be a call, perhaps to me, and in truth I didn't stop to think about it very much, because as I hurried along, frightening thoughts of bad things came unasked into my mind. I imagined Meri picked up through the small of the back and carried away by the lion.

Then suddenly I saw Meri on the trail in front of me. Wearing only her ragged trousers, she was sitting on her heels in a patch of sunlight, her ribs and shoulder blades sharp under her thorn-scratched skin. She had been crying. On her very dirty face were clean streaks, the tracks of tears. I asked, "What are you doing here?"

Her tears began again. "He ran away," she said. "She's gone too. They wouldn't wait for me."

Meri called the wolf pup *he* and *him* and the large wolf *her* and *she*. "Wait for you?" I asked. "Where were you going?"

"I don't know," said Meri. "She came for us. She wanted us to go with her somewhere else. She's not going to live here anymore."

I was shocked. "And you ran into the woods alone? What were you thinking of and why was she howling?"

"She wasn't howling and I wasn't alone," Meri answered, weeping. "I was with her. She waited for me for a while. But she's faster than you and faster than Father or anybody. She gave up waiting and went off, and I couldn't keep up with her."

"Did she take the pup?" I asked, but Meri just sat miserably, wiping her streaming nose and eyes. I saw that the wolf had taken the pup. If so, I thought, Meri could be right that they wouldn't come back. "Well, we must make the best of it," I said, trying to swallow my great disappointment. "We must go back to the lodge now. Night is coming." Meri sulkily shook her head again. "Come on, I'm going. Goodby." I started down the trail. But when I looked over my shoulder and saw that Meri wasn't following, I lost my temper. Thinking, *Now everything is wrong and you are fighting me,* I went back a few steps. "Do you remember those roaring lions?" I whispered. "I see one in those shadows, looking at you!" Meri jumped up and followed me.

When we reached the lodge I went inside but Meri climbed to the she-wolf's place on the roof. "Stay outside then," I said, tired of her stubborn ways and angry because I saw she hadn't even fed the fire but had carelessly let it burn out.

I took my firesticks from their place in the wall. As I was rolling a new fire a wolf's howl rose, wavered, and dropped—the same howl I had heard from far away, now right above me. I dropped the firesticks and hurried outside, glad to think that the wolf was back after all. But on the roof sat only Meri, thin and cold and tear-streaked, hugging her knees.

Late in the evening, Meri gave up and came inside to lie curled on her side, her eyes open. I sat by the fire to think about all the things I had not understood. I had not understood how much we both depended on the wolves. Meri cried for them, though she had never cried for Mother or Father. She seemed to understand them—she could even howl like one. Perhaps they had been teaching her when I was out of earshot; by the time I heard her, she was doing it far too well to be trying it for the first time. I saw that Meri's life and my life here at the Marten had been very far apart. I had been too busy and too worried to think of this before.

Then I saw that the wolf too had a life apart from us, and for the first time I saw how little I knew about her. If wolves live in groups as we do, why didn't she? If they have dens in the earth, why did she choose the lodge, when there were many sandy knolls where the soil could be dug easily? If wolves keep their pups warm, especially right after they're born, why had three of hers frozen? Where was the husband or sister who could have kept them warm?

For a long time I thought about these questions, until at last I saw them as a secret, the wolf's secret, which I picked at like a knot. And when the knot fell open and I thought I saw the truth, it was so like a person's secret that at first I didn't trust myself. Yet there it was: she had gotten pregnant when she should not have gotten pregnant, perhaps by someone forbidden to her, and when her time came to give birth, she had been forced to hide. This explained why she wasn't with her group—she was hiding from them. It explained why she lived in the lodge—she learned that she was pregnant after the ground froze. And it explained why she let me and Meri share the lodge—she needed helpers. Now she was gone, because like me and Meri she was lonely. She heard her people singing far off in the woods and went to find them.

After I became a spirit, when it was too late to matter, I finally saw how close I had come to guessing the truth about this wolf. Sometimes when I sat on the roof of the lodge, bored with Spirit Marmot and Spirit Goldeneye talking of people I didn't know, I would think about her. How lonely she seemed to me then—trying to care for young who couldn't understand her. And if in the form of wolves we went hunting, even as a wolf I remembered that other she-wolf. No matter how strong the wind or how wet the snow, no matter how cold or dark the night or how tired I might be, if I could see the pale hindparts of Marmot or Goldeneye bobbing ahead on the trail, I knew that our hunger and fatigue wouldn't last; we would eat someday, be warm someday, and best the enemies who bothered us. Whenever the cold air held a cloud of odor, or when, like smoke, a scent—perhaps of dung or footprints—crept up through the snow, I would glance at Marmot, the eldest, our leader, to learn what we would do about it. And Marmot and Goldeneye would glance at me, to learn if I thought as they thought.

But if as a wolf I became separated from the others, or had to travel far alone, I would begin to fell unsure, even hopeless. I could keep only part of myself doing whatever the shaman asked, while the rest of me searched for the other wolves. I would search each pool of scent for traces of their scent, and would strain my eyes and ears for a glimpse of them in the distance or an echo of their sound. I would stop as I ran to leave a scat or urine in case they came behind me after the scent of my body had been carried away. And as our scent stays behind to leave a message even if we must go elsewhere, so our voices go where our bodies cannot, to those who are far away. In the evening, when I saw the low sun, I would call them, listen, and call again. Watching the stars come out, I would send my calls to the black place in the center of the north sky where there are no stars, the place that never moves no matter what time of night, no matter what season, like the opening of a den. "Where are you?" I would cry to them.

But all that was far ahead of me that night in the lodge, as I kept watch while Meri slept. During the night I hoped against hope that the wolf would come, or call to us anyway, because I missed her too. *We are really alone now,* I thought when I gave up listening. *We have no one. The wolf has taken her child and gone back to her people; she has forgotten us, our people have forgotten us, we will grow up alone here if we are lucky or die here if we are unlucky. A crane has eaten all the frogs, a bear has eaten the roots and strawberries, the tasty milk caterpillars are now in their shells, and a lion is keeping us off the plain where we might find carrion. Before the bearberries and pine nuts ripen, we will starve.* So I thought, during the night.

A few days later we had no more food, and I decided to visit the plain. I could still find lilies and asparagus there, and I might find carrion by watching the birds. If I went at midday, the lions, if there were any, would most likely be sleeping. Of course I had to bring Meri since the wolf was not there to keep watch, and when, rather than argue with her, I simply started off without her, she ran after me, able to see that if she didn't follow she would be very much alone.

By the end of the day, when I was hot and stuck with grass seeds from digging lilies all afternoon, when I was almost at the end of my patience with Meri for whining and wandering away, we heard the distant voice of one wolf howling from the woods beyond the plain. We listened eagerly. Meri suddenly threw back her head and howled an answer, sounding so like a wolf that if I hadn't known her, I wouldn't have believed what I heard. The first wolf howled again. "It's him," said Meri. "We must go." She tugged at my hand, and I let her lead me, trying to make her go carefully, to look at all the thickets before passing through them, until we came to a grassy place near the edge of the woods. There the pup burst out of the grass and leaped on Meri, licking her mouth with joy. Then he crept toward me very gracefully, his legs bent, his head low, his ears folded, and the tip of his tail wagging. Meri put her arms around his neck and kissed his face.

I looked around the clearing, and found wolf scats and prints and a few chewed bones. The she-wolf, for her own reasons, had made the clearing her camp, as wolves do with their young at the end of summer. I thought at first that the camp might belong to the other wolves, the sound of whose voices seemed to have made our wolf leave the lodge. Did they now live here? Had she come to join them? I looked carefully at the tracks, but found only hers and the pup's. She seemed to have come by herself, perhaps to hide from the others, as they must by then have known of her at the lodge. Then I felt sure that she was trying to keep her pup a secret, and I began to understand why the wolf wanted to bring Meri with her. Meri would have kept the pup company, so he wouldn't try to follow his mother. When we left the clearing, he followed us.

He seemed to have grown, even in the few days since we had seen him, and he was full of excitement and play. When on the way I found a goosefoot with its delicious white tubers and began to dig them, the pup dug too, accidentally filling in the hole. When I got one of the tubers, he seized it and ran around us shaking it, so I thought to give up gathering and go home. He came too.

After dark a wolf howled from the woods where we had found the pup. He seemed eager when he heard the sound, then seemed to think, then howled an answer. Meri joined him with a call that rose, then fell, then faded. After a very long time, the she-wolf came trotting out of the woods. She danced for a moment at the excitement of the pup and Meri, then briefly nuzzled them both. It all seemed so simple. If she had been a person, someone would have angrily made her explain herself. As it was, she lay down in her place on the roof.

During the night we were wakened by both wolves howling, and when we listened, we heard that they were answering many other wolves howling far away. I went out and saw the she-wolf in the moonlight, standing with her pup, both looking into the woods. The pup whined and wagged his tail, and the mother threw back her head and howled. Then the pup joined his voice to hers, and their songs passed each other, his voice high and falling, her voice low and rising, so that their voices passed back and forth over each other like strands in a braid. Their song was strange and beautiful, almost frightening; the voices of shamans when they sing like geese, like eagles, are not more stirring. The hair on my arms rose.

Then suddenly the woods seemed full of wolves. I saw their gray forms, pale in the moonlight, dark in the shadows, moving among the trees. Jumping from the roof, the she-wolf barked sharply once, and the pup dashed into the lodge. Then the mother wolf stood stiffly by the door.

I was afraid of a fight. Meri was inside; I was outside, where I could count four large wolves coming toward us. If, as the she-wolf seemed to expect, they tried to get into the lodge, I would have to help her keep them out, and I wasn't sure how.

But the four wolves showed no sign of fighting. Rather, they danced toward the mother wolf, some tails high, some tails low, while she stood stiffly for a moment to let them smell her lips and mantle. As their furry group crowded against her she suddenly relaxed, and with her ears folded and her eyes almost shut, she touched her nose to the lips of the newcomers.

Then out crept the pup. The newcomers mobbed him. He rolled on his side with the tip of his tail wagging fast and the moon shining white on his belly. He passed urine and made many little whines. The grown wolves loved it. They looked him over eagerly, their waving tails held high, then two of them dashed into the lodge, only to come out again in a moment looking rather surprised.

Until now they had paid no attention to me, but suddenly

they surrounded me, smelling my feet, my hands, my clothes. I stood perfectly still as they pressed their nostrils against me, knowing that in an instant they could tear me to pieces and wondering what they might have done to Meri. But after filling their nostrils deeply with my scent, they merely sneezed and snorted, and then, in their sudden manner, ran away into the trees. The mother wolf went after them. Picking himself up, the pup went too.

"Meri!" I called. "Are you all right?"

"Yes," she answered, crawling out the door.

"What happened?"

"Two wolves looked at me, that's all," she said. "Who were they?"

"The wolf's own people, I think," I answered. "She went away with them. The pup too."

"Look there," said Meri. I looked. Among the trees, against the moonlit sky, the wolves were passing east in single file. We recognized the long-legged wolf, whose shape we knew so well, as the third in line, with two wolves in front of her and two behind. With their ground-covering lope like birds flying low they were over the rim of the valley in a moment, over and gone before we saw the pup behind them. His half-grown figure was small in the moonlight, all legs and feet. His gait was struggling, stumbling.

≪ 8 ≫

NEVER HAD THE LODGE seemed so dark, so quiet. I tried to sleep, thinking that by daylight I would feel more cheerful, more hopeful, but sleep wouldn't come. When I thought of staying alone with Meri in the lodge all winter, the fear of starving and freezing crept into my mind. When I thought of trying to find the Char River, my mind's eye saw lions, saw us drowning, saw us lost. The thought of being lost and hunted by animals was worse than the thought of starving or freezing, but I knew we had to leave—we couldn't stay. I saw that our need for clothing is what makes us different from the animals, who don't need clothing to keep warm. We had both outgrown our clothes during the year since Mother died—our sleeves and trouser legs were much too short. Also our clothes were badly tattered and our moccasins almost useless. Meri, of course, didn't even have a parka. If we didn't have more clothes by winter we would die of cold and I had no way to get more clothes. I had no large piece of leather.

Except for our need of clothes, I saw we would be like small animals while we were traveling—like foxes, maybe. A big group of people can kill a big thing and live a long time eating it, like lions or wolves. But a very small group like me and Meri would have to live like foxes, eating the frogs and lemmings overlooked by the cranes. Big groups of men with spears and clubs can walk where they like in strange country and don't need to fear the dark, but we would have to travel very carefully during the day and at night hide in small places. I remembered a story Mother used to tell about the man who stole fire from the hare and how since then the snow leopard has always come to a campfire, because the hare sends him to get it back. It is true—if you see a campfire, you know that a person is nearby, perhaps sleeping. We would not build a fire.

I wondered how we would find the way. After I became a spirit and traveled as an animal, I always seemed to find my way easily, and even if I couldn't find a place I might want to visit, I could always get home. Sometimes I used the sun, sometimes the stars, sometimes the direction of the wind as it blew my fur, and sometimes a trail of scent left by others ahead of me. I found it easy to remember the scat and urine boundaries made by other animals, the silence made by beds of pine needles, the special squeaking bubbles made by a stream on parts of its course, the clouds of scent made by certain plants—all were useful, even in the dark. But when I was a girl on the Marten River, I understood none of these helpful things.

Instead I sat down to think. "Water flows north," I remembered Father saying. But all he meant was that sooner or later the rivers turn north, or flow into other rivers which go north. Even that wasn't true of the Fire River. Taking a stick, I scratched a line on the ground which I called the Marten River. Meri came to ask what I was doing, and I told her to leave me alone. I put a mark for myself on the south bank, and another mark for Meri.

If I listened carefully, I could hear where the water went around the rocks, and I put a small rock on my drawing. The Marten had to run downhill, from the rising land southwest of us. I put stones for the rising land. I looked at the sun. The Marten ran east, I realized.

I searched my memory for an image of the Char River. It ran west, but just to be sure, I imagined myself on the south bank of the Little Char River on the day I had noticed that Mother was pregnant. I remembered Mother wading downstream toward me, her face dark in her own shadow. If the sun was behind her in the morning, she was facing west. If the water broke over the backs of her legs, it was going west. For sure, the Char River ran west.

In the middle of my stones which showed the rising land I put bigger stones for the hills where we had been when

Mother died. On the far side, from east to west, I drew the Char River. The longer I stared at my drawing, the more sure I felt that it was right, and when I climbed one of the little hemlocks and looked through the treetops at the hills, I knew that my drawing was a good one. "We can go," I said to Meri when I climbed down again.

"Now?" she asked.

"Why not?" I answered. So we made our packs and followed the south bank of the Marten while the daylight lasted.

Many times in my life, I found that things I was sure would happen failed to happen, while things I never dreamed of happened without warning. The trip to the Char River stays in my memory as good and bad surprises like beads on a string.

The first night I was surprised that darkness came so soon, before we were ready. In the dusk I lost all courage and wanted to turn back, but of course we were too far away. We were pushing through the brush by the water in hope of catching a frog, but either a crane had found all the frogs or they knew how late in the year it was and were hiding in their little mud lodges. Instead I found a dead fish floating on its back by the bank, its white belly shining in the evening sun. I took it. Then Meri and I looked at each other. We didn't dare build a fire, so we took bites out of the fish's raw flesh, swallowed with difficulty, and threw the head and guts back into the river. Later we found sedge growing in bare spots between the thickets; we stopped to dig its roots by the last of the daylight. "Tomorrow we'll find food along the way and we'll eat in the sunshine," I promised Meri. "We'll camp before dark, too."

"Where will we go tonight?" she asked. But I didn't answer. I didn't know. All afternoon I had seen no hiding place—the thickets were too open; there were no piles of rocks or blown-down trees with hiding places between them, no trees tall enough to climb. When it was almost dark I noticed how quiet it was, how all grazing animals had left the river, how nothing stirred. I saw that we were in danger. They who eat the deer had started their evening hunting. Then I saw how careless I had been to get into thickets by the river, where hunting animals lie in wait for those who come to drink. As the first stars came out, I stopped walking to think and to look carefully, to push my fear down.

Not far ahead I noticed long follows-fire grass growing on a bank, showing that the ground had once been cleared there. When I went nearer I thought I saw, even in the gathering dark, a darker space behind some of the grass, and when I went up to this darkness I found a hole. Around it in the earth were beds like the ones the she-wolf made around the lodge—it was a wolf den, perhaps the den of our she-wolf's people. I saw many old scats, thick with white hair, a few white, gnawed antlers and white, gnawed bones. There were no footprints except those of mice. The wolves had used the den in the spring and early summer while they raised their pups, and now that the pups were too big for the den, the pack had gone. There were no footprints or drag marks in the mouth of the tunnel. Nothing seemed to be inside it now.

With Meri behind me, I crawled into the tunnel carefully, pushing Father's spear ahead of myself, pausing to sniff and listen, to learn if something else might be inside after all. When I smelled only dust and heard nothing, I went on.

We crawled slowly down a long passage, feeling with our hands the hard floor of the tunnel. The earth got close and warm. We squeezed ourselves through the passage. I wanted to whisper to Meri, but I couldn't turn. My shoulders, my spine, and the top of my head scraped the roof of the passage. Then suddenly I felt space. My breath echoed. I groped with one arm, and finding no wall to my right, moved carefully as far as I could. When I felt the far wall, I realized we were in a little cavern dug out by the wolves, a place where we could sit together, where a wolf could stand up or lie down. Here we could turn, to see the faint gray light up the tunnel and to smell a stream of fresh air. I felt the ceiling and found that it was strong, domed like the roof of a lodge. The tunnel was too small for any animal large enough to eat us. Only a hyena or a bear would bother us anyway— only a hyena or a bear might dig its prey out of the ground. But if something dug for us while we slept, its scraping and snuffling and the dirt rolling on us would wake us, so that we could spear its feet. We saw that we were safe, that nothing could harm us except the many fleas that began to bite us. Relieved and very happy, we hugged each other.

When we went outside to get our packs, we heard a deer stamp and give a loud snorting whistle, its call of alarm. Then many deer slipped past us, quietly hurrying away from the river, and we knew that something large and stealthy was hunting nearby. We crawled down the tunnel again and rolled in the deerskin, warm, safe, comfortable except for the fleas, not even bothering to listen for whatever it was.

We must have slept very well. During the night, unknown to us, the wolf pup found us. When I woke up in the morning, I saw him curled beside Meri. She was delighted, and hugged and kissed him. Outside in daylight we saw that his ears were badly bitten. The other wolves, or perhaps only some of them, must have driven him away after all.

He followed us closely, hunting frogs when we hunted frogs, snatching at locusts which flew up in front of us. Meri dug up a sedge root and divided it in three pieces, one for her, one for me, and one for the pup. Although it is wrong to waste or play with food, I didn't try to stop her, as she had found it.

For many more days we followed the river, until it became a stream running through beaver meadows on high, flat ground. We spent one night in a beaver's lodge that we found in the evening when the beavers were out. Like the wolf's den, it was domed and strong, but it smelled of wet mud and dung and was so small that when we were both inside it, as if we were both together in a parka made of sticks, we couldn't move. During the night a beaver tried to come in with us; when we heard the gush of water in the coldtrap, we shouted to drive it away.

We spent one night in a narrow, hollow log alive with ants and grubs, which crawled slowly over our skin with their tiny soft feet. Another night, on the high ground, we found a perfect cave with a very small opening, a cave used by hares and smelling of hares, grassy and sweet. One night we found nothing better than a cleft between rocks, where we hid ourselves and hoped that no animal would find us.

Each day we stopped to dig roots, and when we were in the high country, to pick berries. On a ledge at the very source of the Marten we found carrion—a scrap of a musk deer's carcass abandoned for some reason by a snow leopard. We carried the stinking scrap far away in case the leopard came back for it, and built a fire to cook it until it smelled better. People later said that we had lived like animals, and I suppose we did, but after all, we had no choice.

One day I felt fullness in my belly, and pain. When I pulled down my trousers to relieve myself, I saw blood in the crotch. At first I couldn't think what was the matter and, very frightened, I called Meri. All I could think of was Mother on the last day of her life, bleeding but not knowing why.

"You're bleeding!" cried Meri, also frightened. "Are you cut? Are you having a baby?"

I didn't know, and my heart was beating so fast that I couldn't reason. I didn't think I was cut or hurt, and knew there had to be a father before a woman got a baby. But was this always true of everybody? Did the geese whose flocks reached between the horizons and the reindeer whose herds covered the hills as far as the eye could see all have fathers? Some did, of course. But all of them? Impossible! Was I gotten with child by a spirit?

The only thing was, my belly was so flat and thin that my ribs and hipbones showed. If a baby were there, we would see the bulge of it. "It's not a baby," I told Meri.

"I smell a baby," she whispered.

She was right. Something smelled like a birth. *I* smelled like a birth, I realized with horror. Would the smell attract bears or tigers?

The smell drew the pup. He came right up to me to sniff, making a brief back-and-forth motion with his hips. And then, of course, I realized what was happening to me—I was only menstruating, like the estrus of deer in the fall, which makes the stags bellow, and like the rutting of tigers in winter, which makes us call the moon the Moon of Roaring. People have it too, only not at any special season, and men are afraid of it. "I must be menstruating," I said.

"Does it hurt?" Meri asked.

"Yes," I answered.

Meri began to cry. "I don't want to go to Graylag's lodge," she said. "If you get married, I'll be all alone."

The idea chilled me. "Married?" I said. "I am married. Didn't you know that?"

"No," she said, weeping.

"Well, I am. Mother told me. But I won't leave you because of that. Not because of that, not for any reason."

Meri seemed relieved. She didn't then ask who my husband was, and it didn't occur to me to tell her.

Only the problem of the stain remained. I found and stripped a birch tree, and with the edge of Father's spear I scraped a mound of fiber to use as a pad. I had more fiber than I needed, it turned out, for the next day my bleeding stopped and didn't start again.

If starting to menstruate was a bad surprise, a good surprise came soon after, when we reached the peak of one of the mountains and saw before us the vast reach of steppe and taiga drained by the Black River, of which the Char and the Antler are west-flowing branches. I saw a gleam of water shining—it must have been the Antler River—and I saw which way to travel to reach the water. I even thought I saw a plume of smoke. It struck me that if we waited until dark, we could see whether or not people had made a campfire in the distance, but the top of the windy mountain seemed very wild and lonely. We decided to hurry on.

We could have spent longer than we did finding the lodge, but given enough time we probably would have found it even if we had never found and followed the Antler River, because if we had kept walking west, we would have come to the Black River anyway. We almost ran during the last few days of our journey, so anxious were we to see the other people. On one of the last nights we hid under a sandy bank in a hole that must have been dug by hyenas. It smelled of hyenas, and like the wolf den was filled with fleas.

"Never mind," I said to Meri. "We'll soon be in the lodge."

"I know," she said. "Mother and Father may be waiting for us."

"What?" I said. "They're not waiting for us. They died. Don't you remember?"

Meri looked unsure. "But I dream they're waiting for us," she said.

I suddenly found myself crying, frightening Meri and the pup with my sobs. So Meri surprised me and I surprised myself. After all, Meri was a child, too young to have sense. Why was I so upset?

But the biggest surprise of the journey, and the reason I remember the journey by the surprises it held for us, came at the end. We followed the Antler River to the Char River, and followed its south bank to the bend. From there we saw the lodge with Graylag's huge antlers standing on top of it, and smoke rising from one of the smokeholes. Where we crossed the rapids the boulders were too far apart for Meri, but the water was slow—we took off our moccasins and trousers, pulled up our shirts, and waded chest deep through the icy water. The pup, after much crying and running up and down the bank, finally plunged after us. Then we dressed and ran to the lodge.

The familiar coldtrap door waited for us, open and dark with the smell of food floating out of it. We dove inside.

When our eyes got used to the dim light, we saw that no one was with us but two strange women, sitting together by Graylag's fire. The cooking smell was theirs, from strips of meat. Although they were older than I, both were young, with sleek bodies, smooth, pretty faces, clean, braided hair, and new clothes. At the sight of us their eyes grew round. "Who are you?" they asked. "Where are your people?"

III

THE LODGE

◄ 9 ►

BONES, HEATHER, DUNG, and trees all seem different, yet all of them are fuel, because they all have fire in them. So it is with times in our lives that seem different while they happen, yet are the same in the end. After I became a spirit and took animal forms, things happened that made me feel as unsure as I had felt when at last Meri and I found the Char River. When I was alone with Meri and the wolves at the Marten River, I rarely felt lonely but, surprising as it seemed, I became painfully lonely after I found the people again. By the time I understood why, it didn't matter anymore, because I was only a spirit with no one to talk to except two other spirits who already knew everything I knew, and more.

One night after I became a spirit, there was nothing to hunt. Red deer were gathered at the fords on the south side of the swollen river, unable to swim across, but the animals of the north side, the bison, the reindeer, and even some of the horses, had long since started for their summer grazing on the steppe. Under the Icebreaking Moon, Teal's trancing figure appeared in the air to beg for food.

"Bring deer," begged Teal. "Make them swim the river so we can drown them. Red deer or reindeer, as long as we can eat." So in the form of a hind I found myself alone, following a trail that wound among the low, scattered spruce that grew along the south side of the river. I raised my head and let the cold spring air, carrying the smells of spruce and meltwater, of lichen and other deer, pour through my head. I also smelled the bitter, heavy smell of

147

the tigress, who had passed recently. Moving slowly, cautiously, I noticed how well the trail was made. When it led among the trees, where someone using it could not see clearly, it also led where the trees blocked the sound of the river, so although I couldn't look for danger, I could listen for it. When the trail got near the river, where the rushing sound of water covered other sounds, it climbed a rise of ground. There, where I couldn't hear danger, I could look for it.

I also noticed that the trail was very old. On a washout by the river, the hooves of passing deer had worn a groove in the stone. Beyond the washout, as the trail traversed a steep bank, the downhill side of the trail was pressed solid into a ledge that now held it firmly. For more time than anyone could know, hinds had passed this way in spring, hinds followed by their children and their children's children, going up the river. Small paths led downhill to wallows near the water, and one small path led up the hill to—ah, its sweet smell came down the wind!—a pine. I hurried to it. Most of its bark was gone, and in places even the sweet-smelling wood had been rubbed away. No wonder! Eagerly I began to rub one side of my nose on it. Ah! The smell of other deer on the pinewood filled my head as I gently rubbed the skin around my eyes, making them tingle. Before opening them again I rubbed my forehead up and down. This felt so fine that I rubbed behind each ear very carefully, setting the crease against the wood, twisting to rub exactly around the curve. With my head feeling wonderful, I could rub my neck with force.

After that I couldn't help but rub my body. Setting my feet firmly, I worked the whole length of each side, not stopping until my skin stung. A great rush of pleasure swelled my throat and made my eyes glaze. Very grateful to the deer whose safe trail led here and whose years of rubbing had made the wood just right, I finished with a thorough shake that left winter hair in piles at my feet, and filling my lungs with pine-scented air, I went along the trail almost dancing.

Soon I reached the ford, now a dangerous torrent. On a mudbank at the water's edge a herd of hinds, some young, some old, some with yearlings, were waiting for the water to go down. Their milky, grassy smell filled me with comfort—traveling by myself, with no one to help keep watch, no one to bark a warning, put my nerves on edge and made me tired; I realized how good it would be to have company. Partly eager and partly shy, I approached them. But several of them raised their chins and looked at me out of the corners of their eyes. One snorted, and one lashed up at me with her front foot.

Disappointed, I stepped back to wait nearby quietly, modestly, my head held low. I nosed a tuft of grass and tried to watch the hinds without seeming to, hoping that they would change their minds and give me the safety of their herd. But they didn't. They stood close together, mothers, daughters, and granddaughters, with their chins lifted and their nostrils flared, keeping me away with their eyes.

By night, when the river was lower, I felt so unwelcome, so uncomfortable, that I told myself the ford was safe, and to get away from the sidelong looks the other deer were giving me, I stepped into the water too soon. I was snatched downstream by the current and dashed against some rocks. Only by running as fast as I could, although there was nothing under my feet but water, did I manage to reach the far bank and drag myself out on it. Cold and bruised, I followed the deer trail up the moonlit terraces, knowing that all the eyes of the night were watching only me. Then it seemed that I had known all this before, when I was a girl with Meri and returned to the Char River.

The two pretty women sat up straight, and without trying to be friendly, slowly ran their eyes over Meri and me, waiting for us to explain ourselves. "I am Yanan," I heard myself saying. "This is my sister. We are from here."

The two young women showed each other puzzled frowns. "From here?" asked one of them. "How from here?"

"Our father, Ahi, belonged to this lodge."

"Ahi?" asked the other woman. "I don't know him."

"Our aunt is Yoi and our cousins are The Stick and The Frog," said Meri.

The two young women looked at each other. "We don't know them," said the first, with her chin raised and her tone very even. I saw she didn't trust us.

Not here? I thought. *Where can they be? Have new people taken over the lodge and killed our people?* "I know the owners of this lodge," I said at last, as bravely as I could. "Graylag, Child of Soossi, is the leader, and his wife, Teal Shaman, is our kinswoman. His daughter is Owl and his sons are Timu and Elho. His first wife is Ina, our father's sister. I don't know where the others are—Yoi and The Stick and The Frog—if, as you say, you don't know them. But our parents are dead, so we are here. I am here to join Timu, my husband."

"Your husband?" asked the first woman, who heard me out with slowly widening eyes. "He's my husband! I'm Ethis, Timu's wife."

"And I'm Ankhi, her sister," said the other, "wife of Elho." She pressed her hands against her swollen belly. "And this is his child, in here."

Meri leaned against me as the eyes of those beautiful sisters crept over us. We were dirty, we were thin, and our torn clothes, now far too small, showed that we had no people. Meri's matted hair was stuck with burrs, and my scalp prickled as I thought of how tangled my own hair must be. It pained me to see Meri humbly gaping at these women, at their sleek braids, at their clean, smooth skin rubbed lightly with fat, at their rounded arms, their rounded legs, their ivory beads, their wedding clothes—more loosely styled than ours, especially through the hips, but new—and Ankhi's rounded belly, where Elho's child lay curled.

When I noticed that the two pretty women were scornfully returning Meri's wistful stare, I remembered that I hadn't told them her name. "My sister's name is Meri," I said, thinking how little this might interest them.

But Ethis said, "We know. When you told us who you were, we knew this girl must be your sister, no other than Meri."

Too much was happening. These women were confusing me. All I could say was, "What?"

"When our uncle found that Meri was not here, he was

THE LODGE

angry," said Ankhi, "but now that she's here everything will
be all right."

"Your uncle? Meri? I don't understand."

"Ah," said Ethis. "Graylag, Child of Soossi, told Uncle
that you would be waiting here when we came. Now that we
know your father died, we understand why you didn't come
before."

These words made no sense. Why was a stranger waiting
for Meri? "Is Graylag here?" I asked. "Are his wives? Is
Timu? Elho? Owl and her husband? White Fox and his
parents?"

"All are here," said Ethis, "except White Fox's parents,
who stayed on the steppe. And Owl's poor little baby, who
died on the way."

"Died? How?"

"Killed by The Woman Ohun. Last summer she sent us
diarrhea."

"Why did White Fox's parents stay on the steppe? Did
White Fox stay with them?"

"White Fox is here," said Ethis. "His parents stayed with
his sister, who is married. Her husband's winter shelter is
on the steppe."

"Where is that?" I asked.

"West of the Hair River cave," said Ethis proudly. "We'd
be there by now, but for you."

The Hair River cave meant nothing to me. "I'm still
young," I said. "No one told me about that place. What
have we to do with your going there?"

"Uncle won't go now, since snow would come while he
was traveling," said Ethis.

"What has snow to do with her?" I asked sharply,
thrusting my lips at Meri.

Ethis and Ankhi made long faces at my rudeness. "As
Uncle came here to get her, he wouldn't go back without
her," said Ethis. "They are betrothed."

"Your uncle and Meri are betrothed?" I asked, shocked.
"Yes."

"But she was betrothed already. Mother told me." In fact,
I remembered very well. It was one of the last things Mother
ever said.

"Someone must have changed that," said Ethis.

Suddenly Ankhi gave a little scream. Then she snatched up her ax. Startled, I turned to see the wolf pup tugging at some pieces of leather which had been rolled together in the coldtrap.

With axes and picks the two pretty women started for him, but little Meri, who had been sitting on her heels with her arms wrapped tightly around herself, as small and thin as a frog and as ignorant of her own betrothal, suddenly jumped up and flung her arms wide. "Don't hurt him!" she cried, as the pup picked up a leather scrap and ran with it.

Ethis and Ankhi looked at us with wide eyes. "Was that a spirit?" asked Ankhi.

"No, not a spirit," I said, as a whole new set of problems rose in my mind's eye. At the Marten, I had put in a treetop anything that a wolf might steal from us. Here, I saw, people might not think to do this until too late. More likely, they wouldn't want to do it at all.

"Then what took the leather?"

I started to explain, but Meri spoke too quickly for me. "A pup," she said. "A wolf pup. Mine."

"Yours?" asked Ankhi, amazed. "What do you mean, yours?"

"Mine, like that ax is yours," said Meri rudely. Now Ethis, Ankhi, and I all gaped at Meri, they no doubt because she was speaking childish nonsense—before you can own an animal you have to kill it, after all—and I because I had never heard her speak so boldly.

"Mind your tongue," I said.

She gave me a long and bitter look, then ducked out the door. I dove after her, and just as I burst out the door I heard her scream.

What I saw outside stayed with me. Sometimes just before I fall asleep the scene flashes into my dream and makes my heart jump. I saw Timu spearing Meri.

How did this happen? When Elho and Timu came to the lodge, the pup ran out. Thinking that they had caught a thief, they kicked the pup to the ground and raised their spears to kill him. Just as Timu's spear started down, Meri burst out of the coldtrap and threw herself over the pup. I screamed and covered my eyes, heard a terrible crunch, and uncovered my eyes to see that Timu, although he hadn't been able to stop his spear, had managed to drive it into the earth and not into Meri.

For a moment nobody moved. Elho and Timu stared down at Meri. Timu started to tremble. Elho, his eyes and mouth wide open, looked stupidly around. When he saw me, he didn't seem to know me. Meri, as if surprised to be alive, looked slowly up at Timu, then down at the pup. Pinned by Meri, the pup was trying to please somebody—his tongue flicked cautiously toward Meri's face; the tip of his tail moved slightly.

Timu slowly drew his foot from under Meri. "By The Bear!" he said.

Meri got to her hands and knees. The pup got up carefully, then dashed away. Timu stared at Meri with a dazed expression. "By The Bear!" he said again. "You're Meri!"

Meri nodded and began to cry. "You frightened me," she said.

Timu's anger came. "Frightened you?" he roared. "I almost killed you!" Elho recovered first. He put his hand on Timu's shoulder. "No one is hurt," he said reasonably. "Be calm until we see what's happening." He looked over my head—I turned to look too—at Ethis and Ankhi, who had crept out of the coldtrap and were gaping at the scene. "Wife!" said Elho. "Please explain this."

But Ankhi could only blink. Finally she asked, "Explain what?"

Surely I was the only person who knew what had happened and why we were all staring numbly at each other, yet no one even seemed to notice me. Suddenly my heart filled with relief at the familiar sight of Elho and Timu. And suddenly the sight seemed very funny—everyone looking as puzzled as bison, with the two men scowling at their wives as if these women were somehow to blame. I began to laugh. "You should see yourselves!" I said. "Timu! Your beard grew! Your mouth looks like a bear's den in a bank. You don't know me. I won't tell who I am!"

Timu stared. "Yanan," he said at last. "It's you."

"Yes, me," I said, wiping my eyes. "Me and Meri. We came home."

Timu straightened himself and pulled his spear out of the ground. "Have you eaten?" he asked as he examined his spear's edge, which even from a distance I could see was chipped, being too brittle to be stabbed into the stony ground.

"No," I answered.

"We'll feed you, then," he said. "And I'll try to fix my spear. Maybe I can use it again. Come, Meri, you too." And Timu led the way into the coldtrap.

At the back of the lodge the two pretty sisters built up Graylag's fire, and we sat by it. As Timu and Elho cut meat and lay strips on the coals, the two women began to chatter, feeling safe because their husbands knew us.

"We're sisters from the cave on the Hair River," said Ethis. "I'm the elder. Ankhi is the younger." She looked at Timu shyly. "We were married the summer before, when our husbands came with Graylag to hunt with our uncle."

"We don't know that place," I said, then added, lest my remark sound like a challenge, "I haven't traveled far."

"The Hair joins the Black River out on the steppe," said Timu importantly. "We found our wives among the people hunting mammoths there. Now you have a co-wife," he added softly, very much surprising me with his tone. Did he feel shy with me? "But where are your parents?" he went on, the shy tone vanishing. "Where are The Stick and The Frog? Where is Yoi? And what is this wolf? Meri, you were almost killed!"

"My wolf," said Meri.

"Yours? How so? Isn't he living?"

"Living," said Meri, "but mine."

"How is it, then, you call him yours?"

"I don't know," said Meri. "But he is."

"Do you see this?" asked Timu, showing her the spear's broken blade. "Do you see what you've done? Why?"

"I don't know," said Meri, growing timid again.

"Your sister will explain everything," said Timu, turning to me.

So I told them of Mother's death and Father's injury, and how The Stick, The Frog, and Yoi, feeling unwelcome by the spirits of the Pine River lodge, had left us there. As I talked, I heard the *tick, tick, tick* of Timu's antler chisel picking a new edge on his spear. But although he was working, he was listening. When I told of Father's death, his chipping stopped. "And then what happened to you?" he asked. "Who took care of you? Who brought you here?"

I said nothing for a moment, because I didn't know exactly how to answer. When I thought about the lodge on the Marten and the she-wolf who once had used it, I couldn't find the words to make it all sound right. It now seemed strange even to me. "We took care of ourselves," I said at last. "First we went to the old lodge of Father's people on the Marten River, and when the summer was over we came here."

At this Timu and Elho and their new wives laughed and praised us, and handed around the strips of roasted meat. Meri took her share and slipped outside with it. "What has happened about Meri?" I asked. "Ethis said she's betrothed to a man from the Hair River. But she can't be. She was betrothed to White Fox long ago. Mother told me."

"Perhaps she was," said Timu. "That's changed. She is now betrothed to Swift."

Then Timu told me that Swift, away for the day with Graylag, was a shaman from the mammoth hunters. Some of his kinsmen were also Graylag's kinsmen, as Graylag had guessed when he and Father parted. Swift was one of the first people Graylag had met after leaving us at the Fire River, and he and Graylag had become close friends. But Swift wanted to become closer still to Graylag.

The winter hunting on the Hair River was never good because animals used the plain only in summer, said Timu. Swift's own winter hunting lands were good some years but bad other years. Swift wanted some of his people to come to the Char, where the winter hunting was steadier. And Graylag liked the summer hunting at the Hair. "You never saw so much meat!" said Timu. So Swift and Graylag decided to join their lodges with an exchange of women.

Swift was an important hunter, a man of meat, said Timu. He should have had two wives, but in fact he had no wife, since he was divorced, and some of his children were dead. Swift caused Ethis and Ankhi to be given to Timu and Elho. In return he asked for a wife from the lineage of Sali Shaman. Only Meri was still unmarried, so Meri was given.

I asked how Graylag could have promised Meri when, for all he knew, Father and Mother were still living. He couldn't, of course, said Timu. And he hadn't. All he could do was persuade White Fox's parents to take White Fox out of the betrothal. When Swift promised to find a wife for White Fox, and when Junco married one of Swift's kinsmen at the Hair River, White Fox's parents gladly broke his betrothal and planned to take back from Mother the flint knife and the necklace with pendants given to her in the wedding exchange. Swift, of course, would have given Mother many good presents in place of the knife and necklace. "Your mother didn't know Swift," said Timu. "He would have given her very nice gifts, and she would have liked him. Anyway, now Meri is free. Since your parents are dead, Swift will give his gifts to Teal and you. And you can share with me."

I listened to this very sadly, not wanting to tell Timu that the very gifts he had named were now in Mother's grave. In a while I went outside.

Far down the terrace, among a cluster of little trees, I saw the tiny form of Meri sitting on her heels, sucking her thumb. I went to sit with her. From her free hand dangled a thin strip of meat. Presently the pup came back, his ears folded humbly, and after looking to see if anyone dangerous was near but seeing only us, he crept forward to beg for a bite. Meri fed him. He gulped the meat.

We sat in silence as the shadows of the little trees reached far over the grass. Ravens flew from the east, circled, landed on the grass, and called. Presently a man appeared on a trail from the east—he whom the ravens had been circling. The pup dashed away. The man was Graylag; we knew his walk from afar. He stopped when he saw us to squint at us curiously. Then his white teeth appeared in his beard and he hurried toward us, laughing. "Aha! My children!" he called. "I wondered when you'd come. Welcome!" As we stood up to greet him, his rough palm raked the top of my head, pulling my hair. I would have told him our story, but in his quick, determined way he was already starting for the lodge. "I'll greet your father," he said, and hurried off. Meri and I sat down again.

I watched the wind move a little herd of clouds across the

sky. When it brought the sound of someone else walking toward us, I turned and saw a big, strange man.

As if I suddenly saw a lion, his looks gave me a fright. His two eyes were pale, like a lion's eyes but blue, and his hair was the color of dry grass. Like a lion, he looked as if he could hide in the grass. As he passed, peering at us, his shadowy face and blue eyes looked like a lion skin with two holes in it where the sky showed through. The sight of him frightened me, as one is always frightened by staring pale eyes.

At last he had to turn to save himself from stumbling. We watched him follow Graylag into the lodge. *He must be Swift,* I thought, and taking Meri by her free hand, I led her quietly to the entrance of the coldtrap so that I could hear what he and Graylag might say to each other.

The coldtrap carried voices as easily as a hollow log. Inside we heard the stranger complaining to Graylag with hard, rasping words like the speech of the strange men we had met near the Fire River. "Zhe is a baby, dirdy and sgrajd," he said in his terrible accent. "Her clodes are in rags or mizzing. A woman who wend inzane had hair like her hair."

"I'm sad," said Graylag. "My son tells me that their father is dead. Their mother too."

"Dead?" asked the stranger.

"He slept at this very hearth," said Graylag. "He was given his wife because of our friendship, just as he would have given his daughter to you."

"Your news is bad," said the stranger in his ugly accent. "Now your people here are few. Your men are few, for hunting in winder."

"Yanan!" said another voice behind us. We turned and saw White Fox, so tall that I almost didn't recognize him. He even had a sparse beard starting, and his wrists stuck out of his sleeves. But he was White Fox just the same, carrying sticks for the night's fire. He sat on his heels beside us, and when I told him about my parents, he sighed. "I too have no parents," he said. "They stayed with Junco at the Hair River cave. I didn't like the mammoth hunters, so I came back here. Graylag likes the mammoth hunters too much." Pointing his lips at Meri, White Fox continued: "Her,

Graylag took away from me to give to one of them. I am no longer betrothed."

If I thought Meri didn't understand about betrothal, I was wrong. Taking her thumb out of her mouth, she looked at White Fox steadily. "Was I going to marry you?" she asked.

White Fox nodded. "Yes," he said.

"Were you going to marry me?" asked Meri.

White Fox nodded a second time.

"When?"

He had to think. "Later. After you grew up. When you were no longer a baby."

Meri put her thumb back in her mouth and sucked it, watching White Fox thoughtfully. He shifted his weight uneasily, then stood. "Now that you're here, you both can help me bring firewood," he said. "If you do, I'll tell you about the Hair River. Come." He tucked his ax into his belt and started for one of the trails.

I followed, but Meri stood still. After a while she called, "White Fox!" He turned. "Don't call me a baby. You're the baby," said Meri.

At dusk homecoming people wound through the valley in single file. Like a herd of deer spotting something hidden in the grass, they stopped in their tracks at the sight of us. Teal wept and hugged both Meri and me, then hurried inside with the others to find Mother and the rest of our group, leaving a strange woman outside, a tall, thin woman dressed in wide trousers. She too had pale, narrow eyes, which watched us suspiciously for a moment before she followed the others.

The strange woman, I gathered from listening through the coldtrap, was Swift's half-sister. The rest of the people seemed to call her Rin. Then I heard Swift breaking sticks for a fire near the door, at the place that once was Father's fire, so I understood that this place was now the strangers' fire, and I wondered where Meri and I would sleep.

In the gathering dusk the wolf pup crept up to us, testing the air, which carried the smell of cooking meat. Darkness fell. In the woods across the river an owl called, one low, trembling note for each of the four fingers of my right hand, then, after a pause, one for each of the four fingers of my left hand. We heard a lion very far away on the plain behind us, above the valley, answered by another lion, much nearer. I tried to think how long it had been since we had last heard lions in the Char valley. Lions made me think of the steppe, of long grass, of summer. We heard them on our summer-grounds, not on the Char. Then Teal called sharply: "Meri! Yanan! What are you doing out there? Why don't you come?" So we crawled in.

Graylag and the strangers were all talking at once about the change in obligations, now that my parents were no longer living to receive Meri's betrothal gifts. Meri and I could not quite fit into the circle at Graylag's fire, because the adults filled all the space. Of course we wouldn't have thought of joining Swift and Rin at the fire near the door. Instead we sat with White Fox behind Mother's kinswoman, Teal, and Father's sister, Ina. I was surprised to hear Ina weeping softly. And I was surprised that Teal didn't speak to me but stared into the fire. Then it came to me that the news we brought was their first news of my parents' death, and I saw how they were grieving.

I might have taken Teal's hand or leaned against her to show I shared her feeling. But White Fox began to tell us under his breath about Teal at the Hair River. "There's a wide place in the river below the cave," he said, "where mammoths wallow. Their shed hair floats and when dust blows over it, it looks like solid ground. Your Aunt Teal almost walked on it. The people warned her just in time. But what if she fell in? You know how she walks." White Fox raised his chin and drew back his shoulders imitating, right behind Teal's back, her proud stance. "I said, 'Don't listen to them, Aunt. Walk where you like!' Not out loud, of course."

I felt deeply ashamed when Teal heard us snickering. "Give me your comb," she said quietly. "I'll do your braid for you!" So I sat humbly between Teal's knees, biting my lip as the comb raked through the knots and tangles. "In the morning we'll start new clothes for you," said Teal as if nothing was the matter. "You can help. We have a skin. Graylag will give you another skin. We must ask Timu and Swift for skins. They must give skins for your clothes now." And so she talked until my braid was done. Now it was too late for me to take her hand, or to show my feelings. I was sorry about that. But I also liked it that she was brave, in the way of the Fire River women.

People began to roll themselves into their deerskin blankets, ready for the night. I didn't know where Meri and I should sleep, and nobody told me. I would have liked to sleep with Teal, but she went to her place beside Graylag, leaving no room for us. The only space Meri and I could find was in front of the coldtrap, where no one else wanted to be.

I woke up before dawn to see Graylag sitting at the fire by the door, where he used to sit with Father, only now he was with Swift. They had the last of a reindeer carcass between them, and were cutting little strips off it with their knives. I could smell the strong, bloody smell of the raw meat, dead many days now, and the smell of some of it cooking. Seeing me awake, Graylag laid a fresh piece on the fire and gestured to it with his knife. He meant it for me. When I opened my mouth to thank him, I noticed, in the opening of the coldtrap, the outline of the wolf pup, its ears and fur lit from behind by the dawn light. Graylag glanced at the pup without much surprise. Swift glanced too. "What does it eat?" he wondered aloud.

Graylag lifted a strip of meat from the fire and handed it to Swift. "Feces, bones, the same as—" he began, but he never finished, because the pup darted forward, snatched the meat from Swift, and dashed out the coldtrap.

Graylag gaped in amazement as Swift leaped to his feet. "I'll kill him!" Swift roared in his frightening accent. "Will wolves grab my food?" And seizing his spear, he lunged after it.

"No!" screamed Meri. Before I could catch her, she leaped from our sleeping-skin and caught the shaft of the spear.

Swift must have been holding it loosely while moving forward quickly—the spear slid through his hand, and the blade sliced his fingers across the first joints. "By The Bear!" he roared, looking at his palm. Then he turned to Meri. Still clutching the shaft, she glanced in terror around the lodge. Then, as the trailing spear scattered the burning branches, she leaped over the fire and ducked out the door.

"She burned me!" cried narrow-eyed Rin in the harsh accent of the mammoth hunters, slapping coals from her legs.

"Stop Meri," cried Teal.

"My spear!" roared Swift, and plunged into the coldtrap.

"Don't hurt Meri!" I shouted, scrambling after him, trying to catch his shirt.

Meri could run like a deer since her legs had grown long, and now she did, dashing for the woods, with Swift close behind her. I ran right after him; the tail of his shirt was just out of my grasp. "Wait! Please!" I shouted above the yammering of all the other people who seemed to be chasing me. Just as Swift reached out for Meri, she dropped the spear. The shaft bounced up between his legs. The next thing I knew, he and I were rolling on the ground with the spear clattering beside us. For a terrible moment we stared at each other, open-mouthed.

Then I felt myself rising. Timu was lifting me by the back of my shirt. Everyone had gathered around to stare at Swift, who didn't get up until Graylag helped him to his feet. Then Graylag picked up the spear and handed it to Swift who, turning his back on the rest of us, walked stiffly, limping slightly, toward the lodge. "He's hurt!" cried Rin.

Then everyone began to talk at once, gesturing and interrupting each other as they followed him. Although Timu wouldn't relax his grip on my shirt, I managed to twist around in time to see a very frightened Meri steal from behind a little spruce and slowly walk toward us. Elho and White Fox ran to her and caught her arms, although she was coming back without even being called, let alone forced.

Inside the lodge the din was terrifying. "Yanan hurt my half-brother!"

"She burned me!"

"She did it for a wolf!"

"The wolf must be killed!"

"She burned my feet!"

"Timu should have stopped her!"

"Swift forgot himself!"

"She frightened me!"

"He threatened Meri!"

"His betrothed cut all his fingers!"

Above the din I heard myself shout, "She isn't his betrothed! We hate him!"

There was an instant of terrible silence before the noise began again, but now Swift's ugly voice suddenly yelled above the others, "If she has a husband, let him take her outside and beat her with a stick!"

Quickly people began agreeing or protesting, each person trying to drown the others out. Terrified by all that was happening and by what might happen next, I cowered with Meri near the wall. Suddenly Timu stepped toward me and reached out his hand. "Come!" he roared. I clung to Meri. Timu seized my arm. I kicked and struggled as he pulled one way while Meri, screaming, pulled the other way. Then, as he dragged us both toward the door, Meri let go of my arm, threw herself at Timu's leg, and bit him. He gripped her jaw and stared into her eyes. "You wait," he said dangerously. "I'm coming back for you. Ethis! Keep her here." Ethis hurried to catch Meri while Timu dragged me out the door. Many of the others tumbled after us to watch us leave. "Let no one touch Meri," called Timu over his shoulder. "Just hold her. I'll take care of this."

Kicking and biting, hitting Timu with my free hand or catching at bushes, I fought for every step, but Timu dragged me down the trail to the riverbank, not seeming to notice my bites and blows. There, in a sheltered place hidden from sight of the lodge by a clump of willows, he sat on his heels and pulled me down beside him. He looked at me for a moment, then brushed my hair back from my face. "So," he said gently. "Be calm." As I stared in surprise at the change in him, he put his hand on mine. Taking a deep breath, he looked straight into my face and said, "Those mammoth hunters, they are quarrelsome. I liked hunting with them, but I could hardly believe some of the things my eyes saw in their camps. How could I hurt you? Aren't you my wife? Won't you soon sleep in my deerskin?"

"What about Meri?" I asked, out of breath.

"Who will harm her? Not my wife's people. They beat their own kin, but they wouldn't dare beat strangers. Anyway, it's you he wants beaten. You knocked him down. You said you hated him."

"But will you punish Meri like you said?"

Timu looked surprised. "When did I say that? Or do you think me a man who would hurt a child? No, the mammoth hunters are different from us—among the mammoth hunters grown men strike people weaker than themselves. We'll wait until everyone grows calm."

No longer frightened of Timu, I grew angry with him. "Why did you drag me here? You made me hit you, and you twisted my arm!"

"Is this your gratitude?" asked Timu crossly. "Would you rather I left you in the lodge for them to punish you?" He sighed. "We must stop all this trouble now," he added. "We didn't used to have such fighting. Even on the last day you were with us, your father left for his old home rather than quarrel with anyone. Your father lived with us in peace."

We fell silent, my anger fading as I thought of my father and thought what a true thing Timu had said. "Why did you marry one of them?" I asked after a time.

"Ethis is a good woman," said Timu. "You'll come to like her. She and I will have children, and you and I will have children. Our people will be many, and we will live in peace, here or in a new lodge. You'll see."

We heard pounding feet. Someone was running toward us. As we stood up to look, tear-streaked Meri burst through the willows with a hafted ax raised high. "Stop!" I shouted. Timu danced aside just as Meri drove the ax into the earth where his feet had been.

He caught her hand and took the ax out of it. "This must stop," he said. "We're people, not animals. Let's remember ourselves."

More people were running. In a moment Graylag came through the willows, looking very worried. Teal ran right behind him, out of breath, followed by Ethis, in tears. "Meri has an ax," they cried. But Meri was clutching me around the waist, sobbing.

Timu stood beside us, the ax dangling from his hand. "What are we beginning in this lodge?" he asked. "We chase each other, we fight, my second wife's kinsman tells me to beat Yanan, someone gets an ax. We didn't used to talk of beating each other. Even small children would listen to reason. Have we found something so hard that we can't use reason? Or have my wife's people come to command us?" He gestured toward pretty Ethis, who looked dismayed.

"We must talk, but calmly," said Graylag. "Your wife's people mean well. They don't know us yet. We must understand that. And you're right. Reason must command us now."

Timu's father and stepmother leading, I followed him toward the lodge. "Well, Timu," said Teal over her shoulder, "a small child almost chopped your leg with an ax. You should think before you say you'll beat someone. You acted rashly."

"Yes, Stepmother," answered Timu with a sigh.

"The trouble is dying down now, Wife," warned Graylag. "Let's not raise it again." He added, "We hear lions every night now. These screams could draw them here."

But more screaming was to come—when we reached the lodge, we found that while we were all out running and fighting, the wolf had stolen the last scraps of our meat. Now nearly everybody wanted to kill the wolf. Meri began to cry helplessly, until I had to pound her between the shoulders.

Teal clapped her hands, exasperated. "No more talk of killing!" she said. "We've had enough trouble. Three times people have risked their lives for this wolf. Are we to harm a person for an animal? Timu was almost killed because of the trouble. Rin was burned. Swift was hurt. We will stop now. No more."

As there was no food in the lodge, Graylag, Timu, White Fox, and Swift got ready to hunt red deer at the ford far down the river where, when the water is low in the fall, the deer swim across. The hunters took their sleeping-skins as if they would be gone for the night. The rest of the people followed the trail along the terrace toward the bushes where bearberries grew, Meri and I behind them. Just as I was about to go around the first bend of the trail, I heard Graylag call me. Stopping, I looked around. He beckoned me back. I obeyed, with Meri following, and we stood respectfully in front of him. "Take axes," he said, "and go cut a fresh pine tree for the door. You chose this wolf. Don't let it rob us."

So we took axes, crossed the river on its bare rocks, and

went into the woods. Selecting a small spruce that we could cut by sundown, we began to chop. Thinking that we should not return without a tree, we didn't rest in our work, even to gather food. But the tree wouldn't fall until after sundown. We dragged it home, hoping that someone would give us bearberries, but no one had thought to gather any for us and we went to sleep hungry.

In bed Meri started to sniffle. "Stop it! People are tired of your crying," I whispered. "This isn't the first time you've been hungry, and it won't be the last." But before I finished my whisper, Meri fell asleep. She looked small and childish with her lips parted and her hands curled. Who would have thought she was fierce?

◄ 10 ►

THE NEXT MORNING Teal took me and Meri to a place on the river where the bank was crumbled and a deer trail led gradually under water. There she made us strip and scrub with sand. She took out our braids and scrubbed our heads, then ducked us in the current, although the water was now ready for winter, cold enough to freeze. Our mouths were blue and our jaws were trembling, but we managed not to cry, even after Teal looked us up and down as we stood wet and shivering, then made us scrub again.

When I reached for my clothes, Teal said, "Your breasts have grown."

I knew this, but I looked down at myself anyway. Then, trying to move casually, I shook out my trousers and held them ready to step into. But before I could, Teal took them from me and carefully examined the crotch. "Has your menstruation started?" she asked.

Could the stain still show, after so many days? It didn't seem possible. "No, Aunt," I said.

"But it has," said Teal. Pinching the stained place, Teal folded the trousers against herself as if they had become her trousers. Over the top of them she stared at me. My eyes dropped.

"Sometimes a girl doesn't understand the signs," said Teal. "Or she is afraid of her initiation or of lying with her husband. It's good we found out. When this Yellowleaf Moon is full, we must dance so The Woman Ohun will protect you. Then Timu can lie with you if he likes." She paused, then continued: "You come from a strong lineage, a

166

Fire River lineage. If you're afraid of initiation or coitus, you mustn't show it."

"No, Aunt," I said.

"Also, we must sew new clothes for you. Meri can have your old trousers." Teal gave back my trousers. "She can also have your outer clothes. We must make her some new moccasins and a shirt. Yours is too ragged. But for now, wear your own." I put the trousers on. "Graylag has promised a skin," she went on. "You can share it with Meri. Today we will start Meri's shirt and your trousers. Owl will give some prepared leather because you are married to her brother. Timu will also give you leather. Ethis has lots of leather from her wedding portions, and she could give some to you."

I didn't think Ethis would want to share her wedding clothes with me, but again I said, "Yes, Aunt."

Suddenly Teal placed one palm on the trail and held up the other hand for silence. After a moment she whispered, "What now?"

We all felt the trail. Something very large walking on our side of the river was making the ground shake. It couldn't be the deer who owned the trail, as deer step lightly.

"There's nothing here to climb," said Teal quietly. "Unless we want to swim, we'd better leave this place."

We walked up the bank to look around the floodplain. At first we saw nothing, but then, as if we saw a hill where before there had been flat ground, we saw a large mound with birds roosting on it. Soon the mound moved, and we saw that it was not a hill but a very large rhino in winter pelt. As it turned a curve of the trail, we saw at its flank a little rhino, a calf of that spring, with straight hair standing out all over it, like a thistle in the morning sun. The birds rode, their heads still on their loose necks, their bodies slowly jolting.

"A rhino," said Teal. "Now where does she come from and what is she doing here? Have you ever seen one in this valley?"

"No," I said. "Only on the steppe."

"I'm afraid of it," said Meri.

"You should be," said Teal.

"I want to go back to the lodge," said Meri.

"It can shatter the lodge," said Teal.

But we went back anyway, keeping out of sight by following a higher terrace. We didn't want the rhino to see us, lest it think we were its enemies and charge us. When we had gone a long way, we climbed the third terrace, looked down again, and saw, far off, the hairy curve of the rhino's back above the bushes. It wouldn't bother us now, I knew, and by the time we reached the lodge I had almost forgotten about it.

At the lodge Teal and Ina built a dayfire outside the coldtrap door, where they could work on the skins in plenty of light. Meri was sent with Ankhi to gather bearberries, while the rest of us spent the day cutting and sewing a shirt for Meri and a parka for me, using my old shirt as a pattern. We used Owl's flint knife and Ina's greenstone knife, scratching the sharp edge again and again across the deerskin, opening the leather a little every time. Owl and Ina couldn't help regretting the loss of the perfect flint knife given Mother in Meri's first betrothal exchange. "If we had that knife, this work would go quickly," said Owl. But the knife was with Mother in her grave.

"Since Meri is now to marry Swift, the knife would have been given back to White Fox's parents," said Teal reasonably. "We wouldn't have it here. But if our work is going too slowly, why can't the mammoth hunter women help us? Ethis!" she called. "Rin!"

"Hi!" called these women from inside the lodge.

"Bring us your scrapers and knives. Bring us your needles. We need tools and helpers if we want to finish this!"

So Ethis and Rin came outside and began to work on my new pair of trousers, cutting them in the style favored by the mammoth hunters, loose and wide, especially in the seat, with extra space over the belly, where mammoth hunter women sew a panel with a decoration. I thought they would also make the decoration for me, and I liked the idea of having one, but the seat worried me—how would I look dressed in such wide clothes? I could say nothing, though; I could only obey Teal, who gave me the chore of making the shirt ready for its stitches by piercing every hole for the needle. I got myself a flat rock to push against, and struggled all day making evenly spaced holes in the very tough leather by twisting a borrowed stone awl.

Ankhi and Meri came back at the end of the day with Meri's shirt, which she had taken off and tied at the neck and sleeves to make a bag, filled with bearberries. I saw how much she had grown up; last fall she wouldn't have picked a handful of berries without eating them, and now she was helping to feed us all. So much food must be shared, of course, and so we saved some for the men. But Meri had thought of this—she had picked extra so she and I could eat a good meal. We were licking the last sweet taste from our fingers when Graylag and the other men came home with pieces of a yearling fawn they had found swimming in the river while a herd of hinds and other yearlings looked down at it from the far bank. It must have been trying to ford with the herd but had somehow been carried downstream by the current.

The men put the liver on our dayfire. While it cooked, we told of the rhino and her calf. The men already knew, having seen their tracks and dung, and were puzzling over why this steppe animal was in the stony, wooded country by the river.

"It's dangerous," said Swift. "Not natural. On the plains we see plenty of them, but not in this country—they don't like rocks under their feet."

"It could be passing through here," said Timu, "or want to go south across the river. Do you think so?" Timu turned to Swift.

"I think so," Swift agreed, sounding as if he said "thing zo." "It wants to go across but doesn't do it."

"How can we get rid of it?" Teal asked him.

"That's easy," said Swift. "They don't like fire."

"Don't hurt them near the lodge," said Graylag. "Leave them alone. Don't make noise. Don't show them fire. Remember how big they are."

"But they don't like fire!" Swift insisted.

In three days' time, working on the new clothes for part of every day, we made new shirts and moccasins for me and

Meri and new if baggy trousers for me, finished except for the decoration. "Put something on the front," Teal said to me. "The front looks strange without a design."

"But I don't know how. And I don't know any patterns."

Teal shrugged. "Do what you can," she said. "After all, those are your wedding clothes." And so, although I had never watched anyone decorate clothing, I sharpened a stick, blackened it in the fire, and drew a small design on the panel. After working out the design in charcoal, I burned it into the leather. It wasn't very good but it was better than I was afraid it might be. In fact I felt a little proud of it.

"What is it?" asked Ethis doubtfully. Her own clothing was beautifully decorated with many fine stripes, both in scratches rubbed with ashes and in black burns.

"A frog," I said. "Those are its ribs."

Ethis and Ankhi exchanged faint smiles. "Why a frog?" asked Ethis.

I felt embarrassed. I had just happened to think of a frog when I began drawing—that was why—but I didn't want to admit as much to Ethis. Instead I said, "My mother told me that snow and ice can't kill the frog. I chose it for its strength."

Again Ethis and Ankhi smiled. "You know," said Ethis, amused and superior, "the panel of the trousers covers your womb. The decoration tells of your womb. Mine"—and she pointed to the front of her trousers stretched over her pregnant belly—"shows all these feathers for the birds that bring children. When I drew this, I meant to show many children. That's how the people of the Hair River draw decorations." She was mocking me. "But a frog? A frog is poor and thin."

"Never mind the decoration," said Teal, cross because talking takes people's minds from their work. "Yanan, give your old trousers to Meri." Teal was already cutting Meri's old trousers to make a pair of winter moccasins. "Meri is cold. Give her your old trousers and wear your new ones. See how you look in the mammoth hunter's style."

Meri stared at me expectantly, hugging her naked knees. So I had no choice but to step out of my old trousers and put the new ones on.

Right away I knew that they were terrible. The decoration

was ugly, but worse than that, I felt the grip of the legs too far down my thighs. I realized that below my waist, the pants were so broad that they stood stiffly by themselves, not touching my body. In dread I peered around. Sure enough, where the seat should be, a great bag hung.

Everyone looked at me. Stupid, horrid Rin even smiled, as if she liked what she saw. Ethis and Ankhi looked mischievous, and Meri looked surprised. Teal merely ran her eyes over me in her matter-of-fact way, then looked at the sun. "Firewood must be gathered," she said, packing her scraps of leather, her scraper, the needle, the sinew, and the awl into her skin bag. Then she stood up stiffly and walked toward the trail, as usual sure that the rest of us were following.

Our way passed some low rocks sheltered by a few spruce trees at a distance from the lodge—the place where, these days, the men sat in the daytime. Most of them, now back from their hunt, were there cooking the marrow bones of the swimming fawn. I heard them laugh, probably at the sight of my trousers. I wanted to hide. Instead I kept walking, hoping that none of them would speak.

But, "Come here, New Trousers!" shouted Timu.

"Come here, Woman of the Mammoth Hunters! I want to marry you!" called White Fox.

"A woman avder all!" cried horrid Swift playfully in his loathsome accent. "I wan du marry you!"

When the moon rose, instead of sitting inside the lodge with the others, I sat alone by the embers of the dayfire, wondering about my trousers. If I had thought I could get rid of them, perhaps explaining that a hyena had taken them while I was bathing, I would have thrown them away. But Teal would never believe that the loss of my trousers was an accident, nor would anyone give me more leather if I ever treated clothing with such disrespect.

Far away in the west the fiery glow of the sun grew dark red, and the wind lifted, showing how cold the night was going to be. Across the river a distant forest fire put a streak of red and a plume of pale gray smoke into the sky. In time, on the plain above the lodge two lions began calling to each other, one far away bellowing loudly to one nearby, who waited a long time before answering, as if unwilling to answer at all. The far lion had to roar over and over, until its voice grew hoarse and even got a high pitch to it, to get a grunt from the near lion. *How like people,* I thought as I listened. *One begs, another begrudges.*

Inside the lodge Swift and Graylag also heard the lions, and crawled out to hear them better. Only recently, Graylag agreed, had lions come near the Char River. They usually chose deeper valleys with caves, or the valleys of rivers that cut through open plains. Swift and Graylag looked thoughtfully in the direction of the roaring. "I hear two," said Graylag. "Perhaps there are more."

"Not more," said Swift, "just two." Graylag looked at Swift doubtfully, which Swift noticed. "The far lion is a male."

"A male?" asked Graylag. "You can tell from the voice?"

Swift laughed. In his mammoth hunter accent he said, "Not from the voice! From the time it takes the near lion to answer!" Now Graylag shook his head, not believing. "It's true," cried Swift. "A lioness gets an answer quickly." He struck his fist into his palm twice, quickly.

Showing me their moonlit backs, Swift and Graylag sat on their heels to listen to the lions. Soon Owl and Ethis on their hands and knees followed Timu through the coldtrap to listen also. While they cupped their ears to catch the fading roar of the far lion, I compared the cut of Ethis's trousers to the cut of Owl's. Owl, of course, wore our kind of trousers. While the people spoke in whispers about the terrible winter that might come, bringing plains animals far to the south, I decided I could make my trousers look like Owl's if someone would give me sinew to make thread and lend me an awl. And while the people sat in worried silence after the lions stopped roaring but as the night wind moaned in the spruce trees—the voice of The Bear reminding us of winter—I crawled through the coldtrap to beg thread and borrow an awl from Teal.

As begrudging as the near lion, Teal took a long time to answer. "You'll waste sinew and leather by changing the style of your trousers," she said at last. "And what will you wear if your cutting ruins them?"

"Please, Aunt," I begged. "I'll treat them carefully."

Reluctantly she took her bag from one of the antler tines under the roof, and reluctantly she reached into it for her awl and a small length of sinew.

"Use the sinew you pick from the old seams," she said.

Because I didn't want anyone to tease me, I waited while all the people outside crawled slowly back through the coldtrap, but when the way was clear I ducked out to the dayfire, kicked off my trousers, and turned them inside out. There I picked open the seams and with the awl pierced a new row of holes for the needle.

After a while I felt someone near, and raising my head saw Meri sitting quietly beside me, holding a small strip of meat. I thought she had brought the meat for me but out of the night the wolf pup, stealthy because most people stoned him, crept to her, gulped the meat, and vanished in the dark again.

Just as I decided to punish Meri with silence for feeding the pup rather than me, we heard the pup bark sharply. Then we heard a terrible loud snort and a stamping that made the earth shake—something was rushing at us! Suddenly, out of the dark the pup dashed up to us, chased by the young rhino. The pup tried to hide behind Meri but we both leaped out of the way, Meri to the right, I to the left, while the rhino's charge carried it straight between us, past the dayfire and into the dark again.

There the youngster gave a sorry bellow as he found himself alone. From the bushes tramped the mother to the rescue, her huge face, as long and plain as the slope of a hill, swinging anxiously from side to side as she came. She seemed to blame me when she saw me—she gave a terrible snort, and the next thing I knew, I was running headlong through the dark with the huge thing pounding after me, her warm breath like wind on my legs. I dodged. She tried to follow, but she was so big and going so fast that she couldn't turn quickly enough. I scrambled up the little cliff behind the lodge, and before I knew it, I was peering over the edge listening to the rhino's thumping feet and to the people all shouting at once. If I had been wearing my baggy new trousers, my legs would have caught in the extra leather and I might have been killed.

The mother rhino must have charged the lodge—the

shouting people scattered. I heard Swift's voice above the rest, then saw a bright torch waving, heard a thump and a bellow, and saw the young rhino running headlong into the night, a spear waving in his side and his long hair burning like a thistle on fire. The mother pounded after him. Sliding down the cliff, I crept back to the lodge.

The mother rhino had shattered our coldtrap as easily as a man breaks kindling. By the light of the moon we saw that the bones and branches of the walls and the antlers of the roof lay crushed into the meat of our fawn stored at the side of the passageway. Also the rhino had stepped on what was left of the shirtful of berries. A dark pool of berry juice oozed into her footprint, like blood. Owl and Ina were weeping. Teal cried, "How will we mend this before the snow?"

"Be glad the lodge is standing!" said Graylag.

"The rhino will be back to trample and kill us," said Ina. "She knows where we are, and now that you hurt her young one, she hates us."

Graylag turned on Swift, who still held the torch he had used on the rhino. "Didn't I say not to show them fire?" Graylag asked angrily.

The anger didn't bother Swift. "They won't be back," he said, and scornfully tossed his torch onto the embers of the dayfire. "They don't like fire."

Swift was right. The rhinos didn't come back. Although all of us except the mammoth hunters decided to sit outside during the night—I sewing my trousers, the others listening to the distant crying of the young rhino, and all of us sure that the mother would come back at any moment to trample the lodge and whoever was inside—the mother did no more than call out a few times. She seemed to be up on the plain above the valley. "You see?" said Swift before going through the broken coldtrap to sleep. "The fire burned the baby. Now the small one is hurt and the big one won't leave it."

Late at night the other people dozed, but I kept sewing. Toward morning, when the seam was finished and I only needed to trim off the extra leather, I heard hyenas calling *m-m-m-mmwoa?*—their call that sounds like a person asking a question. Then I heard more crying, followed by snorting and pounding. Timu and Elho woke up and looked at each other. The hyenas and the rhinos were having a fight.

Right before sunrise I trimmed the last of the leather and put the trousers on. As I did, ravens called in the sky, then dropped out of the clouds to the plain where the rhinos were. When Timu and Elho saw this, they made the hunter's handsign for carrion.

"Wives!" they called. Ethis and Ankhi came out of the broken opening of the lodge, where they, trusting in Swift's experience, had been sleeping unafraid.

"What now?" asked Ankhi.

"Bring your ax and your knife," said Elho. "Hyenas have killed the young rhino."

The two men with their mammoth hunter women set out for the plain, led by the sight of the ravens. Presently Timu turned back, annoyed. "Yanan!" he called. "Are you going to sit there? Come!" So although I was about to fall asleep, I took my ax and followed. It seemed that Timu meant me as well as Ethis when he called his wives.

Letting the others go ahead of me, I stole a look at my trousers. The seat which once had bagged now fit. Also I could feel the reassuring touch of leather all the way up my legs. The insert with its embarrassing decoration was still there, but I pulled the fringe on my belt to cover it. I felt better, not so ashamed, but I must have been walking too slowly, because Timu looked back impatiently. I touched my nose and mouth in a gesture of apology. He nodded—it was all right—then gave me the hunter's handsign to come carefully.

We climbed the terraces to the plain. Over a rise of ground, on a treeless part of the terrace, we saw the rounded side of the young rhino lying still on the heather. Over him stood his mother, her wide hips toward us, her tail raised. Beyond her, just showing above the heather, four hyenas stretched their necks to look at us. The mother rhino shifted her hips restlessly—she wanted to turn around to see what the hyenas saw but didn't dare take her eyes off them. We sat too, hidden in the heather, and moving very slowly began to pull grass tussocks for their clumps of sod.

The wind blew on my cheek, then veered to blow on the backs of my ears. A moment later, the mother rhino spun around to face us. But though she had our scent, she didn't seem to see us, and though she stamped and snorted threats, she didn't dare to charge. The sight of her rear was a signal to the hyenas who, afraid to lose even scraps to the ravens, anxiously moved closer. The mother turned and rushed them. They scattered, then again drew near.

Time passed. By noon the mother's head and tail were drooping, as if she were tired or were giving up. A raven flew down to roost on her spine. By early afternoon she was moving short distances to feed. Each time she did, the hyenas stole up to her youngster, making her charge back again.

By midafternoon the hyenas were goading her to chase them. When she ran after one, the others would close in on the dead calf. When she ran back, the one she chased would lope at her side. This was heavy work for the hyenas, as the heather was thick and springy underfoot and the day was warm. From time to time they would stretch their necks, looking anxiously at us to see whether we were stealing their food. We laughed to ourselves as we sat comfortably hidden in the heather; taking all the risks, the hyenas were going to tire the rhino for us, even though they seemed to guess what we were planning. Then suddenly one of the hyenas led the charging rhino right toward us—we had to jump to our feet and scatter.

"Hyenas are filth!" cursed Timu as he dodged.

At last the rhino no longer chased the hyenas but stood apart from her calf, on whose corpse ravens were feeding. Perhaps when she saw the ravens she lost hope. The hyenas gathered at the corpse, snarling at each other. We let them eat for a little while, waiting for the rhino to move farther away. When she was at a safe distance, we stood up and walked boldly toward them.

The hyenas looked at us, then threatened us with snarls and showed us all their teeth, hoping to scare us. But people can throw things and hyenas cannot. Timu threw a rock at the nearest hyena. We heard a shriek and a sharp crack— Timu had broken its eyetooth! "You tried to get us killed," he jeered while the hyenas, even the one with the bleeding mouth, watched us cut into the meat. "Now see us! Next time we'll kill you."

Back at the lodge, the people fixing the coldtrap had been able to scrape up some of the trampled venison. This, with some of the meat of the young rhino, we broiled on the coals of the dayfire. Teal was still worried that the mother would attack the lodge again during the night. But Owl and Crane, when they went to the river to fill a waterskin, caught sight of the rhino on the south bank. "She swam," said Swift. "She won't be back." Or as he put it, "wand be bag."

"So you say." Teal poked doubtfully at a broiling strip of rhino meat. "Yet she shouldn't have been here in the first place. Since we knew of no rhinos here before, why are you so sure of this one?"

As if Teal's ignorance were hurting him, Swift widened his strange, sky-colored eyes. "This wasn't good country for her," he explained earnestly. "There are rocks here. She's big. She's heavy. Rocks hurt her feet. She didn't want to be here, but she was, because of the river."

"Because of the river?"

"Of course because of the river!" Swift pointed to the meat of the baby rhino. "His mother came from plains in the north. She was afraid the cold winter coming would kill her little one, and she tried to find good plains in the south. But she found your Char River too deep for her baby. She was afraid he might drown like that one." Swift poked a stick into the broiling meat of the drowned fawn. "Now her little one is killed, she can go across and not come back. The deep river doesn't matter to her." Swift's pale eyes took in all of us around the fire. Then he lifted his chin and proudly said, "I tell you one lion is a male; you don't believe me. I tell you the rhino is afraid of fire; you don't believe me. I tell you she won't be back; you don't believe me. But you should believe me—we of the plains are familiar with plains animals." Since he said "Jar" for "Char" and "blains" for "plains," some of us couldn't help but smile, liking to think we couldn't understand him.

"Timu calls you Wife," said Teal to me early one morning as the Yellowleaf Moon, almost full, was setting. She and I were following a deer trail into the hills, on our way to dig lilies. "He watches you when he thinks you don't see him." I knew this, but I said nothing. Teal went on. "He wants coitus."

This surprised me. "He has coitus with Ethis!"

"Ignorant girl. Coitus would frighten the child Ethis is carrying."

I knew that we say "a stranger in the coldtrap" to show the fear a tiny unborn child must feel when he sees his father's penis before he knows his father's face, but if Teal thought that was stopping Timu, I thought I knew better. Anyway, Ethis's pregnancy barely showed. If a baby was there, it was a small one. "I hear them making the noise in the night," I said.

"I have ears!" snapped Teal. "But there are more ways than having coitus to make that noise. As you'll find out. Look at the west." I looked where Teal was looking, at the rim of the setting moon. "Tonight it is full. Tomorrow we will initiate you. If he lies with you after, it won't harm you."

"I don't want to lie with him," I said.

"Some girls are afraid at first, but the fear leaves with experience. Isn't Timu handsome? Don't you like him?"

Not if it meant being initiated first. "I don't want to be cut," I said.

"You mustn't show your fear," said Teal. "The pride of your lineage will be in your care when we cut you. Remember that. If you show pain and fear, people will think that your lineage is weakening and that you aren't ready to bear children. Do you remember how Owl screamed when she gave birth?" I remembered. One night in the lodge, the year before we went to the Fire River, Owl gave birth to her baby with so much fuss that Mother, Teal, Ina, Junco's mother Bisti, and even Yoi scolded her until she wept from the scolding as much as from the pain. "Owl didn't do well," said Teal. "She wasn't ready. Also, Ankhi and Rin will be watching you, and your co-wife Ethis. Also Meri. Do you want to shame yourself? Or do you want to set a good example for Meri and show the mammoth hunter women how it's done?"

But I was afraid to bear children. Mother understood

childbirth and was ready for it, yet she died of it. So did her baby. After all Owl's painful labor, her little boy had died too. What good was it all doing? "I'm too young," I pleaded.

"Not any more," said Teal.

After we crossed the ridge and found the dry leaves of lilies, which showed us where to dig, we sat on our heels and took our antler picks to the partly frozen ground. I wasn't cold but still I shivered, even in the sunlight on the southern hillside where the lilies grew, even in my new parka.

Teal seemed to understand. Resting her pick, she arranged bulbs in her carrying bag. "Listen to me, Yanan," she said. "I went through initiation and childbirth, even though I was afraid at first and both were painful. Your mother did also. Even my mother, no one less than Sali Shaman, went through these things. I didn't show fear, and neither did they. Neither will you. Don't worry about any of it. These women's things—menstruation, initiation, childbirth—they aren't very difficult and don't need skill or knowledge. They're not like finding food or hunting or building or sewing. They just happen. You need only to keep quiet; all can be done without practicing." Teal smiled.

"But why must I?"

Teal grew serious. "We must. It's The Woman Ohun's plan."

That night the full Yellowleaf Moon rose huge and pink at sunset. All night it lit the sky, and set when the sun was rising. At dawn and dusk on this day we call the sun and moon The Woman Ohun and Her Daughter. When the sun was high again, all the women of the lodge, even Meri, carried two deerskins across the river to a southward trail. It led to a meadow among hills where, under some birches, grew short, thick grass and berry bushes. Red deer used this place for grazing. Because we got there when the sun was high, the deer were lying down, chewing. Reluctantly they rose to their feet—hindquarters first, then forequarters— and moved in two groups over the crest of the hill to rest where we couldn't see them. First trooped the hinds, all together in an orderly herd shaped like a spearblade, with lookouts before and behind. Beside them wandered the stags, each one alone but all moving in more or less the same direction. These stags would soon be roaring and fighting each other, gathering hinds.

We built a fire and stripped off all our clothes, even our ornaments (those of us who had ornaments), even the ties of our braids. Then we shook out our hair and began the Deer Dance. Singing the music, clapping the rhythm, we circled the fire, taking two steps forward, then one step toward the fire, letting our hair fly out over the smoke. Meri and I didn't know the dance at first, or the song either, but before we had gone halfway around, following Owl's scarified haunches, we had learned. We circled for a time, Teal screaming in a high bird's voice, and as I seemed to be just one of the dancers, I began to wonder what this had to do with me.

But in time Teal took my arm and drew me toward the fire. Meri tried to follow me, but Teal pushed her back among the dancers. Then Teal spread one of the deerskins on the ground and told me to lie face down. The women clapped their hands to stop the singing and the dancing; suddenly there was no sound but the wind and the fire, and I felt everyone's eyes on me. Then I knew why Teal had said I would be able to chase away my fear—I could either cry or show the pride of our lineage, like the women before me. Almost gladly I took a deep breath, and with a nice slap of my palms hitting the leather, I threw myself on the deerskin. If I had tossed a necklace or a tool in front of the other women as carelessly as I threw myself, I would have been scolded.

But everyone except Teal and Meri wandered off to pick berries. I saw them squatting naked among the bushes, tossing berries into their mouths. Teal took out a sharp knife and crouched beside me. Worried, Meri sat on her heels by the fire. With only Meri and Teal, by now testing her knife on her thumb, I saw that no one was there to admire my courage.

Presently I felt Teal lift a small pinch of flesh on my hip. I looked over my shoulder. Quickly she drew her knife across the pinch, let go, and gathered up a new bit of flesh beside the first cut. By the time she was making the third cut, the first stung badly. Just as I felt tears coming, Teal whispered,

"Relax now. These are the marks of The Woman Ohun to protect you. Soon they will heal and then grow small." I breathed deeply and tried to think of something besides the pain. When the other women came back from their berrying and began to dance again, I made sure to seem as if I didn't care; resting my chin on my two fists, I watched the struggles of a nest of ants whose home, a stick, had been tossed on the fire.

As the day wore on I grew very cold, lying naked on the ground in the autumn air. The pain was bad, and to feel my blood trickling down the skin of my thighs was frightening. Up my right thigh and hip and down my left moved Teal's knife, slitting bits of skin. Although I could keep my face still, I couldn't lie still, and I began to shiver. After what seemed half of my lifetime, Teal made the last of the cuts, then took warm ashes from the fire and rubbed them into the wounds. This last pain surprised me so much that a cry almost escaped me. I bit my lips and squeezed my eyelids shut to stop the tears.

But that was all. Again I looked over my shoulder and saw the marks of Ohun, the two rows of cuts from the tops of my thighs to the base of my spine, like the rows of scars on all other women, like the rump patch of a deer.

I thought I should get up, but Teal pushed me down firmly. "Stay there," she said, so I did, while she threw the other deerskin over me to cover me completely, even my head. Then I lay under it in the dark, hurting and freezing while the dancing women, Teal among them, stamped the ground nearby.

When next they rested, the women talked lewdly. "An erection like a horse's," said Ethis of our husband, and in my mind's eye I saw Timu standing with his penis extended almost to the ground, like a stallion's.

"It could burst a woman," said Rin.

"A trail is marked for it to follow," said Ankhi, speaking of the scars. "Yanan's vagina can be found in the dark."

Owl, Teal, and Ina laughed at these words but added none of their own. Being Timu's sister, Owl couldn't speak lewdly of him, of course, nor could Teal and Ina, being his stepmothers. And not until the next summer, when I watched the initiation of a girl of the mammoth hunters out on the steppe, did I realize that women always speak lewdly when the rows of scars are made. On the steppe I laughed at the jokes and tried to speak lewdly too. But at my own initiation, because only the mammoth hunter women joked, I thought that they were trying to upset me. Under the cape I made up my mind not to move until Teal called me, and then to stand up smoothly, as if nothing had happened, and to show no feeling but pride. I lay so quietly that Meri asked Teal if I was still alive.

"She's alive," said Teal. "When the moon rises and the last red part of the sun is gone, she'll get up." I heard the women's voices fade, probably as they went to eat more berries.

The wind blew cold near the end of the day. I was hungry, stiff, and shivering. I heard the voices of the women coming back, and then I heard, far away, quail calling as they do on a clear evening when the last red bit of the sun goes down. When Teal lifted the deerskin, I leaped to my feet and brushed off my thighs as if I had, perhaps, just stumbled. Taking no special notice of me, the women danced again, and although I began to bleed, although blood ran down my legs into my footprints so that as I circled the fire I could see where I had been, I danced with them. We sang:

> You who give birth to everything,
> You whose children are all the animals and all the
>   people,
> You whose children are the stars,
> You whose hair burns in the northern lights,
> You who walk naked in the snow,
> Don't take our lives when we give birth.
> Let us give birth easily, as the deer give birth.
> Let us walk away from that place without injury.
> Don't kill us.
> Let our children be strong
> Like the deer's children.
> Let them soon walk behind us in health.
> Don't kill them.
> Give us life, Ohun.
> Give us children.

"Well," said Teal when the song was over, "I'm cold." The dance circle broke; in the fading light we went to get our clothes. Trying to dress as easily as I would after a bath, I pulled my trousers over the scars of Ohun, and then, still with no expression on my face, I put on my shirt and braided my hair.

"Good," said Teal as we took up the trail. "No crying. Well done. Now you're different."

◄ 11 ►

PEOPLE OFTEN TOLD the story of the earliest men, Weevil and Wolverine, and The First Woman, Mekka. When Weevil met The First Woman at his summer hunting grounds, he didn't know how to make love to her. Just then Wolverine came along and told Weevil that the woman was meat. Weevil built a fire to cook her, then killed her with his spear. He cooked and ate her, offering some to Wolverine. "That's your wife you're eating," said Wolverine. "None for me. I'm not a cannibal." Weevil got so angry he threw the hipbone at Wolverine. The hipbone struck a rock, shattered, and in its place stood The First Woman with her back turned. She bent over and looked at Weevil between her legs, singing:

> Husband fight your wife!
> Wife fight your husband!

Suddenly Weevil's left hand reached out and struck his right hand. His right hand picked up a stick and beat his left hand. His left hand reached for the ax, but the right hand snatched it and threw it far away. The left hand grabbed a brand from the fire and burned the right hand, but the right hand grabbed the left hand around its neck and choked it until it turned blue. When it seemed that the two hands were going to kill each other, The First Woman sang again:

> Husband, stop fighting!
> Wife, stop fighting!

Now Weevil's hands let go of each other and collapsed on their backs, exhausted. "How unhappy I am," said Weevil. "If my hands keep on fighting, I will starve."

"Clasp them together," said The First Woman. So Weevil clasped his hands. "When they are clasped, they can't fight," said The First Woman.

And Weevil saw that this was true, not only of his hands but of a husband and wife also. So Weevil and The First Woman clasped each other, and after that Weevil knew that The First Woman was there not like an animal to be killed for food but to make his heart glad and to make children.

One night soon after my initiation someone shook me very gently, and I woke up. But for the sound of people breathing and the murmuring voices of Owl and Teal talking from their beds near the embers of Graylag's fire, the lodge was quiet and so dark that I could barely make out the shape of someone crouched beside me. As I tried to see who it was, my skin suddenly prickled. A man! He was large, a faint man-smell came from him, and although I couldn't see him, I heard him breathing and knew he was facing me. Then his warm hand, dry and rough as antler, circled my upper arm, slipped down, and clasped my wrist. I shook Meri, who stirred in her sleep, while the man's hand moved down my arm to my hand, which he lifted and stroked. He spoke. "Come."

It was Timu. Although his voice was very soft, almost a whisper, at the sound of it Owl and Teal fell silent and tossed a few sticks on the fire. In the very faint light I saw that Timu was naked and that his eyes were looking into mine.

Beside me, Meri sat up suddenly and threw her arms around my neck. Carefully Timu lifted them away, folded her hands together, and placed them on her chest. Then, pulling the deerskin over her, he closed her eyes with his thumbs. "Be peaceful, Sister-in-Law," he whispered, soft as breathing. Her eyes flew wide, but she didn't try to stop him as he took my upper arm and pulled me to my feet.

I still remember the clasp of Timu's hand—strong and warm, with pulses in it. I remember realizing that he must have waited for the right moment to come for me, when nobody was sitting by the fire to eat or talk or get warm, when the lodge was dark and everyone was lying down.

Walking very slowly, silently, Timu led me around Swift and Rin in their deerskins by the door, around Elho and Ankhi lying together in the middle of the lodge, around Crane and his wife, Owl, who had tactfully covered her face with her deerskin, around Ethis, alone, quietly curled on her side, around Graylag, asleep between his wives. At his own bed Timu sat on his heels and drew me down beside him, then wound an arm around me, rolled on his side, and pulled his deerskin over us completely, covering even our heads.

Because Teal had praised me for bravery when my scarification was made, I had since tried to walk proudly, without flinching, saying nothing about the soreness and itching caused by the cuts. Then I saw that Timu might have taken my silence to mean that the cuts had healed. What good had my bravery done me if it had led me to this? Would there be a baby? I didn't quite understand what was going to happen next, but I knew I wasn't ready for it. I knew if he hurt me, I might not be able to keep still. What would Teal think of my crying? Or any of the people? Swift and Rin, no better than strangers, would laugh at me.

Just as I opened my mouth to speak, Timu ran his palm over my hip. It hurt! I gasped. He stopped; then, wrapping his arm loosely around my arms, his leg around my legs, he put his lips right on my ear so that only I could hear him and said, "Don't be afraid. Don't fight. This is good, not bad, you'll see."

Suddenly my throat tightened painfully as he began to rub my body from my belly to my throat. "My scars," I whispered.

His face hidden in my neck, Timu stroked my belly with his rough, dry hand. What is happening to me? I wondered; then I heard him whisper, "Will I stop?" I felt the tickle of his breath as he waited for my answer, and as I might feel the earth tremble faintly with the footfalls of a large, advancing animal, I felt his heart. And I tried to answer, but by now my thoughts were darting and hiding like siskins in a forest, and although I could tell that my scars might still bother me a little, by now I didn't care.

Once after I became a spirit, when the Moon of Walking was a crescent but the cold was still so strong that the northern lights hissed like burning spruce needles, Teal tranced to beg for meat. The deer, instead of gathering to start their northward journey to the plains, were scattered through the open woods on the south side of the river. Time and again hunters had gone after them but couldn't find them. Other animals were coming from their wintering places; just that evening a white owl hen floated softly overhead, followed later by another hen, as if the white owls had their own trail in the sky.

Because the shaman promised us a fine reward of fat if we found deer, Marmot soberly agreed to try. But then, instead of taking the form of an animal who hunts widely, like a raven or wolf, or even an animal who hunts by day, since the night was almost over, he took the form of a white owl cock. Rising into the air, Marmot mantled for a moment on the highest tine of the antlers on the roof, then flew silently into the dark in the direction taken by the hens.

A white owl cock! I thought. *What selfishness!* Yet in the lodge below, the people sang a song in praise of Marmot. It made me sad. I tried to brush away this feeling, thinking, *How easily fooled the people are; if they're hungry, they deserve to be.* But after listening a little longer to the sincere, uplifted voices, I slid off the roof in the form of a wolf, nosed for a moment at the people's sparse refuse lying on the snow, then made for the south side of the river.

As I was scrambling up the last sloping terrace of the far bank, dawn came, and in the light I saw ahead of me the silhouette of a large wolf against the sky. He saw me before I saw him, and poised in midstep with his forefoot lifted, he looked straight at me, his gray face in shadow, with the fur around his head lit from behind. Carefully we approached each other, and realizing that we didn't know each other, we tried to circle each other slowly so we wouldn't too quickly get too near.

Soon he cautiously stretched his nose toward my hindquarters, making me tuck my tail, while his own tail, which at first he carried straight out behind him, he lifted into the air. I found a strong, crisp, male smell about him, but it was not completely unfamiliar—he was a young wolf from the large pack who lived in the hills where the Char rose. I had noticed his sign and heard his voice many times before.

In a moment we were frisking. We dropped to our elbows, bounced, danced, nipped each other's ears and faces, and worried each other's necks until I knocked him with my hips and dashed away. He chased me! I lost him! Then I spied him crouched behind a bush, his ears pricked, his yellow eyes bright, and as I turned to run he sprang at me.

All day we played. Late in the afternoon we ate some snow, then stretched out full length in an open glade, back to back, our fur touching. We lay in the last patch of sunshine, and when it faded and the light in the glade turned blue, we stood up, stretched, and shook out our fur. I kissed his lips. Tenderly he caught my muzzle in his jaws. I had thought we would go hunting, but before I knew it I had turned around to show him my haunches, and looking back at him over my shoulder, I drew aside my tail. He threw his gray foreleg over my back. I braced myself to receive him. We joined. Pulling his hind leg over me he turned around, and in a great steaming cloud of our own panting breath we stood still, our rumps pressed together, our faces lifted, our ears low, our eyes shut.

Ah, how fast my heart beat and how gladness rushed through me! When at last we came apart, we danced and kissed and chased each other, although the woods by now were quiet and dark. And then, our hearts filled with love and happiness, we began our hunt.

We stayed together for a long time, my partner and I, mating, hunting, and playing. Whenever the cold air held a cloud of odor, or when, like smoke, a scent of dung or footprints crept up from the earth, we would look at each other to learn what the other thought. Together we followed promising odors and covered bad odors with snow.

One day we hunted up and down the south side of the river until we found a hind who was thin from winter and weak from the swarm of ticks we noticed under her falling winter hair. Sick as she was, it took us most of the afternoon to get her down. Even after we backed her into a thicket, she kept us dodging her terrible kicks by making us keep our eyes on the tip of her nose—where we were ready to grab her—and on her clubbing feet.

Afterwards I realized that a tigress was watching us from the cover of some trees. When the hind broke and ran, with us right behind her, trying to bite her haunches to make her bleed, the tigress must have followed, but we were still too busy to notice. Not until I bit the hind through her nose and my partner bit her rear ankle, not until we stretched her out and wrenched her over so that she crashed down on her side, did I see, out of the corner of my eye, a big striped form slipping among the trees. The tigress! Then a gust of air blew toward me and I smelled her. My hair rose as my heart sank. I tried to get a better look, but my teeth were so deep in the hind's neck that my cheeks were wrinkled up around my eyes—I seemed to see everything over the top of a hill. The hind may have seen the tigress, though; suddenly she bellowed and began to kick harder than ever, snapping my head from side to side. I had no chance to look around for anything.

By the time the deer lay still and our stomachs were hoping for the meat, I remembered the tigress and turned to see her calmly walking toward us. She stared hard at us with her frightening yellow eyes until a big rush of fear made my legs jump, taking me straight over the carcass and off at a run with my tail tucked. My partner followed. At a safe distance we watched the tigress calmly lie down and, as if it was her habit, lick the carcass before eating. We who had done all the hunting and taken all the bruises got no food from our hard work except for a few bites we snatched and the drops of blood on our fur. When we licked the blood off ourselves, our meal was over and we had to hunt again.

Two of us were too few—we knew that. Many of us might have been able to stand off a tiger; many of us could easily pull down another deer. The forest was alive with red deer and roe deer, or so it seemed to us, but we weren't able to start them bleeding. They ran too fast or stood at bay, their backs in thickets. We ate hares and voles.

We followed the river upstream to find a place for a den, a hole that someone had already started and that we could make bigger, because the ground was frozen. We needed to live by water so we could drink and so we would have a way to keep our pups from following us. In my mind's eye I saw myself leaving the den with pups stumbling after me until I crossed the water, so they couldn't follow but had to wait on the bank until I came back. On a sandy hillside we found a hole started by hyenas, too wide for us and too shallow, but since the frozen earth at the bottom of it crumbled easily, we began to dig it out. When it was deep we lay at the mouth with our bellies against the cold, loose earth, rolling out our tongues to cool ourselves. In my mind's eye I saw ourselves next winter, with the pups almost grown and our pack larger.

At dusk the full moon rose. We nosed each other's faces, our tails waving. Again we were ready to hunt! Before we left the den we sang together, softly at first, then with all our hearts, finishing with yells that warmed our blood and filled our heads with triumph.

During the many days that I stayed on the south side of the river with my partner wolf, I never thought of the lodge or the people. As if I had never known them or they had never been, I had no plans to go back. Then one day in early spring we came upon a very strange object: the leg of a hare alone by itself, with no hare attached to it, dangling in a cloud of human scent in an empty space just at head-height above the trail. My partner wolf touched the hare's leg with his nose, then took it in his teeth, and suddenly he flew up to hang in the middle of the air, his feet wildly thrashing. I was so frightened I dashed away to hide in the woods, only to creep back much later, my hair on end. Horrified, I saw him still struggling weakly, hanging in a cloud of his own musk mixed with the smell of his semen and feces. I waited anxiously, but he didn't come down again, and after dark, when the moon rose, I smelled hyenas, so I crept away while a gang of hyenas, chuckling and pushing each other, tugged down his body and cracked his bones.

One last time I crept back to where he had been. Now the earth was all soaked with the stench of hyenas, and no trace remained of my partner wolf but tufts of fur. There was no reason to stay longer, but I didn't want to leave. I stayed nearby for most of the night, and when the sky in the east began to turn pale, I thought I saw his gray face looking at me from a cluster of low spruce trees. Filled with joy, I ran toward him, but after all he wasn't there, nor had he left footprints or a trace of scent. I called, letting my voice go high and loud with a tremble in it, but no one answered.

If I had stayed in the forest, what would have happened to me? Would I have given birth to a litter of pups? One lonely day I fell asleep on a south-facing rock all gray with lichen and silver with mica, a rock that even after dusk still held the warmth of the sun. While I was asleep I dreamed of hunting horses with Timu, and I awoke in human form. The ragged, waning Icebreaking Moon shone between the branches of a spruce tree, and by its light I began my hike back to the lodge on the Char River. I walked all night, as frog song leaped in bursts from the edge of the water, and all the next day, as flocks of calling ducks beat the air around me on their flights in and out of the reeds. When I reached the lodge, Marmot asked me where I had been for so long and why I had walked back in the form of a woman rather than running in the form of a wolf or flying in the form of a raven, and I looked at him scornfully because I didn't want to answer. "What for?" I said.

After I began to sleep with Timu, I became impatient for night to come while at the same time I was anxious all day to be near him. I tried to sit beside him at the dayfire when he scraped a hide, or at least to be within sound of his voice. Hearing him laugh made me laugh. The cloud-ribbed sky made me think of his ribs or the roof of his mouth. I wanted to do everything to please him, and at last saw why some women try to do as their men say.

I was jealous of Ethis and her pregnancy, even though it meant that Timu slept with me. But he would sleep with me anyway, I thought scornfully. I remembered how when we were children I used to try to get him scolded or to shame him or make the other children laugh at him. What ignorance! What had I known about love?

When Timu went hunting with his half-brother, Elho, or his sister's husband, Crane, I took Father's spear and followed them. Why not? I was strong, a fast runner, and good at stalking. One day I wounded a roe deer, which Timu finished killing with his spear. Timu then said that he and I were enough for a hunting team.

So we hunted far and wide together, sometimes stopping at midday to make love, if the frost was not too heavy and we found a good place. I would kick off my trousers and drop to my hands and knees on the smooth, golden leaves of a birch grove or on the rough, sun-warmed needles of a spruce grove, and smile at him over my shoulder. Afterwards we would carefully pick the birch leaves or spruce needles from each other's hair. We thought that if people could guess what we did, they would laugh at us.

But we didn't kill anything and in fact seldom ever saw game. Perhaps my mind was not on food but only on Timu, and if his mind seemed on anything but me, I would tease him until he chased me. On one such day, although he quickly caught me and threw our trousers onto a wormwood bush, he seemed thoughtful. No matter how we tossed about, he seemed to be searching the plain with his eyes. And as soon as we were done he took his firesticks and started a brush fire. Annoyed, I asked why. He answered that here follows-fire grass would most likely grow next spring to lure grazing animals. Giving me a tuft of heather as a torch, he told me to drag the flames a long way so that the field of follows-fire would be very large. Then I went one way, setting fire, while he went the other, and when we were far apart the wind suddenly flamed the wormwood bush with our trousers. Too late we ran back. Timu's trousers were burned.

"Why must you always make love? Now see what's happened!" he cried angrily, pulling on the trousers even though one leg was black and shorter than the other.

I was angry too. "Did I put your trousers there? It's you who started the fire!" I shouted.

In angry silence we strode back to the lodge. The people, who had seen the fire in the distance and were waiting for us, noticed the burned trousers at once. "What happened to your clothes?" they cried.

My co-wife Ethis looked startled, then sullen. "I made his trousers," she reminded everyone.

Swift laughed, showing all his teeth. "Ha-ha!" he cried. "Where was your leg when your pants burned?"

Then everyone laughed, or so it seemed while I stared at my feet, my braid between my breasts. When I remembered to show pride as Teal had taught me, I raised my chin and threw my braid between my shoulders. Then I saw that Meri and Ethis weren't laughing but were staring at me, Meri anxious, Ethis jealous, and that Graylag wasn't laughing but was staring at Timu, furious. "Are you a child to take a woman hunting?" he roared at Timu. "Don't we need hides? Don't we need meat? Do you expect us to hunt for you while you play with your wife?"

Timu looked coldly at his father. "I'm trying to teach her to hunt. Is that playing? Are we so many that we don't need her help this winter?"

"The next time go with a third person," said Graylag. "Go with Swift or me, to keep your mind on your work."

Timu's face darkened, but his expression stayed the same. "Gladly," he said at last. "I thought you and Swift hunted together because of your age. I'm glad you feel I won't walk too fast for you."

Graylag's face turned red and his eyes grew round. "Am I slow like a woman?" he asked, leaning as if to take a step toward Timu. "Am I to be insulted by my own son?"

"Will we fight, Father?" asked Timu. "If you will, I'm ready."

But by now everyone was shouting at once. "Don't fight!"

"Respect your father!"

"Graylag shamed his son."

"Timu can't help his anger!"

"Timu talked back!"

"Graylag is right to be angry."

"Please, good friend, sit here with me a while."

"Please, Brother, come sit with me."

"Please, Husband, don't lose your temper."

"Are we animals, to fight?"

Slowly Graylag and Timu were persuaded to sit at opposite sides of the men's dayfire, Graylag with Swift, Timu with Elho, so the two could relieve their feelings by talking about each other but not to each other. I sat with the other women at our dayfire, where we cracked pine nuts as gently as possible while secretly listening to the men. I was astonished to hear them settle the quarrel by finding fault with me. "Yanan is always begging," Owl's husband, Crane, explained to Swift. "My wife was the same. It happens when girls are new to coitus."

Swift agreed. "Women keep after you. Graylag knows it." Groping in his hunting bag, Swift found a squirrel and laid it on the fire. "Small, but a bite for each man here," he said seriously. "A little food helps anger go away."

It was all too much for Teal. Dropping her pretense of cracking pine nuts, she stood up. "Do you say that Yanan is to blame for Timu covering her and covering her? He was having her before her Woman Ohun scars had scabs on them. You insult me and my lineage when you insult my kinswoman."

The men all turned to look at us indignantly. We stared back. As so often happens, what started as a quarrel between two people was spreading to become a quarrel between the women and the men. "It's lucky for Timu that coitus isn't food," I said to the circle of women, trying to sound spirited, not stiff. "He would die if he got no more food." The women laughed and cheered, looking over at the men's fire to be sure the men didn't miss it. Angrily the men stared back.

And so passed the afternoon and evening, the men not sharing the squirrel with us and we not sharing the pine nuts. Of course the squirrel was very small and we had a great many pine nuts, but our feelings were hurt all the same.

By morning there was no question of Timu hunting with me. While I was still inside by the fire, before I could crack a handful of pine nuts for myself to give me strength for the day, Timu went away with Crane. I found their tracks in the frost. Elho and White Fox seemed to be thinking of hunting—Elho was knocking tiny flakes from the edge of his spear while White Fox looked on—but I had no thought of going with Elho and White Fox, even if they wanted me. Nor did I want to stay at the lodge today, as Swift and Graylag were working a hide by their dayfire and showed every sign of staying. So I decided to go hunting by myself, and went into the lodge for Father's spear. I lifted it. It was, as always, very heavy. I would, as always, have trouble throwing it.

But then an idea struck me. Today I would use a lighter spear to see if my aim improved. In fact I would use a boy's spear, White Fox's, with burned and sharpened ivory for its point. White Fox could use Father's. When I brought Father's spear to White Fox, he gladly agreed to exchange, and I soon found myself crossing the river on the ice, the little spear balancing lightly and perfectly between just two of my fingers. In the heavy frost, reindeer tracks led everywhere. I began to look about for sets made during the night.

It wasn't to be easy, I saw. Although I found tracks, the frost was melting around them, making it hard to tell which tracks were fresh and which were stale. Father could have done it, Graylag or Timu could have done it, and I could have done it if the tracks had been in mud. But tracking an animal in frost was something I didn't do often. I wondered how to begin.

In time I noticed Meri's wolf following me. This was no surprise; he often followed me or Meri whenever we went somewhere. I don't know where he hid himself the rest of the time—we seldom saw him around the lodge anymore—but as soon as either of us set foot on a trail, he seemed to come from nowhere. Right away he chose one set of tracks and followed his nose after them. Off we went, the north wind in our faces, into the lichen-hung woods. The animal, a reindeer doe walking by herself, turned south as if to go into the range of low hills, but where the tracks turned, the wolf stood still and looked north, back toward the river. *This can't be,* I thought; but the wolf's ears were pricked, and he trembled a little as he stared into the woods. *He knows something,* I said to myself, changing my grasp on the spear so I could throw it.

Carefully, quietly, I eased myself through the little trees, and sure enough, a doe was hiding among them, her ears alert. The wolf, I saw, was very interested, his head forward, his eyes wide, and his nose pointing. He surely saw her, and knowing he was about to rush her, I balanced the spear and threw.

The wolf sprang almost as the spear left my hand. As the doe leaped with the spear in her neck, the wolf grabbed her by the hock. I ran to them, groping for the knife in my belt. My spear had missed her windpipe and the big veins—it shook in her neck, then dropped before I reached her, but when she tried to run the wolf jerked her backwards so she suddenly sat down.

That was all the time I needed. Forgetting the knife, I snatched up the spear and jabbed it through her ribs. With a bleating roar she tried to struggle up again, but the wolf held fast, and I threw myself full length on top of her. Her brown eye was not a hand's breadth from my eyes. I looked down into it, saw it swimming with terror, then saw her eyelid flutter and her pupil glaze. But just in case, I took my knife out anyway and cut her throat.

Well! I should do something with this reindeer, I told myself, but all I could think was that I, in no time at all, had found and killed meat all by myself while the unlucky men had been trying for days but had caught nothing. So much for Timu teaching me to hunt! I'd get him to help bring the reindeer home, and then I'd teach him to hunt! I could hardly wait to see him.

The whole hunt went through my mind again—the tracks, the browsing doe, the spear, the strike, the awful bellow! I looked the doe up and down, and saw that the wolf had torn a flap of skin from her haunch and was gulping meat. Perhaps I hadn't exactly killed her all alone; the wolf had helped. I knew the people would be angry when they saw the bites he had taken, but planning to think of some explanation, I let him eat for a while.

Suddenly I thought I heard something behind me. I looked, and saw a large brown animal half hidden in the trees. A hyena! Of course. Perhaps he was also hunting the doe. Surely he would have heard her bellow. Was there only one hyena? Usually they hunt in groups. I wondered what would happen if I now skinned the deer and cut up the carcass. Would the hyena fight me for her? One hyena I could manage. If there were many, I wasn't sure. I would hate to come home having killed a reindeer which I then lost to some hyenas! If the people would mind the wolf having a few bites, how furious my losing the carcass would make them.

I looked at the wolf. Would he help? I didn't think so. He was standing by the doe as if thinking of showing his teeth to the hyena, but his ears were low and his tail was tucked—he was also thinking of running. Suddenly the hyena whooped. Was he calling others? The wolf must have thought so, because he turned and ran. I looked at the hyena. He faded behind a spruce thicket, but since he didn't come out again, I knew he was still there. Perhaps this meant that he was alone.

In case it did, I took off my belt, tied it around the doe's antlers, and began to pull. She moved, but very slowly. Pulling her home would take the rest of the day. I saw I had no choice but to cut her in pieces and put the pieces as high as I could into trees, the way I used to keep food from the wolf at the Marten River. But first I would have to skin her. With White Fox's spear I stabbed a hole in the tough hide over her pubic bone, then I crouched, and with an eye on the hiding place of the hyena, I took my knife to her belly.

I had hardly slit the skin when the hyena cantered from behind his cover and off among the trees. Something had scared him. I turned. Elho was coming up behind me very quietly.

Without a word he took out his knife and bent his long body to skin one of the legs. "Graylag should let Timu hunt with you," he said when the leg was finished. "How can one person carry so much meat?"

These words pleased me very much, but still embarrassed by the burned trousers, I didn't want to talk about hunting with Timu. "Did you see the hyena?" I asked him.

"Yes," said Elho, "and the wolf too."

The wolf? The wolf had left long ago. "Were you following me?" I asked.

Elho hesitated. "No one likes to hunt alone," he said at last. "I decided to come to help you."

Did he? "Before you went to the mammoth hunters you never worried about me," I said. "You used to help my aunt in the woods, though, didn't you?"

Elho showed his white teeth. I smiled too. "We were children then," he said.

"And now we're not children. Not since Teal took us out in the woods and told us the story of our kinswoman Sali."

"Now we're married and getting children," he agreed.

Getting children? "You and Ankhi, perhaps," I said.

Very serious, he waited, looking down at me. "Or you and Timu," he said softly.

I looked at Elho's chest, then at his shoulders, then up at his sunlit face. He certainly was handsome. No wonder my Aunt Yoi had once let him call her "wife."

What was I doing, talking about getting children? Why was I letting Elho stand so near? I took a step backwards. "Me and Timu? When I get a child, I'll tell Timu, not you. I'm not my Aunt Yoi, to spoil my lineage. I remember the story of Sali Shaman, if you don't. If you've forgotten, go ask your mother to remind you."

Elho wasn't listening. Although I hoped I spoke a little sharply, his serious expression didn't change. "Yanan," he said gently. I didn't answer, but I waited, not breathing. "Every night Timu has you. I hear you together and I envy him. And he has you while he hunts with you, the most beautiful of all the women. I want you too."

Far off in the woods I heard a jay. A pulse beat in my throat, and for the shortest moment I stared hard into Elho's eyes. Then, "For shame!" I said, as if I couldn't imagine such a thing. "What will people think when they find us in the woods here? If you came to help me hunt, help me with this carcass. I remember everything our mothers told us, that night in the woods when the tigress came. I care what people say, if you don't!" Seizing the doe by an antler, I jerked the corpse between us to rub out my tracks.

Elho gave me a long look. *Another time,* his eyes said. Then he turned to the carcass in its new position and started to skin another leg. "Go back to the lodge and get someone to help carry this," he told me.

I ran. When I heard the river, I stopped. With amazement I saw I was obeying like a child. And the deer was mine! Elho, not I, should have gone to find the others. I wanted to go back and insist that he go and I stay, but it was too late now. He would laugh to see me angry, and might even take my going back as a signal that I had changed my mind. So, hating myself when I should have been proud, I trudged to the foot of the terrace.

There I looked up at the lodge. It was good I came when I did. Graylag, Swift, and Timu were looking down at me from their places at the dayfire. While they watched me climb the terrace, I felt as guilty as if Elho and I really had made love instead of simply thinking about it. When I reached the top, Timu asked me, rather scornfully, "Have you finished your hunt so soon?"

"Yes," I said.

He looked surprised. "Did you find a carcass?"

"I have meat," I said carelessly. "You'd better help me get it if you don't want hyenas to eat it."

"Eat what? A reindeer?"

"A reindeer doe. A yearling."

"Did you kill it?" asked Timu.

"With this," I said, holding up White Fox's spear. And I turned around and walked off, not looking to see who was following.

When I heard their feet behind me on the trail, I knew the three of them were following. Too late, I saw I should have mentioned that they would find Elho there. As we came near the carcass, they noticed his tracks. "Elho?" said Timu curiously. "Is Elho here?"

"Yes," I answered, as carelessly as I could. "Did you think I left a carcass for the hyenas? You wouldn't wait for me this morning. If no one came along, I would have been all day putting the meat in a tree."

The men said nothing. What were they thinking? That Elho and I had arranged to meet in the woods? Well, they could find out for themselves. I knew better than to keep talking about it.

And they did find out for themselves. When we reached the carcass and Elho, I noticed the three men looking around at the tracks on the ground. Their manners didn't let them crouch down to look at the tracks closely; rather, they tried to scan the ground casually, looking Elho over as well. He worked away with his knife, innocent as a ground squirrel, stopping only to glance at the others as if to ask why they didn't help, as I was now doing. Timu and Graylag took out their knives.

Swift seemed about to do the same, when suddenly his casual manner changed. Giving a grunt of surprise, he looked at the ground with a puzzled, intent expression. Then he began to quarter the space around the deer, then circled us twice, then backtracked me and disappeared among the trees. Timu and Graylag got to their feet. What had he seen? Just in time Elho remembered to get up too. The men were about to follow Swift when he suddenly hurried up to us, rather excited. "Yanan!" he said. "That wolf of yours, he helped you! Did you know it?"

Of course I knew it! Swift treated us as if we were stupid. But, "Yes, Uncle," I said.

"Come here and see this," said Swift to the other men. They did, letting Swift show them how the wolf had followed the deer's trail, where he must have seen the deer, although the trail led the other way, where he stood when he looked at the deer, and how he rushed it. At the footprints where the carcass lay, Swift showed the splash of blood from the wound and the hip mark where the wolf sat the deer down. He saw the hunt exactly.

Graylag and Timu were interested, and Elho pretended to be. But he knew better than to seem surprised—Swift of course found his tracks too. "You saw this!" said Swift.

"Not all of it," Elho admitted. "I came too late to see all of it."

Swift had forgotten any question of wrongdoing. "I want to see it. Yanan! Next time we hunt, I want to go with you." Of course this sounded different in his ugly accent: "I wa ndu go wi dyu."

While we butchered the carcass, Swift asked me many questions about the wolf. Had I known what the wolf would do? Had the wolf known what I would do? While we carried the meat home in single file, I tried to answer the questions Swift called over his shoulder. This wolf had never helped me, I said to Swift's back, but several times his mother had tried to make me help her. Swift must have been listening very carefully. When we were at the lodge, stuffing the meat into the coldtrap, he repeated some of my answers to be sure he remembered what I had said.

The rest of the people fed the fire and got ready to cook the meat. No one cared about the wolf now—everyone waited for me to divide the carcass. Timu helped me, since making a division was something new to me. I had to be sure that my in-laws got the best parts—the hind parts —while making sure that my kin got even shares of the front parts. And Timu didn't act as if the carcass was his, either. In fact he seemed rather proud of me. He made tactful suggestions rather than insisting, and he nicely covered the only real mistake I made—treating White Fox as Meri's betrothed and Swift merely as my co-wife's kinsman—by apologizing as if he had made the mistake himself.

As soon as each piece of meat in the coldtrap had an owner, we cut the liver into strips and laid them on the coals. As we did, a thought came to me. We had just divided the meat as if there were only one hunter. But if there are several hunters, the meat must of course be divided differently. The hide, for instance: the hide belongs to a sister of a single hunter, but if there are many hunters, it belongs to the oldest hunter's wife. If it hadn't been for the wolf, I wouldn't have been able to bring down the doe, and I might not even have found her. I wasn't a single hunter after all—I was one of a pair, and the hide, which now belonged to my sister, should really belong to Ethis, since I was a woman and didn't have a wife, only a co-wife.

No one else seemed to think of this, so I forgot about it. I wanted Meri to have the hide anyway, and I was more interested in Timu, glad that he was pleased with me. No one else wanted to think about the wolf at all, except to be sure that he kept out of the coldtrap. When I told about the hunt, the men were much more interested in the fact that there were a number of reindeer tracks so close to the river. That seemed odd to them; they had been looking for reindeer in the hills. Only Swift was still very interested. Several times he told the other men what he had learned from the pattern of the wolf's tracks and mine as we followed the deer, and from what I had told him afterwards. When no one showed much curiosity, he sat back to think. "Where is your wolf?" he at last asked Meri. She looked around for the wolf, didn't see him, and shrugged. She wouldn't have told Swift even if she had known. "Yanan! Where did the wolf go?" called Swift over the heads of all the people around the dayfire, waiting for the liver.

"He may be looking for scraps where we cut up this meat."

"That's right," said Swift. "I'm going to find him." And standing up, he took his spear.

"Don't touch him!" shouted Meri. "He's mine!"

Swift laughed. "I'm not going to hurt him, Little One. I want to see him, that's all." So Swift went off to look for the wolf, which puzzled the rest of us a bit. But as soon as the liver was cooking and ready, we were too busy filling our stomachs to give the wolf another thought.

Swift came back that night after the rest of us were rolled in our deerskins, I in Timu's again. Trying to control his breath, Timu was stroking the inside of my thighs while waiting for everyone else to fall asleep. When Swift called my name, Timu put his other hand over my mouth so I wouldn't answer. But Swift didn't wait for an answer. "Your wolf has gone away alone," said Swift. "But I want to see him hunting. Next time I will hunt with you."

"What men of meat, these mammoth hunters," whispered Timu.

Before the reindeer was eaten a blizzard came, and with it more reindeer to take shelter in the trees. Snow on the ground was good for us—tracking was easy, and we could walk very quietly. Graylag now had no objection to Timu and me hunting together, so with our spears we started over the fresh snow, wondering if in spite of the cold we could make love by being quick about it and not taking off all our clothes. But when Swift saw us leaving, he came too. He wanted to hunt with the wolf, we knew, and we tried to hide our disappointment. "If it pleases you, Uncle," I dared to say, very respectfully, "let the wolf go alone with you. Then you can watch him better."

"He doesn't want to go with me," said Swift simply. "He wants you." I looked at Timu, who shrugged. To say more would make other people suspicious. Swift and I followed Timu across the river, where in time we noticed the wolf trotting ahead of us, looking now and then over his shoulder to see if he was right that we were on a hunt. Soon he took an interest in a thicket at the bottom of a hill, and Swift made the hunter's handsign for reindeer. Very quietly we crept forward. Suddenly the wolf rushed into the front of the thicket as a reindeer stag leaped from the back, up the hillside, and away, with the wolf right behind him.

Our stalk was spoiled, and I can't say I was sorry. Now

Swift could see that a hunt could be ruined as well as helped by a wolf, and wouldn't insist on coming with us. I was about to start back when Swift barred my way with the shaft of his spear. "Keep still," he whispered. Far up the hill the stag was turning, trying to keep the wolf from circling behind him, slashing hard at the wolf with his forefeet.

Swift poised his spear. *No one can throw that far,* I thought, but the moment the stag showed us his side I heard the spear hum, then heard a thump and a bellow, and saw the stag totter with the spear in his ribs. The wolf grabbed his nose and pulled him over. Swift rushed up the hill with his knife out, kicked the wolf out of the way, and cut the stag's throat.

Swift and Timu were very happy. Up the hill the wolf watched hopefully while Swift and Timu admired the size of the stag and the amount of fat on him, then sat on their heels and started skinning. "Yanan! Go to the lodge and get someone to help carry the meat," said Timu. What else could I do? I went.

The people hurried back eagerly. When the skin was off and rolled into a bundle and the meat was in packs, the people, singing, carried it home. We even brought the antlers to make needles and awls, so nothing was left to reward the wolf but bloody snow and the rumen. The wolf could eat the snow, I thought, but I doubted he would eat the rumen, since there isn't any meat in a rumen, just the cud of chewed lichen, and I didn't think wolves ate that.

While we were cooking the liver, and Rin, Swift's half-sister, was stroking the long white winter hair of the reindeer hide she now owned, Swift had the attention of all the other men by telling them how much the wolf could help them. A wolf could smell trails better than a person, he pointed out, and hear better too. A wolf always knew where the animals were, since he was out in the woods with them all the time and didn't spend the night in a lodge. And if the animals moved away, a wolf saw where they went. On the plains, said Swift, people could catch the animals themselves, but not in the woods. So how is it, he asked pleasantly, that a man from the plains has to show the men from the woods how to hunt in their own country?

Swift was a man of meat, without a doubt. No wonder

all the men respected him. They didn't even mind his teasing—in fact they laughed cheerfully. And now they all wanted to go hunting with the wolf.

So they tried. Each time two or three of them went hunting, they looked around to see if the wolf was near. He never was, of course—they had thrown too many stones at him. Swift thought that hunting with me would bring the wolf. But it didn't; the wolf knew better than to go near Swift after he had kicked him off the stag. The other men gave up quickly, but Swift kept trying, which annoyed Timu, who didn't like to see me spending so much time with someone else. I didn't like to go with Swift either, and wouldn't have if I didn't know that Graylag really wanted me to. Swift ranged very widely, never stopped to rest or talk, but strode all day so fast I had to run to keep up. And if he saw game, he would leave me behind while he stalked it, sometimes forgetting I was waiting, so I would have to make my way home by myself.

In fact, unless I was alone, the wolf usually stayed away from me too. The men became very disappointed in him. Perhaps he became disappointed in us, after all he got to eat was a rumen full of half-eaten lichen. He preferred the feces from our latrine and the food he stole from the coldtrap. The only person sure to see him was Meri, who told us that he sometimes came to find her when she went after firewood. But Meri on a hunt? Meri still sucked her thumb! It wouldn't have occurred to any one of us, not even me, to take Meri hunting.

≪ 12 ≫

THE STORM MOON that winter brought heavy, wet snow. Many times blizzards kept us in the lodge. Sometimes our firewood ran out, and no one wanted to go for more, so we lay under our deerskins to keep warm. Our food ran out too. Soon after I killed the reindeer doe and Swift killed the reindeer stag, most of the reindeer went over the hills to the south slopes, so we had to travel far to find them. That winter we were hungry, cold, and wet, and the storms gave all of us bad tempers. Sometimes we tried not to speak at all, lest we say something awful. We were afraid we would quarrel and then have to stay close together until spring.

One night at the beginning of the Lodge Moon, Swift gave me a beautiful necklace: my share of the betrothal exchange for Meri. I had no gift to give in return, since I owned almost nothing. However, it didn't matter—even the mammoth hunters must be used to waiting a long time to complete betrothal or marriage exchanges. Reaching out my hands to receive this necklace gave me a very strange feeling, since my mind was set that Meri and Swift wouldn't marry. But I took it, of course. When the betrothal was broken would be the time to give it back. It shames me to remember how much I liked the necklace; each bead of polished ivory must have taken many, many days to shape and drill. And it shone by the fire as if it made its own milky light. I would not get a gift like this from White Fox or his people. Wishing I could keep it, I put it on.

Ankhi's baby was born in the Lodge Moon. The birth must have been easy, or so she made it look—she tried to

205

chat and smile not only when a pain took her but even while she pushed the baby out. The rest of us had nothing to do but keep her company and clean up afterwards. She must have noticed how I had borne pain during my initiation; she kept looking at me lest I miss the fact that she was just as indifferent to pain as I had been, but she was having more pain.

The baby was a little girl. Elho was delighted with her and would play with her by the fire when he sat with the men at night. Everyone else was happy at first, then worried, because hunger took away Ankhi's milk. In the Hunger Moon the baby sucked Ankhi dry time after time, and then we had to listen to its whining. We felt sorry for it, but the crying put our nerves on edge. Ankhi's too: during one night of whining I heard a slap, a silence, and terrible crying. At the fire Elho stiffened, then bit his lips to stop his tongue while Rin went to talk to Ankhi in an angry voice, so low we couldn't hear the words. Ankhi's voice answering sounded like a child's.

By the end of the Hunger Moon I was always tired. When we went for pine nuts, I thought my legs would never carry me to the grove. Somehow they did, there and back too. Sometimes I thought of Mother, wondering why she had bothered to seem always cheerful. Perhaps she really had felt cheerful, and hadn't been pretending, or perhaps she hadn't been as tired as I seemed to be. Unlike her, I didn't care. I wanted to sleep.

Ethis, by now very pregnant, wouldn't share her deerskin with anybody, so every night Timu crawled in with me. Once I would have been happy, but now he made me cross, always running his hand over my body. If I told him to stop, he thought I was teasing and would try to force open my thighs. Once I bit him. Furious, he jumped to his feet and took the deerskin blanket with him to another place in the lodge. This left me with nothing but my parka, not warm, but I slept like the dead.

One night I was kept awake by people remembering the past. They sat around Graylag's fire, blocking the heat from the blazing wood I had walked all day to find. By this time in winter firewood is like food—hard to get, and we are greedy for it. If we find food, we eat too much at once just to be satisfied, and if we get wood, we burn too much at once just to be warm. I was still wet from pushing through the snowdrifts for the firewood, and very cold from lying on the floor, but I was too tired to sit by the fire and too bored by the things people said.

The old people were talking about other old people, and listed all their names. I didn't know any of them. Graylag reminded the others of the winter many people had died, among them his three brothers. It should have made me sad, to think of those who had started our lodge only to die helping others. Instead it annoyed me. Were the old people the only ones who knew about hard winters? What did they think we were having now?

Graylag's talk must have made Swift impatient; Swift said that hard winters could be foreseen, and reminded everyone of how he had foreseen this winter when the rhino and her calf came into our valley for the shelter of trees. Or as he put it, "dreeze."

How I hated Swift's endless boasting about how much he knew! He should be back with his kinsmen, not here making us listen to him. I should have held my tongue, but that night I couldn't. "How can animals know how hard a winter will be?" I asked. "Do they know more than people?" Swift's back was to me, but he turned to give me a long questioning look. I propped myself on my elbow and met his sky-colored eyes. "And what if you did tell us a bad winter was coming?" I asked. "Did you think we could stop it?"

"Yanan!" said Teal, shocked. "Respect our guest!"

"Apologize!" cried Graylag.

But I felt sick and sulky, too tired to think of an apology. Instead I lay down again, saying nothing. After a long, embarrassing wait, Graylag apologized for me. "My son's wife has shamed us," he said.

That stung me. "He talks as if we're stupid, Father-in-Law," I said.

"Stop your tongue!" cried Graylag, openly angry now. "Timu should take you outside and give you a big beating for what you said!"

"Are we like the mammoth hunters? I don't care if Timu beats me or not."

What did I know about mammoth hunters? The only ones I had ever met were right here with me: Swift, Rin, Ankhi, and Ethis, my own co-wife. Now they would guess that the rest of us said certain things about them behind their backs.

A shocked silence fell, and the people at the fire wouldn't look at each other. Graylag glared at me. "Now! Now you will apologize!"

I had said things that wouldn't be forgotten. What had Graylag or the mammoth hunters ever done to me that I should insult them? I was so tired I could cry, and I felt sick to my stomach. After an awful silence, Teal stood up, stepped over some people, and sat on her heels next to me. "Yanan, what's the matter?" she asked. "This isn't right." She felt my cheek. "Are you feverish? Why are you lying in wet clothes?"

"I'm tired," I said. "All day I walked through the snow to get firewood. Now people are burning it as if there was no end of it. Tomorrow someone else can get it. I won't go."

"Timu! Your wife must apologize at once to all of us!" said Graylag in a loud voice.

"She will. She's not herself," said Teal quickly. To me she said, "You'd better apologize." When I said nothing, she looked at me sharply. "If you're tired, sleep! Stop this rudeness! And give me your clothes to dry by the fire." So I gave her my clothes and pulled the deerskin over my head. When the talk at the fire began again, the words were slow and stiff from the insults, but the voices pounded in my ears. Although I was exhausted, I couldn't lie still but turned over and over. Perhaps I really was sick, or just hungry. But what did it matter? Only reindeer bones lay in the coldtrap, with so little meat on them that all day none of us had eaten more than a mouthful. It was the men, not me, that people should be angry with. Where was our meat?

One by one, people were leaving the fire to find their deerskins. In time the lodge grew quiet, and I felt Timu beside me. "What's wrong with you?" he whispered. "Why were you rude? Swift was talking to the people at the fire, not to you. And why were you rude to Father? Now everyone is angry with you. I'm angry too."

"Then sleep with Ethis," I said loudly, sorry as soon as the words were out of my mouth.

Timu sat up. "Must I beat you?" he asked, his voice rising dangerously. "Are you angry from hunger? Do you think you're the only one who's hungry? Do you think you're the only one who's tired? I've been walking all day in the snow. The other men want you to hunt with us tomorrow, or they did until you insulted our lodge. And tomorrow you must apologize to Swift and Rin and Father, and to Ethis and Ankhi too." He lowered his voice again so no one else could overhear. "The last time you insulted Swift, everyone knew I didn't beat you but just took you away. Next time they'll want me to beat you right here so they'll know I'm doing it. And I will. Then we'll all be unhappy. Don't force this, Yanan."

All this talk of beating he had learned from the mammoth hunters. Another time I might have said so, but tonight I felt I had already said enough. "I'm sorry, Husband," I told him. "I'm tired and I don't feel right."

"We're all tired and none of us feels right. Remember that. Don't make trouble in winter."

"I won't," I promised.

"And apologize tomorrow. Take time tonight to think of something fine to say, then say it in front of everyone."

"I will," I said.

During the night the wind brought wet snow down the smokehole, and we heard the voice of a storm. In the morning there was no question of hunting, or even finding much firewood—the snow was blinding. Most of us stayed rolled in our deerskins, going out from time to time to look at the weather or visit the latrine. Since all of us were here and most of us awake, I stood up and in a sincere voice I said, "Last night I insulted our guests and the people of this lodge. I didn't mean what I said, and I'm ashamed and sorry. I ask your forgiveness, although I don't deserve it." I waited, listening for an answer from the silent lodge. But no one spoke. This was the moment for me to offer a gift to

Swift or Rin, perhaps a new pair of moccasins I was making to give to Timu, but I let the moment pass. Then I sat down.

As soon as I did, I knew I should have spoken in a tearful tone or made a gift. Graylag saw this too. Wanting peace instead of fighting, he said, "There is her apology. If Yanan makes no more trouble, we will accept it." He waited, expecting one of the mammoth hunters to agree with him. But no one did.

Then Teal tried. "Yanan is young and ignorant," she began. "She seems sick, too. None of us is well. Let's forget her childish talk and think of hunting."

Father's sister, Ina, spoke too. "We are all angry with my brother's child for spoiling the peace of this lodge. In here we are all friendly and we care for one another. Yanan sees what stupid things she said. If her parents were living, they would teach her better. Now that she knows she did wrong, she won't speak stupidly again."

I looked around to see how people took this. Timu looked satisfied; I had done just as he had told me. Elho gave me a cold stare under lowered lids. *How dared you?* asked his eyes. Owl looked soft and forgiving, as if she were asking, *Oh, what does it matter?* Meri looked scared; Ethis looked hurt; Rin looked blank, showing nothing; and Swift gave a shrug and a soft grunt, as if he, at least, was grudgingly willing to accept my apology. What did he care if a young woman wanted to offend him? But Ankhi, covering her baby as if to protect it from me, looked straight into my eyes. "A bird can be snared but a spoken word is loose forever," she said.

I tried not to show it, but I was shocked. Whatever did Ankhi have against me? Last night I was angry at Swift, not her. Ankhi was the last person I thought I had offended. In fact, I hardly thought about her at all. Did she know that her husband, Elho, once had followed me into the woods? Had he said something? And why was she covering the baby? *You slapped it, not me, you bad-mannered squirrel,* I said to myself. *Who are you to act superior?*

But now was not the time to quarrel with Ankhi or anyone else. I was in disgrace, so I hung my head for a while. Then, so I wouldn't have to sit ashamed and idle, I groped around my sleeping place for the moccasins I was sewing, hoping that something sudden would happen to take everyone's attention from me. But nothing did. In a dark corner, Rin snored.

The lodge was so cold I had to wear my parka, and so smoky I couldn't see the holes for my needle. Snow almost blocked the smokehole, and the fire wasn't making enough heat to carry all its smoke up and out. I coughed until my eyes streamed. The men began to complain in rough voices about Meri's wolf, who was robbing their snares. Then they put their heads together to whisper, and I began to suspect that they might have set a snare for him. How like them, I thought. They couldn't make him help them, and now they're trying to kill him, but they don't have the courage to tell even such a little person as Meri. My anger burned.

Yet there I sat, making a present for Timu! Quickly I stuffed the moccasins out of the way. Then I had nothing to do. When Owl asked Teal for a story, I felt hopeful. But when Teal began to tell how Whitefish stole fire from the Hare, I ground my teeth with irritation. I couldn't count how many times I had heard that story before; to hear it again was more than I could bear. I took off my parka and rolled up in my deerskin. Before I knew it, I was fast asleep.

So passed the Hunger Moon. During it we killed only one reindeer, although plenty of them were hiding in the trees across the river. During the Moon of Roaring the tigress came to stalk the reindeer also. The time for tigers' rutting was here again, and at night we heard the tigress call *aao-o, a-a-oo-ng.* As before, we thought the woods more dangerous and formed two groups for hunting. In one group were Graylag with his son-in-law, Crane, and his son Elho, and in the other group were Swift, Timu, White Fox, and I. Swift and Graylag were the leaders. They thought White Fox and I together equaled either Elho or Crane. Perhaps that would have angered me when I felt well, a time that now seemed long ago. Now I was too tired to care.

Because of being tired, I had trouble keeping up with the men. Sometimes when I was out of their sight I sat on my heels, crossed my arms over my knees, and put my head down to rest. Sometimes I had to move quickly onto my hands and knees to vomit without spoiling my clothes. The vomit was a foamy yellow bile that dripped from my nose.

In time the tigress made the reindeer wary. We couldn't seem to get near them. One day, when Swift and the rest of the group were widely spread out among the trees in search of their trails or signs of browsing, I circled the base of a hill, and when I found my own trail again, I saw the tigress's footprints over my footprints: she was following me. Very scared, I found an open place where the tigress couldn't ambush me and gave the alarm call: *lulululululululu!*

The men found me quickly, their spears ready, and although my alarm call spoiled our hunting (and I hoped we could go home), they insisted on backtracking the tigress along the riverbank to learn what they could about her and to find a scat. They found an icicle of urine on a twig where she had backed up to squirt, and a scat full of hair. Not bothering to show me, they broke open the scat, and to their surprise found that the hair belonged to two animals, a red deer and a reindeer. What did the scat mean? they asked each other. This tigress might be hunting very widely, which worried them more than her following me.

After dark at our fire the men had a long talk about hunting and animals. If the other women hadn't gone far away to the pine groves and filled two large bags with nuts, our meal that night would have been snow. I was too tired to crack nuts so, asking Meri to crack some for me, I rolled myself in my deerskin and fell asleep. When Meri woke me I heard singing and realized that a shaman was about to trance. I hardly believed my eyes when I saw Swift naked to the waist and streaked with ocher. Was he really, as he said, a shaman? It seemed he was. To help him trance, we sang.

> You who watch all the animals and all the people,
> Hear us!
> Give us those who carry antlers!
> Give us those with white hair!
> Give us those with round hooves!
> You whose children are the deer!
> Help us under the Moon of Roaring

Help us under the Moon of Cast Antlers
Give us life,
You who give life!
Send us food,
You who give food!
Help us in winter.

How strong Swift looked, I thought. Although he was very thin, the firelight showed the fine hunter's muscles of his back and shoulders. Strange to say, my throat tightened at the sight of him. Around and around he turned, looking up at the smokehole, until he collapsed on the ground. Teal didn't trance with him, but she rubbed his back, his arms, and his legs while he lay unconscious. At last he sat up, wiping his face, and said, "I have seen the spirit of Sali. She's here. She's angry. The deer are hers—she wants to hunt them. We may not take them. That's what she said."

Sali! Sali was our kinswoman, the famous shaman of the Fire River whose daughter was Teal! But how had Swift found Sali? She wasn't one of the spirits of the lodge; hers was the spirit who walked naked in the woods, carrying a baby, or stalked the riverbanks as a tigress, carrying a cub.

No one knew what to make of this. Rather doubtfully, Graylag said, "Hona!" The mammoth hunter woman seemed fascinated, staring at Swift open-mouthed. But the thought of Sali made Meri and me uneasy, and we grasped each other's hands. Swift himself sat perfectly calmly across the fire from us, his elbows on his knees, his hands shading the firelight.

Teal stood straight and tall, lit from below by the fire. As if she didn't believe Swift, she looked down on him. "Tell us, Swift Shaman," she said, "what my mother looked like."

Swift relaxed, the man of meat again. With his pale eyes he looked up at Teal, and in the patient voice he sometimes used to answer women's questions he said, "She looked like a tiger. Stripes, and a long tail on her. She wants to eat the deer herself, you see? She doesn't want us to starve, so instead she'll let us find a sleeping bear."

Teal sat down, looking puzzled. We all felt puzzled. Sali had never appeared like this before, not even to her own daughter. How unusual! Yet the strangeness of it didn't bother Swift, who seemed to be thinking only of the bear. Even with his trance still near him he added, "A tiger doesn't hunt grown bears—not even young ones in winter."

In the morning we found the weather clear. Graylag went hunting, taking Timu, White Fox, and me. Perhaps because he had been married so long to a shaman, or perhaps because he didn't quite believe Swift, Graylag seemed unworried by Swift's message of the night before. Graylag told us that people could say what they liked, but we were going for reindeer, Sali or no Sali. After all, Sali's own daughter was suffering. Her grandson too. Her great-granddaughter was suffering most of all—Elho's little baby, who now cried all the time, weakly and without hope.

Timu agreed. Like his father, he didn't give much thought to spirits, at least not by day. I didn't think we should go against the wishes of a spirit, and I said so. Timu looked at me scornfully. "You think only of yourself and your own fear," he said. "Yet you have less to fear than we do. Sali is your kinswoman, not ours. What about the other people? They're hungry, even if you're not."

But Graylag said, "Your wife is right. If we kill a reindeer, we can leave the spirit's portion for the tigress. That should please her, if she's Sali. She can't refuse food to people who need it. Her own grandson's wife needs it the most. Without food, women can't give milk!" I glanced triumphantly at Timu, and off we went, crossing the river on the ice.

Snow had drifted during the night, covering old foot-prints. All the deer trails we saw were fresh. Before the sun was high we found a likely trail, spotted the deer hiding in a thicket, surrounded the thicket, and killed the deer. *So much for my mother-in-law,* Graylag's manner seemed to say as he cut open the belly. It was a yearling doe, so small and thin that two of us could carry her. We seemed about to take all the meat, but I reminded Graylag of the spirit's portion, so he carefully placed the flesh of the belly on the bloody snow. Then we went back to the lodge, the men with the meat and I with all the wood I could gather, and in the lodge we made a fire and put the liver to roast.

The smell was so good I wept. Rising through the smoke-hole, it brought home all the women, who were nearby, looking for firewood and winterberries. Laughing and talking, they hung their wet clothes from the antlers in the roof and made ready to eat. Ethis with her huge, pregnant belly and Ankhi with her nursing baby sat close to the fire, staring right at the meat as if their mouths were watering. We put aside a large share for Swift and the two men with him, but the moment our shares were ready, we snatched them up and ate them, so hot they burned our mouths. How good they were! Graylag added strips of the foreleg, his own share, to the fire. Soon we were eating them too.

Perhaps I ate too fast, or perhaps my stomach wasn't used to food—in no time I wanted to vomit. Horrified, I lay down on my back, trying to keep the food inside me. But it was no use. Suddenly I had to jump up and hurry out of the lodge, where my stomach heaved again and again, and soon all the bits of liver and foreleg, hardly chewed, were lying on the snow.

I wanted to cry. I thought perhaps I should try to put the food back into my stomach again. What would people think of this waste? I looked around in case anyone saw me, and noticed Meri's wolf watching anxiously from a thicket. He too had smelled the cooking liver in the smoke. Slowly, with his ears folded and his face begging, he crept toward me on bent legs, looking from my face to the vomit. He was starving. Even under his winter coat his bones stuck out. "Eat," I said, moving away from the vomit. I wouldn't have been there at all if his mother hadn't done the same for me. Gratefully he hurried to the vomit, and before I could blink my eyes it was gone.

In the lodge I asked for another strip of meat and ate it slowly. This piece I kept. Later I ate another, and kept that too. Then I lay down to rest, and at last I felt stronger.

After sunset a long time passed, but Swift, Crane, and Elho didn't come. When the moon rose, we went outside to look for them and saw them crossing the river on the ice. They were empty-handed, we saw from afar, but they hailed us gladly. When they had eaten their fill of the reindeer, they told us where they had been and what they had found.

Walking fast, eating birch twigs on the way to stop their hunger, they had gone all the way to the hills where the Char rises. There, as Sali had promised, they found a bear's den from the little smokehole made by the bear's warm breath. The bear inside was probably asleep and probably a female. Listening at the smokehole, they thought they heard a cub.

A bear! Perhaps two! So much meat might last us almost until we traveled to our summerground. How lucky we were to have the reindeer now, to give us strength to walk the long way to the hills, dig out the bear and kill it, and carry the meat home again. Swift and Graylag were already planning the hunt. We would be gone at least two days, perhaps longer, as we would have to camp there and might be slow coming home with the weight of a lot of meat, if we got it. All the men would go except Elho, who would stay to help the women in case the tigress bothered them.

Elho objected, and seemed hurt. After all, he had helped find the bear. I offered to stay instead, since I thought myself as handy with a spear as Elho and I felt exhausted just thinking about the hunt. And hadn't Elho been caught in the act of calling his kinswoman "wife" the last time he had been left alone with women?

But Graylag's mind was set. I could help dig out the bear just as well as Elho, but Elho was bigger and stronger, which would matter if the tigress troubled the lodge. Also he was older and had more experience with animals, said Graylag. And Elho's wife was recently delivered. And if the tigress was Sali, she was Elho's grandmother but only my kinswoman. No—Elho would stay and I would go. The subject was finished.

In the morning, under the waning moon still shining in the clear, pale sky, we set off in weather so cold that our breath froze on our faces. We walked all day, backtracking Swift and the others. Late in the afternoon the trail led to a north-facing slope where Swift showed us a little hole among the roots of a pine. When we put our hands over the hole, we felt a faint, warm draft softly rising: the sleeping bear's breath. The north slope was bad—to dig there we would have to chip the frozen earth in tiny pieces, like ice—but then, the weather was so cold that the south slope wouldn't have been any better. To start digging in the evening would be foolish; we wouldn't be able to do much before dark and might wake the bear besides. We would begin work in the morning. Meanwhile we would camp.

Far from the den, so we wouldn't disturb the bear until we were ready, we chose a small clearing sheltered by low pines. The men rolled a little fire in some tinder, then sent me to gather the firewood for the rest of the night. This was easy, as there was plenty around. Alone in the woods, I remembered crossing these same hills with Meri and being too scared to build a fire. No wonder there was plenty of wood—not even she and I had gathered here before.

When I brought my bundle to the camp, I found that the men had almost killed the little fire by piling it with strips of reindeer meat. They hardly noticed me, but went on with their men's talk, which I soon realized was about Sali. Swift was telling Timu about her, with Graylag adding a few words now and then. It soon was clear that a kinsman of Swift's had been none other than Sali's husband. No wonder Swift knew about her. Was this why he thought he saw her during his trance? Interested, I listened.

Long ago, Swift told the others, there was a man with two little sisters. Their summergrounds were on the Hair River, and their people were mammoth hunters. The two sisters found husbands among their own people: Swift's father and another man. The granchildren of that other man were Ethis and Ankhi.

I now thought that this was not to be an interesting story after all, but a boring list of names I didn't know. And so it was, for a while. By the time the subject of the elder brother came up again, I was looking around for my pack. When I heard that the brother went to the Fire River and married someone there, I unrolled my deerskin. And when I heard that he and his wife were the parents of Sali's husband, I lay down and settled myself for sleep. Who cared about marriages so long ago?

But Swift's droning voice kept me awake, and his accent kept me puzzling, since I couldn't easily catch all his words. When he said "bee-dray," I listened more carefully. And suddenly I was wide awake. Sali hadn't liked her husband's people. Ah well, no wonder, if they were Swift's kinsmen. I drifted off again. Again I was awake! She became pregnant by her own kinsman not because she loved him, as Teal and Mother once claimed, but to spoil her husband's lodge! "Sali thought she could do whatever she wanted," said

Swift. "She was wrong about that. Some things can't be done at all, not by her, not by anybody. But for a while people thought Sali could do anything. She had power. Have you heard how she brought The Woman Ohun to all the people camped on the steppe?"

"Some haven't heard it," said Graylag. "My son hasn't heard it, or White Fox." I hadn't heard it either, and I propped myself on my elbow to catch all Swift's words.

"Sali was a very famous shaman," he began, "whose name was known to all of us along the Hair River. The summer she was pregnant by her kinsman, my father and other men went to find her people's camp, to see if we could exchange women and to get feathers and shells. I was a boy then, and my father was the age I am now. When we found her people they welcomed us and we camped with them on the open plain. We soon learned of the trouble between Sali and her husband. Everyone talked of it, and we did too.

"On the night of the full Mammoth Moon the people built a big fire. Sali told them to start singing, so they did. My father and all the people with him, they obeyed like children, because they feared her.

"But above the singing we heard something new. It sounded like a heartbeat. What was it? We looked, and saw Sali with a little thing in her hands. It was a branch bent round with a swan's skin tied over it, and when Sali tapped it, it sang *ah, ah, ah, ah.*

"'What's she doing?' asked my father.

"'She'll call a spirit,' said a man. 'The voice of that will call a spirit. Wait and you'll see.'

"But now we were afraid of the round thing, and when Sali laid it on the ground, we didn't look at it. We were afraid of Sali too. She was all streaked with ocher and her hair was loose, blowing in the wind. And when she washed herself with fire to heat her power, we smelled burning skin.

"Then we saw what Sali wanted to show us. Out of the fire rose a big cloud of smoke, and in the cloud we saw another woman, as big as a bison. She was so huge, she frightened us, this woman. She was naked too. She had big long shins and big thighs, and a huge belly. This is how she stood, like this, with her arms up and her head back so we couldn't see

218

her face. We just saw the front of her body and the underside of her chin.

"We were surprised, I can tell you. But we were more surprised when she spread her legs and bent her knees to squat. It didn't seem right to watch a woman doing this, even if she was a spirit. But she was showing us something.

"What happened next will scare you. It scared us. She didn't squat all the way down, but stopped halfway. And we saw a head coming out of her body, upside down. It was a baby, facing forward with its eyes squeezed shut.

"We stared at this baby, hoping it wouldn't open its eyes and stare at us. And then we saw it disappearing. The big woman straightened her legs and drew the baby back inside her body.

"The woman waited. We wanted to run but we didn't dare move. As if a lion was right beside us, we made ourselves sit still.

"When the woman was ready, she bent her knees a second time. And again a head slid out to the neck. But now the head was longer, with a wrinkled, blunt snout. And we saw it wasn't a person but a cub! The woman let us look a long time so we didn't miss what she was showing us. And then she straightened her legs and the cub's head slid back into her body.

"A third time she bent her knees. And a third head slid out of her, a narrow head with long, folded ears—the head of a fawn or a colt. The big woman moved very slowly, like a mammoth. When she was ready, she straightened up a third time, and the fawn's head slid back inside and disappeared.

"Then the woman dropped her arms to her sides and bent her head so her hair fell forward. We saw her belly, huge like a hill with we didn't know what inside it. But we never saw her face, because her hair hid it. And the next thing we knew she wasn't there.

"In her place, Sali stood by the fire. Like the big woman, Sali's face was also hidden in her hair. She threw it back and said to us, 'The Woman Ohun. Now you have seen her. Her message is my message. Make of it what you will.'

"What were we to think?" asked Swift. "Even now, most of us don't dare speak of that night. Most of us call it 'the night we first heard a drum.' But we think Sali meant the message for her husband's kin. Like The Woman Ohun, Sali would give birth to anything she wanted. What did she care if The Bear didn't like it? The Woman Ohun gives birth to bears.

"That's the story," said Swift. "You know the rest. When Sali's labor began, she wasn't as strong as she thought she was. From the start she had trouble. The baby was her kinsman's so it lay crosswise, showing its buttocks but hiding its face in shame. It didn't want to be born."

All the men nodded wisely, waiting to hear of Sali's punishment. But I felt awed by what Sali had done and thought the story should stop there. As for the rest, that Sali died in childbirth, I didn't want to hear it from these men.

They talked, though—nothing would have stopped them. For a while they argued about the way Sali died, Timu insisting on a story like the one he must have heard from Elho, that Sali's husband tied Sali's legs together so the baby couldn't come out. That was like the story I believed, but Swift thought he knew different. Sali's husband didn't kill her, Swift told Timu. He wouldn't, because killing causes trouble. Even killing a baby can lead to fighting and sometimes to more killing. If Sali's husband had killed anyone, the shame would follow his lineage even now. But though Sali's husband didn't hurt her, he stopped everyone from helping her. "Let Sali bring The Woman to help. I won't dare stop The Woman," said Sali's husband, according to Swift.

Before the trouble, Swift went on, people from the mammoth hunter lineages and the Fire River lineages married each other. But after the trouble they didn't, or not as much. Each group was afraid of the other. Sali's daughter, Teal, once was promised to the mammoth hunters, said Swift. But after the trouble, both the Fire River people and the mammoth hunters changed their minds. "That's why Teal could marry you," said Swift to Graylag. Graylag nodded. He already knew.

"But good things come from bad things, like mushrooms from dung," said Swift, unrolling his sleeping-skin, as if finished with stories for the night. "Because of the old trouble, our lineages stayed apart. Our people aren't all mixed together anymore, and we can easily find wives in each other's camps. Timu got Ethis and Elho got Ankhi, which is good. All I got was Meri." Swift laughed, having forgotten long ago that I might be listening. "Not so good for me—she's still a baby. But she'll grow."

This talk of Meri must have been hard on White Fox. He poked the fire with a stick to make sparks fly. The angry gesture wasn't lost on Swift, who turned to him and said kindly, "We'll find a woman for you at the Hair River. Do you remember Sasa? Sasa's family will give her to you. Look at Yanan, already asleep. She'll be the only person strong enough to kill the bear." Everyone laughed except me and White Fox.

Timu and Graylag stayed up to talk and feed the fire, keeping watch over the dark woods to see what walked there. I fell asleep, and when I got cold I woke up to see Timu keeping watch alone. So I got up to warm myself, and we sat quietly together. The sky and the woods were bright, with the waning quarter of the Moon of Roaring shining on the snow. And the air was very still, so wind didn't blow away the heat of the fire. Instead its warmth stayed around us, as if we were in a lodge we couldn't see. "Do you believe," I asked Timu, "that we should join our lineages to the mammoth hunters?"

He thought for a moment, then said, "I don't know. Young people don't decide these things. The old people, and the people before them—they know best about marriages and lineages. When we're old, we'll know."

I thought for a while about Timu and me being old together. It was hard to imagine, yet if we lived, it would be so. "If you could choose," I asked him, "what lineage would you have chosen?"

Timu looked surprised. "I did choose," he said. "I chose Ethis." Although this was true, I couldn't help feeling disappointed. But then he added, "That's what I mean about the old people knowing. I chose Ethis, but the old people chose you."

When Timu slept I kept watch alone, thinking how tired I was already, and how sorry I hadn't slept longer. When I felt like vomiting, as I seemed to do often, I ate a strip of meat.

It was the last we had; our next meal would be bear meat or snow. The food helped me stay awake. When Swift and Graylag woke, we saw the morning star rising. The waning moon still lit the sky—we didn't have to wait for day. We took our packs through the quiet woods and found the den, very dark in the shadow of the pine. We studied the place for a while, trying to think how it would be when the bear came out, deciding ahead of time whose spear should be thrown and whose should stab and where each of us should stand. We made two plans to attack the bear, one if she reared and one if she didn't. "Don't forget," said Graylag, "a bear can come out fast." When we thought we were ready, we scraped away the loose snow and began to chop our antler picks on the ice around the opening. The ice was like rock. We pounded away at it, each blow ringing, loosening bits no bigger than beads.

"This bear is really sleeping!" said Swift. "How can she do it?"

We laughed, the men at Swift's joke, I at his accent. I took the chance to rest for a while. Graylag listened at the opening, then beckoned for Swift to listen too. "She's waking," said Graylag. "And she has a cub." Then everyone listened, and with the silence I heard a little voice in the earth—not a loud voice, and not high, just young. I also heard the large bear breathing, lots of air moving, but down in the earth she sounded far away.

"So much meat," said Swift, giving the ice a powerful blow with his pick. It broke. "By The Bear!" said Swift regretfully, fitting the broken pieces together. The pick looked whole, but of course he couldn't use it; he tossed it into the woods and reached for his spear. "I don't think she's so deep," he said. "I'm going to try now."

"Wait," said Graylag. "I think the den is like this." He showed with his hands how he thought the hole curved in under the tree and then up a little. "She's among the roots. If we kill her in there, we won't get her out."

"That's right," said Swift thoughtfully. "Let's get her out." So Swift and Graylag probed with their spears in the hole. Suddenly they stopped and turned to the rest of us. "Don't stand there like horses!" said Swift. "Get ready." So we poised our spears. Swift looked at us again. "And not so close! Do you want to spear us or the bear?"

"She's awake," said Graylag.

"Get ready! Get back!" said Swift. We heard a rumble—the bear was awake! "Watch out!" warned Swift, his spear raised. Gingerly Graylag poked in the hole one more time; then he leaped out of the way. Up came the bear with a deafening roar, bits of earth and dry pine needles dropping off her. Oh, she was big! Like a mammoth! She was standing, not rearing—I should throw at her chest! I threw with all my strength. My spear was gone, so I ran.

After a few leaps I stopped and looked around. At last the bear reared, but now with four spears in her chest, mine near her shoulder. Timu, Crane, and White Fox also had thrown at her chest, and Crane's spear, right in the middle, had gone deep. Blood ran from the bear's nose. From the side Swift and Graylag rammed their spears between her ribs as the bear swung at them. Her swing brought her to all fours, and she ran. We watched her huge rump disappear among the trees, then followed her trail. First she shook off my spear, then Timu's. We picked them up. We found White Fox's—or rather my father's—with blood on the shaft. Then we found Swift's spear, also blood-stained. We followed carefully, ready if she decided to fight us, and found her lying on the snow.

Just in case, we waited at a safe distance for a while. When she didn't move, Swift and Timu, with my spear and White Fox's, slowly walked up to her huge body, threw some snow, gave her a kick when nothing happened, then drove the spears into her heart. She was already dead. She didn't move or groan.

Then we were happy! The pile of meat and fat in front of us was hard to imagine! And a bearskin too! The sun had just reached the tops of the trees, so we had plenty of daylight to work by. Back to the den we went for our packs and our knives, and we saw the cub's face in the opening. Timu killed him with an ax. More meat, and two skins! Teal and Ina would be pleased, since the big skin would be theirs through Graylag. And Owl would be pleased, since the teeth would be hers through Crane. My spear had wounded, I saw when we opened the mother bear, but Crane's had killed. It was buried to three hand's breadths up the shaft, and had pierced her lung.

It took us the rest of the day to get the big skin off and the meat cut into pieces we could carry. Starting a fire, we cut the meat into strips, cooked a few, and hung the rest from branches to lose the weight of the blood. Ravens found us and landed over our heads, calling to other ravens before they flew down to eat the bloody snow. Their calls or the smell must have traveled far—in the middle of the afternoon we saw the wolves among the trees. They were too scared to come near us, although they seemed to be thinking about it, but after all, we were six, and I could see that they were only six or seven. Perhaps they thought we had too much to carry and might not be taking all of it. As it was, we had to strip the heaviest bones. And we talked for a while about cutting the skin in half, since it was very heavy and both Graylag's wives were its owners. It seemed a shame to cut it, though, and when Crane said he thought he could carry it, we gave it a rough scraping and rolled it up in case it froze.

Late in the afternoon all the warmth was gone from the meat, and also the day was turning very cold. We saw that everything would freeze, so we hurried, making packs, gutting the cub, and stuffing most of the guts, the heads, and the heavy bones far down into the den and covering them. If for any reason we needed them, we could always come back and dig them out again.

Then we took up our packs. Mine, the smallest, was so heavy that I couldn't lift it off the ground. Timu had to help me get under it. Using my spear as a walking stick, I followed the men into the forest, very thankful that the way home was mostly downhill. Even so, I soon dropped far behind the others, until I was out of sight and even out of earshot. But the trail was easy to see—it had been used four times now. I found it by starlight. When I was stumbling with cold and tiredness, ready to lie down on the snow, I saw a large man striding toward me through the trees. It was Timu, coming to find me. When he took my pack, I felt as if I was rising into the air. He told me the others were camped, then made me walk ahead to hurry me. It wasn't good to bring a big load of meat through a strange woods after dark.

The trail led straight to a wonderful camp—a small, open cave on the hillside, a place Swift must have scouted on his first trip, knowing we might need it on the way home with meat. In it we could keep the meat through the night and not have to fight off every hunting animal in the forest. The men had gathered wood, had rolled a fire in the cave's mouth, and were cooking. All I had to do was unroll my deerskin and lie down.

It had been a good day, and was a good, starry night, clear and cold, with a yellow glow behind the hills where the moon would rise. The cave soon filled with smoke, but that was no matter. I must have fallen asleep, because Timu woke me to give me my food.

◄ 13 ►

WHEN WE CAME HOME with the bear, we found Elho in front of the lodge with his face bruised but without his parka, and Rin on her hands and knees in the coldtrap with an ax. The heat of Elho's anger must have kept him from freezing— Rin wouldn't let him inside. When we brought the meat to the doorway, Rin backed up to let us through, then sat at the far end of the lodge with Ankhi. Elho hurried inside behind us.

Ankhi was crying. Rin stared grimly at the rest of us but spoke only to Swift. At the near end of the lodge Owl and Meri clung to each other beside Teal, who sat stiffly, looking uncomfortable and very severe. There was no firewood, so we couldn't cook. To talk in privacy about the trouble, whatever it was, the old people sent all the young people out to get firewood, even those of us who had just come.

As soon as we were out of earshot, Meri told me that Elho had beaten Ankhi. Meri wasn't sure why. Elho and Ankhi had argued all morning, and at last he had shouted something about the way she treated the baby. I thought she might have treated it badly, since she once slapped it for crying, but Meri said that she had given it her deerskin and wouldn't let Elho shared. All the women, said Meri, had pulled Elho away from Ankhi so that Rin could club him with her digging stick. When he ducked into the coldtrap to get away from Rin, she got her ax and wouldn't let him back into the lodge again. Why he had gone outdoors Meri didn't know, unless it was just to stand up and catch his breath.

But once he was outside, Rin swore he could stay outside. He could freeze, for all of her.

Trouble so large doesn't go away by itself. Even Graylag couldn't stop it. This was no simple fight where the men side with the husband and the women with the wife—this became a tangle of men against women, lineage against lineage, and lodge against lodge. Most of us felt, one way or another, that Elho had shamed everyone. This made Elho furious, since he had been so badly shamed by Rin. Swift was angry because his half-sister, a guest, had pushed out one of her hosts. Timu was angry because Rin could have killed Elho, keeping him outside in his shirt without even firesticks or tinder. If we hadn't come along to rescue Elho, said Timu, his half-brother would have frozen.

Rin insisted that she had done the only thing possible. If Elho promised to leave Ankhi alone, said Rin, she gladly would have let him inside. But Elho wouldn't promise, so Rin had to keep him out. Timu was senseless not to understand. At least Timu should believe that Rin would have thrown Elho's clothes and firesticks out to him sooner or later. Ethis stopped talking to Timu to punish him for being Elho's half-brother and for being rude to her kins-women.

The women of the mammoth hunters were furious with Graylag's people for leaving a protector who beat one of them instead. Most women of our lodge were angry at Elho too. Hadn't there been a time when he had stolen another man's wife while staying to protect women? Elho insisted he had not. "Ah! You lie!" I shouted. "You took my father's wife, Aunt Yoi!"

But I later took sides with his mother, Teal, since Elho was of our lineage, ours to protect. Teal reminded everyone that Ankhi had a very sharp tongue and had probably provoked Elho. I reminded people that Ankhi's mammoth hunter kin always threatened a beating as a way of forcing someone. Ankhi should be used to her own people's ways. How could a beating surprise a mammoth hunter?

Now Swift took Ankhi's side. Men of the mammoth hunters always gave their wives a long time after childbirth before asking to sleep with them again. Elho's violence could have killed the baby.

"Not so!" cried Teal. "Before my son touched your kinswoman, he took the baby away from her. Ethis held the baby while Elho beat Ankhi and while Rin beat Elho. I was here. I saw the whole quarrel. You were far away, yet you want to tell us what we saw!"

Swift and Graylag sensed a danger to their careful plans of joining our lodges, and, trying to end the fight, they commanded everyone to stop talking about the beating. But matters had gone too far, and people wouldn't stop. After two days and two nights of argument in the dark, smoky lodge, Swift and Timu started a trapline just for something to do, a way of getting out.

The next night, when the lodge was dark, they came back from their snares with a wolfskin. No one but me noticed the skin or saw the men toss it in a corner. Timu and Swift went to Graylag's fire and helped themselves to food, and I, on my hands and knees, as quietly as possible, went to look at the skin. No one saw me.

The skin seemed to have been stripped from a yearling wolf with its head and feet cut off. Wanting to see it better, I rolled it up quietly without anyone noticing and went outside. In the wind and moonlight I unrolled the skin and looked at it carefully. It had the coat of a yearling, and sure enough, it was a male. What wolf could it be but Meri's? Hers was always hungry, looking everywhere for scraps. A bait must have seemed wonderful to him. I looked at the skin for a long time, watching the hair ruffle in the wind. Meri wasn't going to know about this, I decided at last. I would take the skin far away, right now, and get rid of it. Swift and Timu owned it but would have to do without it.

On the moonlit trail the sound of the quarreling people blew away on the wind. Listening to it sigh in the little trees and watching their shadows toss in the moonlight, I thought of the lodge on the Marten, and the lodge on the Pine. Through the smokehole the moonlight now shone quietly on Father's body, with nothing but black shadows of the trees alive, outside on the snow. A year ago he died there; a year ago the she-wolf helped me and Meri—the wolf with long legs and yellow eyes, she who couldn't live with her people, just like Meri and me. All alone she had cared for her pup, and because of him we had lived too. Who knew or cared about our life there? No one. I had never really told anybody. What had come of it? A skin, which would now go under the ice in the river, into a hole over the rapids where the water doesn't freeze.

The wind, from very far away, brought the roar of the tigress: *a-a-oo-ng*. Surely the tigress was Sali, alone with the child her husband would have killed, like me and Meri, whom no one came to find, like the she-wolf, whose pups her pack didn't want.

Below the trail I heard water echoing under the ice—the voice of the rapids. I slid down the terraces one after the other, found a few holes in the ice next to a boulder, and put the skin, head end down, into one of them. The pull of the river took it out of my hand.

When I got near the lodge I heard very angry voices. The quarreling was louder. Meri was crying! I heard Graylag shouting for everybody to sit down. Almost in a panic, I dove through the coldtrap. Everyone was standing except Meri. Someone had struck her! Only Teal stood near her, but still Meri cowered, weeping, her face buried in her hands. "Sister!" I called.

"Sit down, Yanan!" roared Graylag. Meri ran to me and threw her arms around me. "Sit!" said Graylag. "Everybody sit! We will talk, not fight! Sit!"

Even Meri obeyed him as all the people except me slowly lowered themselves to their heels in circles around the two fires. The shouting went on, though. Above the angry voices, Graylag called, "I told you to sit, Yanan!"

But rage was growing inside me. I looked from one person to another, and through my teeth I asked, "What have you done?"

Many people spoke at once, telling me we must not fight, but I heard only Ankhi saying, "Meri took a skin that belonged to me. She was punished."

My rage burst. As ice can't stop the river in the spring, I couldn't stop my voice. "Yes! A wolf!" I shouted. "I took the skin! I, Lapwing's Daughter! Perhaps it was yours, but the wolf was Meri's, and you'll never have any piece of him! His skin is gone where you'll never find it! You'll never have it!

And you'll never have Meri! Meri isn't yours to give or yours to punish and I'm taking her away!" I looked around at the shocked faces gaping at me and felt myself shaking.

Timu stood up in front of me. "Control yourself, Yanan," he said. "Sit down as Father asked you!"

But now I couldn't stop. I shoved him aside. "Who hit her? Who dared? Who but him!" I pointed straight at Swift across the lodge. "You say she's yours, but that's a lie, you animal! You lion! Go hide in the grass where you belong! Look there for another woman!" I tore off the betrothal necklace and hurled it at him. His eyes met mine as he neatly, calmly, caught it.

Timu grabbed my hair. I suppose by now he had no choice—he twisted my braid around his hand and beat me with his belt. I bit him so hard that my teeth met, and his warm, salty blood squirted into my mouth. Hitting and kicking, we crashed together to the floor and rolled right over the fire. Finally people managed to pull us apart, then held us by the arms as we struggled to get at each other. I must have been a terrible sight, my hair all on end, my clothes scorched, and my teeth bloody. Timu too looked dreadful, filthy with ashes and sweat, bleeding from bites and scratches. Without his belt his trousers were sliding, and a flap of his skin stuck up on one arm.

White Fox began to laugh. "Timu! Yanan! You should see yourselves!" he said at last, wiping his eyes. "Hide in the grass? For shame!"

No one else thought anything was funny. Timu and I allowed other people to lead us to opposite sides of the lodge and persuade us to sit down.

What brought us to do this? It was quite a long story. When Timu told Graylag he had snared a wolf, Graylag wanted the skin given to Ankhi to help make up for the beating. Timu couldn't find the skin, and he blamed Meri. So Meri learned her wolf was dead, and cried hysterically. The screaming brought the people to their feet and into a violent argument about Meri and me making so much trouble over an animal. Meri was punished for screaming by Teal, who shook her. At this moment I burst through the coldtrap. Until then, no one had noticed I was gone.

The rage I had felt left me sick and weak. My scalp ached,

and the beating began to hurt. Feeling hopeless, I leaned against Teal, lifting my head now and then to glare across the lodge at Timu. Teal stroked my forehead to stop me from doing this, and talked to me in a soothing voice about spring coming and an end to all our trouble. "Think of the meat you helped to bring, my good girl, my daughter," she said. "And the reindeer doe, when our food was gone. How well you've done this winter."

It was no use. In the morning I stood up in front of everyone and said I was divorcing Timu. The people looked surprised. I reminded them that the bridal exchange was not complete anyway. What had already been given could be returned; I would tell my kin to give back their shares when I went to live among them on the Fire River. And I was taking Meri.

I sat down. As I remember, no one said a word, least of all Timu. I rolled up in my deerskin and went back to sleep. *Let other people gather wood,* I thought. *I won't use their fire.*

Later in the day Teal shook me by the shoulder. "Sit up," she said. "I want to talk to you." So I did, feeling very sulky and pulling up my shirt to show her some bruises. "Never mind that," said Teal. "You must listen now. You're doing a bad thing, and must stop it. Your marriage was made very carefully. Your father-in-law, your father, your mother, her sister, and I, all of us made it. We tied you to this lodge.

"Graylag's lodge is the best winter lodge anywhere. We have food, fuel, shelter from storms, fur animals for parkas, antlers and greenstones for tools. Not many places have all this. Your parents wanted to tie you and themselves to Graylag and his lodge.

"But what of our summerground? You've seen the Grass River, but you have nothing to compare it to. You've never seen the Hair River. You don't know how much meat lies at the foot of the cliffs each summer—more than all the people in the world could ever eat! Graylag wants to tie his people to all of Swift's summer meat. Why else do you think we want Swift to have Meri?

"Her marriage was also made very carefully. Our people want to use Swift's summerground and Swift's people want to use Graylag's winter lodge! Since you and Graylag are tied through Timu, we arranged to tie Swift and Graylag through your sister. You're young and you don't understand yet. Are you listening?"

I looked at my feet and didn't answer. Teal said nothing for a moment, then: "My patience is going, Yanan! I'm trying to talk to you, but you're not listening! You make me glad Timu beat you."

These words made me very angry, but what could I do about it? I might have thought I could be rude to Swift, but I've never talked back to Teal. Still looking at my feet, I waited.

When Teal spoke next, her voice shook. "We old people, we who know things, we tied our people together very carefully. Now you want to divorce Graylag's son, and you have thrown Meri's betrothal necklace right at Swift's face. You want to end our plans and all our work. How do you think the old people feel about that?"

The old people had no right to promise Meri. They weren't her parents. And Teal's own son began the trouble by beating his mammoth hunter wife, for no reason except that she wouldn't have coitus with him. And she was recently delivered! How unfair of Teal to put so much blame on me! I didn't say this, of course—Teal was too angry—but I had to say something. I tossed my head. "I know, Aunt," I said. "I know people are angry. Are Swift and Rin as angry at Ankhi for refusing your son?"

"You do well to ask that question," said Teal. "You would do better to do as Ankhi has done. Swift and Rin took Ankhi aside and reminded her of what I'm trying to tell you. They reminded her that her marriage also ties our people together. It isn't as strong a tie as Meri's to Swift, but a tie, all the same. Unlike you, Ankhi understood. She's not very angry, and she says later she'll be willing to forget the trouble. You, though—you talk of divorce!"

"Yes, Aunt," I said.

"Meri is very young, so Swift will have to wait for her to grow. That's against her. You're so rude that Swift keeps waiting to hear what you'll say next to offend him, and you're Meri's sister. That's against her too. But Swift and Graylag have a strong friendship. Perhaps Graylag can persuade Swift to renew the betrothal. But what use will that be if you're divorced from Timu? Meri is tied to this lodge through you!"

I saw that this was true. I had never thought about it, though. Even now, it didn't matter nearly so much to me as it seemed to matter to Teal. "Swift has ugly eyes, Aunt," I said. "And his speech is strange."

"Yes, he's ugly. And he's the best hunter with the best summerground and the most meat of anyone in all the lodges and from all the lineages! I hope you divorce Timu! I hope you find yourself and Meri some very handsome men! And I'm glad you're a good hunter, since handsome faces mean so much to you. You may be doing all the hunting yourself, with your children trailing after you spoiling your stalk. You think you know everything, but you don't, Yanan. You're stubborn, and you're being stupid. Think about that!" Teal got up and left.

Very unhappy, I rolled into my deerskin again. Did my feelings mean nothing? Did no one care? Did no one see how tired I was, and always nauseated too? Did not one person see how hard I worked for everyone, no matter how I felt? Tears rolled down my face into my hair. I looked at the sky through the smokehole, not brushing them away.

When I was in the woods next day, gathering firewood, Teal came up to me. "Graylag wants to speak to you," she said. "When we go back, I want you to go to him and ask what he has to say. And you'd better be polite about it! We've had enough of your rudeness."

In the lodge Graylag was sitting at his fire with Elho and Timu. I put down my wood and stood respectfully at a distance, waiting for him to notice me. When he did, he motioned Elho and Timu outside so he could talk to me privately. As if he had never done wrong in his life, Elho jumped right up and left, but Timu stood up slowly, giving me a dangerous stare as he passed by. What could Graylag want to say to me? I sat on my heels across the fire and said, "Father-in-Law. I am here. My aunt says you want to speak to me, so I've come to listen."

"That's good. And well said." Graylag smiled. "You're young, Daughter-in-Law, and like many other people, you have a temper. My son has a temper too. You will both learn self-control as you grow older. These tempers are causing your trouble. I'm an old man, but I never saw two people roll through a fire before, as you and my son did. Think now. If you were controlling your temper, would you have done that? No. You would have been afraid of the burns. That means something, Daughter-in-Law."

I nodded respectfully. I agreed.

"Perhaps my son shouldn't have beaten you. But try to remember how it came about. You lost your temper because you thought someone hurt your sister, but you were mistaken. Now I want to ask you this: if you knew she was crying only from anger, not because someone hurt her, would you have forgotten yourself so?"

"No, Father-in-Law." Graylag could always make me feel ashamed of myself, and he was doing it now.

He went on. "You want to take care of Meri. That's why you want to take her to the Fire River. We understand that. But we, the old people, we want to take care of all of you. Such care needs thought and planning. You're trying to take care of your sister rashly, in the same way you rolled through the fire. Rash acts can hurt like burns." He paused for my agreement.

"Yes, Father-in-Law," I said.

"If you had waited to learn what really had happened to Meri, you wouldn't have insulted all the people. Now you should think about our plans before you go rashly to the Fire River. Perhaps the old people know better than you."

"Yes, Father-in-Law."

"Good. Go now. Think of what I've told you."

"Yes, Father-in-Law," I said, out of the respect I felt. But I already knew everything he had told me, so my mind didn't change.

When Timu and I still wouldn't speak, and at night put our deerskins as far away from each other as possible, Teal came to me. "I want you to go with Timu to the other side of the river," she said. "I want you to find a nice place with sunshine, and I want you to sit down and talk until you stop fighting. If you don't, we'll make you talk in front of everyone. You've never seen that—the lodge making two people talk. It can be very shaming. Work this out by yourselves."

"What if I go across the river, Aunt? How do I know Timu will go too?"

"Graylag will make him go," she said.

So Timu and I dutifully marched across the ice on the river, found a sheltering boulder that threw back the heat of the sun, and sat down facing each other. Chins high, eyes blazing, we stared for quite a while. I had no plans to speak first, and he certainly didn't seem to either. But Graylag must have had some very serious words with Timu, or else Timu thought that being the man gave him more responsibility, because he finally said, "We must stop our quarrel if our marriage is to go on."

How true, I thought, feeling the power of my situation. *Say more.*

Timu waited a long time, and when he saw I wouldn't help, he said, "The old people made our marriage. You are hurting and angering them by all you do."

"I'm sorry," I said, sneering. He could hear I wasn't sorry. In fact I was making him burn as if I was feeding a fire. Very satisfied, I waited.

He gave me a long, level stare, then said, "And I'm angry."

"You look angry," I said. "With big round eyes like an animal about to jump."

"An animal, am I? Look at this." He pulled up his sleeve to show his bite, now red and swollen. "This is a bite," he said. "This is the bite of an animal. Now who is the animal? Now what do you say?"

"I say I'll bite you worse if you ever beat me again."

"If I beat you again you'll never bite anybody."

"You say you want to end our troubles. Now you talk of killing me. That's very good. You're doing well. Now we can go home." And I got up and left. Timu came home by a different way.

Everyone could see that Timu and I had solved nothing, so that night, as Teal had threatened, the lodge made us talk. The people made us sit face to face, then sat in a circle around us. Teal, Ina, Graylag, Owl, and Crane all criticized us while the mammoth hunters listened. Elho kept out of it, being in disgrace himself, and White Fox and Meri sat far away, not included because of being young. I thought the criticism was meant more for me than for Timu, and he must have thought so too—although he tried not to show his sneers and triumph, he didn't hide his feelings very well. Anyway, I knew what he was thinking. So the force of the lodge didn't work either, although it was shaming, just as Teal said.

On fair days we dried meat for our trip to our summergrounds—in my case the Fire River, and in the case of the others the Hair River. One day I cut some strips from my share of a stag killed by Graylag and hung them from tines of the long antlers on the roof. There the strips dried as they froze, becoming light to carry. I was about to bring them inside for the night when I heard feet scrabbling on the roof. With spears and axes, many of us crowded through the door of the coldtrap, ready to kill the thief, and to our surprise we saw a wolf standing on his hind feet, tugging down the last and the highest of my strips. He seemed to have eaten the rest.

It was Meri's wolf, without a doubt. He took his time escaping from us, knowing just how far a person could throw a stone. The other people ran after him, hoping for a chance to spear him, but I was so shocked I had to sit down. What had I put into the river?

The skin of another wolf, of course. Yearling wolves look much alike, and without the head and feet to show the face and footprints, I had made a mistake. I had been sure, but wrong. Like a cold spring torrent, the memory of all I had said and done swept over me—my anger, the insults, the fight, Meri's betrothal, my divorce.

Could I mend any of it? Not the breaking of Meri's betrothal, since I had, in a way, returned the necklace, my share of the betrothal exchange. If anything could be done now, Swift would have to take the first step. And even if he did, I had no intention of giving Meri to be bullied by mammoth hunters, no matter what people said. Nor could I undo the insult to Swift. I could apologize, but couldn't call the words back to my mouth. Nor could I stop the fight with Timu. I didn't want to. Just thinking about it made me angry all over again.

At least I could tell Meri about her wolf. She happened to

be away with Teal on a long trip for firewood, so I took the same trail and met them coming the other way just as the sky was getting dark. Taking half of Meri's bundle, I told her what I had seen. She was so happy that my heart ached—in the middle of all this fighting, these doings of the adults, she had been grieving for the wolf all by herself, without a word to anyone. She gave me the rest of her bundle and ran ahead, probably hoping for a glimpse of him. It was now dark and the wolf had run away, so she couldn't have seen him, but when she came into the lodge after everyone else was gathered around the fires to cook, her eyes were shining.

Meri's happiness was good to see, but it didn't right the wrongs of my mistakes. I apologized to Swift for my rudeness, not in front of everyone this time. He shrugged as if to say that no apology was needed. After all, I had been beaten. I waited a moment, half expecting him to mention Meri. But as if he knew what I was thinking, he nodded pleasantly, dismissing me.

I also apologized to Timu, not for biting him but for putting his wolfskin in the river, and at that I spoke stiffly because it hurt me to apologize at all. I thought that in return he might apologize for his part in our fight, but he said nothing.

There was very little else to do, except give another skin to Ankhi. I had no other skin, so I asked Meri for the hide that had been her share of my reindeer doe. At first she refused to give it. "Just do this one thing for me," I begged. "Someday I'll get you another." Very grudgingly, she agreed. I brought the hide to Ankhi, who looked at it a little scornfully. Even though it was a winter skin, the hair wasn't as good as the wolf's—not for clothing. But what could I do about that?

IV

THE MOON OF WALKING

◄ 14 ►

IN THE MOON OF WALKING we heard geese in the night, on
their way to their summergrounds. Before dawn we were on
our way too, our long line of people in single file following
the river to the lake. Graylag led us. After him came Ethis
and Timu, who carried most of Ethis's pack. Her pregnancy
made her walk heavily; I remembered how my mother had
walked on our last long journey through the hills. Rin and
Swift followed, with Ankhi between them to keep her away
from Elho; Ankhi carried her baby, and Swift carried some
of Ankhi's pack. Elho let all the rest of Graylag's people
walk between him and Rin. After a gap in the line behind
Elho came Meri, then me.

Just as I had done the first time I started for the Fire
River, I looked back for a sight of the long antlers on the
roof of the lodge, sure that I would never see them again.
There they were, the antlers, like a herd of deer, like a grove
of trees, with the sun rising behind them, just as they had
been when I had seen them like this so long ago. The antlers
were the last thing I remember seeing, although we traveled
all day.

When we camped that night, Meri and I didn't share the
fires of the other people. Whose would we share? Instead we
gathered cones and branches and built one of our own. As if
we were already gone and forgotten, no one visited us at it.

On the many nights that followed, I remembered the first
time I traveled here, sleeping at night without a care, safe in
a deerskin with Meri and Mother or Meri and Aunt Yoi.

Now I had to sit up most of each night, feeding the coals with heather, listening for sounds from the wide, dark plains around me, and worrying that my fuel wouldn't last until dawn. When Meri and I traveled alone from the Marten River, I chose hiding places where we could sleep safely. Now, although I was alone, I was also with other people. They chose the trail and the campsites. I had to do as they did.

One day we saw in the south the range of hills where the Spring River rises, where we had been visited by the tiger. My way and Meri's led southwest, over those hills, but the way of the others led northwest, out to the Hair River on its grassy plains.

When we camped at night, Graylag and both his wives came to see me. Looking first at Meri to be sure she was asleep, they sat down at my poor fire, only a few sprigs of heather and a lump of burning dung. I couldn't even see their faces, just their dark forms, darker than the night sky; but from the way they moved, slowly and stiffly, I saw that they were tired.

Graylag spoke. "If Lapwing's Daughter will hear us," he began, "we wish to talk with her once more. We want her to know our thoughts and feelings, so she will think well of us when she is among her people."

I didn't know how to answer. Such formal speech, such respectful manners, made me feel as if they didn't know who I was, as if they took me for the oldest member of some other group, perhaps. No one had ever called me "Lapwing's Daughter" before—at first I hardly knew that Graylag was speaking to me. And never had anyone called me *she* before. Just *you*. I thought the old people saved this other form of speaking for themselves.

But, "Yes. Please speak," I said.

"There was never a question," said Graylag very seriously, "that any person now of our lodge could promise one of Lapwing's Daughters in marriage. Only her parents could do that." In a heavy silence, we all waited for a little while.

Graylag went on. "So we ask my son's wife to remember this: when her sister's betrothal was arranged, we thought her mother was alive." In the dark I nodded to show I understood. They may not have seen me. Graylag said,

"Yanan's father, Ahi, would have liked the good hunting on the Hair River. Yanan's mother, Lapwing, would have known that in the past our lineage made many marriages together. My two wives—Ina, the sister of Yanan's father, and Teal, the kinswoman of Yanan's mother—know that Yanan's parents would have been happy, most of all when they saw what a good man we found for their youngest daughter, and how much meat." Again I nodded.

"It surprised us to hear that my son's wife had an objection. And my wives and I are saddened by it. We want her to know that we did not act quickly or without great thought."

Again there was silence. Perhaps Graylag was giving me a chance to speak. But I couldn't. I felt too strange, as if I were floating, or in a wood I hadn't seen before, where I didn't know the way.

So Graylag went on. "Now my son's wife means to join her lineage. That is her right—we will not try to stop her. Nor must we try to stop her from divorcing. If that is her wish, then so it must be." Graylag now seemed very sad, and again paused for a moment. "My son did a terrible thing to fight. The fault is his. We have spoken to him. He knows that his stepmothers and I are angry with him. Young people are not used to starving as we did last winter. We old people know how a heavy winter can cause many troubles. As for my wives and me, the troubles never happened. None of us wishes to lose my son's wife, a good woman from a good lineage, the daughter of good people, who did her work well, even hunting. We hope she and my son can someday forget the troubles too, and come together again. Until then, we hope my son's wife and her sister find food, shelter, and a good trail for their journey."

It made me very unhappy to hear Graylag speak so formally, as if everything were over and he were a stranger. Now he was putting all the blame on Timu, just as if I were a stranger in whom the people of our lodge wouldn't find a fault of any kind. Yet this man who spoke so distantly, so formally, once had been my own father-in-law, who a few days ago had been able to say "Yanan, sit!" The wives he mentioned, they who listened so politely, so sadly, were the old people closest to my parents. Ina just recently had sent me off for firewood. Teal just recently had made me strip by the river and scrubbed me with sand.

What must these women think of me, spoiling not one but two marriages, spoiling the best of their ties with Swift? What must Graylag think of me, he who loved to hear geese keeping their flocks together, fighting the wind and the cold with the strength of their group? Of course people must think of me as a stranger.

As if I heard a stranger speaking, I heard myself say: "Thank you for your praise and good wishes. And thank you for forgetting the troubles of the past. For me, too, these troubles never happened. I, too, want to forget such things. My respect to your son. May he forget the trouble as I have forgotten. Later I will send you gifts for all you have done for my sister and me."

"So be it," said Graylag, with a nod to Teal and Ina. For a long moment their three shadowed faces looked at me closely, sadly. Then Graylag stiffly straightened his legs and stood, Teal and Ina following. My tears came as I watched Graylag with his elderly wives, my mother's kinswoman and my father's sister, slowly winding their way in single file back to their fire. I never felt worse, even on the Pine River.

Before dawn the next day, Elho and White Fox, their packs on and their spears in hand, stepped over the sleeping form of Meri in her deerskin and sat on their heels beside me. I had been awake most of the night—although Meri had got up sleepily now and then to help me keep watch and feed the fire—and I was tired. But then, these days I was always tired anyhow. I looked at Elho and White Fox to learn why they were here.

"We're going with you," said Elho. "I, too, dislike the mammoth hunters, and like you, I want to find our lineage. Perhaps our kin will find me a wife, as I'm tired of Ankhi."

"And I am going with Meri," said White Fox. "Later I'll go to the Hair River and ask my parents why they broke my betrothal."

I made my pack slowly, perhaps hoping that Teal would march up to scold me for divorcing a good man, or even that Timu would come to tell me that the old people knew best about marriages. But it seemed that they were going to respect my wishes. No one came.

Over the tops of the low bushes I watched them getting under their packs, helping each other. Then my heart leaped—Graylag was coming! Ah, but Swift was following. They wanted to speak to Elho, to whom Swift said, "It will be good for you to visit your kin awhile. I'll keep Ankhi for you." Elho gave Swift a weak smile.

Swift then turned to me. "Hide-in-the-Grass! We're glad these men are going with you," he said, then added, "not that anyone forgets how you came alone from the Marten River."

It seemed my last chance to say something to Swift and Graylag, or to any of the people. The others now stood in the distance, waiting with their packs on, ready to leave. "I'm sorry, Father-in-Law," I said to Graylag.

"I, too," he said.

"I'm sorry, Uncle," I said to Swift. He gave a polite nod. I wanted to say more, perhaps about Meri, but he wouldn't talk of that with me now.

"This fine man," said Graylag, putting his arm around White Fox's shoulders, "he'll look after you. We won't worry if you're with him." Glad to be praised, White Fox looked down, smiling modestly. To White Fox Graylag said, "You'll come to us soon, then. Perhaps when the bearberries ripen. And you'd better come, or I'll get you myself. I won't face my nephew or your mother if you don't!"

White Fox grinned at Graylag. "I'll be there, Uncle. You won't have to get me."

Graylag gave him a hug around the shoulders. "Well then," he said, nodding pleasantly to the rest of us. Swift nodded pleasantly to all of us. With long, strong steps they walked back to the other people, then around them, then led them away.

Like two roe deer who happen to be standing near but who are not together, Elho and I watched them out of sight. Then I put on my pack and walked off, taking a direction for the Fire River. Elho, White Fox, and Meri must have followed me.

* * *

"Are they angry at us?" I asked later as we trudged toward the hills.

"They aren't happy," said Elho.

"You were with them—what do they say?"

"We're spoiling their arrangement with the mammoth hunters. They want us to go back, to go on with them."

"Why didn't you?"

"How can I go with them? They're shaming me."

"We fought too much," I said.

"We did," Elho agreed.

Still later I asked, "Why didn't Timu come to see me?"

"How could he?" said Elho. "He has to stay with Ethis, and look happy about it too. Graylag and the mammoth hunters need each other. Now Timu is the only tie they have." He thought for a moment. "Until I go back to Ankhi," he added. We stopped talking then, and wrapped in our own thoughts, we went forward, getting farther from the others with every step. But so it was to be.

After we left Graylag and Swift and their people, we walked for many days, Elho far ahead of White Fox and Meri, me far behind. Elho and I said little to anyone and nothing to each other. White Fox and Meri remembered riddles and jokes to laugh about. Our camping places were always lonely, empty, with one fire every night, a small one. I found myself getting angry at the others for no reason, and not listening when they spoke to me. My thoughts were far away, but I didn't know where, and almost every time I slept, my dreams frightened me. Of course we had very little to eat. We set snares at night and looked for carrion by day, but we didn't catch or find much, and hunger didn't help our feelings.

When the Moon of Flies was the thinnest crescent, we came near the place where we had seen the tiger. I remembered none of the landmarks but everything else about our first trip there, every tasteless bristlecone, every word anyone had said. I remembered Mother and Teal going to find the spring but instead finding the strangers. I remembered their taking Elho with them because they didn't dare leave him behind, and I remembered seeing Elho coming back for us through the birch grove, carrying the strangers' present.

The forequarter of a stallion, it was—a stingy present. My anger grew, huge and cold, until I hardly spoke even to Meri.

We hadn't been able to find the Spring River on our first trip, and we couldn't find it now. Elho, White Fox, and I spread out to look for it, leaving Meri up in a tree. I soon found myself in the birch grove, and saw that I was looking in the wrong place. In my mind's eye, when I saw the tiger circling our camp, I saw spruce trees around him, so I realized that spruce must be growing near the stream. The spruce grew on the north side of the slope. I was too far south to find the stream.

The ground was covered with long grass, damp after winter and very quiet to walk on in spite of the scattered yellow leaves. Even so, I soon sensed something walking stealthily behind me. Then a cold anger overcame me, because without having to turn around to look, I knew who it was. Sure enough, there stood Elho, in his soft moccasins on the soft ground.

Angry to begin with, angrier still to know he had crept up on me, I stared at him as if I was expecting this unwelcome visit, and I didn't speak. Then the skin on my back prickled suddenly. He reminded me of the tiger.

Elho seemed to want to say something. Perhaps he was planning his words. At last he smiled instead and made a soft gesture toward me with both hands. But something in my manner made his hands fall to his sides. For what seemed like a long time I looked straight at him, anger making my back stiff and pushing my chin high. But suddenly I bent, untied my moccasins, and stepped out of them. Then I loosened my belt, pulled down my trousers, and kicked them off. I drew my shirt over my head and threw it on the ground, swung my braid in front where I could reach it, unwound its string, and shook out my hair, all the while looking straight at Elho.

Suddenly Elho too began to strip, moving much faster than I had, shaking off his moccasins, hopping on one foot when his trousers caught. I didn't smile, or speak, or make any move toward him—I just stared at him, my teeth clenched, my hands in fists. The wind blew on my bare skin, freezing me. Soon my jaw was shuddering. When Elho cleared his feet from his moccasins and trousers, I turned my back and dropped to my hands and knees. There I locked my elbows and bent my head so my hair fell over my hands.

Still in his shirt, Elho crouched behind me, and in a moment I felt him enter. I arched my back; he reached an arm over me and pushed my head down; I bent my elbows; he slid his strong arm underneath me, took my shoulder, and pulled me tight against him. My climax soon came; his climax came; he relaxed his grip on my shoulder, drew a very deep breath, and stood up. Once more he looked at me softly as if he was about to speak.

But now I wouldn't look at him. Instead I stared angrily at nothing while I put on my clothes. I divided my hair into three parts, picked some grass out of it, and braided it. When I found the little string that held my braid, I tied it, and then I was finished dressing, so I turned and walked away. But behind me I heard the soft footsteps of Elho, still following. Now I faced him. "Keep away," I said. "Go find the river."

Much later, after I became a spirit, time and again Swift would trance to ask me to bring him Meri's wolf as a hunting helper. I made excuses, but never did as he asked. "Why do you tell me you can't find this wolf, when he's always stealing from us?" Swift once asked. "Why don't you stop his robbery?" I suppose I didn't because I couldn't. Whenever I saw the thin form of Meri's wolf creeping from the woods, filling his hopeful nostrils with the smells of meat, my heart grew soft at the sight of his hunger, and I pretended I didn't notice his taking what he could.

One night Swift felt sure I wasn't trying to find this wolf. "Go get him right now," he said. "And don't come back alone."

"Very well," I answered, thinking I needed to prove my good intentions. And in the form of a wolf I went to the woods to look for signs on the terraces above the Char. Meri's wolf was usually around somewhere, although he hid from me and Marmot and also from the large pack of wolves who lived in the hills. When I found his tracks, I followed him, and in time caught up.

At first he was startled. Perhaps he thought I belonged to the large pack and was out hunting for intruders. But when he saw I was alone, he took an interest in me. Had Swift planned this? It was the mating time of wolves and no doubt my scent drew him. Next he was asking me to play, and before I knew it he had a leg over my back.

I was outraged! Me and this youngster? He might not know me, but I certainly remembered him! And as nothing but a tiny pup! With a furious roar and a flash of teeth I spun around and bit the air where his face had been. He tucked his tail and ran for his life, with me at his heels until I saw he would escape and dropped behind. For a while this spoiled Swift's hopes to have Meri's wolf as a helper, which served Swift right.

Later I often thought about the meeting between me and Meri's wolf. He wasn't my kindred, but at the time he almost seemed to be. So I did to him what I should have done to Elho long before in the birch grove. But instead I had coitus with Elho, gaining nothing but an ordinary climax from the act that in a way cost me my life. Elho and I were hardly on our feet again before I saw I had made a terrible mistake. Here was another misdeed that couldn't be taken back. Yet in the climax itself had been a strange, cold triumph, simple and quick, that punished everybody—mostly Elho and myself and Timu, but also the rest of Graylag's people. Such revenge came easily to the women of our lineage, sad to say.

◄ 15 ►

IF I WAS ANGRY BEFORE, I was furious now. All by myself I found the stream, then went to our camp for Meri. She sat with White Fox and Elho, waiting for me. They had built a fire for warmth since we had nothing to cook, and they were eating fronds of deer ferns, having set aside a few for me. How was it possible, I thought coldly, to find ferns without finding the stream? They must have been a spear's throw from it. "We can go," I said, chewing the fronds. "Come, Meri."

"We didn't find the stream," said White Fox. "We'll have to try tomorrow."

The sun was low in the west, but I picked up my pack and looked at Meri. "Come," I said to her.

"Where are you going?" asked White Fox.

"To the Fire River," I said. "I found the stream while you sat here."

"You're going now?" He seemed surprised. "It's late. We're camped."

"Stay if you like," I said. "Meri!"

Perhaps I sounded dangerous. Instead of getting stubborn, Meri stood up. I walked off, hearing her behind me. Soon I heard Elho and White Fox behind her, complaining to each other that we were leaving a good place and a lot of firewood, but following nevertheless. At last I turned to stare at them. "Are you women that you can't stop talking?" I asked. "Aren't you hungry? Do you think we can hunt with so much noise?" To my surprise, and perhaps to theirs too,

250

they stopped talking completely. And it was just as well. In the gathering dusk we saw the outline of an ear beside a tree, put down our packs, and stalked the animal. It was a musk deer, small, but plenty for the four of us if we could kill it. White Fox screened himself in a downwind thicket while the rest of us moved the deer toward him. When he speared it, it gave a loud, shuddering cry.

Then we had to camp. The place was bad—very brushy and thick, giving good cover for any animal wanting to stalk us or rob us of the carcass, but it was now too dark to go on. Elho and White Fox were angry at me for getting us into this fix, and another time I wouldn't have blamed them.

It was also too late to find wood, if there was any. As we sat in the dark trying to make green juniper burn, with the heavy brush and the strong smell of the fresh carcass all around us, I remembered what Graylag had said about self-control. My lack of it had brought me here in the first place, and my anger could get all of us killed.

In my mind I heard Teal saying that it was up to me to do something about the bad situation. I told her, in my thoughts, that I didn't care. *You do,* she said. *You do. Should I move the musk deer away from where we sleep?* I asked her. *That would be a start,* she said. *Remember the tiger.*

So after we ate our fill of the musk deer, almost raw, I took it by the hind foot and dragged it far away. Elho and White Fox didn't mind—in fact, they must have been thinking of the tiger too. There was no tree tall enough to save the carcass, so I tried to hide it under a bush, but before I was back with the others, I heard two foxes snarling over it. Suddenly there was silence, then the sound of cracking bones. Something large had chased away the foxes. Because all this happened so quickly, we saw that whatever the large animal was, it hadn't been far away.

But what could we do? Nothing but try to keep our fire bright enough to shed a little light, wrap ourselves in our deerskins against the cold, and stay awake with our spears ready. Meri fell asleep first, then White Fox—still sitting up but with his head on his arms—leaving Elho and me awake but not speaking. I didn't even look at Elho, but thought instead about the loud scream of the musk deer. Had pain made it scream? I didn't think so—animals who are hurt are very quiet about it. Fear? Again I didn't think so—we sometimes scream with fear if we think someone will come to help us, but no one would go to help a musk deer. So why? On a cold night like that night, a cry can be heard far away. The large animal now cracking the bones must have heard the cry and come. Had the deer wanted something to come? Could the deer have done what I now saw myself doing—trying to harm others because I had been harmed? *You have killed me,* I heard the scream say. *Yet I have called someone to kill you.*

And the deer almost did kill us—it did, or I did with my anger. Bored and frightened at the same time, both Elho and I fell asleep, although we didn't mean to, and the next thing we knew, the morning star was rising and the sky was turning gray far ahead of the sun. Cold and stiff, we looked around and saw, right next to us, a tiger's footprints. We thought it could be the same huge male who had circled our camp so long ago. The sight of his tracks gave me a sick feeling. If we had been awake, we could have touched him. "I wonder if he remembers us," said White Fox. "It's good you gave him the deer."

That day my anger left me and didn't come back. I wasn't happy, but I was nicer to White Fox and Meri. Elho and I ignored each other, as if we both were trying to pretend that what had happened between us had never been. In time we were acting naturally with each other, almost as if what we were pretending really was true.

Later that spring we found the Fire River, with some whitefish still running but no sign of people. We walked upstream toward Woman Lake for several days, then changed our minds and walked far downstream to where the shallow river wound out onto the plain. When Meri and I were wondering what to do if we found no one, since we had nowhere else to go, White Fox found a trail along the riverbank with people's footprints on it, and we followed it to the camp. To show our good intentions, since in a way we were strangers, we left our spears in a bush when we got near.

The camp was large, with people from many lodges living

in shelters scattered over the plain above the riverbank. Some shelters were copies of bushes, domes of sticks covered with grass, but a few were copies of hemlock trees, cones of poles covered with hides. Many people were in the camp cooking whitefish. Some of them glanced at us, then stood up in surprise when they didn't recognize us. We recognized one of them, though, a tall man with a wide mouth and popping eyes—none other than Kamas, Child of Ina, my cousin The Frog.

I must say it gave me a strange feeling to see him—glad and angry at the same time. And who can say what he felt? He seemed almost frightened to see Meri and me. He probably thought we were dead by now. For all of him, we would be. Perhaps he had lied to the Fire River people to explain why he had left Graylag and Father. But he hid his confusion and came to greet us. Elho and White Fox were very glad to see his familiar face.

Many people gathered around us, among them Cousin The Stick, who looked over our heads to see if others were with us. He asked about his mother, Ina, then asked how Father was. I told him that Father had died soon after he had left us. The Stick nodded; he had expected as much. Aunt Yoi had married another man soon after she reached here, he said. She had known she was a widow. Where was she? I wondered, looking around for her. She was digging sedge root, but would be back soon and very surprised to see us, said Cousin The Frog. Meanwhile we must meet the other people and take food.

Soon we were eating whitefish by a fire with a great crowd of people around us, old and young, men, women, and children, all talking at once, all the adults anxious for news, especially about Teal. They already knew about Mother. They also wanted to hear of their kinswoman's children, Owl and Timu, whom most of them had never seen. Elho embarrassed me deeply when he told everyone I once had been Timu's wife but had divorced him after a fight. I would rather have told people in my own time, when I knew them better. At the news, Cousin The Stick and Cousin The Frog looked at me curiously, as if they wanted to know more, but I added nothing.

When the subject of Meri's betrothal to Swift came up, people grew serious. Presents must be given by Swift's lineage, they said. When they learned that Meri's betrothal to Swift was broken, they seemed disappointed. Swift sounded good to them. White Fox was too tactful to speak of his own broken betrothal so soon after meeting Meri's kin, but he reminded people of the gifts they owed for Owl's marriage exchange. A noisy discussion followed about necklaces, flints, greenstones, shells, ivory, and the rainbow feathers of Woman teals on Woman Lake.

We sat a long time in the sunshine by the fire, with the hazy sky overhead and the wind in the grass around us. We ate whitefish until we could eat no more. I should have been happy, I knew. I hadn't been at a summerground for three years, not since I was at the Grass River with Graylag and the other people, before I knew I was married. And for the first time in my life I was with people who knew me only as an adult and were interested in what I said. Also, although most of the people were strange to me, I was known to them—they remembered Mother perhaps better than Meri did; they knew Timu and Owl by name if not by sight; they remembered Teal and Mother as young girls, and called them by nicknames and pet names. Many of these people were my kin. Even so, I felt strangely sad. At that moment I would have done anything I could to be back in Graylag's lodge, even in winter, even with people fighting. Almost overcome by homesickness, all I could think about was Timu. In my mind's eye I saw his brown face, his handsome, wide shoulders, his long arms and legs, his beautiful back. Something pulled in the pit of my stomach. What was he doing right now? I wondered. I missed him.

A woman with a pleasant face sat down on her heels beside me. Her name was Eider and I was in her lineage, she told me. I looked at her closely to see if she was anything like Mother. Perhaps she was—she had a small, sturdy body with square shoulders, and she was about the age Mother would have been if she were living. Like Mother, Eider had a perfect, glossy braid and white teeth, which she showed often. "Your aunt will be happy," said Eider. "She thought you were dead." Eider called a little boy over to us and told him to go to the river where Aunt Yoi was digging sedge root. "Tell Hama's Daughter that someone has come to surprise her," she said. She then told me how she and I were related. Mother's mother, Hama, had a little sister, Black Wolf, who was Eider's mother. Black Wolf was still living, an old woman now. And she was here, not here at the fire, but asleep by her shelter. She was blind.

Eider took Meri and me to meet Black Wolf. She was lying by her fire on a deerskin blanket, tiny and very frail. Like the skeleton of a bird, her bones showed under her thin, wrinkled skin. Her eyes, which were open, were blue, not sky-colored like Swift's but dark and filmed—ugly eyes. Her deerskin shirt and trousers were too big for her, and her hair, face, and clothes were very dirty; she had ashes on her hands, and had been touching herself without knowing she was making herself gray. When she heard Eider's voice she sat up, slowly turning her head as if trying to find us. Eider sat on her heels beside Black Wolf and grasped her arm. "Your kinswomen are here to see you, Mother," she said. "Yanan and Meri, Lapwing's Children."

"Lapwing?" cried the old woman eagerly, reaching out to touch me. "Is it you?"

"Lapwing's Daughter, Mother," said Eider.

Black Wolf didn't understand. Very softly she said, "I can't see."

"Lapwing's two daughters, Mother, right here." Eider placed Black Wolf's hand against my face.

The dry palm moved slowly across my eyes and nose; the thin fingers felt my eyebrows. "Little Lapwing," said the old woman tenderly. Smiling, Eider looked at me and shrugged. I smiled too, but with the image of Mother here where she belonged, if only in Black Wolf's memory, I felt sad.

Behind me a voice said, "It isn't Lapwing, Aunt. Lapwing died. Yanan, you're here."

I turned. Aunt Yoi stood behind us, looking down at us, not smiling. The surprise of our coming seemed to have upset her. Letting my face show nothing but polite pleasure, I stood up. "Aunt!" I said. "I'm here. Meri too, and Elho and White Fox, all here to visit our kin and lineage. I'm glad to see you."

"Come with me," said Aunt Yoi. "Bring your packs. I'll show you where to sleep." So Meri and I got our packs and followed Yoi to the edge of camp, where in front of a little dome of branches thatched with grass, an old man was sitting. "My husband," said Yoi. The man looked up.

"Uncle. We have come," I said politely.

He and Yoi seemed to be waiting for something. Soon Yoi nudged me. "Offer your greetings," she said. "Where are your manners?"

Embarrassed, I tried to think how. I had never offered greetings at Graylag's lodge, since we all knew each other. In fact, I remembered meeting strangers only twice before —first the people on the Fire River, when my parents would have been offering the greetings, and next when I returned to Graylag's lodge after living on the Marten River, when I was sitting outside with Meri and saw Swift come down the trail. I hadn't even thought of greeting him. Shouldn't Yoi have known that I wasn't used to meeting strangers? Why did she shame me? I suddenly remembered all the other people I had met today, to whom I had failed to offer greetings. What must they think of me? My face grew hot.

Seeing my confusion, Yoi began a greeting for me. "Honor to your lineage," she said. I repeated this, mumbling. "Honor to your mother," Yoi went on.

I looked sideways at her, remembering how, not so long ago, I used to look up to see her face. *I won't do this,* I decided, and instead of repeating after her, I looked openly at her husband and said, "I'm sorry, Uncle. At my home we don't often meet new people. My sister and I mean no discourtesy—we honor you and all your people."

He nodded, giving Yoi a strange little glance. "Welcome to you and your sister," he said warmly. "It will be good having my wife's nieces here in our camp."

"Thank you, Uncle," I said.

"Have you eaten?" he asked.

"Thank you, Uncle. We ate whitefish."

"Yes," he said. "So you did. I was there."

There seemed to be nothing else to say. I sat down, and so did Meri. Some women with children came by on their way to the river. The children, unused to strangers, stopped to gape rudely. A baby wanted to stare too, but it was being carried away. All it could do was turn in its sling to keep its eyes on us like a little owl. In a moment the women gave the children some hard looks to make them leave us alone. Then we got to talking with these women and at last followed them to the river.

Many women and children were there before us, all naked, all bathing at a sunny bend of the river where the water was rushing. In the sunlight the fast water sparkled and the people's wet skins shone like the skins of red deer. These women too bore the marks of The Woman Ohun. But why did that surprise me? Teal, who had put my marks on me, came from here. I took off my clothes and shook out my hair. Then I waded into the water, which was so cold that when it reached my thighs I had to wait.

Yoi and Meri waded in beside me, Yoi as beautiful as ever, with smooth arms and legs. But she looked wrong—a grown woman with a girl's breasts. Suddenly I felt almost sorry for her, still childless among so many women with children to wash and carry, to talk to and sing to—all the Fire River songs Mother used to sing to me. Years had passed since I had seen so many children. Thinking of the people of Graylag's lodge, with only Ankhi's child still living, I watched these children, their wet bodies shining, playing with round stones on the riverbank. They made a little lodge and carefully placed a pile of sticks beside it—a pile of antlers!

I turned to Aunt Yoi to point this out to her, and caught her looking me up and down. On her face was a very strange expression, half angry, half smiling. "Yanan," she said.

"Aunt?"

But instead of speaking to me, she turned to a woman washing herself beside us. It took me a moment to recognize that this naked woman was Eider. To her Yoi said, "Yanan is pregnant."

I was stunned. I couldn't think. I couldn't hear the river or the people, and all I could see in my mind's eye was Elho, Elho over my shoulder in the birch grove.

Yoi smiled and asked, "Aren't you?"

I stiffened my neck to keep from looking down at myself

and stared instead at her, trying not to let my eyes grow round. Was I marked? Did Yoi know about the father? In a terrible confusion, I suddenly realized that I was standing naked in front of many strangers, all now looking at me, all seeing something I knew nothing about. "No!" I said. Then, "Yes!" I was afraid of seeming ignorant. But Yoi still watched me with a strange half-smile. She knew she had surprised me.

There was nothing to do but wash myself. As calmly as I could, I scooped water over my arms, hardly feeling the cold. Then I sat on my heels in the current, up to my chin in the fast water, wishing I didn't have to stand up again so everyone could look at me. What did they see? I bent my head as if to wet my hair and squinted at myself underwater. Was my belly different? My breasts, perhaps? The water was foaming. I couldn't tell. When I waded to the riverbank and found my clothes, I peeked at myself again as I stepped into my trousers. Perhaps my nipples seemed bigger and darker. Perhaps my belly seemed rounder. I caught sight of a faint line running from my navel into the hair of my crotch, right down the middle of me. Was that the sign? Nothing could have made me ask Yoi, and I wished with all my heart for Mother. I could have asked Mother. Then I wished for Teal. I could have asked Teal, too. But of course, if I had stayed with Teal, this would not be happening to me.

At sunset I managed to get away alone into a wormwood thicket. There I pulled up my shirt and looked at myself carefully. My belly was rounder than I remembered, it was true. I pushed and poked at it, trying to feel the baby moving. Nothing. Perhaps it was dead. Considering that Elho seemed to be the father, that might be the best thing that could happen. My belly would be its grave, and someday I would forget all about it. But perhaps it was moving after all, still too small for me to feel, in there with all the fish I had eaten. Sooner or later something would happen, but what? And how long would I have to wait to find out?

By night I was sure I was pregnant. The thought was so frightening that it had to be true. Since I couldn't hear what other people said to me, I went to bed but didn't sleep, and I lay by Yoi's fire, looking at the stars. Yoi's husband, whose name I finally learned was Otter, was away visiting. Yoi and Meri were asleep side by side in front of the shelter. Yoi even took some of Meri's deerskin, just as she used to.

At first I tried to believe that Timu was the father. This wasn't easy. I had been with Timu since the end of summer when we saw the Yellowleaf Moon, having coitus time and time again all autumn and all winter until we had our fight, but not one person had ever noticed a single thing different about me. Yet the moment I had coitus with Elho, it seemed, Yoi noticed a baby right away. Much as I wanted to think that Timu was the father, I felt he couldn't be. And trying to pretend that he was didn't change the feeling.

I then remembered Mother and Teal calling to the tigress, perhaps Sali. I remembered Mother and Teal telling Yoi of babies fathered by their kinsmen—of armless, legless babies put out to die in the snow or left under bushes for the foxes. And of babies born crosswise, like Sali's. And of the men who kill these children, men who want to dash the babies' heads against a rock. And of the Camps of the Dead, where the lineages are angry with such women and refuse them places at their fires. I should have thought of this before I took off my clothes in the birch grove. It was too late to be thinking now. Still, my thoughts wouldn't stop.

But could no one get away with such a misdeed? Many people hid many things; perhaps this too could be hidden. After all, Sali had told her husband about her kinsman-lover. She had shouted out her kinsman's name in vengeance. And when Yoi had let Elho call her "wife," Father had overheard, and caught her. I, on the other hand, hadn't yet told anyone. Perhaps I could hide what others could not. If Mother were living, she would advise me to hide the truth, to lie, as she had advised Yoi.

Why do we look at the night sky when we have questions? In my mind Timu spoke to me. *If you're not asleep, your eyes are open. There's nothing to see except the sky,* he said.

But you don't ask questions you can't answer, I reminded him. *The sky is big, and we don't really know what stars are. All we learn about them is from stories—no one has ever gone up to look. My questions seem small when I see so much darkness.*

What are your questions, Wife? asked Timu.

Even in my daydream I couldn't tell him, of course. Rather I tried to stop thinking about him. I had lost the right to think of him this way. Instead in my mind I heard Teal speaking. *Where will you go next, you who learn nothing from the experience of others? What will you do? You who like handsome men, go find one now to hunt for you next winter. Will you live in Otter's lodge? Where is it? Who are his people? I hope they like rude women or they won't like you, Woman-with-No-Husband.*

I'll find another husband, I said. *I've just come here. I don't know the people yet. I'll make my way.*

Our lineage will marry you to the man who best suits the people here, said Teal in my mind. *Your marriage could be very helpful to them. I hope they're helpful to you.*

Perhaps I'm not pregnant, I imagined myself saying. *What does Yoi know?*

Perhaps you're not. Perhaps Yoi isn't jealous of every sign of pregnancy. You who are always daydreaming, perhaps you just imagined what happened in the birch grove.

Yoi found a husband, I said.

He's old, though, even for her, said Teal's voice in my mind.

I woke from this daydream when I heard Otter coming home. He unrolled a deerskin blanket and wrapped it around his shoulders, then fed the fire as if he meant to sit up for a while. When he noticed me looking at him, he smiled and took two fish out of his hunting bag, holding them up and pointing—one for him and one for me. I got up then and sat with him at the fire while the fish cooked. He asked me about our journey here and what game we had seen. He seemed so kind, so interested, that I found myself telling him about the tiger, and how we had seen the same tiger before, and how we had tried to find the camp here at the Fire River years before. But he knew that—he had heard it first from Yoi. Even so, he listened politely and again told me I was welcome as long as I wanted to visit.

Would he feed me in winter, even if I didn't belong to his

people, even if I brought no useful tie to a good lodge or a summerground? He seemed to be offering just that, and I was about to ask about his lodge when Yoi woke. Otter told her the fish were ready to eat, and she joined him at the fire.

In the nicest way, Otter gave her a fish on the point of his knife, and gave the other fish to me. I tried to refuse it, but he said he wasn't hungry—he only cooked fish to pass time. I was very hungry, and the fish smelled good; I tried to refuse it once more, but when Otter still wouldn't take it back, I ate it. Yoi's, of course, was gone.

Yoi now wanted to know what our plans were, and if it was true that I was really divorced. When I said I was, she was angry. Now she had no place in Graylag's lodge. She might need that place, she said. Who knew what winters The Bear might send her? Who knew when she might starve? Also, she supposed she now would have to return her share of my marriage exchange, with nothing to take its place, since I had no husband. I should cancel my divorce, she said, and solve these problems.

I reminded Yoi that since I had damaged Graylag's ties with the mammoth hunters, I might not be welcome if I went back.

"Not even if you're pregnant?" she asked. "Isn't a child always welcome?" When I didn't answer, she looked at me strangely.

Later she told me that a widower was here from a lodge on Woman Lake where people killed big fish even in winter. If I wouldn't cancel my divorce, I should marry him. Of course, she said, he wouldn't be able to get a child on me for a few years if my child lived. But in the morning she would speak to Eider about the widower and me.

Had Yoi been to his lodge? I asked. No, but people spoke well of it, she said. The people there killed reindeer too, and kept a big pile of all the antlers from all the reindeer next to the lodge. Yoi understood that this pile was something to see. I remembered the pile of sticks like a pile of antlers made by the children at the riverbank. Were these the children of the widower's lodge? I asked. Yoi shrugged. "Perhaps they were," she said. "I didn't notice. Tomorrow I'll bring you to the people of this widower, if Eider agrees.

You can stay with them. We can talk about the gifts they could offer for you."

"Tomorrow?" I asked. I wasn't ready to begin a marriage tomorrow.

"Is something wrong with it?"

"Your niece is here to visit, Wife," said Otter. "Perhaps she doesn't want to marry yet."

"No? Then what will she do in winter? Your brother's lodge is crowded and the hunting is poor. Will she stay with you?"

"She may if she likes," said Otter. "She and her sister too."

"Where do my cousins live?" I asked Yoi, thinking of The Stick and The Frog.

"With their wives' people. Kamas's wife is from a lodge on the Fire River where it leaves Woman Lake, and Henno's wife is from a lodge on the far side of Woman Lake. They're crowded, though. They might take Meri, but they can't take you." Yoi changed the subject. "You haven't seen the lake yet. It's very big. No one has ever walked around it."

Otter laughed. "Of course people have walked around it, Wife. No lake is too big for that." He became serious. "It is big, though," he added. "It takes a whole morning just to walk across the ice in winter." As I began to see how things might be for me, I felt frightened. I didn't want to talk about the size of Woman Lake or the lodges on it. Perhaps I showed this, as Otter changed the subject. "What of the two men with you?" he asked. "Elho, is it? White Fox?"

White Fox a man? I wouldn't have put it that way, but, "Yes, Uncle," I said. "White Fox came to ask our lineage for Meri."

"What of the other man? Is his name Elho?"

What about him? For just a moment I tried hard to think of something to say about Elho. When the silence became worrisome, I hurried. "White Fox was once betrothed to Meri," I stumbled on, as if Elho had not been mentioned. "She then was promised to a man from the mammoth hunters . . ."

But I never finished my speech, because Yoi was staring at me as if a thought had suddenly struck her. "Elho is our kinsman, here for a visit," she answered for me. I glanced at her in dismay. She watched me with cold triumph, seeing something. I tried to smile to cover my confusion, but too late.

During the days that followed I learned much about pregnancy from other pregnant women, of whom there were quite a few, all glad to talk about it. I saw how, when I was a child in Graylag's lodge, the grown women might have talked about these matters with each other. I also saw that, like the women of our lodge, none of the women here said anything to children. If a child, even Meri, came around to listen, the women changed the subject. It seemed enough that children knew who they might or might not marry. In fact the other women seemed to have learned about pregnancy as I was learning, from finding their trousers getting tighter every day as their children grew large below.

Although I always carefully spoke of Timu as the father, Yoi took a deep interest in our trip from Graylag's lodge. She now wanted to know exactly when we had left. Had Timu come partway with us? What moon was in the sky? Was there snow? A lot or a little? Were the rivers open or under ice? What foods had we eaten? Did we find fern fronds by the Char River? Were the winterberries red or black? Did the four of us come all the way together? Did we meet other people?

Since I guessed that she was trying to find out if I had been with Timu when I became pregnant, I lied or answered vaguely, so Yoi got nothing out of me. Sometimes I overheard her questioning White Fox, and I even heard her questioning Meri. But she couldn't question White Fox very closely—she wasn't his aunt—and Meri was afraid of Yoi, so Meri wouldn't answer. Yoi even tried questioning Elho in a whispering, girlish voice, as if to remind him of their own past. But Elho surely had secrets with several women. No old misdeeds would loosen Elho's tongue, especially since admitting to more would add to his trouble. He may not have been a wise or careful person, but he wasn't so careless as to chatter to Yoi. Yoi came away from her talks with Elho looking annoyed and disappointed.

I spent the days sleeping or digging roots and talking with the other women, but I spent the nights awake, wondering what to do. One night I was sitting alone by Yoi's fire when Yoi got out of bed to sit beside me. She tried again to pry from me any adventures I might have had on the way to the Fire River, but as usual I didn't answer. At last she asked me outright how long ago I had left Timu and who the baby's father was. I stared at her as if I was shocked. "You can tell me," she urged. "You have no mother, no one to talk to. But you need someone to talk to. I'm your aunt. Whom can you tell, if not me?"

"There's nothing to tell, Aunt," I said innocently. "I'm going to have a baby—nothing more."

"Then why don't you go back to your husband?"

"The people don't want me, Aunt. As I told you, I broke our ties to Graylag's people."

"You could go back," she said. "If the baby is your husband's, they would welcome you." I said nothing. "Of course, if it isn't your husband's, you should stay far away," she went on. "Have you menstruated since you left Timu?"

"I've only menstruated once in my life, Aunt. That was long ago on the Antler River, when Meri and I were finding our way back from the Pine River where you saw us last. I bled from the cuts of The Woman Ohun instead of menstruating."

If I thought that speaking of her leaving Father would stop her questions, I was wrong. "You know," she said, "you never answer me. What are you hiding? At first I never doubted that Timu was your baby's father. But then I saw that you were hiding something—the real father. He must be White Fox."

"Aunt!" I said. "He wasn't White Fox. White Fox is a child."

Very slowly Aunt Yoi smiled. "Perhaps not a child, but still a youngster," she said. "Of course the man isn't White Fox. The man is our kinsman. Who else? He's Elho, Child of Teal—Teal, Child of Sali. Well, Yanan. We're all in one lineage—Sali, Elho, you, and me!"

I faced her squarely. "Just because you did wrong doesn't mean I did the same," I said. "I've done nothing, and Timu

264

is the father. And I'm tired now. I'm going to sleep. Pregnancy makes women tired. Have you heard that?" Yoi gave me a long look that said, *I haven't finished with you.* But I was spreading out my deerskin for the night.

When I was alone, I again seemed to hear Teal speaking in my mind. *You're going wrong,* she said. *Your aunt sees your secret. Or else she's suspicious. Why does she want this knowledge?*

People are always curious, always prying, I answered.

There's more, said Teal. *Your aunt is jealous. She was jealous of your mother, she's jealous of pregnancy, and she's jealous of you. What will she do with what she thinks she's seen?*

I don't know. I'm afraid of her.

You should be afraid of her. There's good in this for her. Look there for the beginning of trouble. What if she told someone?

That would be bad, I said.

Would you do what she asked to stop her tongue?

I would, of course. I knew it. In my mind I heard more of Teal's questions. *Would you marry someone she chose, and live where she chose, letting her use you and your child, stained and without people except its own kin? She could use you and the child too, for anything, forever. Think how things are with your Aunt Yoi, living in winter where the hunting is poor and the people many, she with no children to tie her to them, and now with no tie to Graylag either. What might become of her? She's still young, still beautiful, but even now she can see herself as an old woman—alone, without children, left to die in the snow.*

Otter is kind. He's good to her.

Otter is old, Yanan. And the lodge belongs to his brother. Did you think to ask if this brother has sons with their own families? When Otter is dead, will they want your aunt living with them if she bears no children to tie them to them? You're giving Yoi great strength, if she can use it. She could have you disgraced and your child put out for the foxes. She needs this strength, and she thinks she sees a way to use it. She's dangerous.

She has suspicions, no proof, I said bravely.

See that she doesn't get proof, said Teal. *Watch yourself and watch your tongue.*

Two days later Meri and I were digging sedge root in the long grass on the riverbank. Hearing the grass rustle, we looked up to see, against the sky and the grasstops, the faces of White Fox and Elho. *Still he follows me,* I thought angrily. I was even angrier when I saw that he and White Fox were carrying out some kind of plan. Without a word to me, White Fox asked Meri to follow the river downstream with him, leaving Elho and me alone. Elho then sat on his heels in the deep grass, facing me across the hole I was digging.

"What will people say when they see us here together?" I asked. "Haven't you the sense to let me be? And what have you said to White Fox, that he helps you?"

"Do you think I'm here to have coitus with you, Kinswoman?" he asked. "People say you're pregnant. I've come to hear if it's true."

"Are you my mother to ask me?"

"Answer, Yanan."

"Why, if it doesn't concern you?"

"Because Yoi is talking of your marriage to a widower."

"Yes?" I kept digging.

"His betrothal gifts won't be many, if he has to wait for years to get a child from you."

Seeing Elho's reasoning, I rested my digging stick. "Your share won't be large," I agreed.

"I need gifts to give for Ankhi. Now you say you're pregnant, so what do you expect my share to be in your next marriage? You leave trouble behind you, Yanan. Have you ever thought of other people before making plans?"

"If I'm pregnant, do you think I can stop it?"

Elho brushed the dirt off a root and bit into it. "You make me tired, Yanan," he said, chewing. "You make people angry." He swallowed. "First you spoil Meri's betrothal, so we get no ivory. Next you divorce Timu, so we must return the gifts we got for you. And then you tell people you're pregnant, so we get very little in your next marriage exchange. How must we feel about that?"

I shrugged, and began to dig another root.

Elho caught the top of my digging stick. "I want something from you, Yanan," he said. "Since you made trouble, you must undo it."

"We're both angry," I said. "You want me to remarry just for presents. You even dare ask if I'm pregnant, because of your greed!"

"Women don't understand the betrothal exchange," he said stiffly.

"You're the one who doesn't understand. That's why you're here, digging roots like a woman and speaking rudely although you've come to beg."

"I told Yoi and Eider I'd persuade you to let Swift have Meri. That's why I'm here. Your aunt will help with my marriage exchange if you listen to reason. I'm doing what I must do."

Suddenly a thought struck me, so that I stared straight at Elho without seeing him. Why indeed was he here? If Yoi and Eider wanted something of me, why didn't they ask me themselves? Did they think I had special feelings for Elho, so he could persuade me when they could not? Or was Yoi setting a snare for us, a snare carefully hidden and baited with something neither of us so far had seen?

She was! I saw it! Suddenly I began to laugh. "Who told White Fox to take Meri away from here, Kinsman?"

Elho looked puzzled. "Your aunt did. She thought I could persuade you better if I spoke with you alone. Anyway, we're talking about Meri. We don't want her to hear."

"You're greedy, Kinsman," I said. "And you're simple. My aunt is greedy too, but she's not simple. She sent you here with the promise of presents. She got rid of White Fox and Meri through you. You and I are alone here for as long as we like. We could have coitus again, as Aunt Yoi hopes we will. Stand up and walk away. Someone else is coming."

"What are you talking about?"

"Do it, Kinsman! Don't stay here by me. Get up and go!"

"Do you think you can command me?" asked Elho angrily, making no move to do as I said, and as we sat glaring at each other, the grass rustled again and Cousin The Frog stood over us. Looking somewhat surprised, perhaps to see us clothed and sitting above a pile of sedge roots, not naked and embracing, he didn't even meet our eyes but seemed to be glancing over the ground as a man will if he comes upon another man alone in the bush with a woman. If we had already done what he came too late to see, the trampled grass would tell the story.

Elho looked embarrassed, as if The Frog had caught us in some wrongdoing, but I smiled. "Cousin! You've come. Perhaps my aunt told you where we were," I said. He grunted with surprise. Perhaps she had! "White Fox and Meri are just there," I went on, pointing with my lips down the river, "and now I'm going to them." I stood up and stretched, then bent and picked up the sedge roots, handing them to Elho. "Take these to my aunt. They're hers—she told me where to find them. I'll get Meri." And I went, leaving Elho and Cousin The Frog ashamed and unable to look at each other.

Perhaps I'm doing better, I said to myself as I followed White Fox and Meri home. *At least I feel better. Now for Yoi.*

I saw what to do about Yoi. I had a plan that would help her a little. But more important, the plan would help me. Yoi didn't know it, but she would get me back to Timu with all Graylag's people welcoming and praising me. I could right all the wrongs and live in honor—well, for a while, if no one ever found out about Elho.

But no one had yet found out about Elho, although Yoi tried to use Elho's greed for presents and women to get proof for her suspicions. But she failed, and instead showed me how useful she herself could be.

My plan made me happy, cheerful, and loving, not just to Meri but to everybody, so that when Yoi brought the widower and some people from his lodge to visit me, these people told Yoi that I was good. They said I had a cheerful nature and would be good company in winter. They would gladly have me, and if years passed before I had a baby by the widower, well, so it would have to be.

I thanked them for their kindness, and with my head bent modestly I promised to speak to my lineage about my betrothal exchange. Yoi seemed a bit surprised—perhaps she didn't think I would agree so easily. Perhaps she was also disappointed. If she needed more time to persuade me, her share of the marriage exchange might have been larger. When the widower and his people were gone, I thanked Yoi for her help.

Eider came to sit at Yoi's fire, seeming pleased with the news. Only Otter looked sorry. A little later he reminded me that I needn't marry in a hurry; I was welcome to stay with him as long as I liked. "Thank you, Uncle, but I'm content," I said.

Meri looked worried. When we were alone she said, "What are you doing? Where are you going? I'm going with you, because I won't stay here."

"You'll come with me. You won't stay here. Don't be afraid—everything will turn out well. Go find Elho. Ask him to meet me where we dug sedge roots when the moon rises tonight. Say it's very important, and don't tell anyone else—not anyone, not White Fox, not for any reason. Do you understand?"

"Yes," said Meri, impressed.

"Good, because if you tell, I'll have to marry the widower and go with him while you stay with Aunt, and we won't see each other, not ever again."

Meri stared at me with round eyes. "I won't tell," she said.

I went to bed early, while the sky in the west was still red after the sunset. "My pregnancy makes me tired," I explained in a satisfied voice to Yoi when she looked at me as if she had a question. When the sky in the east became pale yellow-pink before the moonrise, people had forgotten about me. Leaving my deerskin in a pile as if someone were sleeping underneath it, I crept to the edge of the camp and took the trail to the river, where I sat down in the long grass.

Upstream, bison were wallowing. I listened to them splash and snort. Glad of the sound, since some of the bison would keep watch for lions and hyenas, I saw how The Woman must be helping me. Soon I heard the grass rustle, and raising my chin to look over the top of it, I saw against the rising moon the outline of Elho. He would never have found me if I hadn't stood up.

"You're here," I said as softly as I could.

Even so, he started nervously. "Yanan? What's this? Meri said I must meet you here."

"Get down in the grass," I whispered. "I have a plan and I need your help."

"What is it?"

"We're going back to Graylag, with a wife for Swift. He wants a woman from my lineage, so we'll bring him one. The bridal exchange should be something to see, since she's full-grown and beautiful."

"Who is this woman?"

"Aunt Yoi. Who else?"

"Your aunt? But she's married."

"To an old man from a poor lodge. She left my father because she was afraid of spirits. Think how fast she'll leave Otter because she's greedy for ivory."

Elho thought for a while. "How will you do this?"

"Not I. We! We will do it, and White Fox will help us when he sees how he gets Meri out of it."

"And what am I to do? Do you want me to try to persuade your aunt?"

"Leave her to me. You must describe the Hair River. Tell our kinswomen about the meat and ivory there. Tell them about the presents in your marriage exchange. Be sure the people see what they get if Yoi marries Swift."

"It's good, Yanan. The people here like ivory." Elho smiled, then frowned. "What about Otter?" he asked.

"Don't tell Otter."

"He's a very mild man."

"He's mild, it's true."

"Is it right to take his wife from him?"

"Did something stop you from taking Father's wife or Timu's wife? They were mild too."

"They must be mild, since their women came to me so willingly. Does it never worry the women of our lineage to harm a good man?"

"How am I hurting Otter? Yoi won't share his bed. He's good, but she's not." Elho made me think, though, and I found that I was worried. Otter was so kind to me that it hurt to work against him. I tried to think of a way to soften our deeds, but unhappily, no idea came. "Well, I'm sorry," I said at last. "But after all, he'll be hurt by Yoi, not by us. No doubt she'll pay for it. Swift is so fierce that he'll certainly beat her, and then she'll be sorry she left so kind a man." For just a moment I saw in my mind a very satisfying image: Swift with bite marks up and down his arms, and Yoi striped with welts from a stick.

"Swift might beat your aunt," Elho agreed thoughtfully. "She can be very annoying. Well—let's do it."

"Good. Start tomorrow. I want to see my husband."

"What about the baby?"

"What about it? Doesn't Timu want children?"

In the moonlight we heard the bison leaving the river, water pouring from their sides. Elho watched me as we listened, then said in a soft, strange voice, "Isn't it mine?"

I saw that the time had come to talk with Elho of my pregnancy. "Look at it this way, Kinsman," I began. "Perhaps the baby is yours. I thought so too, at first. If it is, Timu may kill it, Ankhi may divorce you, and both of us will be in disgrace for the rest of our lives. Perhaps Graylag won't let us live with him anymore, even if Teal is your mother. If he doesn't, we will wander where we can, looking for someone else to take us in.

"But if the baby is Timu's, my divorce will be canceled and I will still be Timu's first wife, full of honor, by the wish of the old people. There will be a place forever in the lodge for me and you and Meri and Ankhi, and you will have a niece or a nephew to grow up with your daughter. Now I seem to remember feeling life in my belly even before we left for the Char River. That makes me think this baby is Timu's."

"I see," said Elho.

"Good. We agree. We can go."

"Not yet," he said. His voice was soft, and his eyes were on the neck of my shirt, fastened by the ivory pin his fingers now were gently twisting. He pulled slowly, and the shirt opened. I looked down at my breasts in the moonlight and watched my nipples take form. I couldn't help it—as Elho wanted me, I also wanted him.

Wasn't the harm already done? Couldn't I now give myself to him because of happiness, after throwing myself at him because of misery and anger? But no. I took the pin away from him and closed my shirt. "Do you want to scare this child of mine with coitus?" I asked, standing up. He stood too, but caught my arm. "Haven't you heard of the stranger in the coldtrap?" I whispered, pulling my arm free. Then I walked off in the dark, quickly and quietly among the huge black shapes of the grazing bison. If this baby met a penis, it would meet only Timu's. So it must be.

The next day Elho and White Fox did their work well. By evening, when I told Yoi that Meri was betrothed to Swift only because Swift insisted on having a woman of our lineage, Yoi was more than ready to be that woman. She faced me eagerly, with shining eyes. "Why was a child like Meri offered in the first place?" she asked. "Why didn't someone come straight to me, a young widow?"

"Aunt! People thought you were married to Father. Then, no one knew where you were. Now only Meri stands in the way, because the mammoth hunters don't know of your willingness and are still hoping for her. Remember, her betrothal to White Fox was broken."

"By whose word was that betrothal broken? No one asked me! I helped your parents choose White Fox as Meri's husband, and White Fox that husband shall be! I'll go to the Hair River and fix all this."

Out of the dark Eider came to join us. When Yoi told Eider about her betrothed (as she already called Swift), Eider seemed delighted. She began to talk of ivory, and soon she and Yoi were naming all the people who should give and receive gifts.

But suddenly Eider remembered what the mammoth hunters looked like. In the middle of talking about a necklace, she caught herself. "Think what you're doing, Yoi," she began breathlessly. "I've seen some of them. They have hair like yellow caterpillars and white skin like plucked birds. Just like the animals. It's as if they wanted us to eat them. How do we even know that they're people, since they don't look like people?"

I hated to hear this—Eider could ruin all my plans. I was always very careful in describing the mammoth hunters, and now Eider was blurting everything. Yet what could I say? She spoke the truth—they really didn't look like people. But, "They're not so bad as that, Aunt," I said, "and not all of them look so much like animals. Elho married one of them. And my co-wife, Ethis, looks almost like you. She's just as pretty. And it's not their fault. They're not dirty, just ugly. Some of them can be nice . . ." My voice trailed off. Then I remembered myself. *I must do better,* I thought, and went on in a stronger tone. "Even the ugly ones are not so ugly after you get to know them. It isn't their looks, anyway. It's their hunting. You get used to their looks."

I drew a deep breath of relief when Yoi agreed. "Looks aren't important," she said.

"There's something else," said Eider, "something else I don't understand. Why did Lapwing's Daughter change her mind so suddenly, and what will we tell the widower who now wants to marry her?"

"What does it matter?" said Yoi. "Tell him what you like."

But I felt I owed Eider an explanation. "When I divorced, I didn't know I was pregnant," I said. "But as I was leaving, I noticed the signs. I then decided just to visit here, not to stay. My aunt didn't understand this when she spoke of another husband for me. Perhaps I hadn't told her of my pregnancy, since I felt shy to speak of it. But now I'll go back to my husband. Everyone must keep the gifts of my marriage exchange."

Yoi looked at me very doubtfully. "You learned of your pregnancy when you were leaving?" she asked. "By what signs?"

After all I was doing for her, she still wanted to unbalance me. But she couldn't anymore, not after all I had learned from other pregnant women. "Why, my belly grew round," I said. "My breasts grew large, my nipples turned dark, and I saw a line below my navel, right down the front of me. And I felt life there. We who are pregnant, we know right away."

Yoi was silenced. Sulkily she waited for Otter to come back from his visiting, and when he sat on his heels beside her to offer her a piece of fish as usual, she told him she was divorcing him. "Your people were too stingy to give many presents, so not much will have to be exchanged," she said.

I was watching Otter closely but couldn't tell from his face what his thoughts were. "If you wish, Wife," was all he said.

In the morning we started for the Hair.

‹ 16 ›

IT HURT ME TO say good-by to the people who remembered Mother, especially Black Wolf, whom I would not see again until we met at the fire of our lineage in the Camps of the Dead. Still, as soon as we set off in single file through the long red grass with the morning sun on us, my spirits rose like the swallows overhead. First went Elho and White Fox, then I came with Meri, and last came Yoi. All of us were very happy, and Yoi taught us a song.

After we had walked a way, we heard people behind us. We turned to look, and saw my cousins The Stick and The Frog following, now with their families. Having been so busy with my own problems at the Fire River, I hardly knew their families, and I looked at them closely. Both wives were carrying small children. An older child, a boy, followed The Frog. How was it I knew so little about these people? The older boy must be the wife's son from an earlier marriage, since he was too old to be a child of The Frog's. We stopped and waited for them, and when they caught up with us, we welcomed them. "Father will be glad to see you," said Elho. "He often says you left Ahi's place empty in the lodge."

"We will be glad to see Graylag," said The Frog. "It's been a long time."

"Two years," I reminded him.

He looked at me but didn't speak, and a little chill passed over me. When I thought all my troubles were settled, here was Cousin The Frog following me, he who suspected me, he who had found me with Elho in the long grass. What had

275

Yoi said he might find? But I had carried myself well at the time, and couldn't worry about him now. I was too happy.

"If you won't go first, I will," I said to Elho, and took the lead. But since I didn't really know the way, in time Elho and my cousins were calling to me.

"There. There!" they shouted, pointing. I was far ahead of everyone, but saw where they pointed and tried to find a landmark to walk to. But the plain was flat and grassy. There were no hills and no trees, just the dome of the sky and herds of bison far away. I stopped to let Elho and White Fox catch up with me.

"How am I going wrong?" I asked.

"Look at the sun," said Elho. I looked. "We want to go north."

"No landmarks?" I asked.

"Nothing much," said Elho. "The country is flat and open all the way."

"Have you come here from the Hair?"

"Not this far, but it's all the same."

"How do you know?"

"Wouldn't people tell me?"

"Good. Then you know," I said, and started off, but soon I heard people calling me again. Again I waited, and again Elho and White Fox caught up.

"You're running, Yanan," said Elho. "Aren't there small children with us? Can't you slow down for them?"

"No," I said. "I want to see Timu. Stay behind if you like. I'll take Meri and go on by myself."

"You won't find the way."

"Of course I'll find the way. If I kept going straight north, wouldn't I come to the Hair River?"

"You won't find the people."

"Of course I will. Don't they leave tracks?"

"Yanan," said Elho impatiently, "the Hair is very long. People don't walk the length of it. You won't find the cave."

"Keep up with me, then," I said.

But he didn't, and soon I was far ahead again, with Meri. She was stubborn about traveling so fast, but I insisted. "Think what I've done for you," I said when we were out of earshot of the others. "I saved you from a marriage to Swift.

You didn't like Swift. Now you're betrothed to White Fox again, or you soon will be. Isn't that what you wanted?"

"I don't want to be married," said Meri.

"Well, you won't have to be for years," I said.

"I won't have coitus."

Coitus! How did Meri know of coitus? The sooner she was married the better, since she knew about coitus. But I didn't want to talk of marriage with her now, and reminding myself to ask White Fox what he had been saying to her, I hurried on. In a while she said, "I won't go this fast."

"Yes you will," I said. "We can be there in a short time if we hurry."

"You want to see Timu. I don't," she said.

"Why not?"

"He beat you. He might beat me."

"All that is forgotten," I said. "And he wouldn't beat you." Again we walked without speaking, listening to the wind in the grass and our own hard breathing.

"You're forcing me," said Meri after a while.

"I'm not. Just walk, don't talk if you're getting tired."

"The others won't find us."

"Aren't we leaving tracks?"

"The grass is closing behind us. We might meet a lion."

I stopped and turned around. "What's wrong, Meri?" I asked. "Why are you complaining?"

"I don't want to go to the Hair River," she said.

"No? Why?"

"Because you'll have a baby there. Then I won't see you. I'll have to go away." Meri began to cry.

I sat on my heels and put my arms around her. "What's this? Whatever makes you think this?" I asked. "I won't go away. And when the baby comes, you can play with it. You'll be the aunt." Then I added, "Don't be like Aunt Yoi," hoping to joke her out of her tears.

But Meri clung to me and said, "What if you're like Mother? What if you die?"

So for the second time that day a chill ran over me. "Well, I won't die," I said. "Did you see all the children at the Fire River? How could there be so many if their mothers died? Don't talk to me of death." Then I saw that I was being

277

unkind, and I thought for a moment. "Meri," I said at last, "listen to me. What if I do die? You might miss me, and I would miss you, but you won't be alone. You'll be married, and people will be with you. Do you remember Junco?" Meri looked doubtful. "White Fox's sister. You'd be with her. There are always people."

"I remember Junco," said Meri, wiping her eyes.

"Yes. Well, she's at the Hair River, waiting to see you."

Meri thought for a moment. "We can go," she said at last. So we did, hurrying for the rest of the day and stopping that evening in a thicket of sagebrush to shelter us from the wind. Meri looked for bison dung to burn and I looked for the vines of milkplants so we could scrape the roots and drink the juice from the scrapings, because we were thirsty. I had almost forgotten, while hurrying all day, that on the plain we might not find water.

At dusk Elho and White Fox caught up with us, followed a little later by Yoi. After dark The Stick and The Frog and their families came into our camp, very tired. They had stopped to gather food on the way, and now they shared it, getting in return squeezed root instead of water.

I was a bit sorry to have hurried everyone so much, especially since I could see that people were angry with me. I was truly sorry for the little boy, The Frog's stepson, whose name was Kakim and who now looked so tired, with dark circles under his eyes, that he seemed faint. He looked to be about the same age as Meri, yet she was able to keep the pace. Kakim's pack was very thick and heavy, I noticed, but I also wondered if he was sick. I saw that we would have to think more about the way we were traveling.

"I'm sorry to walk so fast," I said. "I'm in a hurry, but the rest of you don't need to be. I don't mean to hurry the children."

"You should think of others," said The Frog's wife nastily. "Unless you like forcing your sister and listening to children cry."

I felt a little flame of anger. "What I mean is this," I said. "I am going to the Hair River. I'm going to my husband, and the only person I must take with me is Meri. And of course my aunt," I added quickly, "if she wants to hurry. The rest of you are coming by your own choice." I looked at my cousins. "In Father's lodge on the Pine River, I never asked anyone to wait for me." I paused a moment to let them remember. "And no one did. I'm surprised that you think I ought to wait for you. If I get to the Hair River first, I'll tell the people that you're following slowly because of children. I'm finished speaking." And I sat with my chin high, looking at the embers of the burning bison dung.

"This is very rude," said The Frog's wife, breaking the silence that followed my speech. "When people travel, they should stay together." She looked indignantly around at the others, waiting for some reply. But only The Stick's wife seemed to agree with her, and for a long time the rest of us waited.

At last White Fox said, "Yanan can hurry if she likes. If no one minds, I'll hurry with her. I want to see my parents. I haven't seen them for more than a year."

Elho said thoughtfully, "Perhaps we should talk of finding the Hair River in case we separate. Some of us don't know the way."

"Good," I said. "Tell us." So he did, describing how we should use the sun by day and which stars we should follow at night. And when we got to the river, we should walk downstream, looking for high banks. The cave we wanted was in a ravine. "If you meet the river in the ravine, you should go west. You'll be on the summergrounds of mammoths, so be careful," he finished.

"Why should we be careful?" I asked, wondering what dangers we should expect from mammoths.

Elho misunderstood my question. "Yanan—always rash," he said tiredly. "Don't be careful, if you don't want to be."

In the morning Elho, White Fox, and Yoi seemed to be keeping up with Meri and me. By noon The Stick and The Frog and their families had fallen far behind. We rested and ate in a thicket of low-growing bearberry bushes, but the families didn't catch up with us. White Fox asked whether we should wait for them after all. "Not I," I said. "When they were with Father, they didn't wait for him or me." Then I couldn't help but glance at Yoi, who hadn't waited for us either.

Yoi yawned, as if what I said had no meaning for her. Elho seemed a bit uncomfortable to be separating from other people, but he wanted to reach the Hair River as much as I did. At last he said, "They're grown men. They don't need us to take care of their families." And so we hurried for the rest of the way, and never saw my cousins again in all the time it took us to reach the Hair River.

On the night we left the Fire River, the rising moon that lit us was the Bearberry Moon in its last quarter. When we reached the huge, shadowy ravine of the Hair River, the crescent of the next moon, the Mammoth Moon, was following the sun. The distance is very great, but that was how fast we traveled—Elho hurrying to Ankhi and his daughter, White Fox hurrying to his parents, Yoi hurrying to ivory, and I hurrying to Timu.

Elho was right about the mammoths. As we walked on the grassy plain, following the river downstream toward the cave, we saw many mammoths, huge and hairy, with great, sweeping tusks that crossed far in front of them—enough ivory for the marriage exchanges of all the people in the world. Only cows and calves were in the herds; the bulls were alone or in twos or threes, sometimes an old bull with youngsters following him. The mammoths worried us a bit—they were so very big that our spears looked like twigs beside them. We thought that if a mammoth chased us it would kill us, so we kept near the edge of the ravine, ready to slide down where we thought no mammoth would follow. If the ravine was too steep for sliding, we looked nervously at the rocks below, hoping we wouldn't have to choose between the mammoths and the rocks.

When we were within a day's travel of the cave, we met a herd very close to the ravine. We stopped to think about these mammoths, and wondered whether to wait until they moved away, or go around them, or go down into the ravine.

The mammoths seemed to be thinking about us; they were pointing their trunks, blowing air, waving their ears, and rumbling, soft and deep. In the herd were tiny, long-legged infants who peeked at us from under their mothers while older calves trotted back and forth in front of the herd, their ears fanned and their tails high, as if the sight of us excited them. Suddenly one of the calves, its eyes bright with mischief, launched itself toward us in a jiggling trot.

I dropped my pack and leaped into the ravine, with Yoi and Meri right beside me. We clung to bushes to keep ourselves from sliding, and lay against the slope, looking up to see White Fox and Elho soar over the rim and land below us. Above, a mammoth trumpeted.

Since we were almost in the river, we slid the rest of the way down the bank and washed ourselves carefully, then smoothed and braided our hair so we would look nice when we met the other people. While we washed we heard a mammoth whacking something against the earth above us, and when we scrambled to the rim again, we saw my pack flattened. The mammoths who had done this were now grazing far away. Except for my ivory comb, my pack held only things made of leather and stone, not things that could be broken, so I threw away the shattered comb and cleaned the pack a bit, then put it on, and we left there, looking over our shoulders from time to time in case another mischief-maker took it into his head to follow us.

Late in the day we smelled carrion and heard someone pounding something between two stones. Looking over the ravine's rim, we noticed the corpse of a mammoth by the water. Also we saw a trail. Elho led us down this trail, along a wide ledge, and into a great, dim space in the wall of the ravine: the cave of the mammoth hunters.

Our eyes weren't used to the dark. We stood in the cave's mouth uncertainly, trying to see the many shadowy faces of the people inside. There were more people here than I expected—they must be mammoth hunters, surely. Our hearts were filled with happiness to be here at last, and I was looking everywhere for Timu, when to our surprise some of the men leaped up and grabbed their spears! We shouted with laughter. "Shall we fight, Father?" cried Elho.

"Elho! White Fox! You've come!" Graylag's spear thumped on the sandy floor of the cave as he threw his arms around them. "Did you want us to kill you? We didn't expect you! We saw your outlines with spears!"

"It's us, not strangers! You needn't expect us to leave our spears in a bush! We won't harm you!"

"My daughters!" Teal hugged me and Meri and Yoi. "How long it's been since I've seen you. Ah, welcome." I was so happy that I began to cry, and I hid my face in Teal's shoulder.

The cave rang with the voices of the men greeting Elho and White Fox. Suddenly a tall young woman stood in front of me. I gaped. It was White Fox's sister, Junco, strong and beautiful, wearing an ivory necklace. "It's you!" we both cried, hugging each other.

Then Ethis was beside me. In her open shirt I saw a small baby in a sling. It isn't right to shout about a baby, but I put my hand gently on the bulge it made. In return Ethis put her hand on my belly. Our eyes met and she gave me a little, secret smile.

"Hide-in-the-Grass!" said Swift. "Come and eat. You're hungry from traveling." Then he noticed Yoi. He ran his sky-colored eyes from her feet to her face, where he met her brown eyes, staring openly. He nodded politely. "Welcome," he said.

"She is my aunt," I told him. "My father's widow, my mother's sister, Yoi, Child of Hama. He is Swift, Child of Akima, uncle of my co-wife and headman of the mammoth hunters."

As the newcomer, Yoi began the long formal greeting, offering her respect to Swift and all the people with him. Her voice, so often a threatening scream, now had a huskiness to it. Her eyes were cast down. Swift gazed at her even after she had finished her greeting. At last, almost reluctantly, he had to turn to greet Elho and White Fox.

"Why did he call you 'Hide-in-the-Grass'?" whispered Yoi.

"I forget. Perhaps a nickname."

"Why can't he speak right?" she whispered again.

"Hush, Aunt!"

"He's rather white."

"He'll hear you!"

"But his teeth are nice."

Then I heard a voice behind me. "Why are you whispering, Wife?" it said. I turned, and there was Timu.

Now I had no words. I just looked at my husband, and my

eyes filled with tears. "What's this?" he asked, laughing. "Do we make you so sad?"

I laughed too, but it sounded like sobbing. Then I was sobbing! Quickly I drew a deep breath and wiped my eyes and nose. Again I was laughing. He seemed so handsome I could only say, "I'm here."

V

THE CAVE

≪ 17 ≫

DARKNESS CAME QUICKLY in the ravine, but the cave was filled with firelight. We sat eating strips of meat from the mammoth that lay dead by the river, the women at one fire, the men at another. *What a good, safe cave this is,* I thought, looking at its dry walls and high ceiling. *What a good place, with so much food, and what good people.*

And so I ate happily until I was full, hardly hearing what the other women said because I was listening for Timu, glad every time I heard his voice. Even the harsh laughter of the mammoth hunter men had a good sound to it—and why not? Sitting snugly between Junco and Ethis, with Aunt Teal across the fire giving me a smile from time to time, I laughed too.

I always remembered that night, even after I became a spirit. Sometimes loneliness made me think of it, making me wish that once again I was filling myself with mammoth meat among the many people in the firelit cave. But strangely enough, I thought most often of that night after I joined, for a while, the kindred of the very mammoth we ate.

This came about because of something I saw, something that happened because of hunting and meat. At the start of the first summer after I became a spirit, I saw four mammoth cows and one calf walking in bright moonlight on the plain above the ravine. The cave was full of eager hunters, but the mammoths didn't seem aware of the danger. Slowly and carefully, but not fearfully, they started down the ravine, down the narrow trail from the plain to the river.

287

In moments the hunters were out of the cave, and before I knew what was happening, huge rocks were bouncing off the mammoths. With loud cries for help, they crowded together, some trying to turn back while others tried to hurry forward. Suddenly three of them toppled off the trail and plunged to the boulders below. Trunk out and tail up, the fourth cow ran straight for the scattering hunters, and with the calf behind her made for the open plain.

The hunters went in the cave to wait for daylight. No one wanted to walk among injured mammoths at night. The firelit cave echoed with the voices of people praising the shamans, the spirits, and each other.

In the dark ravine the three huge shapes lay still. Feeling almost forced to watch them, I waited a long time. At last, like the back of a trancing person, the back of one mammoth seemed to open like a springfly casing, and a hairy spirit rose out of it. Bracing herself with her trunk and a front leg, then the other front leg, she bent a knee to get a hind foot under herself, then heaved herself up. She hadn't been standing long before the back of the second mammoth split and the second mammoth-spirit got up beside her.

The two touched trunks, then touched the third mammoth lying on the rocks. Nothing happened. The two mammoth-spirits wandered to the river and idly sprayed their chests and shoulders. In time they wandered back to touch the body of the third mammoth again. Still nothing. The two spirits moved toward the cliffs, where they stood swaying, now and then nosing the plants that grew in cracks of the rocks, now and then pulling a little grass to put in their mouths or to toss on their backs. When the moon went down, red and smoky on the dark horizon and the sky in the east became pale gray, the back of the third mammoth split at last and the huge, hairy spirit clambered out of it. By then the other two had drifted quite a way down the ravine, their rumps to the dawn, but as if they knew the third was ready, they now started walking purposefully, and with the third following they went downriver and out of sight.

I was impressed. *Here are animals who understand keeping together,* I said to myself. I wanted to know more about them and in the morning, in the form of a raven, I flew out to look for a herd. I found one easily, and circled for a while.

But the mammoths were grazing on the plain, far from any tree to roost in. And I couldn't find the courage to land in deep grass. When I got tired, I had to leave without learning anything about them. Later I tried again in the form of a long-legged bustard. Now to wade through the grass was pleasant and easy, and I found myself catching grasshoppers chased up by the mammoth's feet. But as a bustard I had trouble paying attention to the mammoths, since my thoughts winked like fireflies on a cold, dark night. Few and dim to start with, they seemed to come from nowhere and I couldn't tell when one might flash or where it went afterwards. Also, the calves seemed to think I was there for their fun, and they chased me mercilessly. At last I saw that to visit mammoths I should take the form of a mammoth, so one night I did, and found myself on four round feet under the rising moon.

Suddenly I realized that mammoths were calling all around me—none nearby, all far away. Mammoths are noisy animals who squeak and squeal, grunt, trumpet, rumble, and roar, but never before had I heard mammoths make these low, rolling calls, like bison bellowing but louder and deeper. It seemed strange to press my nostrils to the earth while looking over the tops of the birch trees, yet that is what I did, listening to the calls. At first the calls seemed unimportant. Some mammoths were just asking where others were and the others were answering; nothing more. But in time I recognized callers by their voices, and soon I could tell how far away each herd was. For no real reason I pulled some grass and tossed it on my shoulders, then set off to find the nearest of those who called.

While the moon sank to the horizon, I walked over the rolling plain, snatching tufts of grass to eat on my way. At last I heard a loud, low call that was almost a warning, smelled fresh dung and the dense, warm hair of mammoths, and heard the loud grunting and farting of mammoths getting to their feet. Caution told me to go no closer, so I stopped, and although the sky was still not quite light enough for me to see the other mammoths clearly, I let the tip of my trunk roam the air.

Suddenly I caught the strong scent of an elderly female, and then, in the gray dawn light, I made out her huge form against the dark forms of the rest of her herd. All were facing me. Very slowly, my head low and turned aside, I moved toward them respectfully.

The elderly leader waited for me to come near. With her head high and her eyes squinting, her chin tight, her cheeks sucked in, and her lips pressed firmly together, the large mammoth seemed strong-minded. Her ears were small and tattered as if they had been frozen when she was young. Her tusks were long, sweeping out and down, then curving inward and upward, with grooves and scratches on them— tusks far older than mine, which were still growing into their downward curve. By the early light her shedding, patchy hair looked black; it was matted on her flanks but sleek on her chest where her summer coat parted over her breasts, which showed behind her forelegs as the breasts of a woman on her hands and knees show behind her arms. When the gathering light shone through this mammoth's hair, I saw its red color.

How should I act? Never before had I met someone so old or so important. The huge, grown cows around her were her daughters and granddaughters. Some of the calves were her great-grandchildren. When Graylag was still a boy, the red-haired leader was grown, having children. She had been to places I had never seen, places farther than my thoughts had ever flown, and she brought others with her, however far, to water and food, to shelter and safety. She had given life or saved it more times than anyone knew, and all the huge cows with their half-grown sons and daughters, their young children and their little babies, were the proof of her knowledge.

Filled with respect, I walked up to her, trying to show that however shy she made me, I knew to be polite. Gently I lifted my trunk, first to her lips, then to mine. Now she could see that I realized she wasn't someone to ignore but someone I should learn about. She stood stiffly while I touched her, but seemed satisfied. Grass I tasted, but also a little acid taste of tension in her mouth. Politely I touched the hole of her temple. Tension there too. I touched her vulva. She was not in season. Was she nursing? Just by looking, I couldn't tell whether her breasts were full. With the finger of my trunk I gently squeezed one of her nipples, then touched my tongue. She had a little milk, rather thin and watery, but then, she was almost too old to have any milk at all. The taste of a calf's mouth was also on her breast. A calf, but whose? It seemed not to be hers. Had a calf stolen a little milk from the red-haired leader, or was she nursing someone else's calf?

Lowering my eyes because of the delicate question, I touched her other breast. Milk was there too, and the taste of the calf's mouth, not from stealing but from nursing. I looked around for the calf and saw a large young male with bristling hair, whose little tusks already showed. He stared at me very boldly, as if he was used to having his own way. Who was he? Not bothering to hide his dislike of strangers, or of watching the red-haired leader with someone else, he looked a bit spoiled. That made him seem like the child of a leader, even if the taste of his mouth was not like hers.

In time the red-haired leader began to touch me. When she lay her trunk across my shoulders, I made no shrug to throw it off. Instead I kept my head low, and when at last I moved, I moved slowly. I wanted her to see that I honored her and her experience. When she slipped her trunk down my neck and stepped by me, letting me go, I eased myself past the rest of her herd and began to pull grass.

And so I joined the mammoths. That very day, when they moved away to graze, I followed them. They were close kin and I was a stranger, so they didn't let me come into their herd. In fact they kept their children away from me and wouldn't call me or wait for me when they moved, but as long as I stayed at the edge of their group and didn't try to walk into the center, they didn't chase me off.

Other mammoths also stayed near the herd: some young males, sons of the females in the herd, stayed within easy calling distance although often out of sight, and a few huge old bulls would visit us every now and then. At the beginning of summer their madness was on them, making them reek of the strong musk draining from their temple glands and of the stale urine soaking the hair of their legs. Long before we heard or saw one of them, we would smell him, and then we would wait while his enormous shape, quiet as a storm cloud lifting over the horizon, would rise from a slope ahead of us. Carefully he would run his trunk over some of us, searching for the scent of season, and if he thought he found it, he would gape and press the tip of his trunk on the roof of his mouth. But as it happened, no cow of the red-haired leader's herd was still in season, although those without nursing babies were pregnant, probably by one of the large, frightening males.

Sometimes one of the large males would stay near us for a while, but the doings of the cows and calves didn't interest any of the males very deeply. In fact the calves annoyed the males, and sometimes we would look up from our grazing to find that our male visitor was gone.

Every morning we grazed. At midday we drank and wallowed in a meltwater pool on the open plain, and in the afternoon we grazed some more. We made as much noise as we liked, screaming when sudden movements startled us, growling at the calves when they ran into us, and calling loudly and often to other herds, friends and sisters of the red-haired leader who grazed on distant parts of the plain. But around us everything else was quiet except for skylarks and insects and the wind in the grass. Other animals moved away when we came near—even lions, even bison, and even a rhino we met one day, who snorted at us but thought better of snorting again when the red-haired leader waved him away with her trunk. He had no business bothering us, and wasn't going to let his disposition get him into a battle with a herd of female mammoths. He trotted off. Late at night, when the world was quiet and everything was still, we lay down on our sides. Every night I slept deeply. Every night I dreamed of grass, with the wind making footprints on it as far as I could see. No lions, no people, were in this dream—just grass. Not even in dreams would anyone dare bother us. Never did I feel so safe or sleep so well.

So the summer passed, with the other mammoths never letting me in their herd and never bothering to answer when I called them, but giving me the good of their grazing and the protection of their number just the same. Then the grass seeds ripened into countless delicious mouthfuls, the wind grew cold, and flocks of birds flew above us in the night sky, where the stars showed the way to winter shelter. Now and then we met herds of other mammoths whose voices we knew, greeted them, grazed near them for a time, then drifted apart. But from the very distant calls I knew that some of the herds were leaving the plain for their winter-grounds. These days we listened carefully to any faraway call, and answered all of them. The red-haired leader didn't want to lose touch with the others.

For the first time her herd seemed somewhat restless, since it was clear that the plain was no place to spend a winter. My mind's eye saw us out in the open, with nothing to break the freezing wind which would soon pack the dead grass in snow, kneeling on the white plain, scraping desperately with our tusks, trying for any mouthful. But the red-haired leader wasn't ready to go.

One cold night the red-haired leader led us straight to the river. Everyone seemed nervous because of the hunters, but off we went anyway. There was no flaw in her judgment, I saw when we reached the river. The cave was deserted. Even the spirits of Marmot and Goldeneye had gone to the wintergrounds by the Char. Still, the fact that people had been here at all seemed to anger the red-haired leader, who with her daughters beside her pushed a rock off the cliff. We listened to the echoes of it bounding in the valley below. Then, in single file, we followed the red-haired leader down the trail into the ravine.

At the bottom we found the partly eaten bodies of the three dead mammoths I had seen fall at the beginning of summer. These the red-haired leader and her daughters nosed for a while. Now the dead cows looked lonely, sprawled in the moonlight. With their drawn tusks and broken bones they seemed defenseless. All their thoughts and memories must have spilled from their broken heads. If a bad animal came near to eat more of them, they couldn't get up to leave on their broken, ruined legs. They couldn't get water to drink or grass to eat. One of them, I saw, must have been the mother of the male calf who now followed the red-haired leader, because he nosed under her arm at the skin of her dry breast. She couldn't even move her elbow to let him nurse.

At last the red-haired leader set her foot on the shoulder of one of the dead cows, and winding her trunk around the foreleg, she gave a great pull. Slowly the leg slipped from its socket. Changing her grasp so that the big leg balanced, the red-haired leader walked off with it down the floodplain. Then I saw that other mammoths were also pulling pieces off the dead and carrying the pieces away, some walking upstream, some downstream. We would help the corpses as best we could, I saw. We would hide as much of them as possible. I helped too, pulling loose the bare thighbone of one of the cows and carrying it on my tusks to a bank, where I strewed gravel over it.

After hiding all the pieces we could pry from the bodies, we drank water from the river, sprayed our ears and chests, and left, taking the trail to the plain and walking a long way in the cold wind, with the dry grass brushing our ankles. I smelled snow. Far away, late at night, we stopped to eat, then walked some more before we lay down. I woke in the black night with snow all over me, and stood up as fast as I could, thinking that the others had left me behind. But no—they lay fast asleep all around me, gently snoring. Still, the thought that they might leave without me troubled me, so I stayed awake in the falling snow, dozing on my feet.

For more days than I could count we followed old mammoth trails, crossing the Fire River by breaking our way through the ice. All the way, a few of the young bulls kept near us. We finally came to a place I had never visited, a plain like the plain by the Pine River but in a range of low hills with spruce and larch. It was the red-haired leader's winterground, and from it she called loudly and long to three or four distant herds of mammoths, who answered her eagerly.

The red-haired leader had chosen her winterground well, since the wind eddied among the hills and kept the snow moving. Almost every day we found a place to graze without much digging. And we didn't need to go far for water, because we were near one of the small rivers that fed Woman Lake. Each morning we broke a hole in the ice and drank our fill.

I grew a winter coat of oily, heavy hair. Except for my ears and the tip of my trunk I was warm, so I kept my ears close against my head and the tip of my trunk in my mouth or under my arm. This I learned from watching other mammoths. And then at last, one day when the others left me behind and I called, for the first time the red-haired leader answered me. *Over here,* her voice said. When I found her, she touched my lips and temple to see how I was. This pleased me very much and left me deeply satisfied.

After the mammoths let me into their herd, answering my calls, noticing how I felt, letting me browse near them and play with their calves, I became so content that I might have forgotten all about the people. But one morning, to my great surprise, I found myself in the form of a raven. Somehow the shamans had discovered me. I saw that I had no choice but to go to the Char, to Graylag's lodge, which I had in life helped join to Swift's meat-strewn summerground. Unwillingly I let the wind lift me into the freezing sky, and with a last look down on the egg-shaped backs of the scattered, browsing mammoths, I began the long flight, squinting against the burning wind and the glare of the sun on the snow.

◄ 18 ►

IN THE SHADOWY, firelit cave above the Hair River, many important things were being said. And so, my mouth greasy with meat, my heart filled with the nearness of Timu and my ears with the sound of his voice, I began to listen to the women around me. I learned that Ethis had given birth to her little boy while on the way from the Char River. Like Ankhi, Ethis had given birth easily, going to find a sheltered hiding place as soon as her birth-water ran down her legs. Ankhi had gone with her and helped cut the cord.

Yoi told Ina that her sons were married and that she had grandchildren, even a stepgrandson from The Frog's wife. Ina wasn't pleased to learn that we had hurried ahead of her sons' families. Yoi said, "You're complaining because you want to see your sons again. But if we waited, none of us would be here yet. You really have no cause to complain." Yoi then smiled, content that Ina couldn't argue with her. Soon she turned to White Fox's mother, the smile gone. "We were forced to hurry," she said, "by our distress at Meri's betrothal being broken! We expect White Fox for Meri, and no one else!"

Taken aback, White Fox's mother admitted that people had been thinking of another girl for her son, the girl named Sasa whose people lived about a day's travel downriver in another cave. Meri, said White Fox's mother, was promised to Swift.

Yoi brushed this aside. "Your son can't have Sasa because he's still betrothed to Meri," she said. "How can the betrothal of children be broken without the consent of the

296

adults who made it? I was one of those people. The others, besides yourselves, were Meri's parents, and they're dead. I wouldn't have agreed to breaking the betrothal, and I wouldn't offer an ungrown child to the strong and honorable headman of this cave. He should father a child, not marry one."

"Since he wants a woman of our lineage, have you someone else for him?" asked Teal dryly.

"I?" said Yoi. "How can I advise you? I just came."

Since I seldom took my eyes off Timu's handsome back, outlined by firelight in the men's circle, I couldn't help noticing that Swift kept turning his head as if to hear what Yoi might be saying. This too made me happy. Across the fire from me, Teal caught my eye and raised her chin very, very slightly to beckon me. I got up and went to sit behind her.

She stood, and I followed her out of the cave and up the shadowy trail to the open rim of the ravine, where there was a pile of boulders, white in the moonlight. A dayfire sometimes burned here, I saw from the ashes. I smelled grass on the fresh wind and saw fireflies. "Well, child," said Teal. "Tell me what is happening here?"

So I told her of Yoi's willingness to marry Swift. Teal thought for a while. "It's sad," she said, "that Yoi is childless. I wonder how Swift feels about that."

I too had considered Yoi's childbearing, and saw that it needn't be a problem. "Yoi is childless now, Aunt," I said. "But think. Father got no child from her because he slept mostly with Mother. I should know, because I slept with Yoi. Without coitus, Yoi couldn't get children."

"Can that be true?" asked Teal.

Take care, I said to myself. *This is Teal, not some young woman at the Fire River.* "It's true, Aunt," I said, and laughed. "I met Yoi's second husband, a man named Otter. He was a very kind man, but she divorced him because he was too old to give her children."

"So?" said Teal doubtfully.

"And without Yoi, the ties you want between Swift and Graylag can't be made. Since Yoi and I are Meri's elders, Yoi won't let Meri marry Swift."

"Not if Yoi wants him herself," said Teal.

"Anyway, what can we do about it? Yoi and Swift aren't children. Who will tell those two that they may or may not marry? They like each other. Watch when we go back. They keep looking at each other."

"So they do," said Teal. "Well, Yanan. Isn't it good that all this came about? If I didn't know you to be rash and headstrong, I might think you helped make these plans."

"Why, Aunt," I said, "Yoi came gladly when she heard Swift wanted a woman of our lineage."

"Someone said good things about Swift, in that case," said Teal. "Was it someone who once called him a lion?"

"I had time to think, Aunt," I said.

Teal smiled. "And what of you?" she asked. "I see you won't be childless."

"No, Aunt."

"When will you give birth?"

I hesitated, afraid to follow this talk. I didn't know when I would give birth. Worse yet, her question had a right answer and a wrong answer, a safe answer and a dangerous answer. I hated to lie to Teal, but at last I took a deep breath and said, "I felt life before we left the Char."

"And still you left us?" Teal waited. I waited too, knowing better than to let more words betray me, as they had with Yoi. When I didn't answer, Teal went on, delicate as a hunter. "If you felt life in the end of winter, your child must be nearly ready. Do you agree?" I said nothing. Teal watched me. "You don't look ready," she said. When I still made no answer, Teal's questions took a new turn. "Did you marry at the Fire River, or will you cancel your divorce?"

"I didn't marry. I was wrong to divorce Timu. I've thought about it ever since. I don't know why it happened. Anyway, I'm back, if Timu will have me."

"He'll have you, especially if the child is his. His father will have something to say about that."

But I had seen from Timu's happiness that Graylag wouldn't have to force him. And as Teal and I found our way along the trail to the cave, we met Timu coming toward us, carrying his spear. "Let me speak with my wife a while, Stepmother," he said, so Teal went on alone and I followed Timu back to the boulders.

In the moonlight we faced each other. "I'm glad you've come," he said.

"I hurried here, Husband. I refused to wait for my cousins and their families, and I forced Meri. I ran."

"And you're pregnant?"

"I am."

"Is it mine, or did you meet someone at the Fire River?"

"Yours," I said, although I felt my tears coming.

Timu must have heard the tears in my voice. "Why are you sad, Wife?" he asked.

His voice was so soft, there in the cool, sweet air with moonlight and fireflies, that I wanted terribly to tell him about Elho. I wanted no lie between Timu and me. I opened my mouth to speak.

But just then I heard the voice of a night bird, a burrowing owl, and a sigh of wind like the breath of The Woman Ohun. I felt Her, She who knows the wombs of all the animals and all the people. She was near. *Silence,* She whispered. *Silence.*

"I'm not sad, Husband," I said.

Timu's hand stroked up the bulge of my belly to my belt, which he loosened. "Is your pregnancy too far along?" he asked. "Or may I have you? I've missed you."

I stood up. "Not here," I said.

Timu hesitated. "You've become shy since you left. Why?" he asked.

"I don't know, Husband."

He took my wrist. "Come then," he said, and led me down the trail to a little grove of small birch trees with bare earth under them, all dark and shadowy even under the moon. On the far side of the grove the enormous white skull of a mammoth rested on its upper teeth, the tusks drawn, the nostril sockets gaping in the forehead like a huge dark eye. "The dancing ground," said Timu, pushing the tail of his spear into the earth to keep it at hand in case an animal came along to trouble us. "The Bear may hear us, but no person will."

Suddenly I heard a short, booming whistle, so deep, so low and quiet, that I felt it rather than heard it, and the hair rose on my skin. "What's that?" I whispered.

"The hum? It's the voice of the mammoth skull. The wind makes it sound so." Timu held me close and slowly drew the pin that fastened the neck of my shirt. So once again in a grove of birch I took off my moccasins, my trousers, and my shirt and set my hands and knees against the cold earth. Timu's hard body was warm against my back, and the feeling of his wrist against my breast when he reached under me to pull me to him almost stopped my breath.

Yet I wept when we finished. Timu sat on his heels, watching me. "Are you still weeping? Why?" he asked.

"No reason," I answered. "Except that while I was away I was lonely and frightened, and now I'm glad."

My answer didn't seem to satisfy him, I saw from the way he watched me. As our eyes met I heard the skull's choked hum, while the whispering breath of The Woman Ohun blew cold on my bare skin. She said, *You thought you would be safe when you found your husband. But he can't make you safe. In spite of all your schemes and haste to come here, you are still in danger. You will never find safety. You will always live with fear and danger.* And I wept again, because I saw that this was true.

Well, there was nothing I could do about the danger but wait, and nothing I could do about the fear but get used to it. In the morning, when I went with the other women to bathe among the mammoth bones scattered in the river, I showed everybody my swollen belly, my large breasts, my dark nipples, and the line down the middle of me. People said a brown, strong line showed that the baby would be healthy. This one thing made me glad. And glad was what I wanted to be, and how I wanted to act. I laughed a lot and showed my teeth and plunged myself several times in the freezing water, then noticed Junco and Owl, Ethis and Teal, all watching me happily, as if they were pleased to have me.

In the days that followed I often overheard people talking about me, saying how right I had been to come back, how happy I seemed, and how well I had managed everything. I was even given credit for the marriage of Swift and Yoi, who began to share a sleeping-skin before the first presents had been given for their marriage exchange. Swift promised me ivory beads to replace the betrothal necklace I had thrown at him. Yoi took to calling me "Hide-in-the-Grass," just because Swift did. I don't think she knew why. And when Yoi and I were alone one day, she gave me an ivory hairpin to thank me. I took the pin in silence, perhaps even with a little shame.

Only Timu sometimes seemed to be watching me as if he were wondering about me. Because of my pregnancy, he slept with Ethis, as everyone, even I, would have expected. And he spent his days hunting on the steppe with the other men or at the dayfire, watching for herds in the ravine. I wasn't with him enough to learn what he might be thinking.

But Ethis and I often found ourselves together very happily. Since I now could feel knees and fists inside my belly, I took a great interest in Ethis's tiny son. One day when we went with the other women to bathe in the river, Ethis asked me to hold him. I reached out my hands for him and cradled him against me. Not since I held my own sister at the time Mother died had I held so small a baby. I sat on my heels to look at him. Like my sister, this one turned his head to grope for a nipple when I touched his cheek. But although my breasts were flat when my sister was born, now they were full, with the nipples standing out, and when the baby found a nipple he snapped at it. To my surprise he sucked, and a strong, sharp feeling close to pain rushed from my breast to my throat. Then the baby looked up at me! Our eyes met! Just then Ethis happened to dip herself suddenly in the icy water and cry out. At the sound of her voice, her baby let go of my nipple to look in her direction. On my dusty breast I saw the wet mark of his mouth and, to my amazement, a smear of milk on my nipple! My milk? "Aunt!" I said. "See here!"

"See what?" Teal asked, leaning her bare and lanky body down for a look.

"I have milk in my breast!"

"Oh? Did you expect something else?"

"But so soon?"

Now Teal looked closely. "It isn't your milk. He had some in his mouth."

"So!" I said, meeting the baby's eyes as he again took my nipple. Then I said, "He's looking at me. He knows me." But Teal had turned her back and was talking with another woman, so I just smiled at him. "Is this your foot?" I whispered, clasping his foot. He smiled! "Look! He's smiling," I said. But the other women were talking, and no one turned to look. That was all right, though. "You little thing," I said, putting my forehead against his forehead and letting him catch my hair. And so we enjoyed each other until Ethis came dripping from the river.

Almost every day I went with Ethis over the plain, gathering mammoth dung for the night's fires. Sometimes she carried the baby, and sometimes I carried him. After we had gathered enough dry droppings we would stop at one of the many firebushes where, standing side by side among its branches, we would pick the red, bittersweet berries and toss them into our mouths. Unlike Ethis, I saved as many as I ate and gave them each night to Timu, pouring them into his hands as he sat at the men's fire, talking and talking of mammoths.

I very much liked to wander with Ethis and her baby under the dome of the hazy summer sky, through the thin red grass that trembled and rippled with the wind as far as the eye could see. Ethis said that late summer was the season of bustards, and sure enough, we often met a herd of five large gray bustards, all carefully poking themselves forward like hunters through the grass. Sometimes, out on the plain, we saw a small brown bustard rise straight into the air, hover and call, then drop into the grass again. But the plain was so flat that we couldn't see far, so usually we saw no other animals and no people. Even so, I was always looking around for Timu, wishing I knew where he was.

"Where are the men?" I once asked Ethis.

"Who knows?" she said, tilting her head to keep the berries in her mouth. "The men care only about mammoths, so they're probably following some of them, watching what they eat, smelling their urine and dung."

"Really?" I said. "Why?"

"To see whether they're finding enough water on the steppe, or if they'll need to climb down the cliff to drink from the river. The pools on the steppe go dry in summer. This year was wet, or the pools would be dry now."

"What if the mammoths climb down the cliff?"

"We push them off."

"The dead mammoth on the riverbank—did you push her off the cliff?"

"Yes, while Red Hair was trying to bring her down to wallow. The dead one had many big maggots of warble flies under her skin."

"Red Hair? Who is Red Hair?"

"Red Hair is a mammoth, a leader."

"Do you name mammoths?" I asked, putting a handful of fireberries into my carrying bag.

"The men name them," said Ethis. "Why are you saving berries? Aren't there plenty?"

"I'm saving them for Timu," I said, surprised.

"Ah yes," said Ethis.

Her tone puzzled me. "Why else would I be saving berries?" I asked.

"Of course you must bring him things," she said, her voice soothing. "Of course you must please him. I can see that."

Distressed, I sat down on my heels under the crossing shadows of the firebush branches. "Sister," I said, "is there a special reason I should please Timu? Because I see no special reason. I gather berries for him because he's our husband. I gather berries for him every time we go out. I ask you, why else should I please him?"

Ethis looked embarrassed, but sat down beside me with her baby in her lap. "I'm sorry," she said. "There's no other reason."

"There is," I said. "There is."

"But you must know it!" cried Ethis in dismay.

"I don't!"

"Why, Yanan," said Ethis, "of course you do! If the child you're carrying isn't his, you want him to forget."

These words should not have shocked me, but they did. I had almost forgotten what other people seemed to remember very well. And I saw how, by always bringing Timu presents, I showed the truth of what Ethis said. Berries grew everywhere. If Timu wanted berries, he had only to eat from the bushes as other men did. I saw that I was the only woman who came every night to the men's fire to pour berries into her husband's hands. But, "Does he think this isn't his child?" I asked.

"Yanan. You went away for a long time and came back pregnant. One day I heard our husband ask Elho what men you were with at the Fire River."

My skin felt cold. "What did Elho say?"

Ethis looked at me carefully. "In a loud voice Elho said he didn't know, since he wasn't with you all the time." Ethis thought for a moment, then added, "The loud voice caused the trouble. Everyone who heard the answer guessed the question. Timu's stepmother reminded Timu of his doings on your people's old summergrounds, and that he of all men should know best about other men's wives. She also reminded him that your father had caught Elho with your Aunt Yoi."

"Which of his stepmothers said these things?"

"Ina, of course. Ina's angry with you. She's angry because her sons and their families aren't here. She knows you made Yoi and Elho hurry away from her sons instead of helping them carry their children."

I saw truth in these words, and felt sick to learn that after all, people still held much against me. "What did Aunt Teal say?"

"Do you think Ina would have spoken against you in front of your Aunt Teal? Would you speak against me in front of my Aunt Rin?" The very thought was so unlikely that I couldn't help but smile, which pleased Ethis. "So, Yanan," she laughed. "Don't be sad."

But I was sad, and angry too. On the way home I shared all the berries in my carrying bag with Ethis, so that by the time we reached the cave, none were left for Timu. Now I was ashamed of giving him berries.

If Timu noticed that I no longer brought a gift for him each night, he gave no sign. Perhaps he, as well as the other men, thought too much about the mammoths. From overhearing the men's talk at night, I understood that the meltwater pools on the plain were drying at last, and that although it seemed the mammoths already knew about us and were putting off their use of the trail down the ravine as long as possible, soon they would be forced to drink from the river. Every night Timu sat in the crowd of men with his back to the women's fire, busy with talk of hunting. The men's voices filled the cave; they interrupted each other while their gesturing hands flew, and over the sounds of talking came the ticking sounds of chisels against flint. They were getting themselves and their tools ready to do a big thing. I saw how much Graylag and his men liked the excitement that their ties with Swift brought them.

After I could no longer give Timu berries, I begged part of a bison skin from Ethis and began to make him a pair of winter moccasins instead. I then worked quietly among the women at the women's fire, trying always to sit beside Teal or Ethis, trying from time to time to catch Ina's eye so I could look reproachful and she could see how wrongly she accused me. The burst of happiness that people might have felt when I came seemed to have passed, and since every woman had her own things to think about, no one paid much attention to me.

I wanted very much to talk with Timu. I thought I could make him forget his doubts about me. But life at the Hair River summerground wasn't like life at the Char—the men never formed small hunting groups which a woman could join, and never helped the women gather fuel. There was never a reason for Timu and me to be together. I asked Ethis to whisper to him at night, to tell him that I wanted to be alone with him. But if she did, nothing came of it.

One long evening in late summer, when the light in the ravine was dim and blue and cliff swallows were flying low over the river, we heard voices on the trail outside the cave. Startled, we looked around at each other. None of us was missing. Who could it be? The men leaped to their feet to stand with legs apart and spears ready, facing the mouth of the cave as if they would welcome any excitement, even a battle. But very cautiously around the corner came the unmistakable figures of Kamas, The Frog, and Henno, The Stick, lit from behind and empty-handed, moving slowly and looking very polite. Ina gave a great loud cry and ran forward to embrace them.

Then we all got up to greet them. In came their wives and children, shy at first, to greet Yoi, one of the few people who knew them. For me the wives had only sharp glances. Soon

Ina was embracing them all, welcoming the children, and settling them near her sleeping place between the back of the cave and the women's fire. And soon after that, since the meat of the men's last kill seemed to have been eaten, Ethis and I were on our way down the trail to the river to cut meat from the dead mammoth for the newcomers' evening meal.

The flyblown meat was quite badly spoiled, even for the tastes of the mammoth hunters. So we cut strips from deep inside the ragged carcass and then washed ourselves and the strips in the river to get rid of the maggots and the smell. I thought with some satisfaction that my cousins' wives would find fault with this food, having grown used to fresh fish every day in summer. But I had forgotten how long they had been on the trail. All the newcomers ate so gratefully, so eagerly, that they shamed me, and without anyone asking me to, I went alone to the carcass to get more meat for them.

By now the ravine was filled with darkness and the echo of the wind. The waning crescent of the Mammoth Moon lay on the slowly moving water, and a white fox slipped away from the carcass as I got near. I heard someone behind me, and turned to see Timu's head and wide shoulders against the night sky. He was carrying his spear. He had come to protect me from large animals who might be here in the dark. *Ah, Husband,* I thought. *Welcome.* And when he stood beside me, I put my hand on his arm.

But he stood stiffly, looking down at me thoughtfully, without speaking. I leaned toward him a little bit, as if I were yielding, and took the ivory pin from the front of my shirt so the neck fell open. "Timu," I whispered.

"What's this? Isn't your pregnancy far gone?" he asked rather harshly. "Are you so greedy that you would lie with me now? Do what you need to do, and do it quickly. Lions come here." So although his words and manner hurt me very much, I turned to burrow in the carcass, then hurried to wash the meat in the river while he looked on. Although I didn't want to cry, my tears came anyway, and I brushed them from my face with my sleeve.

On the trail to the cave Timu walked ahead of me, letting

me carry the meat. Halfway up I heard the voices of the people above, and saw my chance to speak disappearing. I stopped as if I needed a rest. He walked quite a way before noticing that I wasn't behind him, then didn't come back. I leaned against a rock to show I wouldn't follow quickly. In time he walked down the trail to me. "What now?" he said.

There he stood, the light of the low moon on his forehead, and suddenly my words left me. I wet my lips. He waited. "I wonder why you have nothing to say to me," I began fearfully. "Are you angry? Should I not have come here?"

"Why not?" he asked. "Aren't you my wife?"

"Is it the baby? Has someone said something to you about the baby?"

"Am I a woman, to talk of your pregnancy?"

"No, Timu. I'm wondering what you think."

"I think about hunting, not women's business," he said.

"I want to talk with you now."

"Then talk." But he seemed so forbidding that I couldn't. Instead I took his hand and placed it on my belly so he could feel what was inside. Our eyes met, and he took his hand away. "Come," he said. "Your cousins are waiting." And he turned and led off again. I followed, wondering if I was tear-streaked. Perhaps I should have thought of that at the river, where I could have washed my face.

It was easy to slip unnoticed behind the people, all talking eagerly at the fires. I rolled myself in my deerskin but lay awake listening. Timu sat far away—I heard him laugh from time to time. Near me the wives of The Stick and The Frog fed small bits of meat to their children. The Frog's little stepson, Kakim, had found a place right beside mine and was already fast in an exhausted sleep. When I heard his shallow breathing, I propped myself on my elbow to look at his face. In the dim light reflected from the cave's low ceiling I saw how very thin he was, how lightly his eyelids lay over his eyes, how tight and blue his skin seemed, and how his face quivered faintly even in sleep. He looked worse than when I saw him as we left the Fire River. Had he eaten? I didn't think so—I noticed no smell of meat on his breath, and his face wasn't greasy. Quietly I reached out to touch him, which made him stir but not wake. His skin was cold and dry. He was sick with an old sickness. I felt someone watching me and looked up to see Ethis, whose eyes met mine. We exchanged a glance of understanding. She too had noticed this child.

Talk at the women's fire that night was strained because of the new women. Only Yoi knew them well, and I got the feeling she didn't think much of them. She seemed to ignore them and often interrupted when they tried to speak. Of course, for Yoi such behavior wasn't unusual. But the two newcomers didn't make talk easy. Rather, their offerings were nothing but complaints about the distance they had come and the lack of good water on the plain. Their praise was for the people they had left behind, and sometimes they even whispered to each other, as if about us. I'm sure that Ina had built them up in her mind before she met them, since they were her new daughters-in-law, and I wondered if she was now disappointed. She made much of the two babies who were her grandchildren. Little Kakim, Ina learned from questioning the new women, was not only the stepchild of The Frog, but also the stepchild of The Frog's wife—the child of this woman's first husband, who had been a widower. Surely Yoi knew this, but perhaps her interest in the two new women was so small she forgot.

Talk and laughter at the men's fire echoed from the walls. The Stick and The Frog had wonderful news: herds of mammoths were drinking from the river upstream. No doubt more mammoths would soon drink in the river here. The Stick and The Frog were very interested in how mammoths were hunted, since at the Char, the Pine, and the Fire rivers, people for the most part left mammoths alone. All talking at once, the other men described how mammoths took the narrow trail down the ravine while people threw stones on them from above, frightening them and making them crowd together, hurrying them so they lost their footing. Then they fell, and most couldn't get up again. Because there wasn't much to eat on the riverbank, the other mammoths couldn't guard the injured mammoths for more than a day or so. Then we could kill the injured mammoths easily. "We cry from so much eating," said Swift. "And we laugh from so much ivory."

In the morning The Stick and The Frog willingly joined the other men in carrying a great many large rocks from the river. All day they worked in groups together, resting when the sun was high, bathing in the afternoon. My cousins stayed with Timu, I noticed. The women made blinds of branches cut from thickets; most of us were caught up in the excitement of hunting. Swift now felt sure that the herd of mammoths led by Red Hair wouldn't wait much longer to use the trail. Little Kakim was not thought too young to help the men, and often I saw him staggering patiently up the trail, each time with a rock too heavy for him. He tried to rest in the cave for a while, but his stepfather, The Frog, called him out again. Often Kakim had to leave his work to squat in the bushes. I saw that his sickness was caused by diarrhea.

By nightfall even the two new women felt happy and hopeful. As the mammoth hunters put it, the time of meat was coming. But little Kakim fell asleep before he ate, just as we lay meat to cook. Sitting side by side, Ethis and I exchanged more glances. At last I couldn't help myself, and spoke to The Frog's wife. "Your little boy needs food," I told her. "May I wake him?"

"What makes you care about him now?" she asked. "Is someone watching your manners?" Her rudeness was no more than I expected. What did it matter? I shrugged. When I caught Ina's spiteful stare, I smiled pleasantly to annoy her. I would have no more to do with any of the newcomers, who could fetch and cook their own food for all of me. But later, when we were eating, I noticed that Ethis had found the boy and was shaking him gently. She let him wake slowly, then put her arm around his shoulders and fed him a strip of meat. He looked up at Ethis so humbly, so gratefully, that I felt a pang of sadness. Still later I noticed that he had fallen asleep again, leaning against Ethis.

In the middle of the night I heard him crying. The sound shocked me, and I sat up. He was sitting on his heels beside his stepparents, tearfully insisting that he needed to move his bowels. Hardly awake, neither of them wanted to get up and go out with him. "Please," he begged, afraid to go alone.

"Take the trail a way. Nothing to hurt you," mumbled The Frog. So at last, slowly, the little boy began to make his way among the sleeping people to the mouth of the cave. I got up. "What now?" murmured The Frog.

"I need to relieve myself," I said. "I'll take him to the latrine."

"Good," said The Frog, as if in his sleep.

Outside in the starlight, with the burrowing owl calling in the grove of trees and the faint watery sound of the river below us, I took Kakim's thin, dry hand in mine and led him to the plain. He squatted for a long time, passing only a little mucus. I heard him breathing, panting. He seemed very tired and sick. At last he stood up. "Are you Yanan?" he whispered.

"Yes, Kakim."

"I'm ready to go back."

"We'll go," I said, and again took his hand.

"Is there any more meat?" he whispered when we were inside. "I'm very hungry."

"I'll see," I said, and trying to move quietly, I looked on all the flat stones by the fires where a piece of meat might still be lying. I found none, but accidentally woke Ethis. She looked out from beside Timu's naked shoulder under the deerskin.

"What do you want?" she asked.

I sat on my heels beside her bed and whispered very softly. "Poor little Kakim is hungry. I'm trying to find something for him."

Careful not to wake Timu, Ethis got up with her baby, stuffing her breast in his mouth so he wouldn't start to cry. "I'll help you," she said. So we both searched, but found nothing.

Now we looked long into each other's eyes. There was nothing for it—one of us would have to go down to the carcass. "I'll go," I said. "I'm not tired."

"I'll go with you," whispered Ethis. We sat on our heels by little Kakim. "We'll soon have food," she said. I got my spear, and we left.

The ravine was very dark. Partway down the trail we threw a few stones ahead of us to startle anything that might be waiting there, then thought to sing.

Save my life, hunters!
Kill ten horses,
One for each of my fingers!

The echo of our song rang from the ravine walls. Ethis
and the baby kept watch while I again took off my shirt and
dug inside the carcass. I had forgotten a knife, and had to
cut with the spear. Only the lower side of the mammoth was
useful anymore, and with the spear shaft catching awkwardly in the ribs, the digging took quite a while. "Sister!"
whispered Ethis suddenly, as if alarmed. I backed out
of the mammoth's ribcage. There stood Timu, facing us
without speaking, looking so severe that he frightened
me.

"What is it, Husband? You startled us," said Ethis.

"Why are my wives here, at this time of night? You woke
everyone with your singing! People wonder what you're
doing. I came to find you!"

"What does it seem that we're doing?" asked Ethis,
perhaps annoyed by his tone.

"Come. We're going back," he said.

"Are you finished, Yanan?" asked Ethis.

"Almost," I said, and leaned into the ribcage to dig some
more.

Timu caught the shaft of my spear. "We're going," he
said.

"A piece of meat is almost loose. I'll get it quickly." But
Timu wouldn't let go of the spear.

What had happened to me? In my mind's eye I saw this
taking place a year before. I saw myself bracing my legs,
seizing my spear with both hands, and giving it a great yank.
Now, as someone struggled in my belly, I stood anxiously in
front of Timu, not sure what had displeased him, dreading
to find out, dreading even to speak for fear of displeasing
him more.

"Finish," he said, and rudely gave the spear a shove. So I
did, then went to rinse the meat and myself in the river.
While I was there, I heard Ethis and Timu talking urgently
and angrily in very low voices. I stood up. "Why do you
listen to everyone with bad will?" Ethis was saying.

"I don't listen to everyone," said Timu. "But since Elho is

my half-brother, I know what he does. Why shouldn't I believe The Frog?"

Elho and The Frog. I guessed, of course, what had happened. One way or another Timu had heard whatever it was that people thought they knew about Elho and me. Or since Timu already suspected my pregnancy, perhaps The Frog had only to tell him the story of finding me and Elho talking in the grass by the Fire River. I saw all this with a dull, dead feeling. Yet I saw something new as well, although to see anything new at that moment surprised me. I saw that Elho hadn't told Timu. If he had, Timu would feel different-ly. Timu would be sure of what had happened, which would put him in a pure, high rage. Instead he showed the dark, sullen anger of suspicion, with the cloud of his anger covering everyone, Ethis as well as me.

I didn't know what to do except to walk back to them slowly. They stopped talking and looked at me. "We can go now, Timu," said Ethis. So we did, climbing the dark trail, feeling the way with our feet—Timu first, then Ethis, then me.

Ethis let Timu get far ahead, then whispered, "He's sure he's not the father of your child. The Frog told him that you used to go away alone with Elho."

"I know. I overheard Timu," I said.

"Such trouble is too much for one person," said Ethis.

"Yes."

"I'll help you! And I'll divorce Timu if he doesn't show more respect for his wives! As you tie us to Graylag, I tie him to Swift. Remember that."

"If you help me too much, he could divorce both of us."

"And turn everyone against him? I don't think so," she said.

Inside the cave Ethis and I cut the mammoth meat into very thin strips so they would broil quickly on low embers and also be easy to eat. When we brought them to little Kakim, we found him asleep. Since it was almost morning, we decided to give him the meat when he woke. Then Ethis with her baby crept back into bed beside Timu, who was too quiet to be sleeping, and I crept into my own bed, where I felt another person inside me turning over and over. In time everything was still. Then my thoughts gathered in my womb, right in the center of me. The child who had been turning now lay quiet, warm and safe, knowing nothing of anger or danger or of anything that had happened or that could yet come. It might know me, though. Perhaps it could hear me. Perhaps it already cared for me, as I once had cared for my mother, as I still cared for my mother, wherever she might be.

≪ 19 ≫

THE SECOND SUMMER AFTER I became a spirit, when Marmot's brother, Spirit Goldeneye, happened to be with us and the Moon of Flies was new, a pride of lions camped in one of the empty caves above the Hair River. The lions had plenty of trails to follow up the terrace to the plain and down the terrace to the water. When the people reached the Hair River that year, they met lions everywhere, and wondered if they were drawn by the carrion left behind in the fall.

Then people began to hear them roaring, sometimes so loudly that even we, the spirits, thought the echoes booming in the valley would split our heads. At first we thought that the lions were trying to frighten the people, but later we saw that they were simply living as they liked; they were comfortable enough to snore and purr, to cough threats or spit scoldings at each other, without thinking about the people at all.

After a few days of moving around very carefully in fear of being surprised by a hidden lion, the people sang and the shamans tranced until Swift and Teal stood in the air above the empty mammoth skull that lay by the birch grove. The shamans didn't even speak to us respectfully but scolded and threatened us for letting the lions come at all.

"We couldn't help it," said Goldeneye.

"Just get rid of them!" said Teal. "They'll eat all the food. Then they'll eat us! Don't say anything to me! Just do it!"

Her anger shamed us, and we found ourselves agreeing to

314

try. That same night, in the form of lions, we set out while the sky was still black.

On large, soft feet, our ears flat, our tails stiff, our heads and shoulders low, we crept along the terrace. Above us the morning star crept stealthily toward the reindeer stars, reminding us that the time for hunting was near. As the dawn wind lifted and birds began to sing, we climbed to the valley's rim above the lions' camp and stopped to test their scent, heavy with musk and meat.

With alarm I realized that I was smelling a great many lionesses, some in milk and some in season. Marmot and Goldeneye noticed this too, and rumbled very softly to each other. Then my nose told me that the lionesses had with them only one lion. His musky smell was not heavy and male like the smell of Marmot and Goldeneye, but light and fresh. He was still young. Then my skin crawled and my face grew tight; on the wind came the healthy smell of cubs—his cubs. Suddenly one yowled angrily. One of the lionesses spat a warning, then began a faint, rhythmic scraping with her tongue.

I knew I shouldn't be near these lionesses. They owned the cave. I was nothing but a stranger. They might tear me open if they found me on their land. As their slow, even breathing changed to yawns and rumbles, my fear grew. I began to tremble hard, and soon could no longer keep still; in the gathering light I crept from the valley's rim and crawled toward the open plain. But Marmot and Goldeneye didn't follow me. Rather, side by side, the two of them stepped back from the edge of the terrace and gave a double-voiced, challenging roar that brought the young lion and all his lionesses swarming onto the plain. I bolted.

From a sheltering patch of juniper, hoping to keep my teeth from chattering, I listened to the horrid roars of fighting. Up the river the terrified people were listening too, not daring even to build a fire—they made no smoke and no sound. After what seemed like a very long time, I heard something gasping and rustling the long grass, and I turned to see the pride's male lion hurrying away, alone. Red with blood, trying to hide and run at the same time, he was so busy looking over his shoulder to see whether Marmot or

Goldeneye was following him that he never saw me. At the overpowering scent of his trouble, his sour breath, his musk of fear, his urine, and his newly opened wounds with their smells of opened skin, fresh muscle, and even fresh bone, I grimaced.

Then, believing that Marmot and Goldeneye were getting rid of the pride, I waited for the lionesses to follow the lion. But when the sun rose higher and the lionesses didn't follow, I crept back to learn more and saw the lionesses held at bay by Goldeneye—some licking wounds, all watching Marmot clamber up the trail from the cave, carrying a little spotted cub. It hung limp, its head rolling. Blood oozed from its nose. Marmot opened his jaws and dropped the cub like meat. With an easy, loping bound, Marmot swung himself down the trail once more and came back with another little cub, but now a few older cubs rushed past him and scattered over the plain. My tail twitched with discomfort and the wish to run too, but knowing that the lionesses would chase me if they saw me, I stayed low.

Marmot dropped the second cub, and with a great, coughing roar hooked his paw at one of the youngsters dodging past him. He caught it a blow that left it twitching. Another cub flattened itself, trying to hide in the grass. Marmot pounced on it and bit the nape of its neck. Its cries hurt me as he shook it. Then it too hung limp, its tongue between its teeth, blood dripping from its nostrils. Some of the lionesses rumbled dangerously, but none of them moved. The smell of their heavy, frightened anger burned in my nose.

Knowing that if they caught me now, they would punish me for what Marmot and Goldeneye were doing, I tried so hard to keep from moving that I ached. Dizzy with fear, I waited while Marmot and Goldeneye, their chins held high, slowly circled the lionesses. Some lionesses spat roars at them, and one struck Marmot hard on the ear, making his head snap sideways. He bellowed at her. But soon another lioness was smoothly rubbing the length of her body under Marmot's chin. I heard purring. Suddenly Marmot set his open mouth over her neck, clasped her waist to pull her hindquarters between his legs, and thrust his hips quickly a few times. "Hiow!" he cried in climax.

Then I saw that the lionesses in season were too tempting for Marmot and Goldeneye. They no longer wanted to chase away the pride, but were trying to join it. Alarmed, and wondering if they would lead their new lionesses in a hunt for me, I felt my hair bristle and my eyes stretch, and before I knew it I was running, belly to the ground.

I didn't go far before the long grass rattled behind me, and I spun around, ready to fight for my life. But I saw only a cub looking at me hopefully—a little male not yet a yearling, with a long neck and big ears. I hissed at him and bounded away. He followed. In a thicket of juniper I turned. He was right behind me, looking at me for a sign to tell him what to do. Although I wanted to roar, I didn't even dare to spit loudly. Instead I stretched my lips to show him my teeth and hissed again. He backed off, but doubtfully.

By now both Marmot and Goldeneye must have been coupling. Each meow of climax startled me. But I knew I could escape while everyone was busy, so I stretched my neck to look above the juniper, and seeing a line of standing grass and low brush far out on the plain, I made for it. The cub ran behind me. On the way I heard flies buzzing, and when I crossed the trail of the wounded lion and saw that the flies were drinking from spatters of blood on the grass and pools of blood in his footprints, I knew he wouldn't live long. He too was making for the line of brush. I felt no fear of him—he was weak and wounded and I was still strong—but then the thought of the other lions hunting him down made me change direction. Over the plain I ran, keeping as low as I could, the cub behind me. But the farther I got from the lionesses the faster I ran, until I was bounding freely. Soon the cub dropped far behind. That was good, I thought. Now I could hide safely, without him running out to greet any lionesses who might come hunting for me. In the middle of the day I found a heavy patch of sagebrush, and ignoring the cries of a gray shrike who watched me, I went into the patch and lay down.

Ah, this was better. The bush in the middle of the thicket was dry and crumbled, making a space where I could stretch on my side. And the bushes around were leafy, with a smell that hid me from insects. I could see out through the branches but no passer-by could see in to notice me. Now quiet, the gray shrike clung to the highest branch. In a fork below him I saw the drying carcass of a beetle. His prey, I thought. He lives here like a leopard. If he sees another lion, he will tell me. I suddenly felt lonely, but also easy and sleepy in the sunshine, warm as spring.

Just as my dreams began the shrike scared me with a loud scream. I sprang to my feet, ready to fight, but saw only the cub who, his forehead wrinkled, pushed slowly and politely through the sagebrush as if he wanted to come inside with me. I looked over his head, searching the plain for other lions, but he was alone. He must have tracked me. Angry, I showed him all my teeth, putting my face near his face so he wouldn't miss my meaning. He looked worried, and stepped back. *He'll go now,* I thought, and lay down again, settling my tongue comfortably, feeling the good sun.

But he didn't go. Waking up when I felt cool, I found him sleeping beside me. I looked him up and down. The fur on his neck was matted as if it had once been wet. *Marmot or Goldeneye must have had his jaws on this young one,* I thought, sniffing the place. Marmot, it was. I smelled Marmot's dried breath. I licked the matted fur to put it in order. The cub woke, twisted onto his back, and patted my face. I flattened him with my paw to hold him down while I licked his belly, nosing between his hind legs to learn what had passed from his food. Around his anus and penis clung a faint smell of bison and milk. *Eats meat, but still a suckling,* I thought, lifting my paw. The cub pushed under my thigh and I felt a sudden tingle all the way from my nipple to my throat—he was trying to nurse. His warm body felt good to my body, and his rough tongue soothed as he tried to clear my nipples of fur. I lay back, lifting my thigh to make a place for him. Feeling more relaxed and less lonely, again I slept.

I woke suddenly to feel teeth in my tail. The cub was playing with me. I lashed my tail out of his reach. He frisked in front of me, but I didn't want to play. Instead I looked through the screen of brush at the plain beyond. Perhaps something to eat was walking there. Yes! I saw a line of bison making their way to the river, but very many of them, very large and strong, and out on short grass with nothing to hide me. Anyway, I wouldn't try to kill a bison alone. They were walking one behind the other, making it hard to ambush any but the first. And of course the first had to be the largest and the fiercest of them. Also, bison wouldn't be good like reindeer, who might let you alone while you killed one of them. Bison would bother you. You might be pulling a bison right off its feet, only to be hit from behind by another bison. The line of bison even seemed to want to hunt me, because they stamped and snorted and looked around for me when they caught my scent. I didn't like them.

Disappointed, I looked farther. Saiga like to walk with bison. But today the saiga were somewhere else. Red deer? None. Reindeer? None. Was there nothing on the plain for me? Far away I saw the cloud of dust made by a herd of mammoths. But I wasn't after mammoths—they could stamp me flat and scatter all my pieces.

With my neck sunk between my shoulders and my head low, I walked heavily out of the thicket, sad because I saw that my food would be hard to find. The cub followed. Soon he got bored and bounced ahead of me, which made me cross; if I was lucky and saw something, he might spoil my stalk. But there was no one to keep him away from me, and feeling lonely again, I set out for the horizon as the sky grew red and the night wind began to blow, cool and smelling of sage.

Suddenly something bit my head! I looked up. The shrike had stooped on me. Angry, I leaped at it, but of course it flew out of my reach. The cub thought I was playing and ran between my feet. My patience was gone. I growled at him. Then I remembered the large pride nearby, who now were probably hunting too and who might hear me, and I regretted the noise.

What could I do but keep walking? This I did, keeping the wind in my face. Far over the plain I went, crossing the tracks of many delicious animals, although their trails were cold. Even so, my mouth watered at their smells. The cub ran ahead of me or lagged behind me, pouncing on grasshoppers or anything that moved. Then he disappeared for a long time and I thought I'd lost him, but after all, he wasn't mine, so I didn't look for him. I walked on. But he was only hiding, and when I passed a little wormwood bush he jumped out at me. He startled me, so I smacked him.

Just before the light faded, I reached a rise of ground, where I stood as tall as I could and stretched my neck as far as I could and saw a herd of horses. Now I felt hopeful, and I quickly got down low to make for another little wormwood that I noticed, which would screen me. Down behind that, I peeked out, looking for another. I saw a patch of tall grass, and quietly, slowly, keeping my ears flat and my eyes on the horses, I crept up to it, feeling with each foot to keep the grass from rustling. Beside me the cub crouched too, his ears up and his eyes opened wide.

Hidden in the tall grass, I watched the stallion. His head was down. He was eating. Around him his mares fed too, their tails to the wind, their heads to me. With the wind behind them, they would come toward me, so I waited. And I waited. I picked my horse—the young mare nearest to me—and stared at her until my eyes burned. My tail twitched. My mouth watered. The nearer the horses came, the closer I gathered my feet under me, until the muscles in my haunches ached. I could see my mare's eyelashes, and flecks of saliva at the corners of her mouth. The sound of her chewing excited me so much that I could hardly hold myself, but I managed. I was angry to hear the cub breathing heavily. Would he spoil this? Suddenly my mare lifted her head. Did she see him? Her ears were high and her eyes were wide—she looked worried. Yes! She saw him! Out of the corner of my eyes I noticed the cub stretching his neck to see her better. They were looking at each other! *Now!* I thought, and I leaped out of the grass.

With a loud snort, my mare jumped backwards. The other horses threw up their heads, then all dashed away with me behind them, the grass whipping my face, the turf from their hooves pelting me. My heart began to pound from running, but I saw I was closing the distance, gaining a little, a little more, until my mare's round haunches were shining wide and gray in front of me, and with the last of my running strength I leaped.

My belly thumped hard against her hips. I gasped. My

claws shot out and hooked in her ribs. She screamed and bucked under me, kicking. I felt myself slipping, and scrabbling to hook my back claws into her thighs, I tried to climb higher, out of danger from her feet. The world leaped up and down with her bucking, and her mane whipped my eyes, but I clung tight, reaching for her face. Just as one of my hind feet tore free and bounced helplessly in the empty air, I felt her cheek under my claws, then the pull of her flesh tearing against my fingers. I groped for something hard under her flying mane and when my tongue touched skin, I bit. Blood squirted. She plunged and I slipped, and we were falling. With a terrible jolt we hit the ground, she almost on top of me. She screamed right into my ear, making my head spin, but I twisted myself over her and set my teeth in her throat.

I'm getting somewhere, I thought, feeling her screams rattle in my skull. But she shouldn't be screaming! I took a deep breath and quickly moved my hold higher, so my eyeteeth locked through the flesh of her neck and my side teeth squeezed her windpipe. She thrashed and kicked but my hold was solid, and although my whole body called my mouth to open, I didn't do it but tried to force my bursting breath through my nose. I knew I wouldn't have to clench much longer.

In a little while I let go, then slowly got to my feet and looked around. My mare lay still, smelling of grassy dung and blood and horse sweat. I stood for a moment, satisfied, catching my breath and filling my tired nose with these sweet odors. The other horses watched me from a distance, the good creatures, never even thinking to threaten me. Soon, like obedient youngsters who hide when you look at them, they ran away. The cub watched me too, his eager head on his stretching neck showing over the grass.

Darkness had come. In the east a pale light in the clouds showed the moonrise. Overhead the evening star crept toward another star, which tried to drift always out of reach, just as a horse might do. As I looked down at my mare, my heart filled with a grateful feeling. How nice she was, steaming quietly in front of me. How round her belly was, and her haunches. I bent my head and pressed my nose to her soft nose, then slowly walked around her. I sniffed her haunches, then her belly. Perhaps I would start at the haunches. Heavily I lay down, getting myself ready to eat.

But what was this? The cub ran up and set his teeth into her belly! I jumped to my feet. *Out! Out!* I roared at him. He quickly backed himself into the grass. Peaceful again, I ran my tongue a few times over the haunch, then took a bite out of it. The sweet flesh tumbled down my throat. I took another bite, and another. Soon my teeth hit bone, and licking my lips, I shifted myself to eat a little higher on the leg. Here the flesh was hotter and thicker. More meat fell into my stomach. I began to feel very fine. But when the cub crept back to try again to eat at the belly, the flesh of the belly seemed to be better. I should be eating there, not he! Again I chased the cub, shouting *Out! Out! Out!*, and I bit into the belly myself, freeing the guts. I like the large gut, and was squeezing it through my clenched front teeth to force out the feces when I saw the cub creep to the haunch. *Out!* I barked, getting angry and showing all my teeth. I grew angrier when he showed his teeth to me. *Out!* I snarled. *Out!* said he. We glared, crouching face to face and swallowing meat as fast as we could, although I like to lie down when I eat, so my food slides easily.

Then the hair prickled on my neck and I raised my head to listen—I thought I heard the slowly rising call of a hyena. The hyena was far and was alone, or so it seemed until I heard another. Then I heard many, and I knew they were ganging together, whooping before their hunt. I stood up, not sure what to do. We were on the open plain here, my mare and I, where our scents would carry on the wind and where, after the moon rose, anyone could see us. I didn't like it. We would be better in the wormwood thicket where I had hidden when I first saw the horses. With the faint voices of the hyenas in my ears, I walked to the mare's neck, and setting my teeth through her throat, I began to pull.

The cub took a hind leg and did as I was doing, but he didn't know where we were going or why we were pulling the horse, so he dragged in another direction. This spread the horse out so that even I couldn't move her. Enraged, I ran at the cub, making my worst snarls and roars. He scampered. When I stopped to take a breath, I noticed that the hyenas were suddenly quiet. I stood still, listening hopefully. *Surely,* I thought, *soon they'll call some more.* But they didn't. The cub crept back to steal another mouthful.

My worry grew. I took the mare again, this time by the nape so that her knees folded nicely, not sprawling as before, and setting her between my legs, I walked, spraddling, toward the wormwood, the horse's back bumping against my belly. The thicket I had in mind was farther than I thought, but I struggled on, my jaws hurting from the weight of my mare. I felt tugs and knew that the cub was stealing bites behind me, but I didn't know what the hyenas might have heard and didn't want to take time to chase him. I struggled on, listening for the hyenas but hearing only an owl. At last I heard other lions, very far, many voices quarreling angrily: certainly Marmot and Goldeneye with all their lionesses, eating up a kill. I tried to think of the hyenas going to the lionesses instead of coming to me, but since their voices told that they were many, while the cub's voice and mine told that we were few, I couldn't make myself believe it. I tried to trot to the thicket but my mare was stiffening, making me slow.

Suddenly the cub gave a frightened meow and dashed ahead of me. Letting go of the horse, I whirled around. Many pairs of big green eyes were bobbing up and down in the moonlight, and many dark, hunching forms were galloping after me, almost caught up with the mare. Hyenas!

OURS! I shouted at them. They scattered, whooping. Without giving me time to think, some lunged at the mare and some slipped behind me. Panic gripped me, and my head swam. *Perhaps the cub will help me now,* I thought. *OURS!* I roared. But the cub was nowhere. Instead I felt a hyena breathe on my hind leg. *OURS!* I roared again, spinning to face him, swinging my paw with all my strength. But suddenly he wasn't there—again he was circling behind me. *OURS!* I shouted, turning back. Many blunt faces were all around me, some looking for a way to bite me, others pulling the mare. Her head slid right from under me. I saw her open eye and the claw marks on her cheek—my claw marks! *OURS!* I roared, trying to sit, protecting my hindquarters. *OURS!* I swiped at another hyena, and *OURS!* at another. A terrible pain burst in my haunch: I was bitten! I spun again, catching one hyena a blow that sent him tumbling, but he jumped up as if unhurt and my leg felt broken! Now I cared nothing for the mare, I was so scared of the hyenas. With all my strength I leaped as far as I could, right over their backs, and landed running.

I thought my heart would burst with running. When I was dizzy, I stopped and looked around. No hyenas were following. But why would they? They had what they wanted. I heard them whooping and snarling; I heard pops of tearing meat and loud snaps of cracking bones. My meat! My bones! I grieved.

My rump hurt. I sat down, and lifting a hind foot high, I put my head between my legs to see my haunch. Now it had holes in it. Slowly, carefully, I ran my tongue over the holes—first one, then the next, then the next.

Just as I began work on the last hole, I thought I heard someone calling. I lifted my head. The cub was calling, not with pain or fear but with a question. He had lost me. How strange! I was right here, sitting in the grass. I took my tongue to the hole again. The cub kept calling. *He'll bring the hyenas to himself,* I thought, listening for his voice to change when the hyenas found him. At last his calls grew faint. *He's going the wrong way,* I thought. *Why?* And standing up, I put my head near the ground and roared. Under my feet the earth shook. I roared again, this time working up to the loud part slowly, letting my voice gather strength as it grew. Then, although my wound still hurt a little, I walked in his direction, and soon he came bounding up to me, full of greetings, and lifted his little face to mine. Our noses touched. We kissed. Then I walked on, slouching, listening to him scramble after me. On a rise of rocky ground I stretched out to rest myself, and he stretched beside me. Before he went to sleep, he helped me clean the holes in my leg.

The air grew cold during the night and mosquitoes swarmed on us. The moonlight blazed. I could still hear the other lions in the distance, fighting over the last of the bones. I wondered what animal it was. Perhaps a big animal; perhaps a bison. Probably something good, with plenty of meat. Any hyenas trying to rob all those lionesses couldn't take their prey by force but could only hope for scraps. The lionesses would eat their fill, and if anything was left, Marmot or Goldeneye would guard it for them while they slept. Hearing them eating all together made me hungry, but I had no hope of eating now, and besides, a long time had passed since I rested. I dreamed of horses. I lay in the middle of many dead horses and had only to move my head to eat from any one of them.

Before morning I stood and stretched, yawned a few times, backed up to a grass tussock and squirted urine on it, scratched backwards, left a scat so small it was hardly worth passing, scratched backwards again, and started walking. Later the cub woke too. In time I heard him scrambling after me. Having no place to go, I went straight ahead, looking hopefully over the plain as I traveled. I saw only far-away herds, all worried now because the dawn was coming. In each herd someone had her head up, looking around for me. Hunting was hopeless when all the herds were so selfish about themselves, thinking only that someone might be trying to catch them. And then when the sun rose, ravens saw me and came screaming around my head, selfishly insisting that I catch their food. I decided to spend the day sleeping.

The days passed like that. Followed by the cub, I walked and slept, walked and slept, trying to get near herds as I saw them. On the second day I spotted ravens flying around something and ran to it, hoping that someone for some reason had left a kill, but only broken bones were left of a huge feast; hyenas had killed a spotted deer. But the hyenas had finished the meat and foxes and ravens had eaten the rest, even stripping the antlers of velvet. Very disappointed, I squirted urine on this uselessness.

Near dawn on the third day, at the edge of a wood, I found a trail used by a roebuck and lay in wait beside it, and I didn't have to wait long before the roebuck in the wood came picking his way, testing the air and looking everywhere as he tiptoed toward the grass on the plain. What good did so much caution do him if he always took the same trail? I had him in an instant, choking him so quickly that his little feet had no time to kick. Remembering the hyenas, I dragged him into a heavy thicket. There I began with his haunches, but of course on a roebuck these are small. Soon I had eaten both. Then I moved to his belly and took out the large gut. Fat clung to it. I swallowed the back end of it while feces popped out the front. The roebuck had a big grass-stomach that the horse lacked. I took his out carefully and dragged it aside. I wouldn't eat a grass-stomach—I didn't even want to see it. I was afraid that I might lie on it by mistake and break it and then all the slimy grass would stick to my fur. The roebuck was so small that I could reach across it from any direction, so this time the cub couldn't rob me but had to sit quietly, watching me eat. At last I took a bite of the neck, which I could hardly swallow, I was so full, and I pushed myself up, took a few steps away from the carcass, and dropped. *Ough!* I was asleep before I knew it.

The cub must have taken the chance to eat while I wasn't watching. When I woke up, the meat was gone. The cub held a legbone in his paws and was licking out the marrow. I growled at him, but I was still very full—my heart wasn't in it. The warm sun made the sage smell sweet. Now I slept a long time and woke in the dark. The cub was sucking my nipple.

The moon is a stomach that fills with meat, then grows small with digestion. While I lived with the cub, the moon ate itself full, then grew small again. A fire came with clouds of smoke, making the grazers on the plain half-close their eyes and turn their tails to it. In so much smoke we are all unhappy, but the grazers got more confused than I—I had no trouble catching a horse from behind. So I ate from time to time, not as much as I wanted, but enough, and except for worry about the lionesses, I was all right.

The cub was all right too. One day when I was cleaning my belly I saw something I didn't see often: my last two nipples showing, pink and cleared of fur. Thoughtfully I ran my tongue across them. To my surprise, I found on the tip of each a tiny drop of milk. I licked the milk away. There was very little of it, but I saw that the cub hadn't been suckling for nothing. *The little thing,* I thought. *No wonder he follows me.*

One day I saw some torn grass and bits of dirt, and found the backwards scratch of feet that showed a scentmark. On a tussock was a squirt of urine left by Goldeneye. I made a face. The cub nosed the tussock too, and sneezed. *Now*

Goldeneye is marking all this land for the lionesses, I said to myself. *I'd better go away.*

We walked for two days, which made the cub very tired. But the only land I found had scentmarks of another pride. At least in the land of the first pride I knew where I was and where to go hunting, so I went back again and lived as best I could, sometimes eating but always uneasy. The cub seemed nervous too, and helped me by keeping watch. Two of us were better than one when listening or testing the air. When I saw his head rise and his ears or whiskers twitch, I made sure I paid attention.

Sometimes we played. Perhaps I was too old to play, and I wouldn't have thought of doing it without him, but when he felt frisky and chased my tail, I found myself chasing him. Then we stretched our mouths and touched our teeth together, as if we were really fighting. I liked the way he washed my face and the feel of his breath, two little streams of it in my belly's short fur. And I liked his young smell. Cubs don't know about their smell—so good it makes your heart soft and your anger leave you. I was too busy playing with him and thinking about the grazers on the plain to remember who I was or why I was there. I never even thought about the shamans.

Then one night at dusk, when the lion star was crawling near a horse star in the west, I suddenly turned into a person. There I stood on two legs but in a cloud of lion musk, near a wormwood thicket on the middle of the plain, not even sure where I was. At my feet was a lion cub. It gave a great hiss of surprise, then bolted. I saw its green eyes where it crouched in the long grass in the starlight.

Lions! I thought. Then I remembered the shamans. *This is Swift's work,* I said to myself. *He won't let me stay away longer.* So I knew I had to return. But I didn't know the way. Since the night was dark and the cave was probably very far, I thought I should fly, and I tried to take the form of a large owl. Instead I became nothing more than a little brown owl with barred feathers. Then I saw how angry Swift really was.

Even so, I had wings, and so I floated up into the dark air. In the grass below I heard the rustle of vole and stooped on it. Its blood ran between my toes. But when I put its head down my beak, I couldn't swallow. *Swift won't even give me time to eat,* I thought sadly. *He must be in a hurry. I had better get home before he gets more angry.* And so I flew high until I saw the moonlight shining on the river, then flew up the river to the cave.

There Swift's trancing spirit was waiting for me. I landed in a tree in the spirit-grove, and when Swift wasn't looking, I quickly turned into a person. Rather fearfully I greeted him. "You?" asked Swift sharply. "Where are your uncles? I sent for all of you."

I couldn't answer, of course. I hadn't even heard my uncles' voices, except from far away. I was just as glad they weren't near, since the fear of them still clung to me. "They're coming, Honored Shaman," I lied.

But of course Marmot and Goldeneye did not come. The Moon of Flies left the sky and the Bearberry Moon showed as a crescent. Still they stayed away. Lionesses were around, though, in plenty, hunting out most of the game. The people did the best they could; they were now more worried than ever, because they sometimes noticed two large male lions stalking them. And the roaring, if anything, was worse than before. The people, trying to be careful not to make loud sounds, might have saved themselves the trouble. Whatever noise the people made the lions drowned out. And worst of all, so much roaring drew hyenas, who followed the people's trail right into the cave and stole a deerskin. During the Bearberry Moon the people talked of going to the lodge on the Char River even while summer lasted, to get away from the lions.

In the form of a raven I tried to satisfy the shamans on my own, flying high into the air, keeping watch, calling warnings. Out on the plain I found foals and calves of every kind being eaten by lions, or hyenas, or wolves. Picking the bones were birds and foxes. On a baby bison I ate until I could hardly fly.

So much food made me think of the cub. Was he also eating? With all the carcasses he might scavenge enough to live on, if he could keep away from Marmot and Goldeneye. He might find food, just as Meri and I had found food the year we lived with the wolf. The next time I flew out as a raven, I looked everywhere for him, expecting to see him at any moment.

Instead I saw three huge male lions drinking from a buffalo wallow in the river, quite far upstream. None of these lions was Marmot or Goldeneye; these lions were newcomers. From the way they rubbed and kissed each other after drinking water I saw that they were brothers, perhaps born together—much more than friends. I also saw, from the way they left the river with the slow, even strides of fullgrown lions, that they were old enough to mate. But at the top of the trail one lion suddenly pounced on the sweeping tail of the lion scrambling in front of him, who turned with a bellow and a swipe of his big left paw. Then I knew that although they were fully grown, they were still young enough to be playful. So when they became serious again and walked in single file toward the cave where the lionesses lived, I knew that Marmot and Goldeneye would soon have more than they could handle. Sure enough, after a bad night of roars and battle calls, Marmot and Goldeneye appeared in human form to sit in the spirit-grove, wrapped in their deerskins, cross and quiet, refusing to give any explanation of what had happened to them or why they had been away so long.

But I knew they were sorry to be back. Very soon, in voices so low that I could hardly overhear them, they began to talk about the lionesses. When a lioness killed something, Marmot or Goldeneye would chase her off the prey and eat his fill, it seemed. "I showed her this," said Marmot, stretching out his big palm and looking at it.

"That's what they understood," agreed Goldeneye. "They didn't give unless you forced them."

"Did you see me get this?" asked Marmot, showing Goldeneye a slit in one of his ears. Goldeneye nodded. "Did you see me swat her?" Goldeneye looked wise. "I made her think," said Marmot. "She never bit me again."

"Then how did you get that?" asked Goldeneye, pointing with his lips to long scars on Marmot's leg.

"That was someone else," said Marmot.

"The one you mated first?"

"One of the ones I mated first."

"We ate and we mated. We mated and we ate. Now here we are, no better than two roosting birds. Yanan! What were you doing all that time? Did the three lions find you?"

"No, Uncle," I said. "I ran away from the lionesses and lived on the plain with a cub. You learned more than I did about the three lions." I liked my joke and laughed.

Goldeneye turned angrily to face me. "What impudence!" he said. "How is it you make fun of your elders?"

But Marmot thought for a while. "You say with a cub? How with a cub? I don't remember any."

"There were cubs at first, Uncle."

He thought again. "Perhaps there were," he said. "I wonder what happened to them."

"We had more to think about than cubs," said Goldeneye. "We were trying to please their mothers. That's gone now. We should take the form of rhinos and trample the life out of those lions and lionesses."

"With only two of us?" asked Marmot. "I wouldn't go near them with only two of us. Let the people go themselves, if they like. I'm staying here."

By morning I was tired of so much selfishness. Because of Marmot and Goldeneye, the people might have to leave the summergrounds and live at the lodge before animals took shelter in the woods there. The people would be hungry. Yet if they stayed, the lions might kill someone. And how was it, I wondered, that Marmot—and probably Goldeneye too— could kill cubs and then not even remember, when I remembered so well? What had happened to those who ran, and to the cub who followed me, whom I could never find?

In the form of a raven I tried again. I found the sagebrush thicket where I had been hiding when he joined me. I found the place where I had killed the horse and the place where I had killed the roebuck. It wasn't easy to find my old trail, since when I made it I was on the ground and now I was in the air, but finally I found the place where I had turned into a person. Of course the cub wasn't there. Then I lost hope of finding him, thinking that long ago he would have gone. But in a dense willow thicket not far away I found his bones. The willows hid his carcass, which the sun had dried. Birds and ants had eaten his flesh without scattering his skeleton, so I saw that hunger had killed him; he died curled up in his hiding place, with his hind legs tucked under him and his little jawbone resting on his arm.

After that my sadness began and wouldn't leave me. Until

the people went to the Char River, I lay wrapped in my spirit-deerskin near the mammoth skull. Sometimes I lay on one side, sometimes on the other. I didn't speak to Marmot or Goldeneye, and they didn't speak to me, being too busy remembering their life with the lionesses—how they had taken whatever the lionesses hunted, how they had mated whenever the lionesses asked. They remembered filling themselves with bison meat, food which even as people they hadn't eaten very often. They spoke pleasantly of mauling the young male lion whom they found with the pride, and forgot the three male lions who in time mauled them. A good life, they agreed.

In my mind I saw the cub still hiding in the willows. Perhaps he had died waiting for me. Although he didn't matter anymore, the thought of him troubled me.

Before the people left for the Char, the shamans tranced to honor The Bear. The shamans' fire brought us a spatter of burned fat, but I left my share in a tree until a bird came and ate it. Was I lonely? Angry? I couldn't say. But when it was time for us to take the form of birds and follow the people to the Char, I watched everyone else out of sight, then lay on my back looking up through the birch leaves. Not until a day and a night passed did I become a raven and follow unwillingly.

◄ 20 ►

LITTLE KAKIM DIED in his sleep a few nights after Ethis and I went into the ravine to get mammoth meat for him. I learned of this in the morning when I saw The Frog lifting him to carry him outside. His arms stuck out like the branches of a bush and his withered buttocks were stained with the last of his diarrhea. I began to cry, then couldn't stop, and put my fist in my mouth to muffle my sobs. Everyone else stared at me strangely. Some people's eyes were moist with tears, but no one else, not even his stepparents, lost control of themselves over Kakim.

I saw that I was embarrassing myself and others. Still I couldn't stop. In the silence I heard my ugly sobs echoing from the cave's rock walls. I vomited suddenly. Then I felt someone pull me to my feet. It was Teal. Gripping my hand, she stared fiercely at the other people, even at The Frog, who, with Kakim in his arms, stood bewildered in the mouth of the cave. Some of the others stood up slowly, gathered their picks, and followed The Frog outside to help him dig a grave for Kakim.

Teal led me behind the little procession up the trail to the plain. But while the others took The Frog in one direction, Teal took me in another. My crying went on by itself, my eyes streaming, my breath catching, as if I had nothing to do with it. I began to hiccup. Slowly we walked a long way beside the rim of the ravine, until we came to a large, flat rock with juniper around it. On top of this rock, hot from the sun, we sat down.

"It's time," said Teal, "for you to talk to me. You're going to have a baby which your husband doesn't think is his and some think is Elho's. You're very frightened, with good reason, and the fear is making you sick. You must tell me everything as best you can, and we'll see what must be done." My crying left me empty of all feeling, even of caution and shame. So I told Teal all that had happened, beginning with stripping off my clothes for Elho in the birch grove and ending with Timu's anger.

When I finished, panic took me. If I could have called back every word, I would have. My heart beat so fast it made me dizzy, for I saw how my words could ruin me. Rather than speak I should have fallen on my spear or jumped from the ravine to the rocks below. I was a coward, and stupid too. My mind's eye saw our people carrying an infant out of the lodge to leave it in the snow.

Teal said, "You speak of one thing, but there are two things here." Then she paused and gave me a shake. "Listen, Yanan!"

When I looked up, she began again. "There are two things here. First, there's what you did with Elho. He's as much to blame as you, and you're both very much to blame for such wrongdoing. Even in the Camps of the Dead, we in your lineage feel fury to learn of it! We must atone for your misdeed. All of us, even Meri, will come to this rock today and shed our blood into a fire. And the smoke will travel to the top of the sky and the far ends of the world to purge our lineage of the stain you and my son brought on it. Yoi once stained us. Now you have stained us. But my son has stained us twice. The first time he was young, and the second time he was far from home and badly tempted, but if he does it again I will know he's insane, and I, with others, will hunt him down and kill him like an animal. He may not continue. That's the first thing."

I was astounded. How could Teal say such terrible words but show no feeling? She waited to be sure that I knew she meant what she said.

When she saw she had shocked me, she went on. "The second thing is the question of the baby's father. Children conceived in winter are born in the fall. Children conceived in spring are born in winter. You don't seem to know this, but it's true throughout the year, for all children born alive, with no exceptions. Your belly is very large for a child conceived only last spring. I think Timu is the father, even if you and he do not. Still, no one can say when a child was conceived just by the size of the mother's belly. So we must wait for the birth. Then we can be sure, if as you say you lay only with Timu and Elho." Teal took my chin in her hand and looked straight in my eyes. "You told the truth, I think."

"Yes, Aunt," I said numbly. But now I began to cry again, this time from fear that I would give birth too late to say that Timu was the father, and from relief that, after all, he might be.

"A child lies in your belly a while before you notice," said Teal. "I remember how you used to vomit and sleep and get angry easily last winter. After the Moon of Roaring, I think it was. Vomiting and sleeping are signs. So is easy anger. So when Yoi noticed your pregnancy, it was far along. As I say, I think Timu is the father."

Teal left me lying on my back on the rock while she went to send Yoi and Meri to me and to bring Elho herself, after talking with him. In the warm sun, with the hum of tiny yellow wasps in the juniper around me, after all that had happened and all that Teal had told me, my head was empty of any thought or feeling, and I fell asleep. I dreamed of Kakim. Then I dreamed my child was born—a boy who could walk and talk. He was Timu's, I saw, with the strong, square body of Timu and Graylag.

Something woke me. I looked up into the gray faces of two large wolves. With their front feet on the rock, they looked at me curiously, and leaped away when I suddenly sat up. As if they thought I couldn't harm them, they turned their hindquarters to me, and without a backward glance loped on their way.

I saw that this was no place for sleeping, and I looked around over the plain. While I slept, a herd of bison had drifted near. Perhaps too near; if I held my fist at arm's length, it was just a little larger than one of them. But instead of worrying me, the sight of these bison nearby calmed me greatly. Yellow wagtails flew up and down around them, catching insects trying to escape the bison's feet and teeth. I heard the bison breathing and chewing.

Perhaps the wolves had come to learn whether the herd held anything for them, then noticed me. Beyond the bison I saw a herd of saiga, almost hidden by their color: tan against the short, tan grass, with white, shadowy bellies.

So many animals, I thought. Here all along. Perhaps Ethis and I rarely saw any when we went gathering dung because we never went this far. But of course the animals who left the dung didn't stay, because of the hunters. Also, the grass was long near the cave but short here, and many animals liked short grass better than long grass, although this went against reason. Even so, they did, and kept hunters burning the long grass. On the horizon I noticed the smoke of one of those fires.

Then, in the great distance, I saw mammoths. They didn't seem to be doing anything, although in the shimmering air that rose from the plain at this time of day, it was hard to see them clearly. Most of them seemed to be very far apart, and some of them might have been walking slowly. Their heads were up, and their huge curved tusks gleamed faintly.

A bison snorted. The bird on its back hopped into the air as the whole herd turned and cantered stiffly for a short way, raising dust and grass seeds behind them. I tried to see what had started them, of course, and when I couldn't, I thought to let the bison show me. They soon stopped, then turned and stood. Presently their heads drooped and they went on with their grazing, whisking their tails. What they saw hadn't worried them much. Perhaps it was a wolf or one hyena or a woman, since they seem to know women from men, and run farther if they see men. Ah, yes. Here came Yoi and Meri.

I felt ready to meet them. If, as Teal said, I had been sick, I saw that sleep, sunlight, the peace of the plain, and the thought that what I had done could now be mended had made me well.

Meri didn't seem to know what was about to happen or why she was there, but I could see that Teal must have told Yoi. We sat quietly together on the hot stone in the sweet smell of the sun-warmed juniper, watching the bison and waiting for Teal. I was very grateful that Yoi didn't pry at me with questions or accuse me. Instead, after we had waited a long time, she began to sing. Meri and I joined—it was Yoi's Fire River song, to be sung by at least two people, since the idea for this song came from wolves' songs, with two parts. Yoi began and Meri and I followed, singing strongly, although the song seemed to be drawn away from us by the huge sky.

When the sun was low, we got hungry. We would have gone gathering, but were afraid to miss Teal. Instead Yoi took from her bag a long strip of meat from the dead mammoth, lightly cooked and bad-smelling. A small piece of it was enough. Yoi thought we might soon have something better. After burying Kakim, she said, all the men had gone hunting. Teal had gone to look for Elho, which explained why she was taking so long.

Just as we were wondering how far to let the sun go down before starting back to the cave, Teal and Elho came up behind us, walking quietly over the grass. Teal was calm, but Elho looked stricken. His eyes were red and his face was swollen from crying. I felt a stab of pity for him—it must have been terrible to hear his mother say that she and others, unnamed others, would hunt and kill him. It also must have been frightening, since he must feel (as we all felt) that if Teal wanted him killed, she would see him killed, and not even Graylag, his father, could stop her. And it must have been surprising, in the way that learning that someone has died is surprising. We looked to Teal to help and protect us, each of us feeling that part of our safety lay with her.

None of us needed to be told what we were about to do after we had stripped off our shirts, except perhaps Meri, to whom Teal said, "This is a lineage thing. One of us will explain it to you sometime. What we do today, you may not tell to others." Meri nodded, looking grave and ready, and Teal took out her firesticks and tinder and rolled a fire on the rock. The rest of us gathered grass and dry juniper, and when the fire burned high, Teal drew her knife from her knee-high moccasin.

She scratched the blade across her left arm, and blood ran down her hand into the fire. Then she scratched the blade across her right arm. Yoi took the knife and did the same, and I did the same, not flinching from the pain but almost glad of it. Teal, I think, would have made a small nick on

Meri's breastbone as she had once done long ago, but before she could, Meri took the knife from me, and with her jaw set and her eyes wide, scratched her arms just like the rest of us. Then Elho took the knife and cut both his arms deeply. Blood dripped into the fire. His hands became slippery, but grasping the knife so hard that his knuckles bulged, he cut his chest and shoulders. His mother might have stopped him there, but before she could, he drew the knife straight up his body from his navel to his chin, then stood over the fire so that his blood made smoke.

Then we all stood over the fire to let our blood drop on it, and we danced in place, swaying. We sang:

> You who live in the sky,
> You whose burning hair makes the clouds,
> You whose voice is in the storm,
> You who are the mother of all the animals and all the
>   people,
> Find our blood in the smoke.
> We want something for it.
> We want life.
> We want food.
> Do not harm us, Ohun.
> Give us children.

"We'll go to the river now," said Teal, "where we can wash and drink. We'll sleep here. By morning these cuts will have scabs and our shirts will cover them. Elho, thank you. You could have shed less blood. But instead you showed yourself a strong son of our lineage, and I'm pleased with you."

Down in the ravine, the water was not as clear as the water below the cave. Even so we bathed and drank our fill of it. Then we noticed mammoth and bison dung, and we saw that many animals drank and wallowed here. Teal and Elho, who had learned the country the year before, told of a wide place farther west, where the plain swept low until it almost met the river. Here the animals could find water without using a steep trail. From the number of tracks we suspected that animals who had once used our trail might now be crowding near the low place. This year our trail might not be used, and we might not get as much meat as we hoped for. We planned to tell the others this sad news.

The light in the ravine was blue with evening, but on the plain the sky was still bright. In the long twilight we roamed around looking for berries, eating them as we found them. We also gathered dung and heather for the night's fire. The bison had moved far off, facing the wind but with their heads down, their thick hair red in the evening sun. The yellow wagtails flew away. We made our camp beside the rock, and since we had no sleeping-skins to roll in, we slept on the rock, because heat was still in it.

During the night we heard bellows, snorts, and splashing in the ravine, and we knew that bison were wallowing. Later we heard groans, more splashing, heavy bodies rolling, then trumpeting and squeals. Mammoths too were wallowing. On the plain we heard lions roaring one after the other, leaving long pauses between roars. Because they were spread out over a great distance and took turns calling—the farthest lion first, then the next, then the next—they sounded almost like one lion moving toward us over the plain with huge, flying bounds. The lion who roared last was very near. He made our ears ring. What were they doing? Were their hunters like our hunters, who sometimes spread out in a row?

When the lions fell silent, perhaps not needing to call more, a nightjar began with his *bak! bak! bakbakbak!* almost as loud as the lions. Far off we heard hyenas, and nearby we heard the bison breathing and chewing, pulling and crunching grass with their large jaws. Because the bison were so many, their chewing made a soft, rolling sound like water running.

Late at night the last waning crescent of the Moon of Mammoths lifted slowly from the plain. With it rose a cold wind carrying the bison's smell, dense and grassy. Sighing, they began to lie down. This was the dead time of night, the time like midday, when nothing moves or calls, when everything is still. Now nothing moved even in my belly, and my mind's eye saw a child curled and quiet, like the moon on its back among the stars.

Then the eastern sky turned pale and light began to

gather, and although it was too dim to see, we heard large bodies moving. The bison were heaving themselves to their feet. We heard them bellowing, calling and answering, and with a little more light we saw their large dark shapes slowly drifting west, perhaps on their way to their trail down the ravine.

In the dawn we saw that we were no longer bleeding. We scraped off whatever blood had dried on us at night, put on our shirts, and began the long walk back to the cave, finding and eating berries on the way. We didn't reach the cave until midmorning. A heavy blue cloud of smoke rolled from the mouth to meet us. Inside, our noses told us, the people were cooking fresh bison.

We waited in the mouth with the light behind us to let the people see us, not wanting to surprise them. "You're here," said someone, and we went in. Although many people gave us curious glances, especially at the scratch that reached to Elho's chin, we didn't explain. Meri seemed filled with a sense of the importance of what we had done; her young face was calm, without expression. Like an adult, she found a place at the women's fire and sat down, waiting for someone to offer her meat as if she had never been away. No one would learn of our affairs from Meri.

Yoi joined the crowd at the women's fire but sat back to back with Swift at the men's fire. They began to chat over their shoulders, passing to each other morsels of their shares of the meat and turning now and then to exchange affectionate glances.

Teal stood alone, her flat, bored gaze slowly roaming the faces of all the people looking up at her. In her own time she bent her long legs and sat. There seemed little hope to learn of our doings from Teal. In search of hints, Ankhi and Timu looked at Elho and me, the people least likely to give any, and while once I might have been frightened by their searching, I now felt safe.

Not since I had found the Hair River cave had I been so happy as I was for the next few days. Doubt about my pregnancy might still linger in the minds of some, I knew, but not in my mind. I wanted the child to be Timu's and it would be Timu's, no matter when it was born. Well, not if it was born in winter. But it wouldn't be born in winter! And what if it was? Hadn't we taken away the taint?

I worked until my eyes burned and my fingers grew sore from the awl to finish Timu's bison moccasins. And they were beautiful! With brown fur curling out of the tops, they were as soft and tough and warm as moccasins could be. With every step he took in winter, he would thank me.

So I brought them to him. He and Ethis were sitting at the dayfire in a group that included The Stick and The Frog and their wives. Timu wasn't surprised by the moccasins, since he must have seen me working on them. But when I handed them to him proudly, he took them almost reluctantly, and instead of thanking me, gave me a long stare. This wasn't what I expected. Embarrassed, I sat down, waiting for the group to go on talking.

But no one said anything. Instead, my cousins' wives exchanged sly glances. The others looked stern. Even The Stick and The Frog looked as if they disapproved of me—they who had left my father to die! Then The Frog's wife took one of the moccasins and examined the work. Limply, Timu held the other. Ethis looked at me with pity, and my face burned!

I stood up to leave. "Thank you for these," said Timu awkwardly, lifting the moccasin.

"They were easy to make," I said, and left.

When I went to gather fuel that afternoon, I didn't try to find anyone to go with me. Instead I went all by myself, and walked far out over the plain, alone under the blue sky. *So this is how things are,* I thought, *and how things will be.* The interesting question of my misdeed was tightening the group around Graylag and pushing me far outside it, which must have satisfied Ina, since I had once showed how willing I was to do the same thing to her sons. Now they and their wives were in the center of the group and I was at the edge.

I expected others to feel what I felt, which was stupid of me. How could Timu feel pleased just because I felt pleased? Why should he forgive my misdeed just because it had been put right in my lineage? If he blamed me and not Elho, why should he blame Elho, his half-brother and willing partner in misdeeds with the women on our old summerground? And who could say what Elho had been telling people all this time? He seemed to be on good terms with everyone, yet how did he stay so? By telling part of the truth! By saying that Yanan had indeed lain with another man. Like a fox in a snare, I was caught well.

The next day I went gathering with Ethis. We talked about Timu. I told her that I carried Timu's child, although I knew that others thought differently. I told her what Teal had told me, adding that I had felt life before I left the Char. And I told her what was almost true, or might just as well have been true ever since our lineage had shed blood in the fire, that I had never lain with another man.

I saw she didn't believe me. By now The Stick and The Frog and their wives, with Ina adding her part, would have talked so much and so often with so many other people that my untruth was almost hopeless.

But though Ethis didn't quite believe me, she still wanted to help me. "Whatever happened, people will forget," she said. "Be calm. Stay by your Aunt Teal. Stay by your Aunt Yoi and my Uncle Swift. He's headman of all these people here, and all the plain for many days' walk is his to hunt in. How can it matter to him what your people say? When your child is born, Timu will see that it's his. He'll love it. He loves mine." She smiled, thinking of this.

On the way back I saw the lonely figure of a tall woman against the sky. "There's Teal. I'm going to talk to her," I said to Ethis. Then I put my arms around her. "Thank you, Sister. I was afraid of you when I first met you. But you have helped me," I said.

We could scarcely hug because of the bulging children between us, but we tried. "I was jealous of you," she whispered, as if embarrassed to admit it. "Remember not to worry."

Well, she wasn't jealous now. Letting her go on by herself, I waited for Teal. When we were together, I said, "People are openly scorning me."

"Some people are scorning you," said Teal. "I'm not."

"Could Timu divorce me?"

"Of course. But he won't."

"Can't you help me?"

"Not yet," she said. "After all, what they're saying is true.

341

But if the baby is Timu's, we'll know. Then I can help you, if you still need help. Why do you think we wear the scars of The Woman Ohun? They remind us to be brave, even for a long time, if need be."

One evening soon after, I came back from gathering fuel to find many people building a fire by the mammoth skull. The shamans were going to trance to bring mammoths, Ethis told me. I noticed Swift already streaked with ocher, wearing a shaman's shirt copied from Teal's shirt with fringed sleeves. He saw me and called. "Hide-in-the-Grass! Did you find fuel? Don't take it to the cave. Bring it here. Tonight I'll show your Aunt Teal a new thing!"

I doubted very much that anything Swift might do as a shaman would surprise any of us, let alone Aunt Teal, but, "Yes, Uncle," I said, and brought my bundle of dung and heather to the fire near the skull. Leaning on the skull was something new after all: three long, straight branches from a redberry bush of the kind that grows in thickets by a river—a kind that grew nearby, in fact—but these were hollow, like bones without marrow. Someone had pushed out their cores. How was this done? I wondered. And why?

Ethis found a place in the circle of people around the fire. When she beckoned me, I gladly squeezed in beside her and sat down to watch. "What are we doing?" I whispered.

"This is our dance," said Ethis. "It's not like you do at the Char. You'll see." Ethis dangled her baby as if he were standing and bounced his feet on the ground. "Like this," she said. The baby gave a happy scream. Around us men were taking off their shirts and rubbing their arms with fat. Ethis rubbed the baby's arms, as if with fat. He kicked to show he liked that too.

When she started to put him in her shirt, I asked to hold him, and Ethis let me. Under my shirt he rested on the bulge made by his kin. Both struggled at the same time, as if they felt each other. At least these two would play together one day, I thought, if all went well.

The evening wind was lifting, carrying the first of the dry birch leaves into the yellow sky. People began a song like Aunt Yoi's song, a song for many voices which wove like wolves' voices, some rising, some falling. I listened to Ethis for a moment while I learned it, then sang too. We kept time by clapping. Behind us the men began stamping the mammoth dance, swaying the tops of their bodies, their arms out and stiff like mammoths' tusks.

Then I noticed a deep sound all around us, as if a voice were rising from the ground. It was the voice of the skull, made loud by three men blowing down the hollow redberry branches into its nostril. The sound was strange and chilling. My skin prickled. It was good to be singing and clapping among a big group of people doing a big thing— my own troubles seemed small, and I felt that I belonged. So I sang and clapped as loudly and carefully as I could. When Ethis's baby fussed, Ethis and I took him from my shirt and stuffed him into her shirt quickly, so we didn't miss anything.

Suddenly we heard roaring! Scared, I caught Ethis's arm. "The blade," she said into my ear. "The voice of the ivory blade!" *Aaong! Aaong! Aaong!* it went, getting loud, getting soft, but never stopping. Cupping my hands under my chin to keep the firelight out of my eyes, I looked over the heads of all the singers, out into the dark. There, among the birch trees, I saw one of Swift's sons whirling something thin and white on the end of a string. It wasn't large, and it fluttered like a moth's wing, but the sound that flew out of it almost overcame the singing.

Swift and Teal took off their shirts, loosened their hair, and washed their arms with embers to heat up their power. Above the singing and clapping, above the voices of the skull and the ivory blade, Teal sang in the voice of an eagle, with high, piercing screams. Almost with triumph I watched this strong woman of my lineage. Would others push her kinswoman aside? We would see!

Swift rolled his eyes into his head so the white parts stared at us. On a person with dark eyes I might have found this stirring, but on a man with pale eyes like Swift's I had to look twice to see what he did. Even so, Swift was exciting. With his loose hair like a mane and his muscles gleaming red in the firelight, strange, strong power shone from him, as if a lion with no skin was dancing. *"Bak! Bak! Bakbakbak!"* he cried, as the pale pupils of his eyes rolled down where we could see them, like the eyes of a corpse alive again, like two reflections of the moon.

With their arms wide like the wings of flying birds, Swift and Teal danced back to back, turning slowly, their trances growing. Then, locking their arms and planting their feet, the shamans turned like a firestick whirling, showing us first Swift's face, then Teal's, a man's face, a woman's, until they came apart, reeled, and dropped unconscious. Swift fell on one side of the fire, Teal on the other. And suddenly it came to me why Swift had been so eager to marry one of us. What a child he might get from the lineage of Sali! In all the world of the living, even in the Camps of the Dead, people would stand in awe of such a shaman-child. Why had I never thought of that?

As hard as we could, we sang and clapped to help the shamans, to show their distant spirits how to get home. When the shamans sat up again, first Swift, then Teal, to bury their faces in their hands until their heads cleared, Ethis and I hugged each other, scared and excited because The Bear could not be far.

"I have seen The Bear," said Swift at last. "He promises us mammoths." And we were sure that the mammoths would soon come where we could hunt them. But now was no time to stop singing. We sang and clapped while the men danced and the voices of the skull and the ivory blade roared. When the new crescent of the Yellowleaf Moon rose we drew power from the moon, and when the sun rose we drew power from the sun. I didn't want the night to end, and was one of the very last people to keep singing.

In full daylight we went back to the cave, threw ourselves on the cool floor, and fell asleep, relaxed and exhausted. In the afternoon we woke up and cooked bison meat, then went to the river to wash and drink, and at night slept some more.

While we slept, the mammoths walked down our trail and drank from the river. In the morning we found big piles of dung and great round footprints. The mammoths who had left these signs must have come like shadows, as only mammoths can. Angrily the men hurried into the ravine to see if this was the work of Red Hair, while the women peered over the ravine's rim. Red Hair it was! No other mammoth made that half-sliced right rear footprint! We saw Red Hair as clearly as if she were standing before us—Red

Hair and many others with her, ten or more. She made all our work of cutting bushes and piling boulders useless, since not even Swift would hunt mammoths in the dark.

The next night mammoths came again, and again on the third night. But they no longer came quietly. Humbly we crouched in the firelit cave, listening to the roaring and trumpeting of mammoths on the plain above us, mammoths on the trail, and mammoths wallowing. Even when they didn't roar, the earth shook and little streams of dust poured from cracks in the cave's ceiling. Perhaps they were quiet, but they were there! On the fourth night, after we thought they were gone at last, we heard boulders crashing into the ravine. Our boulders! Red Hair was destroying our ambush.

Swift didn't like being humbled by an animal, and with each new outrage he shouted, "By The Bear!" Even Graylag was disappointed. Last year many mammoths were in the summer's catch, but this year, he could see, there would be just one. A madman might hunt mammoths at night, but not Graylag. And the time had come to start for the Char, if we wanted to be in the lodge before the snow.

Soon we who were going to the Char made up our packs. At the last moment White Fox decided to stay with his parents. He now had no fear of losing Meri, and said he didn't want to spend another winter like the last. I couldn't say I blamed him. I too dreaded the winter in the lodge, in my case because of Timu's anger, but what could I do? After taking great trouble to bring Aunt Yoi to Swift, I now had no close kin on the Fire River except people who had no room for me. And the only really good person there was Otter.

Sometimes I wondered if Yoi remembered our promises of huge piles of meat and ivory below the cliffs in summer. But if she was disappointed, she gave no sign. Rather, she and Swift seemed in very high spirits. As we packed, they teased and jostled each other until Yoi snatched Swift's ivory pin, making him chase her to get it back.

Speechless, Ethis and Ankhi watched their uncle tussling. I watched too, slightly embarrassed by my aunt and sad as well, since I remembered tussling with Timu. Wondering if he remembered, I looked for him in the dim, daylit cave, but saw only his back. His pack was ready. He was planning next summer's hunting with Swift's sons and saying good-by to them as well, since they and many other people were going to the new husband of one of Swift's divorced wives, who controlled the hunting near a winter cave far down the Hair River.

When Swift and Yoi saw that the rest of us were ready, waiting only for them to end their play, they became serious and finished packing. And so we said good-by to the other people and followed Swift to the plain, where a cold wind blew, moving a herd of clouds so that their shadows rushed past us from behind, as if they were making fun of our slow footsteps.

Not far along the way we passed a place of disturbed earth: the grave of little Kakim. Some of the rocks piled on the grave he himself may have carried from the river. Not even his stepparents stopped to look at the grave. Kakim had been an orphan, after all, and surely his spirit was also traveling, not east with us but west all alone, to the place of his lineage in the Camps of the Dead. In my mind's eye I saw the burrowing owl gliding over the short grass ahead of little Kakim, standing on the grass to let him catch up, then gliding on again.

VI

THE REINDEER MOON

≪ 21 ≫

AFTER OUR WAY LED south from the Hair River, we started across the plain, taking our direction from the sun by day and from a big dim star at night. That star, said Graylag, was the Spotted Deer, and would show us to his lodge. In our minds' eyes we saw the lodge with the spotted deer's antlers standing on it, long and dark, with something triumphant in them, like a stag with his head up.

But the lodge seemed far, at least to me. My body was heavy, and my spirits too. Since it seemed best that I travel at the end of our line with Yoi and Meri, all I ever saw of Timu was his back far ahead of me. And the only words I heard from him were spoken to others. He stayed mostly with The Stick and The Frog, who remembered all the old jokes they used to share together. At night Timu shared a sleeping-skin with Ethis among the many people at Graylag's fire, leaving me to sleep with Meri; it was lonely with no one but Yoi and Swift and Rin at Swift's fire.

Also our travel was slow, even though all the children with us were being carried. I was slow, Ankhi and Ethis and my cousins' wives were slow with their packs and children, and the older children easily grew bored with travel, so almost every day we stopped early. Wherever there were fireberries, we stopped to eat all we could. Far up the Hair we stopped to hunt, since the plain in the fall, unlike the plain in spring, isn't littered with carcasses. We killed a saiga, losing a day's travel on it. And after we left the river, we had to stop to dig milkroots as we found them for the water inside.

My cousins' wives complained that the food we found on the open plain upset their stomachs. When Ethis's baby began to show signs of an upset stomach, I went with her to look for the soft, curling grass that works best underneath a baby, glad of a chance to speak with her alone. I begged her to try again to talk to Timu for me, and in her warm, giving way, she seemed eager to help. But the next day, when I asked if she did, she shook her head as if she had lost interest, and I saw that she was crying. "What is it?" I asked, afraid she had bad news for me.

"My milk isn't good," she said, opening her shirt to show me the baby. He was fussing, crying. "He doesn't want my milk." To prove this, she put her nipple in her little boy's mouth. He turned away.

I remembered the complaints of my cousins' wives. "Can it be the berries? Perhaps your milk tastes of them."

Ethis squeezed a drop of her milk onto the palm of her hand and licked it. "It's sharp," she said, taking my hand to squeeze milk onto my palm.

I tasted and found it mild. "The sharp taste could be on your hand from the berries. Perhaps he isn't hungry."

"Perhaps," she said doubtfully.

"Let me carry him. Maybe he's tired of being in the same place." So she handed him to me in his sling and I put him in my shirt. Hot, he tossed and cried. I gave him back, and just as Ethis took him, he passed diarrhea.

"Do his stools come often?" asked Rin when, at our camp, Ethis took her baby out for Rin to look at.

"Yes," said Ethis.

"Next time he has one, show me," said Rin.

"He always has one," said Ethis, pulling the grassy pad from under the baby and handing it to Rin. Rin glanced, then threw it away and turned to Teal to speak of the constipating deer's-eye. But deer's-eye is only found on tundra or low plains where fine grass grows. We would find none here, in the dry tussock-grass of this high plain. We looked around at each other in case one of us had a piece of its root. My cousins' wives hesitated. They had it in their packs, I realized. Perhaps they had been feeding it to Kakim. Unwillingly, The Frog's wife brought it out. Ethis chewed it and smeared the paste in her baby's mouth.

Noticing this, Timu came to sit on his heels beside us, stretching out his hands for his baby, then holding him close while he cried weakly. Very tenderly, Timu rocked him. But there wasn't much else to do—when Ethis reached for him, Timu gave him back.

Everything happens suddenly with babies. One night later Ethis's baby was much too quiet. He lay on her arm with his head limp and his parched mouth open. Teal told us to build the fire and sing so she could trance and beseech The Woman Ohun, then called Her name in the loud voice of a pine grouse. Swift took from his pack his thin blade of ivory, which he fastened to its string, then whirled around his head until it roared like a mammoth.

These sounds went far, but The Woman and The Bear were farther. When Ethis and Timu and then their sisters, Ankhi and Owl, began to wail during the night, we at Swift's fire knew that something terrible had happened. Miserably we waited for morning. When it came, cold and windy, with many flocks of small birds scattering overhead, Ankhi asked me to bring my pick and follow her. Owl came too, her eyes red with crying, and as we dug a hole at a place Ankhi chose, Owl told me that Ethis's baby was dead. Of course I knew, but to hear the words shocked me. When Timu brought the little body, wrapped in its carrying sling, and placed it on the ground beside us, I couldn't look at it or at him. Timu couldn't watch, and went back to camp.

When the hole was finished, Owl and Ankhi waited for me to put the baby inside. So I did. He weighed no more than a dry leaf, but his stiff, cool stillness seemed to travel up my arms, numbing them. Ankhi opened her shirt and with her knife made a scratch on her breast. "I mourn you, my sister's child," she said. Then we pushed earth into the hole, packed it down, and walked slowly back to camp, not looking at each other, none of us knowing which child would be next. On the wind we heard the voice of a child in camp—probably Ankhi's, wanting her back. And inside me someone kicked and struggled, as a frog might struggle in my hands. But on this plain Owl's baby, dead a year now, also lay in a grave. I realized that wherever people lived or traveled, the earth was burrowed with little graves. Grass grew over them or spruce needles covered them, but they were there, hiding the babies too young to have names. How many there were, no one knew. But all the wisest people in the world together couldn't count them.

"Where are your tears for your co-wife's child, since you had so many for Kakim?" asked The Frog's wife when I was making my pack.

Shocked, I turned to face her. "I am crying," I said.

She looked wise, then said nastily, "It's only right."

While I puzzled over her manner for a moment, something quick happened inside me, like a pine nut bursting in the fire. As if a stranger, not me, were in my clothes, I noticed that I was rising to my feet. I saw how I was going to rip the braids off this woman! But someone clasped my shoulder and pushed me down. It was Swift. "Be peaceful, Hide-in-the-Grass," he said. "We're all unhappy."

Then I cried hard, with angry, ugly sobs. And other people began crying. But Swift exchanged a glance with Graylag. Graylag looked serious, then told The Stick and The Frog to follow him, bringing their wives. The rest of the people also started. When Rin touched Ethis's elbow, Ethis moved after the others as if in her sleep, as numbly and obediently as a mare might follow her herd. I'm sure she didn't know whose heels she followed.

I tried to follow Ethis, perhaps to comfort her later if I could, but Swift stopped me. "Stay with us a while, Hide-in-the-Grass," he said, not unkindly. "Let the others go on a way." Did he think I would find The Frog's wife's braids too tempting?

But without a word I did as he asked. Knowing how far I already was from Timu, I saw how much further this death would take me. More threatening than helpful, I was almost like a stranger again. Months would pass before Timu would forget the baby I had helped put under the ground. Until then, the loss of his child would increase his anger. What would come from so much anger? In spite of Teal he could divorce me. And if he did, where would I go? To some crowded lodge on Woman Lake, where people like The Frog's wife would begrudge each bite I ate? If I didn't have a good place to live, what had just happened to Ethis would happen to me.

That day we traveled very slowly. All morning the wind tried to loosen my braid, my shirt. By afternoon the air was filled with snow. We tried to walk faster to reach the shelter of the woods, but because we had lost too much time that morning, by night we were still on the plain.

The night was the worst I've ever spent. Our fuel was hidden with snow—we found enough for only one small fire. We had nothing to eat but a handful of plains-peas, and no water but scrapings of snow. I didn't want to lie down—to be covered with snow made me think of being buried, and though some of us were too unhappy to speak, the others quarreled miserably. The three children who were still living, who could still feel cold and hunger, cried because of it. Their parents pinched them, making them cry more. And we heard lions. "They may come here," said The Frog's wife.

"Let them," said Timu, the only words I heard him speak all day.

The next night we were among the trees that grew in the basin of the Black River, camped under the shelter of a hemlock. The night was clear and the light in the woods was blue. We found bristlecones—not good food but enough to kill our hunger—and many little runs used by small animals, in which we set snares. By morning, we thought, we would be eating well. And of course we had plenty of firewood, so we built a great fire.

The low-lying woods were colder than the plain, but alive with animals. We heard footsteps and the *tsi! tsi! tsitsirivi!* of a hazelhen. We heard wolves in the distance, and then, very near, the loud rutting challenge of a red deer. Swift cupped his hands at his mouth and drew a deep breath.

"Stop," said Graylag quickly. "Don't call him! We can't get him tonight!"

"I know stags," said Swift. "We'll get him tonight." And cupping his hands again, he gave a great bellow, which brought the stag crashing toward us, a loud roar jolting in his throat as he ran. The men were on their feet in an instant, spreading in a circle to surround the stag. We heard stamping and branches breaking. Soon the men came back again. They had lost him. "We'll get him tomorrow!" said Swift, as if hunting the stag in the morning were his idea. "He wants this place. He won't go far."

During the night I knew that Ethis was crying. I couldn't hear her, but my skin prickled suddenly, and I guessed why. Perhaps I heard something after all—Ethis sniffing back her tears, or sighing. Timu spoke, very low. I tried to overhear. "It flows. Look," whispered Ethis. Shocked, I hated to think what she meant. But I knew anyway: her milk was still running. Timu said nothing. After a long silence he made a choking cough, as if he cried.

Rin must have overheard them too. "Nurse your sister's baby," she whispered. "It helps the soreness. It helped me. When I lost a child, I nursed you."

At the first light the men set off through the woods, their breath making clouds and their footsteps crunching on the frost. The stag must have heard them. Unwisely, he challenged the sound with a bellow so loud it rang from the trees. We saw that we would soon be eating him.

The women didn't go for firewood or food that morning, but stayed to give advice to Ethis. Of the ten of us, I realized, only three had never lost children—me, Yoi, and Ankhi. We sat at the edge of the group and listened, as girls who don't yet have their Woman Ohun scars listen to older women. I didn't think the other women gave Ethis any comfort, but at least they reminded her that she wasn't alone.

"The sooner a dead child is forgotten, the better," said Teal.

"One dies, another begins," said The Frog's wife.

"It's worse the first time," said The Stick's wife.

"You still have your sister's baby to play with, and Yanan's on the way," said Rin.

"We all lose children—one day we get used to it," said Ina.

"I hope your baby isn't like mine, born over and over to keep hurting you," said Owl. That was the first I had heard of Owl's losing more than one baby. Others must have died on our old summergrounds at the Grass River. Had I ever been too young to notice such a thing?

"Ethis and I had a brother like that," said Ankhi to Owl.

"Four times he was born and died, never once living long enough to have a name."

Ethis cried, then said her breasts hurt, and Rin again suggested that she nurse Ankhi's little girl. Ankhi thrust the child at her sister.

The little girl wasn't sure what to do at first, but Ethis cradled her in a nursing position until the full breast by the child's face gave her the idea. When at last the child sucked, Ethis looked grim, as if she were removing a splinter. The little girl stopped sucking and stole a glance at Ankhi. *Am I making a mistake?* her eyes asked.

Ankhi also seemed grim. So the little girl twisted away from Ethis and held out her arms to Ankhi. But Ankhi turned her head and wouldn't look at her daughter, to show her daughter that there was work to be done. Then Ethis made the mistake of jerking the child from one breast and forcing her at the other, and the child began to cry. Angrily, Ankhi snatched the poor child back as if something were the child's fault, which made the child cry all the more, with her mouth open and her wide, tear-filled eyes fixed on Ankhi. Ethis had to empty her breast by squeezing her milk into the fire.

In the middle of the morning all the men but Swift came back, carrying the bull's forequarters, hindquarters, flanks, and sides, with The Stick carrying the good winter hide and Timu dragging the head by an antler. We built a big fire and cooked the liver, wondering what had happened to Swift. The other men couldn't say. While they had been cutting up the stag, Swift had gone somewhere else.

Soon we saw him through the trees, carrying something over his shoulder. When he flung his bundle down beside our camp, we saw that it was a wolf.

Surprised, people asked him why he had brought the whole of it. Why not just the skin? Was he going to eat it? When it moved, we saw that he hadn't even killed it. What now? But Swift didn't stop to explain. Instead he hurried off again, leaving us gaping.

The wolf was very young, I saw when we went to look at it: a pup of last spring, a male. With his four feet tightly tied together and his head tied to his feet by a thong that also held his jaws shut, he couldn't move. Only his tail was free, but that was tucked tightly. Although his eyes were open, he didn't seem to be looking at anything; he was just staring. But when we stood over him, he stole a glimpse of us out of the corner of his eye, then looked quickly away, as if what he saw was so bad that he didn't dare see more.

Well, he belonged to Swift. We would have to wait to learn what Swift wanted with this wolf. While we waited we ate the stag's liver, and at last we saw Swift among the trees, again carrying a bundle. This too was a wolf, also tied tightly. With a thump, Swift flung it down beside the first.

"Hide-in-the-Grass!" cried Swift. "Now see how we'll hunt this winter! You'll have to show us how!" I must have looked down at my belly, because Swift added, "Later." Then he looked hard at Meri. "My wife's younger niece must leave these wolves alone. They're mine, not hers," he said severely.

We threw more meat on the fire and cooked and ate while Swift told us how he had caught the wolves. While hunting the stag, he happened to notice a clearing, he said, a place where trees were tipped over. Thinking it was a place that wolves might like, he went back to it. There he saw something twitch beside the upflung roots of one of the trees—something gray, an ear. He crept forward, his ax raised. Three young wolves were curled up in the shelter of the fallen tree, and flattened themselves in terror when he loomed over them. One, two, three, he clubbed them on the head, then sat on one while he trussed another. He couldn't work fast enough—the third came to its senses and ran. But the one he sat on didn't stir, although it opened its eyes. It even lay limp while he tied it.

We looked at Swift's captives. They seemed dead to me. Swift might have clubbed them too heavily. Not so, he said. They were very much alive. To prove it, he untied them, and although they hardly moved, he put the thongs around their necks and tied them to a tree.

A third time we threw meat on the fire, glancing at the wolves from time to time, wondering if we would have to share our food with them. "Hi!" cried Timu suddenly. We looked. Both wolves were gone. Swift ran to the tree, then laughed. They were hiding behind it, but because he found them chewing at the thongs, he again tied their jaws together.

Late in the afternoon we cut all the uneaten meat into strips and hung them from branches to drain the heavy blood. Our camp reeked of deer. We would draw a bear or worse, said Graylag. Timu and Elho climbed the tree to put the meat higher, and we gathered plenty of firewood, to be ready to fight for our meat if we had to.

During the night we heard the rising voice of one wolf calling far away in the woods. Near me, Swift said to Yoi, "The grown wolves are back in their camp. I should have set a snare. I wasn't thinking."

"I want the skins if you change your mind about the two you caught," said Yoi.

"Yes, if I change my mind," said Swift.

Later that night we saw wolves all around us, their eyes green in the firelight, their shadowy gray shapes pale among the trees. Swift seemed delighted. I heard him remind Yoi that wolves keep bears away.

When I saw the morning star, I woke Meri, rolled our sleeping-skins, and made our packs. Remembering the Black River from our travels to our old summergrounds, I knew that if we left soon, by sunset we would reach a shallow place on the river where water rushed through a tumble of large, flat stones. There we would ford and camp on the far side. I wanted to be ready to start this hard day, to be helpful and pleasing to others, so no one would have reason to be impatient with me. When I heard someone climbing the tree, I groped my way to it to see if I could help pack the meat. But The Stick and The Frog were in the tree, handing strips of meat to Timu and Elho below. Timu seemed not to want my help. Rather, as if I weren't there, they went on with their work, so I went back to Swift's fire and sat down to wait.

Yoi was still asleep, but Swift was tying his pack strings. "Hide-in-the-Grass," he called, "you know wolves. Help me tie mine." So as gray light spread through the misty woods, I followed him. From afar we saw the dark shape of the male wolf at the very end of the thong that held him. He lay flat on his side, his head and tail limp on the ground, his feet stretched in front of him, as if he thought himself already a carcass. But the female wolf was gone. Her leather thong lay bitten through, and in the dim light we found large round footprints, which showed how other wolves had helped her. "By The Bear!" cried Swift. "I should have brought them to our fire."

The male seemed more scared than ever without his sister. When he heard us, he twitched an ear, then raised his head a hand's breadth for a glimpse of us. At the sight he couldn't help but startle, then crept to the far side of the tree, where he cowered.

Swift looked at the bitten thong, disappointed. Then, because the thong was still good leather, he sat on his heels beside the tree and began to pick at the knot. "Don't stand there," he said. "Tie him up."

It hardly seemed worth the trouble. "You won't get much help from this wolf. You should skin him," I said.

"Why?" asked Swift, as if the thought surprised him.

"He's too scared. If you untie him, he'll run away. And you wasted the female."

"Wasted?" asked Swift, sounding irritated. The other people were awake now, all talking, perhaps waiting for us. They could become impatient with me after all, so I didn't answer Swift. Instead I pushed the male wolf onto his side, gathered his four limp feet together, and wound a string around his ankles. Although he humbly folded his ears and tried to raise his thigh slightly, he didn't dare watch what I did to him.

My remark seemed to be bothering Swift. "I wasted?" he repeated. "How did I waste her?"

"You didn't take her skin."

"No, because I didn't catch her for the skin!"

"Well, it's gone now," I said. "She'll starve with her jaws tied shut. So would you."

"Ah, Hide-in-the-Grass," said Swift, laughing. "Who is strong enough to tie my jaws shut?"

◄ 22 ►

By the time we forded the Black River, the long summer days were over. We didn't have enough light to travel as far as we wanted before making camp, although every day we tried. By evening of the last day some of us were exhausted, but we were still far from the lodge. In spite of the meat, which gave us much strength, our group could no longer be hurried. On the floodplain of the Char we heard the tiger.

All day I had been so tired that I trailed far behind the others, so when people paused to listen to the tiger, I sat down. Ethis sat beside me. "Yanan must rest," she said fiercely. "If she stops, I stop." The Stick's wife looked back at us, perhaps remembering how, on the way to the Hair, I hadn't waited for her. The thought struck Ethis too. "Go ahead, if you want, if you can find someone to show you where the lodge is. Nobody minds." So The Stick's wife said nothing.

Swift's pack was leaning dangerously. On top of it he carried his string-wrapped wolf, which must have moved during the day. Now he took off his pack, put the wolf on the ground, put his pack back on, and asked for mine. "Give it," he said to me. "I'm tired of creeping like an insect. I'll come back later." Then, without waiting for me to give it, he tugged it off me. As usual when a heavy pack comes off after a long day, I felt I was floating. With my pack now on top of his, Swift strode off for the lodge on his long legs and soon was out of sight. I then remembered how he had used to make me go hunting with him, only to walk so fast that I trailed far behind.

"He'll get firewood on the way," said Graylag. "Any of you who want to follow Swift are welcome to go. All of us don't need to wait for Yanan. But I will." So Ina with her sons and their wives and children and Owl with her husband walked on, leaving the rest of us.

Swift's wolf lay very still. Without food or water since he had been caught, he might be dead. If so, there was no reason to carry the carcass. "We could skin this quickly, Father-in-Law," I said to Graylag. He nodded, and knelt to help me do it. But the wolf flinched when the knife touched him. "Let's untie him while we rest. Perhaps he needs water."

"Don't lose him," said Graylag. "That wouldn't thank Swift for his kindness." I untied the string that held the wolf in a bundle. Then, seeing how he might run if he knew he was free, I tied the string around his neck before untying his feet. "Let's hurry," said Graylag. "We should go or camp." He thought for a moment. "Yanan can't camp, since Swift took her sleeping-skin." The others stood up, ready to leave.

But now I had it in my mind to let the wolf drink water, and lifting him to my shoulders, holding his front feet in one hand and his hind feet in the other, I carried him to the riverbank. There I put him down, keeping a tight hold on the string.

The wolf stood unsteadily, and I saw how he couldn't drink with his jaws tied together. So I made a noose, slipped it over his jaws, and untied the thong. Now I could open the noose a little, and the wolf could open his jaws enough to put his tongue out. So the noose wouldn't drop off, I tied the other end around his neck.

Suddenly the wolf gave a great leap, almost pulling the string from my hand. But I held tight, so the leap only left him thrashing on his side, half in and half out of the water. I saw that I would have to wait until he understood what to do, and I said to the people behind me, "Please don't wait here. I know my way home and I'm not afraid."

"We can't go off and leave you," said Timu. "Didn't you hear the tiger?"

"It won't find me. Hasn't there always been a tiger?"

"Hurry, please, Wife," said Timu.

"I will," I said, but I didn't.

Time passed. "Yanan!" called Timu.

"I'm coming," I answered.

"Think of the distance! Look at the sky!"

I didn't need to look at the sky. The valley of the Char was already so dark that I could hardly see the wolf standing in the water. "I said I was coming," I called. But I wasn't—I was listening to the wolf's tongue carefully lapping water.

Timu was tired too, or by now he would have come to get me. Instead he called again. "Wife!" But I didn't answer, because my shout might stop the wolf from drinking. "If you don't come, we'll camp, and you can sleep on the ground," said Timu.

"I'm getting a drink of water," I said. So I did. Then I tightened the noose on the wolf's jaws and again lifted him to my shoulders, feeling the water in his fur run down my neck and under my clothes. "I'm ready," I said, and off we went.

We had gone hardly any distance before we met Swift coming back for us. "Here you are," he said to the men. "You must be women. You didn't get far!" He laughed at his joke, not noticing the other men's silence. Swift gave a grunt and a nod when he saw how I was carrying his wolf, then took the packs from Yoi, Meri, and Ethis and vanished into the night again. Yoi took Elho's sleeping-skin and Ethis took Ankhi's, and we went along faster, following the floodplain. The familiar river slid quietly among its rocks, black water with the Yellowleaf Moon trembling on the surface.

Sometimes the wolf struggled, and sometimes he lay limp. I felt his breath on my face, warm and quick. I felt his heart beating against the back of my neck. The smell of his wet coat and the feel of coarse, short hair on his bony ankles made me think of the long-legged female who once had helped me and Meri. I tried to remember everything I could about the wolf and her people. Did Swift's wolf belong to them, who lived so far to the east? I felt sure he did not. Even so, the smell of his fur brought the long-legged female to my mind very clearly. As if she were watching me, I saw her yellow eyes.

A third time Swift appeared on the trail. By now we could smell smoke and see the tall antlers against the stars above the lodge, so we knew we were near. We didn't need help now. Even so, Swift took Ankhi's pack from her and the wolf from me and vanished again. We caught up with him in front of the lodge.

Somehow he had found the time to make a thick ring of brush near the dayfire, and inside this his wolf was tied, where other wolves couldn't free him if they came this far. Some of us were nearly speechless because we were so tired, but Swift seemed full of life. When I thought to remind him that the wolf had only a noose to keep him from chewing his tether, he said, "I tied his jaws again. Don't let anyone tie mine!" He laughed, then he thought for a moment. "And don't let Meri untie him, please," he added. "If her wolf had been tied, the things you left in the lodge last summer wouldn't be ruined."

"Did he eat our things?" I asked, hating to think of the trouble that might come of it. "Any animal could have done it."

"Tell that to the others when they tell you what he took. Now we'll snare him, whatever fuss your sister makes."

Swift didn't see Meri in the dark behind me. "No, you won't," she said.

That Meri overheard him bothered Swift not at all. "We will," he said. "And your sister won't be able to stop us. Think of that!"

Meri seemed to see how things were with me as well as Swift did. "Aunt Yoi will stop you," she said.

Swift laughed loudly, then laughed again. "If she doesn't want the pelt," he said.

Inside I saw The Stick and The Frog and their families with Ina at Graylag's fire, where they had every right to be. Owl was there with her husband, sitting where they had sat for as long as I could remember. Elho and Timu with Ethis and Ankhi went there too. I saw that I wasn't to go with Timu; if he wanted me, he would call me. Instead, I saw, someone had put my pack beside the fire near the door, where I used to stay with Father and Mother. I was too tired to mind.

I was almost too tired to eat, but Rin gave the last of her cooked meat to me and Meri, so I ate my share, then unrolled my sleeping-skin and lay down on my back, my great belly like a hill above me. No one said a word about Meri's wolf. Meri lay down beside me, and before I knew it, I was fast asleep.

During the night I felt someone shake me. It was Ethis, sitting on her heels beside my bed. Outside I heard muffled wailing: Swift's wolf trying to call without opening his jaws. Ethis too was crying. I sat up.

"Sister! What's wrong?" I asked.

"Look," she said. I saw milk oozing from her breasts. "Even the crying outside starts this. Come to the river with me. I'm afraid to go alone." So I got up and followed Ethis out the coldtrap. Neither of us troubled to put on our clothes, so the cold bit us as we listened carefully for night noises and sniffed the air for the musky smell of tiger. But we heard only water moving softly in the river and wind in the spruce trees, and we smelled only spruce needles in the clear air. Swift's little wolf made no sound. Then we walked quietly down the stony, moonlit terraces to the river, where Ethis splashed freezing water on her breasts. "I'm tired of people telling me I'll have another child," she said, "because I know I'll have another child. Our husband keeps bothering me and bothering me."

This surprised me. How could he? I asked, "Doesn't he grieve too?"

"Yes," said Ethis. Then she added, "Men are different from women, or they are when they grieve."

"I had a sister who died soon after birth," I said. "Father grieved." I then remembered the trip from the hills to the Marten River and added, "But he soon lay with Aunt."

"Your Aunt Teal?" asked Ethis.

"With Aunt Yoi. She was his wife then."

"Was the child her child?"

"No," I said.

Above us, Swift's little wolf began to cry again. Ethis waded into the river and sat on her heels, gasping from the cold water that foamed over her shoulders. "My breasts don't seem to know what happened," she said between chattering teeth. "Now they will." I bathed too, just dipping water over my arms and legs at first, then sitting on my heels by Ethis. Unlike her, I jumped right up and scrambled out.

Ethis followed slowly, looking down at herself. "I'm all right now. We can go." So we did. When I crawled into my sleeping-skin, my icy body startled Meri.

In the morning, large footprints around Swift's wolf showed how Meri's wolf had visited him. All day Swift's wolf cowered under the brush pile around him. No one fed him, since only shreds of meat were left, and no one took him to the river for water. Some of us thought he would be dead by morning, and Yoi made plans to use his skin. But by morning only his tracks and the tracks of Meri's wolf were in Swift's ring of brush.

I thought the little wolf had managed to work the thong down over his nose and bite through his tether, but the others thought that Meri's wolf had freed him. The doings of the wolves weren't clear from the tracks, and they seemed to have eaten the thongs.

Swift shrugged off his disappointment. He could find another pup next spring, he said. The woods were full of wolves. But the other people were furious that once again Meri's wolf had robbed us. When all the people started for the hills above the Char, the men to hunt and the women to find pine nuts, Timu took a snare and a scrap of marrow. I started to follow Teal, not wanting to fail to do my share, but also thinking that I could learn where the snare was set and later spring it for Meri. But Teal told me to stay behind and rest.

The long walk from the Hair had taken all my strength. I was too tired to argue. Then Meri said she was going for winterberries, and vanished into the woods. Alone, I sat at the lookout below a south-facing rock, getting hot between the sun and the dayfire, roasting one of the stag's bones, then cracking it with a stone for the marrow. From the size and weight of my belly and from the way the fists and feet inside made my shirt jump, I knew it wasn't too soon to look for a place to give birth. A hemlock on a warm southern slope would be perfect—but hard to find, I saw, as my mind's eye roamed the landscape. The hemlocks were mostly in the valley, in cold, dark places. A pine on a high southern slope might be better. But my mind's eye looked up through the pine branches and saw lots of blue sky. *Too open,* I thought, and went back to the valley. Perhaps I could find winterberries growing near. Perhaps the valley wasn't so bad, because I didn't own a waterskin but might want to drink water. And if I cried, the river would cover the sound. I knew I might cry, and my bowels might open. My mind's eye saw many people listening and laughing. I had no plans to give birth in the lodge, unless snow fell before my labor started.

Meri came back with only three winterberries, which she gave to me. But she hadn't gone for winterberries, she admitted. I wasn't surprised. In the woods she had met her wolf, she said. He didn't come near her as he used to but instead traveled along beside her for a while, keeping at a distance among the trees. And she thought she had seen another wolf with him. She wasn't sure, but she guessed it was Swift's.

That didn't surprise me at all. Where else would the youngster go? Who else would he follow? What surprised me was Meri, whose eyes shone. "Those two are like you and me," she said. "Or they would be, if they were sisters." Of the three berries that lay in my palm, she took one back and ate it. "Do you remember living with the wolf, just you and me?"

"Of course," I said.

"Why do we have to live with Timu? He doesn't like us. Why can't we go back there? We might meet her." Meri meant the she-wolf, I realized. "And we could raise your baby. I told you not to go back to Timu."

Deep inside me something moved—a feeling, not the baby. I put my arms around Meri. "We can't," I said. "I wish we could. But we might not live. We almost didn't live, even though we only spent the last part of a winter. We'll be all right here. And we'll stay together."

"Oh, I know that," said Meri. "That's not the trouble. This isn't a good place for us, that's all. Think of the snare!" But thinking of my own trouble made me lose interest in Meri's, so I closed my eyes and didn't answer. Meri persisted. "Sister, wake up!" she said.

"You know," I reminded her, "people already set many snares for that animal but never caught him. Don't you remember the night we thought Swift had caught him? Do you remember why Swift calls me Hide-in-the-Grass? Anyway," I added, "perhaps Timu's snare was for a ptarmigan."

"Not if it was baited with marrow," said Meri.

When everyone but Yoi and Rin joined Graylag to crack pine nuts at his fire, I knew I should have gone to the hills with the women. So far that day I had eaten no food but a bit of marrow and two of Meri's winterberries. The men had caught nothing, so there was no pile of meat, and the women had really been gathering only for themselves. Of course they gave handfuls to the men who sat at the fire. So it was one thing to have people against me when I felt strong and could walk far for pine nuts or do my own hunting, but another thing now.

"Will you give us pine nuts?" I asked Yoi.

"You could have come with us today," she said, but she gave me a few.

I cracked and ate them, then went to Graylag's fire to sit on my heels behind Teal. "Will you share pine nuts with me, Aunt?" I whispered. Teal was talking, but she gave me a handful absently.

"I'm hungry," I had to say at last. Then the other people at Graylag's fire had to share with me. But nothing forced them to be generous. Their lack of interest hurt, but I didn't criticize them. In turn I shared with Meri, who could always surprise me by being satisfied with very little food.

In the morning I still felt tired from the long trip to the Char. My back hurt and my hips felt weak. I didn't feel like walking all day to the hills and back for pine nuts. Hoping that the men would kill something, I went with Meri into the nearby woods for winterberries. There we saw Meri's wolf again, shadowy among the trees. He stood to look at us a moment, then ran. I saw no other wolf with him.

At midday, when animals are still and hunting is almost useless, Timu came from the woods carrying a wolf's limp body. Of course it was Swift's captive. With no parents to feed him and no food for all the days with us, he was almost sure to be caught by Timu's baited snare. Timu flung the body by the dayfire and took out his knife. Then I saw where Swift had gone wrong trying to tie the pup—Swift hadn't tied the string to the bushes carefully. The young wolf's jaws

were still tied shut and the string was still around his neck.
He must have tugged at his tether until he was free, and later
the bait must have tempted him, although he couldn't eat.

After he was caught, a fox or a marten had bitten him and
spoiled his pelt. If not for the wolf, Timu's snare would have
caught a marten. I couldn't help it—I laughed. "This was
well done! Your snare caught a hood for Aunt," I said.

As if the many faults were Timu's, he angrily tossed the
knife at my feet. "Skin him," he said.

"May I have the meat?"

"Wolf meat?" asked Timu. "Why? It's disgusting!"

"But I'm hungry, Husband," I said.

"My snare, but Swift's wolf. Ask Swift," said Timu.

So I did. "Reindeer are already in the woods," said Swift.
"By tonight or tomorrow we'll have plenty to eat."

"Are you refusing me?" I asked, surprised.

"No, I'm not refusing you! Of course you may eat that if
you want." Swift turned to the other men. "Yanan's hunger
shames us," he said.

Perhaps it did. I couldn't help being hungry. I cut strips of
meat from the young wolf and laid them on the fire. When
they were cooked, I didn't know whether or not to offer
them to others. I might insult people by offering such meat.
So I placed the cooked strips on a rock and said, "This meat
is not mine. I thank Uncle for it." Then I ate alone while
others watched me scornfully, and I too was ashamed.

I should have waited. That evening, by moonlight, when
the men came across the river jumping from stone to stone,
we saw that they carried on their shoulders the cut-up
carcass of a reindeer, as Swift had foreseen. In no time
people were cooking the liver. Unluckily for me, Timu's
spear had killed the reindeer, so the liver was his to share,
and the portion he gave me was insultingly small.

Teal started to speak, but I stopped her. "I'm not hungry,
Aunt," I said. Not wanting to remind people of how I had
humbled myself by what I ate before, I added, "Meri and I
found winterberries."

My excuse didn't satisfy Teal in the least, and she spoke
anyway. "Husband!" she said, surprising Graylag with her
tone. "Look what your son gave his wife."

When Graylag saw, he said to Timu, "Come now, son.

Don't anger women." So Timu cut another small piece and threw it at my feet.

Sensing a fight and hoping to avoid it, people suddenly pressed meat into my hands. But too late. Teal stood up, stared down at Timu, and said, "You may not insult a woman of my lineage. Apologize now, and give your wife a share that shows how you respect her."

Timu glanced at the others around the fire to see what to do. Enough people must have shown him that he needn't obey in a hurry. He waited, meanwhile staring rather rudely at Teal. "Do it, Son," said Graylag calmly.

So Timu said in a low voice, "I'm sorry, Wife," then picked up the meat at my feet, threw it in the fire, and cut a new piece for me.

"Good," said Teal, folding her legs to sit down.

Perhaps Graylag feared that Teal's demands were shaming to Timu. "My son may not be to blame for his feelings," he said.

"You're right, Husband," said Teal. "He may not. And you're right to speak openly, since this is no longer a matter between your son and my kinswoman, but a matter for the lodge. People of my own lineage are to blame, because the man responsible for the trouble, your son Elho, is my son too."

It was frightening to hear Teal speak so boldly of things that could lead to great danger, things better left unsaid. Even so, Teal showed Graylag that Elho was threatened, and Graylag took Teal's meaning. Their eyes met. We all sat quietly for a time, everybody thinking. I waited, wondering if Teal was sure of herself. I hoped so, since the life in my body was in her hands.

She seemed perfectly sure. Her eyes swept over the firelit faces watching her. Then, with Graylag warned, with the people of our lineage alert as deer, and with the other people ignorant of what was really being said, Teal went on. "Our son is responsible for the trouble because he told people that Yanan lay with a stranger at the Fire River. Is it true, Yanan?"

"No," I said.

"Elho," said Teal. "Did you say this thing?"

"Perhaps I did, but I don't remember," said Elho. I could

hear from the uneasy way he answered that he didn't see where Teal was leading us, any more than I did.

"Did you or didn't you? Other people here remember, if you don't."

"Yes," said Elho quietly.

"There you have it," said Teal to Graylag. "Yanan says she did not take another man, and our son says she did. Yanan has reason to lie, but our son doesn't. For my part, I believe Elho. I'm sure you do, too." Graylag watched Teal closely, saying nothing. Teal went on. "But here's my question to you. Suppose she did—what does it matter?"

"Who was the man?" asked The Frog's wife.

"That you ask anything about Yanan surprises me," said Teal, "you who came so recently to our lodge. Yanan was born here, as her child will be. But I was speaking with my husband, who can ask his own questions. You needn't help him."

"My son's wife has a right to speak," said Ina.

"My wife asked an important question," said The Frog. "I know the answer, and it spoils our lodge."

"Why then, tell us," said Teal.

"The man was Elho," said The Frog. Thinking that they had Teal and me too, Ina and The Frog exchanged satisfied glances. I blinked, as if I had no idea what they meant, and Teal looked surprised. "My son?" she asked. "Did you see my son and Yanan together?"

"I saw them sitting in the grass at night, alone."

"Sitting in the grass may be coitus to you," said Teal, "but not to women. Ask a woman what is meant by coitus. She might surprise you." Swift laughed loudly. No one else breathed.

But The Frog was now unbalanced. "Yoi told me about Yanan and Elho," he said.

"If she did," said Teal, "our lineage is even more to blame. So I ask Yoi if she saw Yanan and Elho together."

"No, Aunt," said Yoi from the edge of the group. "I didn't see them. The Frog is lying."

"Did Yanan or Elho tell you they lay together? Did someone else tell you?"

"No, Aunt," said Yoi.

"In that case, I agree that someone is lying. But perhaps

Yanan lay with another man at the Fire River. Now, Husband, I again ask my question. If she did, what does it matter?"

"It may not matter to you, Wife," said Graylag very seriously. "But it must matter to my son. My brothers and I found this place and built this lodge. With our children, we own the hunting. How can we live in winter without hunting? We haven't agreed to let the child of a stranger hunt with us."

"No stranger's child will. Yanan says her child is Timu's."

"Are we to believe the word of a young woman who may or may not take other men?"

"You should, although you don't," said Teal. "How can the child be other than Timu's? What man was with Yanan to be its father? If at the Fire River a man tried to get a child on Yanan, he had her too late. She conceived her child in winter. Didn't the rest of us have to listen to Timu having coitus with Yanan last winter?" Some people laughed uncomfortably, but Teal ignored them. "Look at Yanan. She will soon give birth. If the child is born soon, it was got in winter, right beside us while we tried to sleep."

People having coitus do seem to make the kinds of sounds other people remember. Embarrassed as I was to think it, I knew that most people might remember exactly how and where they had heard the sounds.

But though I was embarrassed, and saw that Timu was also embarrassed, I now wanted to speak. "My child's father is of this lodge," I said. "I don't know what people say about me. No one has the courage to tell me. The child was not fathered by a man from the Fire River. Whoever says different is lying. I'm finished speaking."

But then I wanted to say more. "My place in this lodge may be spoiled," I added. "If so, rather than live in the corner by the door, rather than beg food from those who left me and Meri and Father to die on the Pine River, I'll go to Woman Lake next spring, this time to stay. And I'll take my child of your lodge with me. Now I'm finished."

That night The Frog spoke last. "Yanan is wrong to say my brother and I left her to die on the Pine River. We knew her father was sick when we were forced to go. He was our mother's brother, our kinsman, our lineage. We tried everything to take him with us. Yanan may not remember. Yet what I say is true. Her Aunt Yoi came with us, but her father refused. Could we take his children without his consent?"

Once I might have cried to remember the time of Father's death. But by now I felt calm and almost happy. And The Frog's speech didn't stir me, so I ignored him.

In the morning I went to search for my hemlock tree on the southfacing slope. As I left the lodge in the cold air, I met Timu carrying firewood. We both stopped and looked at each other, not smiling, then passed each other and went on. From the feel of my hips as I walked, I saw I wasn't searching for a tree too early. With each step I swayed. Something was softening my bones.

All my life I broke branches from the trees around the Char without thinking that one might shelter me in childbirth. Remembering a few on the north bank, I went to see them. But their branches were sparse, or the slope was too steep, or the earth below was rocky. I didn't want to cross the river—my balance didn't seem good enough to jump from stone to stone—so I gave up the thought of a sunny hillside and went down the terraces to search the floodplain. Near the first bend of the river the trees came almost to the water. And there I found a hemlock with wide branches and a thick bed of needles below.

The woods around were cold and dark but not so dense that I couldn't see through them. I didn't want a hunting animal to surprise me. The river was near and not yet frozen except along the bank; I could wash off the blood if I needed, and drink all the water I liked. And moss softened the partly frozen ground. I could bury the birth matter in the moss. But best of all, thick patches of newly ripened winterberries lay everywhere, shining red in their smooth green leaves. Satisfied, I gathered moss to soak up any blood and broke dry branches from the nearby trees so that I could feed a fire.

As I worked, I heard someone coming. Was it Timu at last, to talk to me? But I wasn't sure I wanted to hear anything from Timu, not today. Anyway, it wasn't Timu but Swift, the man of meat, who walked out of the woods to lean on his spear and look down at my pile of firewood. "So,

Hide-in-the-Grass," he said. "Here you are, making a nest for yourself to have your baby."

I wouldn't talk of childbearing with Swift. "No, Uncle," I said. "I'm gathering wood for the lodge."

To my great surprise, Swift softly touched my hair. "No," he said, "you're gathering wood to have your child here. You're too proud to have it in the lodge!"

In my face he must have seen astonishment. "If I am, Uncle, it's women's business," I told him.

"Women's business," he agreed, "but mine too."

"And why is that, Uncle?" I asked stiffly.

"Because I came here to find you, Hide-in-the-Grass," he said. "I know what you're doing and why. I came because I won't see you wasted on the men you'll be with next spring, the fish-eaters at the Fire River and Woman Lake. But there you'll be. I saw it when Timu threw the scrap of meat at your feet. I saw you picking fish heads in the corner of a crowded lodge. But instead you must come with me."

Because I wasn't sure what he meant, I said very simply, "Perhaps I'll go to the Hair, then. Thank you, Uncle."

"No, Hide-in-the-Grass, if you come, you won't call me Uncle. I want to marry you."

The strange accent rang in my ears: "I wan du marry you." I folded my legs and sat down slowly, carefully watching this man while my thoughts struggled to make sense of what he said. At last a useful thought popped up. "What of my aunt?" I asked. "You can't marry an aunt and a niece."

Swift sat too. "Your aunt had two husbands before me but is still childless," he said. "By now, many people have reminded me of that. And I want children from your lineage. Only from your lineage. I'll divorce your aunt."

Just when she seemed content at last? What would happen to her? "You might divorce her," I said, "but not because of me. She's my mother's sister."

"I won't desert her," said Swift. "Men at the Hair River envied me when I married her. So if she likes, she can choose one of them. She's beautiful, like you."

What was I doing, calmly talking about plans for Aunt Yoi? Even in the deepest part of me, I hadn't foreseen Swift as my husband. In my mind I tried to give myself a shake, but nothing happened. At last I said, "I don't know how to answer you."

"Meri will go to the Hair," Swift went on. "White Fox is there now. Isn't he the man you wanted for Meri? So if you come with me, you'll be with Meri."

"Well, what of my child?"

"If this child isn't mine, the next will be. I'll call your child mine although I'm not the father."

"Yours?"

"Yes, Hide-in-the-Grass, I will for this reason: I want you. The men in your lodge are worried about the father. But this isn't my lodge, so why should the question trouble me? You're as strong as a man, your hands are skillful, and you're beautiful. You know much about hunting, and you're fearless. I thought you might come back to Timu after you cooled your anger over the pelt he snared. But when he threw your food on the floor, I laughed inside. Do you remember throwing the betrothal necklace across the lodge?"

"You don't let me forget," I said.

"While the necklace was still in the air, I said to myself, 'Let White Fox keep the little girl. I'll take the sister.' And I will."

I couldn't help but see how Swift's offer might be tempting. Once his looks made me think of a lion, but who could dislike his great strength and white teeth? I watched him for a while, perhaps understanding why others admired him. Anyway, I liked his summergrounds—I liked the grassy plains and the great pale sky over the Hair River, and the cave. And I liked the thought of starting over, of leaving behind all the old troubles that could cling to me if I stayed here. Timu might never feel that my child was his child. So a doubt could stay with the child too. Doubt can lie hidden a long time, and like a bad sickness that begins quietly, it can be dangerous. Even so, there was much to consider before I answered Swift.

"Don't forget," he said, noticing how I hesitated, "Timu would have to call you Aunt for the rest of his life. That alone should please you." So I couldn't help but smile.

"Well, then, Hide-in-the-Grass," said Swift, clapping his hand down hard on my knee, "we'll speak more of this later. Think about it. You won't be sorry."

"I'll think about it if you find another name for me!"

"Never!" said Swift. At that we both laughed.

Nothing was decided, so there was nothing to say. In the evening people might have been surprised to find Swift alone with me, talking at the embers of the dayfire, watching the sun go down. Timu walked by as if he didn't see me while Swift and I were talking about the wolves. I was pointing out to Swift the many mistakes I thought he had made with his captive, and telling him about the time Meri and I stayed alone with the she-wolf in Father's old lodge.

Except for Meri, no one had ever heard that whole story before, although Swift might once have pried some of it out of me. In return, Swift told me about the western reaches of the Hair River and how it goes over a fall down to a short-grass plain. He spoke of the hunting there, and of his people's winter caves and lodges. If I married him, I realized, I might see some of these places. I especially wanted to see a waterfall. When Swift stopped suddenly, because he overheard Graylag speaking of going hunting in the morning, I was strangely disappointed. I wanted to hear more.

This was how things were with me the day my labor began—Timu and I trying not to look at each other but Swift and I quite friendly. By then I even liked his lion's eyes.

That day the men went hunting and the women went for pine nuts. A bad pain in my back had kept me awake the night before, but I didn't know what it foretold. As soon as the people were out of sight, the men going west and the women east, the pain moved around to my belly, and I knew I should visit my hemlock tree. Perhaps Swift's offer had made me sure of myself again, or else I put much trust in the marks on my thighs, the marks of The Woman Ohun, which protect women. For whatever reason, I felt no fear.

I didn't need to explain where I was going, because the only person in the lodge with me was Meri. Putting on my parka and wrapping my sleeping-skin around my shoulders, I took my knife and a coal from the fire and left for the bend in the river. Meri followed, making a cloud of breath with her excited talk. Soon she would have a niece or nephew to play with, she thought. I was worried about my trousers and moccasins, since I thought I felt a trickle of water. Soon, although the air was cold and the ground frozen, I stopped and took them off. And none too soon; a great gush of steaming water warmed my legs and feet. On we went until we came to the tree, where I put the coal into some tinder and blew on it. When my fire was burning, I took a deep breath, then wrapped myself tightly in my sleeping-skin and sat with my back against the tree.

The pains were much worse than I had ever expected, and they went on all day. A huge, dry stone inside me seemed to be forcing my bones apart. How did women do this, not once but again and again? At the first very strong pain, a pain so bad that I didn't feel my teeth sink into my knuckles, a pain that forced feces out of me, I swore by The Bear I would never again have coitus. When I thought I could stand no more, I looked up through the branches and saw the dazzle of the sun. It was still morning, though I thought it must be night. And then it was night, with the woods cold and blue. No baby came, but I was exhausted.

If we had a waterskin, Meri could have brought me a drink. Instead, on my hands and knees I crawled to the river. While I was there, a new pain caught me, and I lay on my side with my teeth clenched, shivering with cold and waiting. As the pain faded I heard the splash of something wet moving noisily, and I saw an otter watching me from the bank, cautious but interested. She was small, with brown eyes and long, pale whiskers. Our eyes met briefly. Then, on the far side of the river, a stag called in the woods. The otter and I turned our heads at the sound. Out of the woods came a large stag with dry grass draped on his antlers. Stretching his throat, he gave a full-voiced call that echoed in the valley. When his voice broke like a young man's, he wet his mouth with a drink of water, then called loudly again. No one answered. The stag waded into the river where the water was low, heaved himself across without needing to swim, and came out on our side to crash away through the woods. When he passed my tree, he stopped and stamped his feet. But I had nowhere to go except the tree, so when the stag left I crawled there, noticing that I was leaving a trail of blood on the ground.

When a pain slackened I fell asleep, and when a new pain gathered I woke. For a while I thought Meri was speaking to me; then I thought Meri was gone. I tried to call to her but couldn't, then suddenly I saw how unwise I was even to think of making noise while reeking of blood and birth-water and lying on the ground. Even the place was chosen unwisely. By now, if I could be warm and safe in the lodge, I would gladly let the people watch and even laugh at me. I wished I hadn't set my heart on the privacy of a hemlock tree. Again a pain took me and kept me staring at the sky until it faded. When a new pain woke me, I heard the stag far away and saw, thin and yellow, the new moon through the branches—the Reindeer Moon, so bright it lets the reindeer travel at night where men can hunt them.

When I woke again, I saw in the shadows many people sitting around me. I thought I might be in the lodge, but no, firelight shone on the hemlock branches. I tried to smile when I saw Teal and Ethis, but they took off their shirts and crowded together between Owl and Ina, who bent my legs to raise my knees. Why did Teal and Ethis take their shirts off? I understood when I felt a new, sharp pain as Teal pushed her hand into my vagina. I saw that they didn't want to soil their sleeves. And I felt afraid, because I also saw that what had happened to Mother must now be happening to me.

Someone's hands reached under my arms. It was Yoi, pulling me upright to lean against her. Between my knees, Teal and Ethis were working hard, frowning and biting their lips, pushing something harsh against me. Teal pushed her fists into my sides. Ethis leaned forward, then leaned back holding a baby—a small, thin, blood-streaked baby with a thick, dark, twisting cord fixed to its belly. Ethis's milk began to run in two arching streams.

The pains went on, very long and very deep, fading only to begin. I flinched at Teal's hand in my vagina again, then felt her tugging. Later I heard men's voices. After a long time Timu lifted me up and carried me. I heard him speak, but didn't remember what he said. Very far he carried me.

Someone dragged me along the ground. Then I was tumbled back and forth as someone slid my arms out of my sleeves. I saw firelit antlers in the arch of a roof, with Yoi's ivory necklace on the tine of one of them, and I knew I was in my own place by Swift's fire. I saw sunlight in the smokehole, then moonlight again. People were singing. The pain moved far away. As if I were in a lake in winter, I was cold, numb, almost asleep—a fish barely moving under black ice in stale, dark water. Ethis wept and Meri called my name, and then, as if high above me, Teal began to sing in the fierce, blooming voice of a pine grouse.

◄ 23 ►

MARMOT THE SPIRIT knew little of childbearing. He was
following the reindeer migration when Ina bore The Stick,
and was digging out a bear when she bore The Frog. Not
that he would have watched his wife laboring—in his time
as in mine, men sat as far away as possible from a woman
giving birth inside a lodge. And I would never mention, not
to a man who was my senior, anything that leads the mind
to private parts. So neither Marmot nor I ever spoke about
what happened to me.

Instead I found out for myself. Lying face down on the
roof, hanging my head over the smokehole, I watched what
went on below. In Ethis's shirt, next to her full, warm
breasts, curled a little baby, a boy—the one I bore under the
hemlock. Ethis and Timu, their heads together, would smile
down at him and put their fingers in his fists to feel the
power of his grasp.

I couldn't help being somewhat jealous. For a while I had
thought that Timu and I would raise Elho's child, with only
me knowing the father. Now I saw that Timu and Ethis
would raise Timu's child, with everyone knowing the father.

And Timu's child he was. Soon after my death Teal lashed
the people in the lodge with words, showing them what fools
they had been to think that any other man could be the
father. What better proof of it, she asked, than the second
child, the child born dead, the twin?

So! Teal had pulled a double-child out of me under the
hemlock! I didn't have time just then to think about what I
had heard, because Teal's angry voice went on. "If Yanan

lay with a stranger after lying with Timu, maybe the stranger was the twin's father," she said. "But Timu's child was the first out because he was the first in!"

The people tried to calm Teal because they understood her anger at the loss of a kinswoman. They knew Timu was the father, they said. They had never thought he wasn't! They were glad about the baby—Timu's baby—and sorry things had turned out badly for Yanan. They also were sorry that Timu had to feel the painful shame of doubt, now that they saw no doubt was necessary. And they were even sorry about the other baby, not that he mattered.

But he mattered to me. Where was he? One day I went back to the hemlock to look, but I didn't find his body or his spirit. Somewhere, someone had buried all the birth matter and him too. And who could say about his spirit? It wasn't around me, I knew. Nor did I see how a bird could have found his spirit in my belly to bring it to my lineage. But the spirit had to be somewhere.

At last I remembered the otter whose eyes met mine on the bank of the river, and the tussles and splashes of otters mating in early summer. That meant otter kits were ready for spirits, there inside her long, strong body. Was my child now on a wild ride, speeding and twisting through the water? I didn't see what else could have happened to him. Of course I wouldn't meet him later, because he wouldn't be a person. Even so, otters surely have their own lineages, since in every other way they seem to do well. Who wouldn't, with plenty of food even in winter? Nothing seems to hunt them, not even people, since getting their pelts is too troublesome. I didn't remember ever seeing a dead otter. So I was content.

Sometimes I thought to go as an otter to visit him, but the otter with kits might not want to meet another female in the river. So I left them alone, except to hunt for sign. And of course I left Ethis and Timu alone to raise the baby, which they did very well. Through the smokehole Marmot and I would look fondly down at our children, he at his boys, as he called The Stick and The Frog (although these great, hulking men were older now than Marmot), and I at my son, who in time learned to talk and said many little things that made the people smile at him.

After three years the people named him Spotted Deer. I liked that. I liked to think of him growing tall and strong to fill the name brought to mind by this great creature. And after three years, if I judged otter sign rightly, my otter child was fully grown and owned a nice long stretch of the river.

Swift acted differently toward me when he knew me as a spirit. No longer did he call me Hide-in-the-Grass and no mention was ever made of the fact that we had spoken of marriage. I was also more respectful to him, since only after I became a spirit did I fully realize his power. Once at the Hair River, when he saw me asleep in some dry birch leaves after I had stayed very long with the mammoths, I suddenly found myself bolt upright, rigid, unable to move or speak or see. I could still hear, though. "What stands behind the lodge, naked in winter and clothed in summer?" a faraway voice was saying. "If I ever come back, I'll know where to find you."

However long he left me as a birch tree, it seemed longer, rooted to the earth with insects crawling up and down my skin. I had nothing to do but think, as I'm sure he planned, but if his plan was to make me think about the lesson he was teaching me, the plan went wrong—all I could think of was fire. Then suddenly I was sitting collapsed at Swift's feet, again in human form but limp from the experience. I looked up at him, my mouth agape, and in those lion-colored eyes of his I saw a truth: that we who are spirits have owners.

Or those of us who used to be people have owners. Who knew about the rest? Into Swift's birch grove at the Hair River, the spirits of animals used to come at night in human form. Twice I saw this—two pairs of animal spirits who, each pair for its own reasons, wanted to see the mammoth skull. The first pair were lion spirits in the form of a man and a woman. Looking more like Swift than Swift himself, the two walked boldly from the plain straight up to the skull and peered into the eye sockets. What they thought to find in there, I couldn't tell. They didn't spend much time—in a moment the lion spirit turned his back and faced a bush. Did he mark it? Both left right afterwards, one behind the other, shoulders straight, heads up, bodies swaying.

The second pair were mammoth spirits in the form of women. Both were tall and strong, and their dry, brown skins were covered with fine wrinkles. Both had long, coarse hair in hopeless braids, made with no skill at all, like the clumsy braids that little children make when no one helps them. But the minds of these women were far from their braids. Moving slowly to the skull, they ran their hands up and down its forehead. In time they wandered to the hunters' boulder piles and brush screens. The screens they examined carefully, looking long at how the branches stood in the ground, then pulling up a few to taste their cut ends. At last their slow but constant movements brought them to the plain again, and I watched them growing smaller in the distance. They walked quite far apart and side by side, not one behind the other as we would do. For a while one carried a branch, then dropped it.

These spirits weren't owned by our shamans. In fact, Swift shivered when I told of them, and wondered what gifts he could offer. The lions might like fat, the same as us, but not the mammoths. Grass? There was too much grass already, and it was easier to get right where it grew than wherever we might put it. "We already know they don't want us to kill them," said Swift. "But how can we not do that?"

One day, followed by all the people, Swift and Teal visited the mammoth skull, sang into its nostrils, and decorated its forehead with ocher. I never knew whether this show of respect impressed the animal spirits, since if they ever came back to see the skull, they didn't come as men and women, or not in the years I was there.

In my third year as a helper to the lodge and the living, I was sent away for good. No more did I see Spotted Deer or my otter son, or the shamans or the people, or the animals in the woods or on the plain. I was sent away because of trouble brought on, as usual, by a bad winter and much hunger. Part of the trouble was my fault, but part was not. After the trouble was over, a man was dead and the shamans didn't want to keep me.

The bad year began in summer, which was very dry and so cold that the berries never ripened. Since there was so little to eat, many of the migrating reindeer didn't stay in our woods but kept going. No snow fell to help the people, to cover the lodge from the wind, to show tracks, or to make the red deer flounder. Instead the noisy, frozen earth made stalking very difficult for the people and escape very easy for both red deer and reindeer. And the tigress kept them scattering.

Goldeneye was with us in the early fall, but as if he foresaw the winter to come, he kept an eye on the long lines of geese as they passed overhead. How he recognized his old flock I couldn't say, unless he knew their voices. But suddenly one day, with much calling and a clatter of wings, he rose into the air. Up he flew, reaching a high place just as a flock was passing. Those were the geese who had made him break trail for them through the wind when he had last traveled with them, so now he timed his meeting to join the flock at its tail. He might have unbalanced a few geese before and behind him when he burst into their line, but if so, they were too busy flying to do anything about him. In moments all were gone.

As autumn turned to winter the cold deepened. Trees split, startling people at night. And when the ice boomed far away in Char Lake, the people in the lodge felt the vibration. The cold came through the people's heavy clothes, freezing their toes and fingers. And ice on the river was so thick that people couldn't keep an open waterhole.

By the time of the Icebreaking Moon, the weather got warmer, but too late. People were almost starving. In the scattered refuse around the lodge they looked for broken, frozen bones to crush into powder or to pick for scraps of marrow. At the first creaking of the ice on the river, the sound that told us the water would soon be free, the shamans pleaded with us to start the char running. Knowing how much the people must need food to beg for fish instead of meat, it hurt us that we couldn't. But The Woman Ohun starts the char, out in water as deep as the sky and almost as far as the Camps of the Dead from the river. Helpless in the face of so much hunger, Marmot escaped in the form of a wolverine.

Then the people sang and the shamans tranced and asked me for a bear. But they didn't ask nicely or call me Honored Spirit. Rather, Swift promised that if I didn't bring news in three days' time, he would root me to the earth forever. The next thing I knew, I was a great sow bear making for the hills where the Char rises.

I might have seen how the plan would fail. It was too early in the year; I was confused, sleepy, cold, and hungry because there was nothing to eat. Nothing. Other bears were safe in their dens, but I was wandering in the barren, frozen woods with my strength leaving me and no place to go. I walked without stopping for a night and two days, found my own tracks, and saw that I had made a circle.

Meanwhile, the hunters didn't wait for me to come back. Perhaps I had too often failed them. The next thing I knew I heard people close on my trail, and tired as I was, I began to run. But not fast enough—the hunters on their long legs overtook me. I looked over my shoulder into their staring eyes, their eager, fearsome faces, and before I knew what I was doing, I spun around and charged them. With a swipe of my paw I laid a man down on the snow. The next swipe raked the clothes off the side of another man. A spear bounced off my shoulderblade, but I hardly felt the blow as I bolted from the people, amazed that they fell back to let me through.

As suddenly as I became a bear, I found myself as a person again, now alone in the woods and lost. Heartsick, I walked south until I found the river, then followed it to the lodge, where I heard people singing. By now it was dark. Sitting on the roof of the lodge wrapped in his sleeping-skin was Marmot, home at last. I was very glad to see him.

But the news he had for me was bad. A sow bear had hurt The Frog so badly that he now lay dying in the lodge. The Frog! Marmot's son killed by my hand! Marmot would not forgive this. Might he do to my son what I had done to his?

I listened at the smokehole, praying to The Woman to spare The Frog, or if not, at least to let people think another bear had killed him. But I heard people talking of his burial. Since the earth was still frozen, people were trying to decide in which tree to store him. Suddenly his wife and many other people began to cry, and I realized that he was gone.

Just as I turned to Marmot, planning the speech I would make to admit my guilt and beg his forgiveness, the spirit of The Frog suddenly appeared beside us. Since he couldn't yet know what had happened to him, he seemed amazed to see me and didn't recognize Marmot. But Marmot was delighted, and soon, in his most fatherly way, was explaining matters to his large, confused son. I thought to let the shamans decide whether or not to point out who killed him. So instead of speaking, I waited quietly, dreading what was to come.

I didn't wait long before I saw the trancing spirits of Swift and Teal slowly take form like rising heat in the air above the smokehole. In their most respectful voices, they greeted Marmot and The Frog. It seemed that Teal had captured him. While she began to tell him of the people's need and ask him to go as a reindeer to lead another reindeer to the hunters, Swift took me aside.

"Honored Spirit," he began, "what can I say? The people are angry that we promised them a bear, only to have it kill this man and destroy my parka. The Frog will never hunt again, and I can't hunt in this weather until a skin can be found to make a new parka. The people blame us. Yet they are hungry and need our help, as we need theirs. How can we trance without their singing? And why would they sing if their songs bring them death but not food? You are harming us. So your cousin will replace you. Now you must go to find your lineage where they eat the sun. Speak well for us if you find the place. I've finished talking."

I didn't want to leave the lodge I had known all my life, and I didn't want to leave my two children, but what could I do? The shamans owned the air.

I gathered all my things, my grave goods, and said good-by to Marmot very humbly. I even said good-by to The Frog. When the sky turned gray, I slid off the roof and started west. It would have been easier to fly as a bird, but my power to change form seemed to lie with the shamans. Now it was gone, so I walked. In the form of a falcon, Marmot slowly circled me a little while. I was glad about that—it seemed to show that he didn't want to see the last of me. Perhaps he even knew what had happened and forgave me. Then something far off must have caught his attention—with a flash of white under his wings he rose high, became a tiny thing, and vanished.

I didn't know where to go, so I followed the Char. In the afternoon I reached the plain on the far side of the Black

River, with no idea where to go next. But suddenly a ptarmigan must have noticed me standing there—it burst noisily from under a bush, then dragged itself fluttering over the ground, asking me to follow. So I did. It led me.

I came at last to a vast, treeless plain, free of snow, where berry bushes and high grass were growing. Far away I saw the camps of many people, with shelters meant to look like bushes, made of grass laid over branches, and shelters meant to look like hemlocks, made of hides laid over poles. As I got near, many people stood up to see who came.

I asked a stranger for the camp of our lineage, and with his lips and chin he pointed. As I passed among the people, they realized they didn't know me and sat on their heels again. But when I saw Mother, all the people near her remained on their feet. "Yanan. You've come," she said.

"I'm here," I answered, glad to see her. Of all the people at the camp of our lineage, she was the only one I knew. But I noticed which shelter was hers from her antler necklace with pendants, which hung inside. I also noticed an awkward silence growing.

One by one my relatives began to sit down again. I stood uncomfortably, trying not to stare. Even so, I couldn't help but notice that not all my relatives were dressed as I was. A few wore clumsy one-piece garments made of sewn skins, as if the wearers were trying to look like animals. Others wore only loincloths, while still others, although they were outdoors in the daytime, were completely naked, with loose, matted hair. Those small people were strangest of all as they clustered nervously at the far edge of camp, openly staring. At last, as if he found his courage, a little bare-naked man stepped forward. "You spoiled a hunt," he said.

I didn't know who he was or what to call him, so I answered as simply as I could, "Yes, Uncle." When no one spoke, I added, "I'm sorry."

"Let me talk to my daughter," said Mother to the people. And she led me to her shelter where others wouldn't overhear. "The elders had great hopes for you, and want you to know they're disappointed," she began.

I felt sure they were, whoever they might be, but thinking that explanations would be useless, I said, "I'm sorry about The Frog."

"Never mind him," said Mother. "Let his own kin worry about him. The elders are worried by things that hurt us."

"What things?" I asked, remembering many and feeling uneasy.

But Mother didn't answer right away. Instead she said, "It's their own fault, to my way of thinking. They expected too much of you. They expected you to die on the Pine River, but you surprised them. When the elders saw how well you took care of yourself and Meri, they became greedy. That's why they sent the spirits of two people instead of one. That's why you had a double-child. I say the mistake was theirs, because you didn't understand child-bearing, but they say it was yours, because you chose an unsafe place to bear those children."

I nodded to show I understood. Mother went on. "And we noticed the smell of our burned blood on the wind and realized that you lay with a kinsman. You were taught not to do that. What if your misdeed had divided the lodge?"

"If I lay with anyone, it was after I was pregnant."

"But you didn't know! What if someone had killed the child or made the people of our lineage leave the lodge? Were there so many of us in Graylag's lodge that we could lose one to an angry husband? Could some of us live without the others?"

I knew she was right. "I hid my misdeed," I said.

"Teal hid it," said Mother. "Teal took care of everything. The elders are pleased with Teal. Of course, for years they've been pleased with Teal. And except for those things I told you, they should be pleased with you. After all," she said, "perhaps you didn't add to our number, but you didn't lessen it. That's what's important. If the elders used their fingers to work it out, they'd find you did well. What really bothers them is that you lost one of us to the otters. Sometime you might apologize for that." She smiled. "Well then, Yanan. Welcome. Tomorrow I'll help you pull grass for a shelter. Or you can sleep with me in mine. I'll take you to the elders later, and they can greet you."

I looked around her shelter and saw her familiar deerskin on a pile of grass. "Thank you, Mother," I said, very content. Then, since the account of my misdeeds seemed to be over, I couldn't help but ask, "Who are the little naked people?"

Mother touched her finger to her lips. "Speak softly when you speak of them!" she whispered. "They're the elders!"

"Ours?"

"Ours," said Mother. "They hate to see waste, like a spoiled hunt, and because they're poor, they think we disrespect them. But otherwise they're simple to please." Mother moved close to my ear and whispered, "When you get a chance, look at their grave goods, if you can find them. Only easily pleased people would keep grubs and sticks and old eggshells for grave goods. Just like ravens." She moved back far enough to let me see that she was smiling. "The elders led strange lives, though, so they tell good, strange stories."

In the evening a large group of men with spears and axes gathered in one place as if they were expecting something. People who were sleeping then sat up, sharpened their knives, and talked excitedly, as people do with a meal in sight. Hungrily I asked Mother where our food was, and she pointed above us at the sky, where the sun was setting.

The sun was huge, as big as a mammoth, all hot and flaming and coming down fast. Fearlessly, the people speared it. When it collapsed struggling on the ground they clubbed it with axes, then cut it up and gave a piece to everyone. Hot and crisp, mine burned my mouth but tasted good because, just as I thought, it was mostly fat. What else can make such a fire?

SOURCES AND ACKNOWLEDGMENTS

TWENTY THOUSAND YEARS AGO, when much of the Northern Hemisphere was glaciated, Siberia was not, or not much. Nor was it forested, as it is today. Rather, it was covered with a mosaic of forest, tundra, and steppe—a cold version of the African savannah with a fauna to match. On the Siberian savannah, as the Soviet paleontologist N. K. Vereshchagin has pointed out, lived northern forms of lions, hyenas, rhinos, and elephants (woolly mammoths), with bison in place of buffalo, horses in place of zebras, dholes in place of wild dogs, foxes in place of jackals, wolves as the coursers in place of cheetahs, and many kinds of deer in place of many kinds of antelope, with the giant deer *Megaceros* (the spotted deer of this novel) browsing the treetops in place of the giraffe. I have no idea whether *Megaceros* was really spotted; it is herein because its ecological counterpart, the giraffe, is spotted, as is its closest living relative, the fallow deer.

I have tried to portray the animals in this novel carefully. No reptiles are included because I thought the climate was too harsh for them, and frogs are included with much trepidation only because the wood frog and a river frog now live near Hudson's Bay. All except one of the birds are modern Siberian birds whose ranges I tried to adjust to fit the ancient climate. Many small plants and some small animals have fictional folk names but are real nevertheless. Very little is known about the insect life of the U~

389

Paleolithic, and less is known to me. But since the populations of very small animals show much about an environment, I hope my displays of ignorance are limited to poetic license and don't dynamite the poetic pond.

The habits of extinct animals are of course purely fictional. My mammoths, drawn from elephants, have a breeding season like many other ungulates, although elephants do not. My cave lions were drawn from modern African lions and thus are plains-dwellers. Some live in prides which own territories including the limited number of sheltering caves where year-round reproduction could have been possible. Some lions, however, are lonely nomads who can't command territories or caves and can't hope to raise young in winter, if at all. So with successful reproduction by prides in caves and unsuccessful reproduction by nomads without caves, my lions lack a breeding season. Such is my fantasy. My tigers, on the other hand, are forest-dwelling Siberian tigers who have a breeding season and even today rut in February. My spelling of the roar was drawn from George Schaller.

The people are not meant to represent any particular Paleolithic culture, except that their lodges resemble those found in the Yenisei-Angara Basin. Their tools and clothing are intended merely to be compatible with the time and place. Their group size and way of life, including the distances they travel and the way they spend their time, were drawn in part from real hunter-gatherers, the Ju/wa Bushmen of the Kalahari, among whom I lived for several years in the 1950s. The personalities of my fictional people, and their culture, both spiritual and material, are not intended to resemble the Ju/wassi or any other people in any way but are entirely my own inventions. Mention of a parka troubled several early readers of this manuscript, as the word seemed to evoke contemporary sports clothing, yet the garment is surely very ancient and its name is Innuit.

The coordinates of this novel happen to fall near Lake Baikal, but I felt that the presence of a lake the size of Baikal would so influence the action of the novel that I left it out. Since the specific terrain is largely fictional, a smaller lake was substituted.

Nancy Jay encouraged me to begin this book. I am deeply

grateful to her, because I have had such a good time working on it. Megan Biesele, Naomi Chase, Joan Daves, Lexi Eliot, Eleanor Gerber, Ingrid Honaker, Bill Langbauer, Lorna Marshall, Katy Payne, Claire Ritchie, Peter and Susannah Schweitzer, Stephanie Thomas, and Ramsay Thomas have helped me greatly with advice, information, and/or critical readings of drafts of this book. Katy Payne and Bill Langbauer, who are my colleagues and partners in an ongoing field study of elephants, greatly helped me by generously shouldering much of my share of the work of our partnership while I finished writing *Reindeer Moon*.

Many people helped me obtain information about the USSR during the Sartan Glaciation. In this context I would especially like to thank Charles Fishman. I am also grateful to Robert Hoffman of the University of Kansas at Lawrence, Alex Hromockyj of the Science and Technology Division of the Library of Congress, Beverley Kaemmer of the University of Minnesota Press, and Patra Leaming of the Quaternary Research Center at the University of Washington.

I would especially like to thank the editor of this book, Peter Davison, for his poet's eye and his faith in my project, and my husband, Steve Thomas, for his immeasurable help in obtaining hard-to-find sources, for his excellent translation from Russian of much of the material listed below, and most of all for his encouragement and enthusiasm for this work.

I am indebted to the following sources for information on the Siberian climate, ecology, and populations during the Sartan Glaciation, and on modern fauna and ecology from which those of the past have been extrapolated.

Alekseyeva, E. V. 1980. Mammals of the Pleistocene of Western Siberia's Southeast. Nauka, Moscow. In Russian.

Darling, F. F. 1937. A Herd of Red Deer. Oxford.

Flint, V. E., Y. V. Kostin and A. A. Kuznetsov. 1984. A Field Guide to Birds of the USSR. Princeton.

Giterman, R. E., and L. V. Golubeva. 1967. Vegetation of Eastern Siberia During the Anthropogene Period. In:

The Bering Land Bridge. Ed. David M. Hopkins. Stanford.

Kuz'mina, I. Ye. 1977. On the Origin and History of the Theriofauna of the Siberian Arctic. USSR Academy of Sciences, Institute of Zoology. Trudy 63, 18–55. In Russian.

Levin, M. G., and L. P. Potapov. 1964. The Peoples of Siberia. Chicago.

Markova, A. K. 1984. Late Pleistocene Mammal Fauna of the Russian Plain. In: Late Quaternary Environments of the Soviet Union. Ed. Andre A. Velichko. Minnesota.

Payne, K., W. R. Langbauer and E. M. Thomas. 1986. Infrasonic Calls of the Asian Elephant *Elephas maximus*. Behavioral Ecology and Sociobiology. 18: 297–301.

Powers, R. 1973. Paleolithic Man in Northeast Asia. Arctic Anthropology. Vol. X, No. 2, 1–50.

Praslov, N. D. 1984. Paleolithic Cultures in the Late Pleistocene. In: Late Quaternary Environments of the Soviet Union. Op. cit.

Schaller, G. B. 1967. The Deer and the Tiger. Chicago.

Soffer, O. 1985. The Upper Paleolithic of the Central Russian Plain. Academic Press. Orlando.

Vereshchagin, N. K. 1971. The Cave Lion and Its History in the Holarctic and within the Soviet Union. In: Materialy po faunam antropogena USSR. Nauka, Leningrad. In Russian.

Vereshchagin, N. K. 1984. Late Pleistocene Mammal Fauna of Siberia. In: Late Quaternary Environments of the Soviet Union. Op. cit.

Vereshchagin, N. K., and G. F. Baryshnikov. 1983. The Ecological Structure of the Mammoth Fauna of Eurasia. Zoologichesky Zhurnal, vol. LXII, No. 8. In Russian.

Yermolova, N. M. 1978. Theriofauna of the Angara River Valley in the Late Anthropogene. Nauka, Novosibirsk. In Russian.

Zeuner, F. E. 1963. A History of Domesticated Animals. Harper and Row.

Finally, I feel a special debt to Joseph Campbell, whose work must inspire everyone who tries to imagine the cultures of human beings long ago. Through the stories and images that remain with us today, some of our past is preserved. I cite in particular his work of 1983, *The Way of the Animal Powers, Vol. 1,* published by Harper and Row.

Part of this book was originally planned as a nonfiction work to discuss the relationship of hunter-gatherers to their environment. The work of that portion was completed under fellowships from the Mary Ingraham Bunting Institute at Radcliffe and the National Endowment for the Humanities.

Peterborough, N.H.
June 1986